WINCHESTER: 1887

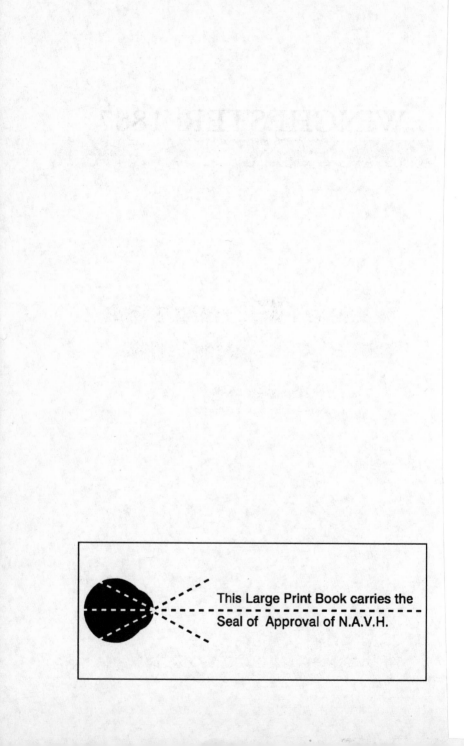

WINCHESTER: 1887

WILLIAM W. JOHNSTONE
WITH J. A. JOHNSTONE

WHEELER PUBLISHING
A part of Gale, Cengage Learning

GALE
CENGAGE Learning·

Farmington Hills, Mich • San Francisco • New York • Waterville, Maine
Meriden, Conn • Mason, Ohio • Chicago

GALE
CENGAGE Learning®

LIBRARY OF CONGRESS CATALOGING-IN-PUBLICATION DATA

Names: Johnstone, William W., author. | Johnstone, J. A., author.
Title: Winchester 1887 / William W. Johnstone with J. A. Johnstone.
Description: Waterville, Maine : Wheeler Publishing Large Print, 2016. | © 2015 | Series: Wheeler Publishing large print western
Identifiers: LCCN 2015040296| ISBN 9781410486486 (paperback) | ISBN 1410486486 (softcover)
Subjects: LCSH: Large type books. | BISAC: FICTION / Westerns. | GSAFD: Western stories.
Classification: LCC PS3560.O415 W563 2016 | DDC 813/.54—dc23
LC record available at http://lccn.loc.gov/2015040296

Published in 2016 by arrangement with Pinnacle Books, an imprint of Kensington Publishing Corp.

Printed in the United States of America
1 2 3 4 5 6 7 20 19 18 17 16

WINCHESTER: 1887

PROLOGUE

Tascosa, Texas, late spring 1895
He swore softly and chuckled again. "That was . . . some . . . journey."

And Jimmy Mann closed his eyes one last time.

CHAPTER ONE

Randall County, Texas

Usually, Millard Mann found the sight of his home comforting — not that it was much of a place. A converted boxcar, the wheelbase and carriage long carried off, the rooms separated by rugs or blankets. The only heat came from a Windsor range, and when it turned cold — winters could be brutal — there wasn't much heat.

But the lodging came free, compliments of the Fort Worth–Denver City Railroad, although Millard figured he and his family would be moving on before too long. He wasn't even sure if he would get paid again since the railroad had entered receivership — whatever that was — during the Panic a couple years back, and although it was being reorganized . . . well . . . Millard sighed.

The landscape didn't look any better than that makeshift home. Bleak and barren was the Texas Panhandle. Rugged, brutal. Sometimes he wished the white men hadn't driven the Comanches and Kiowas out of it.

His horse snorted. He closed his eyes, trying to summon up the courage he would need to face his family. His wife stood down there, trying to hang clothes on the line that stretched from the boxcar's grab irons to the corral fence. She fought against that fierce wind, which always blew, hot during the summer, cold during the winter. Out there, the calendar revealed only two seasons, summer and winter, the weather always extreme.

Libbie, his wife, must have sensed him. She turned, lowering a union suit into the basket of clothes and dodging a blue and white striped shirt that slapped at her face with one of its sleeves. Looking up, she shielded her eyes from the sun.

Again, his horse snorted. Millard lowered his hand, which brushed against the stock of the Winchester Model 1886 lever-action rifle in the scabbard. A lump formed in his throat. He grimaced, and once again had to stop the tears that wanted to flood down his beard-stubbled face.

He would not cry. He could not cry. He was too old to cry.

Facing Libbie was one thing. He could do

that, could tell her about Jimmy, his kid brother. He could even handle his two youngest children, Kris and Jacob. But facing James? Sighing, Millard muttered a short prayer, and kicked the horse down what passed in those parts for a mesa, leaning back in the saddle and giving the horse plenty of rein to pick its own path down the incline.

He figured Libbie would be smiling, stepping away from the laundry, calling toward the boxcar. Yet Millard couldn't hear her voice, the wind carrying her words south across the Llano Estacado, Texas's Staked Plains in the Panhandle. Kris, the girl, and Jacob, the youngest, appeared in the boxcar's "front" door and then leaped onto the ground.

The horse's hoofs clopped along. Millard's face tightened.

Next, James Mann, strapping and good-looking at seventeen years old, stepped into the doorway, left open to allow a breeze through the stifling boxcar.

The sight of his oldest son caused Millard to suck in a deep breath. His heart felt as if a Comanche lance had pierced it. James looked just like his uncle, Millard's brother, Jimmy. Millard and Libbie had named their firstborn after Millard's youngest brother.

Millard himself was the middle-born. The only son of Wilbur and Lucretia Mann left alive.

His wife's face lost its joy, its brightness, when Millard rode close enough for her to read his face, and she quickly moved over to stand between Kris and Jacob, putting hands on the children's shoulders. James had started for him, but also stopped, probably detecting something different, something foreboding, in his father.

"Whoa, boy." Millard reined in the horse and made himself take a deep breath.

"Hi, Pa!" Kris sang out.

Even that did not boost Millard's spirits.

"What is it?" his wife asked. "What's the matter?"

He shot a glance at the sheathed rifle and then lifted his gaze, first at Libbie, but finally finding his oldest son.

Their eyes locked.

Millard dismounted. "It's Jimmy."

Jimmy Mann, the youngest of the Mann brothers, had been a deputy U.S. marshal in the Western District of Arkansas including the Indian Nations, the jurisdiction of Judge Isaac Parker, the famous "Hanging Judge" based in Fort Smith, Arkansas. Jimmy had been around thirty-five years old when he had ridden up to the boxcar Millard and his family called home sometime late summer. When was that? Millard could scarcely believe it. Not even a full year ago.

Sitting at the table, he glanced around what they used as the kitchen. It was hard to remember all the particulars, but James had been playing that little kids game with his younger siblings, using the Montgomery Ward & Co. catalog to pick out gifts they would love for Christmas — James doing it to pacify Jacob and Kris. Millard had been on some stretch of the railroad, and Libbie had been in McAdam, a block of buildings and vacant lots that passed for a town and served as a stop on the railroad.

Jimmy, taking a leave from his marshaling job, had found Millard, and they had ridden home together, to surprise the children. James had been interested in a rifle sold by the catalog, a Winchester Model 1886 repeating rifle in .45-70 caliber.

Millard frowned. What was it Jimmy had said in jest? Oh, yeah. "In case y'all get attacked by a herd of dragons . . ." Millard smiled at the memory.

Most rifles out there were .44 caliber or thereabouts. A .45-70 was used in the Army or in old buffalo rifles, and those were single shots. The Winchester '86 was the first successful repeating rifle strong enough to handle that big a load.

Millard's weary smile faded. A rifle like that would cost a good sum even considering the discounted prices at Montgomery Ward, but Jimmy had given James a lesson shooting Jimmy's Winchester '73 .44-40-caliber carbine. Millard couldn't understand it, but there had always been a strong bond between James and his uncle. Jimmy had always seen something in Millard's son that, try as he might, Millard just could not find.

His right hand left his coffee cup and fell against the mule-ear pocket of his trousers and Jimmy's badge that was inside. His eyes closed as he remembered Jimmy's dying words back on that hilltop cemetery in Tascosa.

"You'll give . . . this to . . . . James . . . you hear?"

Millard looked again at the beaten-up Winchester '86. Jimmy's head was cradled by that sharpshooting cardsharper Shirley Something-or-other. He couldn't recall her last name, and never quite grasped the relationship between her and his brother. But he knew that rifle. Jimmy had tracked the notorious outlaw Danny Waco across half the West trying to get that rifle. Danny Waco's lifeless, bloody

14

body lay in a crimson lake just a few feet from Jimmy.

Millard said softly, "I hear you."

Other men from Tascosa climbed up the hill. Waco and some of his boys had tried robbing the bank, only to get shot to pieces. Jimmy would have — could have — killed Waco in town, but some kid got in the way. Jimmy took a bullet that would have killed the boy, and then went after Waco.

Jimmy killed Waco, but Waco's bullet killed Jimmy Mann.

Death rattled in Jimmy's throat. Townspeople and lawmen stopped gawking and gathered around . . . like vultures . . . to watch Jimmy breathe his last.

"Might give . . . him my . . . badge, too." The end for Jimmy Mann was coming quickly.

Millard didn't see how his kid brother had even managed to get that far.

"Maybe . . . Millard, you . . ." Jimmy coughed, but once that spell passed, his eyes opened and he said, "Gonna be . . . one . . . cold . . . winter." He shivered. "Already . . . freezing."

On that day, the temperature in Tascosa topped ninety degrees. Winter would come, but not for several months.

"You rest, Jimmy," Millard said. The next words were the hardest he ever spoke. "You deserve a long rest, Brother. You've traveled far."

Millard had learned just how far. From the Cherokee Nation in Indian Territory to Kansas, north to Nebraska, into the Dakotas, to Wyoming, New Mexico, and finally in the Texas Panhandle. Chasing Danny Waco and the Winchester '86 that the outlaw had stolen during a train holdup in Indian Territory.

If only he had ordered that foolish long gun from the catalog, but Jimmy knew how tight money came with Millard. Through his connections in Arkansas and the Indian Nations, Jimmy had promised that he could find a rifle cheaper that even Montgomery Ward offered.

That had brought the oldest Mann brother, Borden, into the mix.

He'd worked for the Adams Express Company, usually traveling on Missouri-Kansas-Texas Railroad — commonly known as the Katy — trains. In Parsons, Kansas, he had found the rifle, not a .45-70 — which Millard thought too much rifle for his son — but a .50-100-450, one of the first Winchester had produced in that massive caliber.

Jimmy and Borden had decided it would

be a fine joke, sending that cannon of a rifle to their nephew. So Borden agreed to take it by rail and have it shipped up to McAdam for James.

It never made it. Danny Waco had robbed the train and killed Borden. Murdered him. With the big rifle.

It was why Jimmy had trailed Danny Waco for so many months, miles, and lives.

Again, Millard thought back to that awful day on that bloody hill in Tascosa.

"He'll be a better man than me, Millard," Jimmy said. "Me and . . . you . . . both. Badge and . . . this rifle. You hear?"

"I hear."

Heard, yes. Millard could hear his brother. But understand him? No, not really.

"That was . . . some . . . journey," Jimmy said, and then he was gone.

Millard could hear the younger ones, Jacob and Kris, sobbing through the old blankets that separated the kitchen from the children's bedroom, Libbie trying to comfort them. James sat across the table from Millard, tears streaming down his cheeks. Sad, but his eyes were cold, piercing, frightening. Like Jimmy's could be when he got riled.

"Where is he?" James said at last.

Millard frowned. "We buried him. In Tascosa."

"You left him there?" James sprang out of the chair, knocking it over, bracing himself against the table with his hands.

The crying in the children's room stopped.

"Yes," was all Millard said.

James swore.

Millard let it pass, no matter how much that language would offend Libbie.

"You told me yourself that Tascosa's dying, won't be anything but memories and dust in a year or two. Why did you bury Uncle Jimmy there? Why didn't you bring him home?"

Because, Millard thought, *in a year or two, all that will be left here are memories and dust.* "It's not where a man's buried. Or how. It's how he died that matters. More important, it's how he lived. You've got your memories. So have I."

Reluctantly, he pushed the rifle toward his son. "He wanted you to have this."

"I don't want it." Tears fell harder, and James had to look away, wipe his face, and blow his nose.

"I don't have any shells for it," Millard said.

18

"I don't want it." The anger returned. His son whirled. "I want Uncle Jimmy. I want him alive. You don't know how it feels. I lost —"

"I feel a lot more pain than you, boy." Millard came to his feet, only the rickety table separating the two hotheads. Out of the corner of his eye, he saw the curtain move, saw Libbie's face, the worry in her eyes. He ignored his wife.

"You lost your uncle. I lost Jimmy, my kid brother. I also lost Borden, my big brother. Two brothers. Dead. Murdered. Because of this gun! Because —" He stopped himself, choked back the words that would have cursed him for the rest of his life.

Because you wanted this gun.

He started to sink back into the chair then remembered something else. His hand slid into the pocket and withdrew the badge, a tarnished six-point star. He dropped it on the table, read the black letters stamped into the piece of tin.

**DEPUTY
U.S.
MARSHAL**

"Jimmy wanted you to have this, too," Millard said. He had to sit. His legs couldn't support his weight anymore.

James Mann sat, too, after he righted the chair he had knocked over.

Letting out a sigh of relief, Libbie returned to comforting Kris and Jacob.

"The man who killed Uncle Borden —" James began, but stopped.

"Danny Waco," Millard said numbly. "Rough as a cob, a cold-blooded killer. Posters on him from Texas to Montana, and as far west, probably, as Arizona Territory. He killed Jimmy, too, but Jimmy got him." *Revenge,* Millard thought. *Was it worth it?*

"He took a bullet, Jimmy did, that would've killed a kid. Stopped a bank robbery. Stopped Waco. The law's been trying that for a number of years. Folks in Tascosa, even Amarillo, said Jimmy was a hero. Died a hero."

The curtain drew open, and Libbie came into the kitchen, her arms around Jacob, a sobbing Kris close behind.

"Maybe," Kris said, "maybe we can buy a monument — one of those big marble stones — and put it on Uncle Jimmy's grave."

"Maybe," Millard said. Jimmy's grave had been marked with only a busted-up Winchester, another '86, that he had used, somehow, to end Danny Waco's life. Not even a crude wooden cross or his name carved into a piece of siding.

"Put a gun on it," Jacob said, still sniffling.

"Maybe." Millard managed a smile.

"A gun on a tombstone?" Kris barked at her brother.

"Uncle Jimmy liked guns!" Jacob snapped back.

"That's ridiculous," Kris chided.

"Hush," Libbie said.

The children obeyed. Millard stared at his oldest son, who sat fingering the badge, his shoulders slumped, at long last accepting the fact that Jimmy Mann was indeed dead, wouldn't be coming back ever again.

Jacob became interested in the badge and left Libbie's side. He moved toward his big brother and looked at the piece of tin. "Why'd Uncle Jimmy want you to have this?"

James didn't answer, probably had not even heard, and Jacob looked at his father for an answer.

"I'm not sure," Millard said.

"Uncle Jimmy didn't make James a lawman, did he?" Jacob asked.

Millard tried to smile, but his lips wouldn't cooperate. His head shook. "No, he couldn't deputize anyone. At least, not officially."

"Was Uncle Jimmy a good lawman?" Kris asked.

Millard shrugged. "I reckon. He did it for some time."

"Can we go see his grave?" Jacob asked.

"Sure. Sometime." Millard, however, had little interest in seeing the dead. Maybe that was why he left Jimmy in Tascosa. He had not gone to Borden's funeral, mainly because of the expense and time such a journey to the Midwest would have taken. He had never been to the graves of his parents. Never had he cottoned to the idea of talking over a grave. The dead, he figured, had better things to listen to than the ramblings of some old relation.

James left the boxcar without speaking.

"Where's Jimmy going?" Jacob asked.

"James," his sister corrected. "You know he don't like being called Jimmy. That was Uncle —" She stopped and brushed back a tear.

"But where . . . ?"

"Just for a walk," Libbie answered with a sigh, stepping toward the open doorway.

Alone with his grief.

Millard felt some relief. His son had walked out with the badge, turned toward the corral. Walking away his troubles, his thoughts. But at least — and this really

made Millard feel better — James had left
the .50-caliber Winchester '86 on the table.

CHAPTER TWO

Mountain Fork River, Choctaw Nation

An ounce of lead ripped into the hardwood, sending splinters of bark into Jackson Sixpersons' black slouch hat. The old Cherokee dived to his right just as another slug tore through the air and thudded into a tree. He rolled over and brought up the big shotgun, not lifting his head, not firing, just listening.

Many years earlier — too many to count — he had learned that in gunfights, it wasn't always the quickest or the surest who survived, but the most patient.

Another bullet sang through the trees.

Sixpersons freed his left hand from the shotgun's walnut forearm and found his spectacles. He had to adjust them so he could see clearer, but all he saw above him was a blur. "Sweating like a pig," is how that worthless deputy marshal he partnered with, Malcolm Mallory, would have described it. Idiot white man. Pigs don't sweat.

He found one end to his silk wild rag and wiped the glasses free of perspiration. His right hand never left the Winchester, and his finger remained on the trigger.

A Model 1887 lever-action shotgun in twelve-gauge, it weighed between six and eight pounds and held five shells that were two and five-eighths inches long (ten-gauge shells were even slightly bigger). The barrel was twenty-two inches. When Sixpersons got it, back in the fall of '88, the barrel had been ten inches longer, but he had sawed off the unnecessary metal over the gunsmith's protests that the barrel was Damascus steel. Thirty-two inches was too much barrel for an officer of the U.S. Indian Police and the U.S. Marshals.

"Did you get him, Ned?" a voice called out from the woods.

"I think so. He ain't movin' no-how," came Ned's foolish reply.

"He was a lawdog, Ned," the first voice, nasally and high-pitched, cried out. "I see'd the sun reflect off 'n his badge, Ned."

"He's a dead lawdog now, Bob."

"Mebbe-so, but you know 'em federal deputies — they don't travel alone."

That reminded Sixpersons of his partner. Where in the Sam Hill was Malcolm Mallory?

Footsteps crushed the twigs and pinecones as someone moved away from Sixpersons.

The Cherokee lawman rolled to his knees and pushed himself up. He was tall and lean, had seen more than sixty-one winters, and his hair, now completely gray, fell past his shoulders. His face carried the scars of too many chases, too many fights. He kept telling his wife he would quit one of these days, and she kept telling him as soon as he did, he would die of boredom.

In the Indian Nations, deputy marshals did not die of boredom.

Sixpersons rose and moved through the woods — like a deer, not an old-timer.

Tucked in the southeastern edge of Choctaw land just above the Red River and Texas, that part of the country could be pitilessly hard. The hills were rugged, the ground hard and rocky, and trees, towering pines and thick hardwoods, trapped in the summer heat. The calendar said spring. The weather felt like Hades. He didn't care for it, but passed that off as his prejudice against Choctaws. Cherokees, being the better people, of course, cared little for loudmouthed, blowhard Choctaws.

He could hear Ned and Bob lumbering through the thick forest, thorns from all the brambles probably ripping their clothes and their flesh.

Sixpersons figured where they were going, moved over several rods, and ran down the leaves-covered hillside, sliding to a stop and disappearing into another patch of woods. Ten minutes later, he pushed through some saplings and stepped onto the wet rocks that made the banks of the river.

The country was green. Always seemed to be green. The water rippled, reminding him of his thirst, but Jackson Sixpersons would drink later. If he were still alive.

He stepped into the river, the cold water easing his aching feet and calves, soaking his moccasins and blue woolen trousers as he waded across the Mountain Fork. A fish jumped somewhere upstream where the river widened. He had picked the shallowest and shortest part of the river to cross and entered the northeastern side of the woods. He moved through it, heading back downstream, hearing the water begin to flow faster as he moved downhill.

How much time passed, he wasn't sure, but the water flowed over rocks — running high from recent spring rains — when he dropped to a knee and swung the shotgun's big barrel toward the other side of the Mountain Fork.

Bob and Ned burst through the forest, fell

to their knees, and dropped to their bellies, slurping up the water, splashing their faces, and trying to catch their breath.

Through the leaves and branches, Sixpersons could see the two fugitives clearly. Luck had been with him. Well, those two boys weren't bright or speedy. He wet his lips, feeling the sweat forming again and rolling down his cheeks.

"C'mon, Bob," Ned said as he pushed himself to his feet. "This way."

Sixpersons waited until they were near the big rock in midstream, not quite waist-deep in the cool water. Only then did he step out of the forest and bring the Model 1887's stock to his right shoulder.

He did not speak. He didn't have to.

The two men stopped. Their hands fell near their belted six-shooters, but both men froze.

Slim men with long hair in store-bought duds, they had lost their hats in the woods. Their shirts were torn. One of them wore a crucifix, another a beaded necklace. Not white men, but Creek Indians — Cherokees didn't care much for Creeks, either. Jackson Sixpersons didn't consider these two men Indians. Not anymore.

They were whiskey runners, selling contraband liquor, some of it practically poison,

28

to Indians, half-breeds, squaw — men, women, even kids. Jackson despised whiskey runners. He had seen what John Barleycorn could do to Cherokees . . . and Creeks . . . and Choctaws . . . and Chickasaws . . . and all Indians in the territories. He recalled all too well that wretched state liquor had often left him in.

He had, of course, been introduced to bourbon. Grew to like it, depend on it, even became a raging drunk for twenty-two years. Until his wife told him that if he didn't quit drinking, she would pick up that Winchester of his when he passed out next time and blow his head off.

No liquor, not even a nightcap of bourbon, even when he had an aching tooth, had passed his lips since '89.

Ned and Bob could see the six-pointed deputy U.S. marshal's badge pinned on Sixpersons' Cherokee ribbon shirt. Sixpersons figured he didn't have to tell those two boys anything.

"He can't kill us both, Bob." Ned, the taller of the two Creeks, even grinned. "He's an old man, anyhow. Slower than molasses."

Jackson Sixpersons could have told Ned and Bob that they would likely get two or three years for running whiskey, maybe another for assaulting a federal lawman, but Judge Parker, being a good sort, did show mercy, and probably would have those sentences run concurrently. It wasn't like those two faced the gallows.

Instead, he said nothing. He never had been much for talk.

"Reckon he's blind, too." Bob grinned a wild-eyed grin.

Silently, Sixpersons cursed Malcolm Mallory for not being there, but waited with silence and patience.

"Die game!" Bob yelled. He clawed for his pistol first.

The shotgun slammed against the Cherokee marshal's shoulder. His ears rang from the blast of that cannon, but he heard Bob's scream and ducked, moving to his left, bringing the lever down and up, replacing the fired shell with a fresh load.

Most lawmen in Indian Territory favored double-barrel shotguns, and Jackson Sixpersons couldn't blame them. There was something terrifying about looking down those big bores of a Greener, Parker, Savage or some other brand. With cut-down barrels, scatterguns sprayed a wide pattern.

Yet that master gun maker, old John Moses Browning — old; he had turned thirty-two in '87 — knew what he was doing when he designed the Model 1887 lever-action shotgun for Winchester Repeating Arms. That humped-back action was original, even compact considering the '87s came in those big twelve- and ten-gauge models. When the lever was worked, the breechblock rotated at lightning speed down from the chamber. Closing the lever sent the breechblock up and forward, with a lifter feeding the new shell from the tubular magazine and into the chamber. This action also moved the recessed hammer to full cock.

A double-barrel shotgun could fire only twice. The '87 had four shells in the magazine and one in the chamber. It fired about as fast as a Winchester repeating rifle.

Jackson Sixpersons didn't need five shots. Ned's shot hit nothing but white smoke, and the big twelve-gauge roared again.

When the next wave of smoke cleared, Ned lay on the rock, faceup, his chest a bloody mess. The current had swept Bob's carcass downstream a few rods before he got hung up, facedown, on some driftwood on the far bank.

Birds had stopped chirping. Sixpersons set the shotgun's half-cock safety notch, rose, the joints in his old knees popping, and stepped into the stream.

He reached the rock, closed Ned's eyes, and looked for the pistol the Creek had carried, but the weapon must have fallen into the river. It was likely nearby, but Sixpersons wasn't bending over to hunt for some old pistol. Likely, he would get wet enough just dragging the dead punk across the cold, fast-flowing river.

Cursing in Cherokee, then English, he moved toward Bob's body. At least this one had the decency to die near the bank. Sixpersons laid his shotgun on dry ground and pulled the dead whiskey runner onto the bank. The blast had caught Bob in the stomach and groin, and he had bled out considerable. Still heavy, for a corpse. Probably from all the buckshot in his belly.

Sopping wet by the time he got Ned onto the bank, out of breath, and sweating, the deputy cursed the two Creeks. "Die game." He shook his head. "Die foolish."

After wiping sweat from his forehead, he looked at the woods he would have to travel across. Getting those two boys to Fort Smith would prove a big challenge, and that caused him to laugh. He had taken Deputy U.S. Marshal Jimmy Mann deer hunting up in the Winding Stair Mountains where Jimmy had bagged a twelve-pointer with a clean shot from his Winchester. But it was Sixpersons who had butchered the deer and hauled it those grueling four miles back to camp.

Shaking off the memory, he reloaded the Winchester before he drank water from the stream or wrote in his notebook — still dry — what would pass for a report on the attempted arrests and subsequent deaths of Bob Gooty and Ned Yargee, whiskey runners, Creek Nation.

He found a couple corndodgers, stale but salty, and a tough piece of jerky in his pocket. That was all he had to eat. The rest of his food lay in his saddlebags on the horse he had tethered to a pine back near where the whiskey runners had camped. Their horses had run off when they started the ball after Sixpersons had demanded their surrender.

Three miles. Not as many as he had had to cart that deer Jimmy Mann had killed. But there were two carcasses this time.

It would have been easier in the old days. All he would have had to do was cut off their heads, stick those in a gunnysack, and carry them to the Indian court. But Judge Parker and the Senate-confirmed U.S. marshal, Mr. Crump, frowned on such things in the civilized word.

And the ground was too hard to bury the

Creeks and come back later with horse and pack mules.

Sixpersons was ready to call it quits, just leave them there for coyotes and ravens, and forget any reward that might have been posted, when he heard a horse's whinny.

He came up with the Winchester, aiming at an opening in the woods a quarter-mile downstream. A dun pony stepped out and into the water, and the shotgun was lowered.

The rider eased the horse out of the river and up onto the bank, grinning at Jackson Sixpersons. "Howdy," Deputy Marshal Malcolm Mallory said.

Sixpersons didn't answer with word or nod. The fool hadn't even ridden out of the woods with pistol or rifle ready.

"Dead, eh?"

The Cherokee's head bobbed, though it was one stupid question.

You kill 'em?"

He answered. "No, Wild Bill Hickok shot them."

Mallory laughed like a hyena and dismounted, which was one good thing.

"I'll hold your horse," Sixpersons told him. "You put the bodies over your saddle."

"But —"

"How else are we getting them back to Virgil Flatt's tumbleweed wagon?"

■ ■ ■ ■

Deputy U.S. marshals did not work alone. At least, they weren't supposed to. It was too dangerous. But sometimes Jackson Sixpersons wondered exactly what U.S. Marshal George J. Crump, appointed and confirmed by the Senate back in April of '93, was thinking.

Working with Malcolm Mallory and Virgil Flatt, Sixpersons might as well be working alone.

It was Flatt's job to drive the tumbleweed wagon, which was basically a temporary jail on a wagon bed. Iron bars were affixed to the reinforced wooden floor, with a padlocked door swinging out from the rear of the wagon. The roof leaked, and if the prisoners got too rough, they could be chained to the floor. Painted on the side of the wagon was U.S. COURT.

Under Judge Parker's orders, the driver of the wagon was not allowed to carry a gun. So in essence, the party of deputies was limited to two — Jackson Sixpersons and Malcolm Mallory. The way the Cherokee did his math, basically one.

The sun was setting, but the day had yet to cool by the time Sixpersons and Mallory reached Flatt's camp. The two deputies had found the dead whiskey runners' horses and transferred the bodies to those mounts. Ned and Bob were pretty much bloated by the time they reached camp, causing Flatt to curse and moan.

"We'll pack them down in charcoal when we reach Doaksville," Mallory said, the one sensible thing he had spoken all day, maybe all week.

"Who kilt 'em?" Flatt asked.

Mallory tilted his hat toward Sixpersons, who was rubbing down his horse.

"Got coffee boilin'." Flatt did something unusual. He filled a tin cup and took it to Sixpersons.

The Cherokee knew something was wrong. Besides receiving the coffee, he could read it in the tumbleweed wagon driver's eyes. He accepted the cup, stepped around his horse, and waited.

"Trader come along, headin' for Texas," Flatt said.

Sixpersons waited.

"I give 'im some coffee and a bit of flour." Flatt's Adam's apple bobbed. "He give me a paper. Newspaper, I mean." He reached into the rear pocket of his duck trousers, pulled out and unfolded a newspaper. "*Democrat,* only two weeks old."

Sixpersons took the newspaper.

"Second page. Well . . . it's . . ." Flatt stepped away.

Sixpersons opened the newspaper, saw the story just above an advertisement at the bottom of the page for Straubmuller's Elixir Tree of Life.

"What is it?" Mallory asked.

Sixpersons read.

Flatt answered. "Ex-marshal, Jimmy Mann. Seems he kilt Danny Waco, the old border ruffian, over in Texas, but he got hisself kilt doin' it."

CHAPTER THREE

Greenville, Arkansas

To the teller at the Greenville Independent Bank, the gun in the hand of the man in the hood looked like a cannon. Five other men inside the bank also wielded guns — one a rifle, the others revolvers — but those weapons weren't four inches from Mike Crawford's face.

"You tell me there's a time lock on that safe again," Wheat-sack hood said, "and I'll wallpaper this place with your blood and brains."

Crawford had seen shotguns before, but nothing like that one. It had no stock, but a pistol grip that ended just beyond the lever. The wooden fore end was covered with beaded leather and the case-hardened, blued barrel had been sawed off just in front of the tubular magazine. He had done enough dove and deer hunting to know that the bootlegged Winchester shotgun was a ten-gauge. It wouldn't just wallpaper the back wall with his blood and brains; it would blow his entire head off.

He had already lost his watch. The man with the pistol-grip Winchester '87 scatter-gun had ripped the Waltham out of his vest pocket and dropped it into his own pocket. To Mike Crawford, that watch — a gift from his dearly departed father — was worth more than all the money in the bank, though he knew his boss would disagree with any such sentiment.

Crawford nodded just slightly and backed away from the counter. One of the hooded men with a revolver hurdled over the gate and followed him to the vault door. As soon as he turned, he felt the barrel of the pistol ram into his back. He flinched, but at least the man did not shoot. Slowly, he pulled open the heavy vault door, walked inside, and easily opened the safe.

"Payday, boys!" the man said, pushing Crawford aside. "Come and get it."

Two other men rushed through the gate, into the vault, and began filling sacks and saddlebags with greenbacks and coins.

Crawford found a handkerchief in the pocket of his waistcoat and wiped his brow. He heard the man with the shotgun say from the bank's office, "You. Empty the tills. Now, or you're a dead man." He was talking to Spencer Tillman, assistant cashier.

Crawford returned the soaking piece of cotton to his pocket and stood ramrod straight as the men in the safe stuffed money into their bags, not even bothering to pick up the bills and coins that fell onto the floor.

Greenville, Arkansas, was not a big town, and the Greenville Independent Bank was not a big bank. The town was located between the St. Louis & San Francisco Railroad and Indian Territory, southwest of Fayetteville, practically due north of Van Buren. The bank held maybe $2,500, if that, between what was in the vault and in the tills of the tellers. It hardly seemed worth the outlaws' time, but Crawford wasn't about to tell anyone that — especially the man with the cut-down Winchester '87 shotgun.

He just wanted to get out of there alive, back to his wife and three little girls. He was praying that if he did survive, well, he would even stop seeing that Cherokee soiled dove over in Flint, and might — no he *would* — rejoin the choir at the Methodist church.

The bank robbers had no reason to kill him. He had opened the safe, wasn't doing anything, and there was no way he could identify any of them with those wheat-sack masks they all wore. He frowned, remembering the shotgun. There couldn't be two like that west of the Mississippi River.

Five seconds later, he heard words outside the bank that he had prayed he would not hear until the robbers had left the Greenville Independent Bank.

"Robbery! Robbery! Robbery!"

The words were followed by a gunshot. Then another. Moments later, the streets of the small town sounded like Gettysburg on July 3, 1863.

Glass shattered somewhere inside the bank.

"Time to hit the trail, boys!" the man with the shotgun yelled.

The first man, wearing a linen duster, ran past Crawford without a second glance. The next shoved him against the wall, cursed, and spit tobacco juice on the floor. The third tossed the saddlebags over his shoulder, walked past Crawford, then stopped and turned. "Don't get no foolish notions, bub."

"N-no . . . s-sir . . ." Crawford stammered.

The masked man slammed the barrel of his Remington revolver against Crawford's head. He saw stars, then nothing at all.

Outside the bank, Stoney Post yelled, "It's

hot out here, Link!"

Those were his last words. A blast blew him through the plate-glass window as Link McCoy opened the door of the bank.

He cursed and sent a shotgun blast across the street. "I told you this was a mistake, Zane," he told his partner, who checked on Stoney Post and then cut loose with his Winchester rifle.

"You told me!" Zane Maxwell yelled and began feeding cartridges from Stoney Post's shell belt into the Winchester '73. Post wouldn't have need of those shells anymore.

"Get out!" McCoy yelled to the gang members. "We get separated, we'll meet at the Salt Works."

"Get killed," Maxwell said, "we'll meet in Hell."

Even McCoy had to laugh at that, but he focused on business as soon as the boys bolted into the streets, trying for their horses tethered by the bank and funeral parlor. He fired the shotgun, levered another round, and fired again. He and Zane crouched at the shattered window, and Zane made his .44-40 rifle sing. As soon as McCoy's sixth shot finished, he fell back from the window and began reloading the cut-down Winchester. He had only two shells in when he saw that fool teller, coming at him, a little brass-framed Sharps derringer waving wildly in his shaking hand.

"Don't be a fool," Maxwell yelled at the idiot, but did not wait for the teller to lower the four-shot, .30-caliber rimfire popgun with the fluted barrel group. That old relic, made before the War Between the States, might not even fire, but Link McCoy was not one to take chances or give fool bankers second chances.

The shotgun roared, and the teller went flying against the counter while the Sharps Model 2A sliced across the room, bounced off a desk, and fell into a wastebasket.

McCoy jacked the hammer and finished reloading the shotgun.

"Corey's bought it," Maxwell said, as he fell back and reloaded the Winchester. "And I think Tawlin got hit."

"Rest of them?" McCoy levered a fresh load into the chamber of the ten-gauge.

"Hard to tell. Made it, maybe."

"Let's you and me make it, maybe." Link pushed himself up and bolted through the open doorway, blasting away with the sawed-off shotgun.

Farmers mostly, in that part of the country, not that it was worth growing anything other than corn. Farmers and city folk, if you could call Greenville, Arkansas, a city.

43

The people were full of grit. McCoy would give them that much, but not much when it came to brains. Too nice for their own good.

All they had to do was kill the outlaws' horses, but the good folks of Greenville prized solid horseflesh, so McCoy swung into the saddle of his piebald mare, fired his last round from the Winchester, and waited until Maxwell found the saddle. Both men spurred their mounts and rode west toward Indian Territory, leaving two of their gang dead on the streets, poor old Stoney Post dead inside the bank, along with the corpse of a fool bank teller with a chest full of buckshot.

Mike Crawford's head was splitting. The knot on his skull felt like it would split his scalp, at least the part of his scalp that hadn't been split wide open by that buffaloing hoodlum in the wheat sack. He held a rag trying to stanch the flow of blood, trying to ease the agonizing pain in his head, and trying — and failing — to hear everything Grover Cleveland, president of the Greenville Independent Bank but no relation to the president of the United States, was saying.

"You opened the vault, you fool! How many times did I tell you that if robbers ever demanded money, you were to tell them that the safe is on a time lock? How many times? Those rascals have absconded with one thousand seven hundred and ninety-three dollars and sixty-seven cents! Because of you. A time lock, you fool. You were to tell them about the time lock."

"I did," Crawford moaned when Cleveland stopped to catch his breath. He wanted to tell that idiot that no intelligent robber would believe that time lock lie anyway. Safe on a time lock? How would the bankers get money out if they needed to cover a withdrawal? He wanted to tell Cleveland to drop dead, but his head ached too much. Why didn't he send someone to fetch a doctor? Crawford was bleeding, for goodness sakes!

"Spencer Tillman lies dead," the president roared. "He died a hero. Defended my money — the money of our depositors — defended it carrying the pistol I carried during the War for Southern Independence."

Leaning beside him, County Sheriff Whit Marion turned his attention to the small derringer he held in his left hand, thinking *you carried* this *during the war*? And suddenly, he recognized Grover Cleveland for a liar, a fraud, and a blowhard.

Cleveland decided to turn his rage onto the law. "Sheriff, why are you here? Why aren't you pursuing those murderous, scum-sucking thieves?"

Marion said calmly, "U.S. marshals will be goin' after 'em, I expect."

"Marshals? Why? Ain't it your job?"

"For one, those bandits will be in the Nations, by now. My jurisdiction ends at the state line. For another, they didn't just kill your teller, cashier, manager or whatever that boy was. They shot Don Purcell dead in the streets. Don wasn't just my deputy. He had a commission as a deputy marshal. Judge Parker, well, he frowns upon folks killin' his deputies. So we'll get 'em. Rather, the marshals will."

"How?" Cleveland spoke with contempt. "How can we even identify them? They wore masks, and you said none of the vile fiends killed in the raid had any identifying marks. Nothing. Nothing but bullets, gold watches, and horses they had stolen in Rogers."

Whit Marion shoved the .30-caliber Sharps into his vest pocket, then realized he had no use for it, and handed it, butt forward, to the bank president, whose meaty hand swallowed the pocket gun.

"I know who they were," Mike Crawford said at last.

The sheriff eyed him curiously.

46

Cleveland leaned closer to Crawford's face. "Who were they, my good man?" he demanded, his breath reeking of cigarettes and brandy. "Who were they? How could you recognize any of them when they all wore hoods?"

"Let him speak, Grover," the sheriff said.

Cleveland stiffened at such a rebuke.

"One of them had a shotgun, a sawed-off Winchester lever-action with a pistol grip. I remember reading about such a weapon in . . . a newspaper." The latter part was a lie. It had actually been in a dime novel he had picked up over in Flint when he was with the Cherokee soiled dove.

Some truth must have been in that piece of fiction, because Sheriff Whit Marion leaned backwards and whistled.

"What is it?" Cleveland demanded.

"Congratulations, Grover," the sheriff said, "you just made history. Your bank got robbed by the McCoy-Maxwell Gang."

Mackey's Salt Works, Cherokee Nation
Folks had been producing salt there for longer than Link McCoy could remember, likely before he was even born. Indians had been going there before the Cherokees had been kicked out of Tennessee and Carolina or wherever they hailed from.

McCoy stood by the campfire, watching with interest at the commotion below the hillside. Old Sam Mackey and his boys had had a good business. Pay a lease to the Cherokees and then send salty water from the springs into hollow logs, dump the water into giant brass kettles, boil the water until there wasn't anything left but salt, pack up the salt, and sell it. 'Course, with the Katy railroad coming through the Nations for the past twenty or so years, a body could buy his salt elsewhere. Link wasn't sure how much longer old Mackey could stay in business. Nobody went there anymore for salt, and Mackey had only a handful of hired men to mine the works.

That was why Link McCoy, Zane Maxwell, and the boys met there.

"Not much of a take, was it, Zane?" Jeff White said.

Maxwell shrugged. "Would've been better, but some sodbuster killed Clete McBee on the way out of town and I couldn't catch his horse." He spit into the fire, frowning at the bad memory. Clete had wrapped his war bag heavy with gold coins around the saddle horn.

Maxwell's dark hair had lightened over the years and was streaked with gray. His girth had widened, too, and no longer could

48

he mount a horse as quick as his slim, balding partner, Link McCoy. Yes, age had begun to show on both men. Outlawing wasn't getting any easier.

"Clete McBee," Jeff White muttered. "Stoney Post. Pottawatomie Jake. Three good men. Dead."

"More money for you, Jeff," McCoy pointed out.

White let out a mirthless chuckle and brought a bottle of rye to his lips.

Tulip Bells came out of the tent and took the bottle from White. "Vann's done fer."

White let out a curse. "Four men dead. Killed in some hayseed town by a bunch of square heads. Give me that bottle, Tulip. I need to get good and drunk."

"Ain't that redundant?" Tulip Bells asked.

"Huh?"

Tulip pushed back his bell crown hat and sniggered. "I's too intellectual fer yer way tiny brain, White."

"Shut up."

Tulip Bells laughed again and sat beside McCoy. "He's right, though, Link."

Bells was a lithe man with a crooked nose, pockmarked face, and graying droopy mustache and underlip beard. Two fingers on his left hand had been shot off during a robbery in Kansas back in '89, and he had been

49

walking with a limp since taking a slug in the hip in Creek Country two years back. Tulip had been riding with Link and Zane as long as either could remember. He carried an Arkansas toothpick sheathed on his left hip, a double-action Starr Army revolver in .44 caliber on his right hip, a pearl-handled, nickel-plated Smith & Wesson No. 3 stuck in his waistband to the left of the buckle on his gun belt, and a Remington over-and-under .41-caliber rimfire derringer in the pocket of his linen duster. He was a man that took few chances.

"Rode in to Greenville with ten men." Tulip drank, and then tossed the bottle to Link. "I count four left. You, me, Zane, and Mr. White."

McCoy did not drink. He cleaned the cut-down Winchester shotgun. "Smith and Greene got out of town, too."

"Yeah." Tulip's lean head bobbed. "But they've seen the light. Won't be seein' 'em weasels no more."

"Good riddance to them," Maxwell said from across the fire.

"Four men ain't much of a gang," Tulip Bells said. "Law'll be ridin' after us pretty soon."

"Imagine so." McCoy worked the action of the empty shotgun then wiped the casehardened steel with an oily cloth.

"We can pick up some new boys," Maxwell said. "Territory's full of eager beavers."

"Like Smith and Greene," Tulip said, shaking his head.

"They left their cut for us," Maxwell said.

"Yeah." White kicked at the saddlebags McCoy had escaped with. "Instead of six ways, four ways. To split four hundred dollars."

"Makes the cipherin' easier," Tulip Bells said.

"Shut up," White snapped.

A minute passed then he spoke again. "We can't stay here."

"Why not?" Bells said with a chuckle. "Make it easier on the law. They can use the salt to help preserve our corpses for the trip back to Fort Smith."

"Shut up," White said again.

Tulip Bells morosely laughed.

"Where to?" White asked.

McCoy had been doing some thinking. "South. We'll change our duds, become respectable cattle buyers. Buy our tickets in Muskogee and ride down to Texas. Law won't expect us to ride a train out in the open. Anybody can lose himself in Denison."

Tulip Bells cackled again.

51

"What's so funny?" Maxwell demanded.

Bells shook his ugly head. "Buy a train ticket?" He howled harder.

Link McCoy, Zane Maxwell — and even Jeff White — joined in.

CHAPTER FOUR

Randall County

As soon as the coyotes began their singsong chatter, James Mann sat up in the straw-tick mattress and held his breath when Jacob rolled over and muttered something. It was too hot for covers, and Jacob said something again. James breathed easier, understanding that his brother was merely talking in his sleep. A short distance away, Kris slept like a rock.

He rose, moving cautiously through the darkness, found his hat, and the sack he had been hiding for a week. Carefully, he peeked through the slit in the rug. It was too dark to see anything in the kitchen, but he didn't need to see anything. He could hear his father's snores through the rug divider. Still, he took a deep breath, held it, and finally exhaled before he slipped into the kitchen and made his way to the open door — open to let in air, not rattlesnakes or skunks —

and found the Winchester '86 leaning against the wall. Even empty, that rifle weighed a ton.

He leaped onto the ground and waited, listening. Nothing. Everyone remained asleep. He took a step then stopped.

Regret paralyzed him. Fear. Uncertainty of what awaited him. At seventeen years old, he was too old to run away from home, something he hadn't done since he was seven. Then, he had wanted to find somebody with a pony he might ride.

His father and mother hadn't whipped him when they caught up with him a half-mile from wherever they were living back then. They had merely laughed and walked him back to their house, or tent, or whatever they had been calling a home.

James looked back at the outline of the boxcar. His memory wasn't that good, but he was pretty sure they hadn't lived in something like that when he was seven.

Uncle Jimmy gave me his badge, he told himself. *For a reason.* The rifle he could explain. James had wanted a rifle, a Winchester '86. Maybe not the particular rifle in his hand, but his uncle had promised that he would get a rifle for him and it was what he had found. And paid for. With his life. And the life of Uncle Borden.

But the badge?

The way James saw it, his uncle had seen that look, that wanderlust, in James's eyes and knew that James was not cut from the same cloth as his father. Millard could spend his years working for the railroad, living in boxcars, bossing gangs, laying track, moving from place to place across an endless prairie of nothing. James needed more. He needed to find a purpose in his life.

Like being a lawman.

A deputy marshal, just like Jimmy. He owed his uncle that much.

His right foot stepped forward, followed by his left.

With each step, he breathed easier, listening to the coyotes, hearing the night birds, and feeling the wind on his back. He kept up a quiet conversation with himself. "Move south to the railroad, but not to McAdam. Too close. That's all you have to do. Go south. Pa knows when all the trains will be rolling through or at least scheduled to roll through. You've studied those maps he always pores over, burning coal oil.

"Pick up the southbound at the water stop near the North Fork. Find an open boxcar, and slip in. Make yourself as comfortable as possible. When the train reaches Fort Worth, just jump off. A little before the train reaches the town. Pa says that's what the railroad bums do to avoid getting clubbed with a nightstick carried by some yard boss or railroad dick.

"After that?" James stopped walking and frowned. He looked around, shrugged, and kept going.

"Well, that's where things might get a little peculiar. Pa works for the recently rechartered Fort Worth–Denver City Railroad, and that line doesn't go to Fort Smith, Arkansas. Green as I am, I know many railroads go to Fort Worth. Surely one of them will head northeast for Fort Smith."

It took him two hours to make his way to the tracks. Once, he heard a rattlesnake's whirl, making him stop — almost scaring him out of a year's growth, as Ma might say, but he figured, at seventeen, he was as big as he was going to get. He gave the serpent a wide berth and moved on toward the tracks — and almost missed that train.

The whistle screamed, startling him, and his heart quickened as he heard an Irish voice call out, "Let's get this thing rollin', Quint. We're behind schedule!"

James had no idea what time it was. Had he misread the timetable? Had it taken him longer to make it there? He didn't have the answers, and none mattered at that point anyway.

He came up out of the wash to find the train pulling away from the water tank. Moving south. Definitely, it was the train he wanted to catch, so he began hoofing it, leaping over the prickly pear and shrubs, moving desperately toward the train. Smoke from the big locomotive burned his eyes, but he reached the grading, feeling the gravel crunch underneath his boots. There was no moon — perhaps that had slowed him, too — and the only light came from the caboose and the Baldwin engine. He was between those two, but the train was picking up speed.

He saw the boxcar — reminded him briefly of home — and the open door. That was a bit of luck. Never would he have been able to open the door as the train sped away. Coming up to it, he hurled the Winchester through the doorway, followed by his bag. He stumbled, barely caught his feet, and had to find some extra effort to make up the ground he had lost. Not until much later did he think about how things could have turned out. He could have fallen underneath the train. His father had worked on railroads long enough to tell stories of men who had died those grisly deaths.

Reaching up, he grabbed the iron handle, grunted, and felt himself slipping. "No!" he screamed, thinking he would fall. Be left alone. Wouldn't even have Uncle Jimmy's badge — in the sack — or that Model '86 rifle — somewhere in the boxcar. And he would have to face his father, his mother . . . if he wasn't killed.

Something grabbed his arm, almost crushing his forearm, just as he let go. The toes of his boots dragged along for a brief moment, and then he felt himself being pulled upward, heard a massive grunt, and suddenly felt himself landing inside the car on ancient hay and horse apples.

His heart pounded. He smelled the manure, but did not care. He was alive. He was on the train.

Someone grunted, and James quickly rolled over, his racing mind suddenly aware of what had just happened. He slid across the hay-carpeted floor until his back pressed against the wood-slated wall. The boxcar rocked as the train picked up speed.

A match flared, briefly illuminating the bearded face of a dark man. Then a giant hand shook out the match, and all James could see was the glow of the end of the cigarette when the man inhaled.

"You owe me," a haggard voice said.

James was too scared to reply.

"Got victuals in that sack, I hope. Ain't et in three days."

The only sounds that followed were the clicking of the wheels and the pounding of James's heart.

"Answer me, boy. I saved your hide."

"Some . . ." James tried to remember. "An apple. Can of peaches. Some jerky."

The cigarette glowed for a long time and then the glow died.

"I'll have the apple. And jerky. Peaches hurt my teeth. They's rotted, most of 'em. My teeth."

Again, the cigarette shown orange, revealing just a shadow of the man.

"I said," the voice returned after the glow died, "I ain't et in three days."

"Oh." James moved in the darkness. "Let me find my bag." He fumbled in the darkness, feeling like an idiot, feeling petrified. For a moment, he wished he had not run off from home. His hand touched the cold barrel of the Winchester, and he froze.

"Find it?"

"No," James said, and moved over the rifle, remembering where it was. "I stepped in something else. Well, my hand did."

Sniggering, the man drew on the smoke. "Reckon they dumped a load of horses up north, right afore I gots on this train."

"Yes, sir."

He found the bag and opened the sack, reaching in, but the man's voice stopped him.

"You tossed something else in here, boy. Somethin' heavy. Like maybe a —"

"Walking stick," James sang out. "It's gotta be somewhere around here."

"A stick?"

"Walking stick. You know . . ." Something about the stranger James didn't like. He didn't trust the man, even if he had pulled him aboard the boxcar.

"You a cripple?"

"No, sir."

The man laughed. The cigarette flared again. "Run like one. Iffen I hadn't been headin' fer that door to take a leak, you'd never be ridin' with me. Might have even gotten a bath of my pee."

The thought soured James's stomach, but he said, "Yes, sir," and found the apple, then two pieces of jerky. He figured he would leave the third for himself, not quite certain how long it took to travel to Fort Worth. He saw the glow again, and realized his eyes had adjusted to the darkness. He could see a bit better as he weaved across the rocking floor of the car, getting his bearings from the cigarette. He stopped, knelt, and held out his offerings. "Here you go. Name's Mann."

He smelled tobacco smoke. A rough hand snatched the jerky, disappeared, then came back and took the apple. The man did not say his name, and James knew it would be rude to ask.

"That all you got?" the man asked.

"In the bag?" James fell back on his haunches. Cigarette wasn't all he smelled on the stranger. Months must have passed since the guy had felt soap and water. "Just some extra socks."

"Where's yer hat?"

He reached to his head and realized his slouch hat was gone. Probably had fallen off as he had scrambled to make the train. He smiled, although he doubted if the man could have seen it. "Lost it."

"Get sunburnt in this country, kid."

"I'll get another."

"With what?"

That caused James Mann to stop and let out a long breath. He was an imbecile. He had left home with an apple, some jerky, an empty rifle, and a tin star. He hadn't thought about money. Rarely did he have any and he could never have brought himself to borrow — no, *steal* was the word — some

61

of the cash and coin his ma and pa had stashed away in the coffee can.

The stranger, however, thought the silence meant something else.

The smoke turned orange again and then went straight into James's cheek, burning just underneath his right eye as a wicked left fist that felt like a hammer slammed into his jaw.

Down went James, blinking back pain and surprise, feeling the breath explode from his lungs as the stinking man leaped onto his gut. Giant hands fell to his throat, squeezing, squeezing, squeezing.

James couldn't breath. Couldn't move. The man had pinned James's arms with his knees. He laughed. Saliva dripped into James's eyes and onto his nose.

The curve saved his life. The boxcar tilted, just enough that the man lost his balance. He had to let go of James's throat with one hand and brace himself against the floor. Using that to his advantage, James turned with the man, and the crazed killer fell to the floor.

He made himself get up, run, though where he had no idea. The man's hand got his foot, just enough to send him sprawling through old horse dung and stale straw.

"Give me yer money, boy," the man said.

James wanted to scream at him that he had no money, just one more piece of jerky, but the fiend was on his feet, moving slowly. James backed away, past the sack with his uncle's badge and that jerky, those socks, when he felt the Winchester's stock.

The man laughed. He sounded like a hydrophobia coyote. "Ya gots to pay to ride with me, kid. That's why I pulled ya aboard. Gots to pay. One way or —" The laugh and words died in the man's throat when the metallic clicking of the Winchester being cocked filled the entire boxcar.

"Stop or I'll blow your head off," James said in a hoarse voice.

He prayed, prayed that the man wouldn't call his bluff. In the week since his father had returned with the Model 1886 and the news of Uncle Jimmy's death, no one had bothered to find any shells for the .50-caliber repeating rifle. His pa never had been much for guns anyway, except for hunting. The way James figured things, his pa never wanted him to have the rifle.

"Boy," the voice called out icily, "you ain't got the guts." Another crazed laugh. "But I sure do."

A flash blinded him, and the bullet clipped off a strand of hair. James screamed. There was a new smell of brimstone and gun smoke in the boxcar. The man laughed again, but James came up as the second shot slammed somewhere into the floor. Somehow he grabbed the bag with that piece of jerky as he ran, thinking he never would make it, never *could* make it.

Those two shots from the revolver had blinded the killer and thief more than they had blurred James's eyesight. The man began cursing as he heard James coming toward him and spun around, jerking a shot. It went into the ceiling for the man had lost his footing and was falling.

So was James. Falling through the open door. Into the night. Into eternity.

CHAPTER FIVE

Randall County

Nothing but bitter disappointment. Millard Mann came riding back to the boxcar when the sun reached noon-high, feeling as if he had been in the saddle for a week. Slowly, he eased his body to the ground, the leather creaking, and led the bay mare to the corral. He removed the saddle and turned the horse into the corral. Pulling his hat low, he walked toward the boxcar.

Libbie lowered her head as he walked inside.

Kris asked, "You didn't find James, Papa?"

His head shook and he took the cup of water Libbie had filled from the bucket on the table.

Millard did not speak until he had finished two cups of water.

At last, he gestured toward the east. "Trailed him to the tracks. Found his hat. Nothing else."

Jacob stepped back, his eyes wide with amazement. "You . . . trailed . . . James?"

Despite how he felt, Millard smiled and tousled his son's hair. "Wasn't that hard, son. Pretty easy."

"But you didn't find him," Kris said.

"I will." He looked at his wife. "He jumped the southbound."

Their oldest son had taken the rifle and probably Jimmy's badge. He hadn't robbed them. Maybe some food, socks, a shirt. Millard thought of something else. *An extra hat would come in useful.* He frowned. That was a stupid joke.

"Where would he go?" Jacob asked.

"South," Kris answered.

Wordlessly, Millard moved past them, stopping only for another cupful of water, and then heading through the kitchen and into the bedroom.

"What's Pa doing?" Jacob asked.

"He'll be along," Libbie said. "Come help me with the laundry."

"But I want James!"

"Hush."

When he stepped back outside, Millard Mann had changed. Not just clothes — although he wore trail duds and a linen duster that, surprisingly, still fit him — but the weapons he carried.

His family was surprised. They had seen him as a railroad boss and with the Jenks, a .54-caliber carbine he had handled since the Civil War that he used when hunting deer.

That was long ago . . . when he was but a mere button himself, much younger even than James. He had only used that carbine for deer hunting; ducks and other game he usually opted for the Colt twelve-gauge shotgun, but those weapons he had left behind.

He had opened the old trunk in the bedroom, pulled out the blankets, the heirlooms, the clothes, and keepsakes until he had found the long fringed leather rifle sock and withdrawn a rifle Kris and Jacob didn't remember having ever seen.

It was a Winchester Model 1873 repeating rifle. One of One Thousand. The dream rifle of just about every shooter in the United States.

Something else was different.

He had buckled on a long-barreled Colt Army .44. That, too, had been used during the Civil War, but back around 1871, a man who'd worked for Colt, Charles Richards, had gotten a patent for his plan of converting the old percussion cap-and-ball Colts to cartridge revolvers. A year later, William Mason, who had also worked for Colt, improved on Richards' methods.

To Millard's surprise, the Richards-Mason conversion model .44 felt natural. As if he had been wearing it all his life. He would buy shells for it in McAdam, clean the pistol, and ride south.

"Where you going, Pa?" Kris asked.

"To find James."

No one mentioned the short gun strapped to his hip, but every eye kept falling to it.

"Will you take the train?" Libbie asked.

Millard nodded. "I'll ask Luke to bring the horse back. And check on you every now and then. I expect James to go all the way to Fort Worth — providing no brassy railroad dick tosses him off for freeloading — but he might get off in Wichita Falls, Henrietta, Bowie . . . just no telling. But I'll find him." He leaned over and kissed Libbie's cheek, and knelt to hug his youngest son and daughter.

At forty-five years old and after years of railroading, he felt different, too. Hadn't felt this way since those few years after the war, when he and his brothers — the dearly departed Jimmy and Borden — had sown their share of oats in the wild Panhandle as Texas went through Yankee Reconstruction.

Some words from Jimmy ran through his mind. He couldn't remember when Jimmy had said them, certainly before Jacob had been born. He smiled at the memory.

"You ain't cut out for this life, Brother."

Millard sipped his whiskey. "What kind of life you think suits me, Jimmy?"

Jimmy smiled that devilish smile of his. "Like mine."

Millard shook off the memory and looked at the horse. Probably shouldn't have bothered unsaddling the mare, but, well, the notion hadn't struck him until he had finished that second cup of water.

"I'll write you," he told his wife. "You kids be good." Hurriedly, he made his way back toward the corral before his resolve faltered.

Fort Smith, Arkansas

"You were not surprised by the death of Deputy Mann?" Judge Parker asked. "I should say, former Deputy Mann."

"No." Jackson Sixpersons did not care much for being in the judge's chambers. Too stuffy and being in the room with the powerful white man gave him an uneasy feeling.

"I see." But clearly, the judge did not.

69

Sixpersons knew there was no reason to tell him what he was thinking. *I knew Jimmy would not return when he left. I could see the death in his eyes.* He thought back to the time at the depot in Vinita up in the Cherokee Nation. Remembered telling Jimmy, probably his best friend, *"This is something you have to do. But I can't go with you." Jimmy was going on a vendetta, not for justice. He had no jurisdiction in Kansas, nor anywhere else he went.*

Strange as it seemed, the white man's law meant something to Jackson Sixpersons. Yet he thought of that day, watching Jimmy Mann take the train and leave him, his job, his career, going after Danny Waco. Jimmy had told Sixpersons to take care of his horse, and Old Buck was back in the barn at his place near Webber's Falls.

"May I see your shotgun, Deputy Sixpersons?"

Nodding, he handed the weapon to the judge.

Parker was an old man, hair, mustache and beard completely white, having served as U.S. district judge for twenty years. The May term had just finished. Old Parker wouldn't have to bang that gavel or do what he did so well, and fairly often, condemn some ruffian to swing on the gallows erected

70

outside the courthouse, until August. "I haven't been bird-hunting in ages." He looked weak.

Sixpersons had heard someone whisper that the judge was suffering from Bright's Disease, whatever that was.

"Twelve gauge?"

Sixpersons nodded then remembered he was supposed to show respect to a white man like Parker. "Yes, sir." *Bird-hunting?* He pondered at the idea. The Winchester Model 1887, the barrel tightly choked, and with that three-inch drop at the heel . . . well, it wasn't really made for hunting doves or quail.

John Moses Browning had designed it. Considered the best gun maker in the United States, he had done a lot of work for the Winchester Repeating Arms Company and had made his pile. Plenty of piles. Since Winchester was known far and wide for its lever-action rifles — the 1866 Yellow Bow; the 1873, likely the most famous, most popular rifle on the frontier; the 1876 Centennial; and that cannon, the 1886 that got Jimmy Mann killed — well, the boys that ran the company decided that Winchester needed a lever-action shotgun. To keep up appearances.

The '87 had a two-and-a-half-inch chamber, held five shots, and had the Winchester Repeating Arm Company's monogram and the company's address in New Haven, Connecticut, engraved on the receiver. It was the perfect shotgun, with a powerful rolling-block design. Of course, Jackson Sixpersons had made his shotgun even better by sawing off ten inches of barrel.

Although he had designed Winchester's 1885 single-shot rifle and the '86 repeater, John Browning, the story went, did not care much for the idea of Winchester's shotgun. A shotgun would work better with a slide, more like a pump, action. Not levers. The slide action would be easier to operate, Browning had argued, but levers were what defined Winchester Repeating Arms Company. And, well, Winchester was paying him good money — old Browning had earned $50,000 for the patent to the 1886 Model rifle.

Naturally, he took it and told the Winchester boys he could get a lever-action shotgun design to them in two years. It took him about a year, and in June of 1885, the patent on what became the Winchester Model 1887 was filed.

Oh, it wasn't the first repeating shotgun. Others had been tried. As early as 1839, Samuel Colt's Patent Arms Manufacturing

72

Company had produced a few revolving shotguns, improving on the design with its Model 1855. About 1,100 1855 models had been produced, and you could still find a few of those ten-gauges in the territories. Back in 1884, Christopher Spencer had designed a pump shotgun for New York–based Bannerman's in ten- and twelve-gauge models.

Yet Winchester's 1887 was the first truly successful model.

A Mormon, John Browning hung his hat in Ogden, Utah. The Latter-Day Saints sent their people out on missionary work, and Browning had gone with another Mormon to Georgia. In some Southern city, he and his accompanying Mormon missionary had passed a sporting goods store and seen the Winchester '87 on display in the window. Bearded, dusty, and tired, the two had entered the stop, asked to see that shotgun, then, before the store clerk could tell him no, Browning picked up the Winchester Model 1887, worked the lever, checked the action, the balance, and smiled.

The clerk had scratched his head and said that Browning knew his way around that shotgun.

Browning's companion had grinned. "He oughta. He invented it."

The clerk, already suspicious of the two bearded men who looked like vagabonds, took the shotgun from Browning's hand, replaced it on its case in the window, and told the two "liars" to get out.

Judge Parker finished his perusal of the shotgun and held it out to Sixpersons. The deputy U.S. marshal took it from the judge's trembling hands and butted it on the floor.

"Most deputies carry Winchester repeaters. Or double-barrel shotguns. Why the lever-action twelve gauge?"

Sixpersons could only shrug. It was a simple design, made of only sixteen parts. The barrel was Damascus, and the stock had fancy checking and a rubber butt plate. On the other hand, the shotgun was affordable. Sixpersons had paid thirty dollars for his twelve-gauge. The most expensive models he had found cost forty-eight dollars. More than a double-barrel or single-shot and pricier than many rifles. But that's not why he had picked the shotgun. He pointed at his spectacles. "I'm an old man."

The judge laughed. "So am I, old friend."

Still laughing, Parker found some papers on his desk and coughed.

Time for business, Sixpersons figured.

"I have read your report and the prosecutor Clayton's affirmation," Parker said.

Sixpersons waited.

"Your actions were just. Those Creek Indians were a couple of fools."

"Yes, sir." That fact seemed undeniable. Dead fools.

"Likely, you'll be wanting to return to home . . . where is it, Honey Spring?"

"Webber's Falls."

"That's right. Silly of me. My mind is boggled from this term of court. See your wife. Family."

The Cherokee knew what was coming. The last time Judge Parker had called him into this office and mentioned his wife, Jackson Sixpersons, Jimmy Mann, and six other deputies had found themselves in the Winding Stair Mountains for three weeks.

A knocking sounded at the door, and a bespectacled man pushed it open a crack, saw the judge wave him in, and entered the room, followed by the U.S. marshal.

U.S. marshals were political appointees at the mercy of the party in power. They did nothing more than talk to newspaper reporters, give speeches, and kiss babies. The deputies did all the work. The deputies did all the dying.

The clerk handed Judge Parker the writs, who signed them, and held them up for Jackson Sixpersons to see. "You've heard of

Link McCoy and Zane Maxwell?"

"Yes, sir."

"They robbed a bank up in Greenville. Killed a citizen. Killed . . ." He looked at the marshal for help.

The fat dog cleared his throat. "Don Purcell." He coughed slightly and shot Sixpersons a stare. "Know him?"

Jackson Sixpersons' head shook. There were plenty of deputies in Judge Parker's court. Too many for an old Cherokee to count.

"Three gang members were cut down in the streets. The rest got away with" — he paused to check his notes — "one thousand seven hundred and ninety-three dollars and sixty-seven cents."

Sixpersons did not comment.

"They entered the Cherokee Nation around Flint along the Illinois River," Judge Parker said. "Might have crossed the river by ford or ferry. Might have headed for Kansas. Might have gone south. That, old friend, is for you to find out."

Marshal Crump spoke up. "You will take your tumbleweed driver and Deputy Mallory immediately, cross over, and head for Eufaula. We have men already at the Kansas border between Baxter Springs and Coffeyville, but we think they are heading south.

Maybe for Texas. A group of Indians will meet you in Eufaula, as well as another group of deputy marshals led by Boston Graves."

Sixpersons nodded. *Boston Graves. Another worthless man with a badge.*

"The McCoy-Maxwell Gang have been a burr under my saddle for a decade," Judge Parker said. "They have killed, robbed, and plundered. I haven't long left on this bench, but I would like to see them delivered to justice before someone takes my place."

"I understand." Sixpersons felt as if he had talked enough for six months.

Marshal Crump was still saying something, but Sixpersons had heard all he needed to hear. He picked up the writs, tucked them into his trousers pocket, and walked out carrying the Winchester shotgun.

The last words he heard came from Crump and Parker.

"Where's that impertinent Cherokee going? I wasn't done talking."

"Easy, George. He knows what to do. And he'll get it done."

Greenville
He knew better than to follow orders. If the bank had been robbed in Greenville, why should he go to Eufaula — maybe a hun-

77

dred miles southeast. Oh, Jackson Sixpersons followed orders, but within degrees. He sent Malcolm Mallory and Virgil Flatt to Eufaula and told them not to hold their breath until Boston Graves showed up. Then he rode to Greenville.

The bodies of the dead outlaws had been planted in the town's potters field, but an itinerant photographer had snapped a few good photographs of the corpses and charged the county ten cents a pop. Sixpersons looked over those photos at the sheriff's office. He nodded.

"You recognize someone, Deputy?" Sheriff Marion asked.

Sixpersons nodded. "Stoney Post." Another nod. "I guess you were right. It was the McCoy-Maxwell Gang."

"Not me. The teller. Feller named Mike Crawford. That skinflint of a banker, Grover Cleveland, fired him. Said he should have give his life like the assistant cashier done."

Sixpersons tossed the photo back on the sheriff's cluttered desk. "Grover Cleveland?"

The sheriff snorted and spit tobacco juice into the cuspidor.

"The teller recognized them? But the report I read said all the men wore masks."

"He recognized the shotgun one of them boys held. Lever-action Winchester. Like yourn. Only cut down more. Even had the stock sawed off like a —"

"Pistol."

"Yep. I reckon. Tell you the truth, lead was flyin' so thick, I didn't get a good look at nobody."

"Somebody did. You left three of them dead."

"Thought it was only two at first." The sheriff leaned back in his chair. "One of 'em we found on the road in a ditch. His horse come a-trottin' back. Cleveland, the bank ramrod, sent Crawford after it, see if there was any money on it. That's how tight that miser is. Poor Mike comes back, says it was just a bloody horse and a lathered-up zebra dun, and that's when Cleveland fired the boy. Just told him he was finished, to get out." He spit again. "Don't seem right by me. Ain't worth dyin' over, money, I mean. 'Specially if it ain't your money."

"What is?" Sixpersons asked.

"What's what?" The Cherokee had stumped the sheriff. Not that that was hard.

"Worth dying for," Sixpersons answered.

The sheriff nodded.

"The robbers get anything else?" Sixpersons asked.

Marion's head shook, but then stopped. "Yeah. Crawford, the teller who Cleveland fired, said one of the robbers — the one with the fancy shotgun . . . that would be . . . ?"

"Link McCoy," Sixpersons said.

"Uh-huh. Well, Crawford said they taken his watch."

"A watch." Sixpersons perked up. "Anything special about it?"

The sheriff laughed. "I reckon so. If Mike Crawford could have described them bad men as well as he talked about that watch of his . . ." He pulled open a drawer and began sorting through papers, pulled a few out and tossed most of those aside or into the wastebasket until he found what he was looking for. He laid the paper on the desk, put his head in his hands, elbows on the desk, and read. "A sixteen-jeweled Waltham five-minute repeater, hunting case, MRC engraved in a shield on the checkered-design case. Sunken porcelain dial, Arabic numerals, and solid gold."

That, Sixpersons figured, might be the best bit of information he had gotten from his visit. Watches like that were scarce.

The sheriff laughed. "He wanted that watch back something fierce."

Sixpersons said nothing, although he was thinking *A solid gold repeater? I don't blame him.*

80

Of course, he had never owned any watch.

The door opened, and in ran a telegrapher, from the looks of him. Jackson Sixpersons had learned to read white men, especially town folk.

The little runt handed the fat sheriff a yellow paper.

The sheriff read it. and grinned. "Reckon maybe we kilt four of them bad men." He held the telegraph out for Sixpersons.

Sixpersons took the telegraph and read.

A dead body had been found in a tent at Mackey's Salt Works. He had a bullet in his back and had bled himself out. Plus, some of the men working the old salt diggings had seen a bunch of men — well-mounted, well-armed men — hanging around that tent.

Sixpersons rose.

"You'll send the body back, won't you, Deputy?" the sheriff asked.

Jackson Sixpersons picked up his shotgun. "For the reward? Or the photographer?"

The old sheriff laughed and wiped the tobacco juice off his lips.

"Grover Cleveland won't put up a dime for no reward, Deputy. And the photographer done left. Headed up to Fayetteville where the pickin's might be better."

"I see." Sixpersons pushed through the

door. Sheriff Whit Marion was no fool. Grover Cleveland, president of the local bank but not the United States, might not offer a reward, but plenty of others would. Trains, banks, express companies, and stage lines had offered plenty of rewards on the capture, death, or conviction of known criminals to have ridden with the McCoy-Maxwell Gang.

Jackson Sixpersons didn't care about a reward. He just had a job to do.

CHAPTER SIX

Somewhere in the Texas Panhandle

No hat for protection from the sun. No bullets for the Winchester '86. No food. No water. He had not thought to bring a canteen with him. No brains, either.

James Mann knew what he should have done. Once he had leaped from the boxcar the previous night, and the train had passed — carrying the stinking thief and would-be killer south along the rails — he should have followed the tracks. Eventually, he would have come to a water tank, and there he could have slaked his thirst, found a good hiding place, and hopped the next freight train that rumbled along south. Yet he hadn't. He'd figured his father would come looking for him, and the idea of being caught by his pa sickened him.

Smart enough, he'd found the North Star and walked east, away from the tracks. Fort Smith lay east. All he had to do was keep going in that general direction and cross through Indian Territory.

In the heat of the day, he sat, and knew he was a fool. Cross the reservations of the Kiowas, Comanches and Apaches? Long before he even reached the land of the Five Civilized Tribes, those Indians, even the peaceful ones, would probably kill him for the Winchester.

He reached into the sack and found the badge, which he stuck into his pants pocket. He pulled on the extra pair of socks, but had to fight to get his boots on over the two pairs. At least, that would minimize the blisters he was getting. The extra shirt, he put on after tossing away the one he had worn, the one ripped to shreds from his tumble on the gravel and brush alongside the rails. That emptied the sack. The hobo from the boxcar had most of his food, and James had eaten the last bit of jerky hours earlier.

He wrapped the sack around his head, made himself stand, and, still refusing to concede defeat, to give up and return to the railroad, he walked eastward. Walked. And walked. Moving blindly, but smart enough to use the sun to find his way east.

No clouds shown in the sky.

The temperature, he guessed, had to be

approaching eighty.

Onward, he walked.

Eventually, he came to a river, or a creek, but it had water, red, muddy, and brackish, but it tasted better than the sarsaparilla Pa and Ma had bought for him that time at the store in McAdam. Yet he wasn't completely stupid. Uncle Jimmy had warned him about drinking too much Texas water, and James did not want to get sick. Not out in the middle of nowhere.

He followed the riverbed, since, for the time being, it seemed to be flowing eastward. Only an occasional lizard came into his view; James saw no game, not even a scrawny jackrabbit or soaring raven. No fish jumped in the river, but as sorry as that water had tasted, that came as no surprise. On the other hand, he rarely heard the warning of a rattlesnake.

How far had he traveled? He couldn't fathom a guess, but not far from home — not considering that he'd expected to be well beyond his father's grasp and iron hand. Was he too old to get a whipping from his parents? James didn't want to find out.

Texas turned bleaker, more rugged. The treeless plains seemed endless, and every mile or so, he had to squash that urge to return home. After a while, even that would have been hopeless, he realized. Oh, he could follow the river back a ways, but after that? Finding the railroad tracks would be a poor gamble.

So . . . James kept walking.

His feet ached. He knew that the sun had already burned his neck, and, even with the sack for a bonnet, his head felt like a scorched hotcake. Around dusk, he found a grove of trees. The only place a person could find trees in that part of the country came along riverbeds, so it would have to be his first camp. Without food, his stomach rumbled and his belly tightened.

How long could a man go without food? He recalled Uncle Jimmy talking about that. A week? James wasn't sure. Water was more precious — just a few days, he remembered his uncle saying, before you died a miserable death — but he had water, as bad as it was.

It didn't matter. Not yet. It was as far as he was going. He crawled to the river, cupped his hands, and slaked his thirst, wondering if the sand and grit he swallowed along with the water might be considered food then moved back to the small cottonwoods.

Uncle Jimmy had also told him a habit many cowhands got into before they bedded down. It was probably nothing more than superstition, but cowhands and many wayfarers, would throw a lariat around their bedrolls. They believed that snakes and other night crawlers would respect the rope and never cross it.

"Why even think about that?" he said aloud. The rawness of his voice surprised him, especially after he had just reduced the swelling of his tongue and the dryness in his mouth with that awful water.

Refusing to speak again, he thought *I don't have a lariat.* Besides, he didn't want to get into the habit of talking to himself.

If a snake came along at night, he could always bash its head in with the butt of the Winchester rifle. Or maybe stab it to death with the pin on the back of the deputy's badge.

He sat there, legs outstretched, crossing his weary feet every now and then, leaning against the tree, watching evening become night.

Off in that not-too-far distance, a wolf howled. Not a coyote, but a wolf. It sang out again. Definitely a wolf.

He thought about home. *Ma would be scrubbing the dishes clean, and Jacob and Kris would be already in bed, their bellies full of salt pork, beans, maybe fried potatoes.*

After that chore, Ma would go over their lessons they should have studied in their McGuffey's Readers. Pa would be checking on the livestock, gathering the dried manure for the breakfast fire in the morning. When full dark came, they would turn in. Kris would lead the prayers, with Jacob following.

James shook off the thoughts, knowing he would be mouthing the words . . . if he'd been there.

What was I thinking? Running away. He closed his eyes and immediately fell into a deep, hard sleep.

All the next day, James saw the clouds forming, darkening the skies way off in the horizon, which did not bother him. At least, not at first. After all, those thunderheads loomed low, but well behind him, off to the northwest, and he kept walking, more or less, in an easterly direction, still following the river.

By noon, he felt a cooling wind on his back, and he could hear the distant rumbling of thunder. Every now and then, he would stop to look behind him. Lightning flashed, and he could see where torrents of rain were flooding the Panhandle somewhere well behind him. *Good,* he kept thinking, *empty those clouds now.*

Those clouds were a lot closer than they had been the last time he had looked.

A few hours later, the wind whipped him along as if urging him to hurry up. He needed no motivation. The thunder, the lightning, was all he needed to know he would soon be in trouble if he did not find shelter.

Soon.

Once, he stopped underneath a creaking cottonwood, and found shelter under a canopy of leaves. He stayed there only a few minutes before he remembered all of those trees he had seen, splintered, scorched, split, or killed by lightning. He moved again, quickly.

He could see blue all around him, but right on his back was an ominous black. By three o'clock, his hair began to feel frizzy, and the electricity in the air became palpable.

Soon, the clouds had overtaken him, and he thought he might just luck out. Maybe the storm would pass over him, dump its contents, and send its lightning well ahead of him. He hoped that would happen. Prayed for it.

Thunder boomed, and he ducked, scanning the Llano Estacado — the Staked Plains of the Texas Panhandle — for some sod house or makeshift shelter left by a buffalo hunter who had traveled that country decades earlier. Or a cave, some hole in the ground, an overhang in some arroyo. Anything.

Nothing. No coyote den. No overhang. Not even an anthill.

James swore, and God must have heard that curse, because it had scarcely passed his lips when cold, hard, icy rain drenched him.

It happened almost instantly. The wind took off his sack, but he no longer felt the need to protect his head from the sun, for there was no sun. Just low, black clouds. Or so he assumed. He couldn't see anything but white sheets of rain, and those giant drops stung him like buckshot. He brought the rifle close to him, and felt chilled.

The barrel was casehardened steel. It could attract lightning, and he remembered hearing stories of men caught out in some brutal Texas thunderstorm. Cowboys had been struck dead with their horses, their spurs melted onto their burned boots. Or that farmer who had been carrying a shovel. Or that man down on the Pease River who had been sitting in the edge of his covered wagon, eating beans with a spoon.

"Throw the rifle away," he heard himself

say. "It's not worth dying over."

But he just couldn't do it.

He even tried to wrap it underneath his waterlogged shirt, protect it from the rain, and potential rust.

The river had carved a bit of a canyon across the ground, and that might have protected him from some of the risk and rain, but as he walked, he soon realized he had cleared the canyon and kept moving across open prairie. Sagebrush scratched his legs, but he kept walking. Perhaps a hundred yards later, he realized another greenhorn mistake. Back in the canyon, there had been protection, if only moderate, from the rain, wind and lightning. He could have leaned against the canyon walls for shelter.

Go back.

He tried to change his course, but the assault of rain and wind, turned him back, kept pushing him onward. James relented, let the storm drive him — like storms often herded cattle and wild mustangs. Let the storm guide him . . . to his death.

I couldn't find that canyon anyway, he thought. He wasn't even sure he was following the river. He could see maybe a few feet in front of him, and that was it.

Late afternoon had turned pitch black, except for that brilliant sheet of white rain

— which abruptly changed.

At first, the hailstones were maybe the size of his pinky fingertip. They stung, but his body had been so numbed by the freezing rain and brutal wind that he found the hail less painful than the rain. Moments later, however, those hailstones had become larger, growing into the size of dollar coins, mothballs, and a few even larger. One slammed into his shoulder and knocked him into the mud. He wanted to lay down, stay there, but if he did, in minutes he would be covered by thousands of hailstones, so he used the Winchester to push himself up, noticing the stock of the rifle sank three or four inches into the muck. It took all his strength to pull the rifle free.

He grimaced as stone after stone smashed into his head, his back, his thighs and calves. Finally, he was moving, slowing down, his teeth chattering.

So this is how it ends, he figured. *Either freeze to death or catch my death from pneumonia.*

Just when he thought he might as well just sit down and die, a new sound came to him. The roaring of a locomotive.

His eyes widened with hope. He figured he had somehow made a crazy loop and come back to the Fort Worth–Denver City tracks. He could hop the train, if he could just find it. Searching for the locomotive's headlamp revealed nothing, but the hail had stopped as abruptly as it came. The wind hit the side of his face. Then the other side. The wind blew him down . . .

And he understood that he had not circled back to the railroad line. It was not the roaring of a locomotive that he heard. "Tornado!" he yelled.

The wind drove him back into the rain.

He rolled over and crawled across cactus and sagebrush, ripping his shirt, hauling the .50-caliber rifle with him. Crawled desperately for his life. He couldn't see anything. His ears seemed to pop with pressure. But he sensed that he was moving.

Keep moving.

Keep moving.

Stop and you're dead.

The wind intensified, and the rain — thankfully no longer huge chunks of awful ice — washed all over him. He had no sense of time, not anymore. Could not recall how long he had been in the storm. James Mann just knew that he had to keep crawling.

His shirt was ripped open. He wasn't sure if that was blood running down his chest or just icy rainwater. The roaring of the twister seemed to die away, but the rain came down and down and down and down.

He moaned, prayed, begged, but, mostly, he crawled. Kept crawling and pulling the Winchester with him. He thought he had lost one of his boots, but did not stop.

Suddenly, his head bumped into something solid. He reached out, fingered wood, then air, something cold, then another piece of wood. Slats of some kind. No. Not slats. The wood felt round.

Wagon wheel spokes.

He gripped them with his right hand and pulled his body along. Sensing shelter, he dragged his battered, soaked, freezing body underneath the wagon. What kind of vehicle, he couldn't tell, but decided that it had to be some old buffalo hunter's wagon, left behind so many years ago or maybe some abandoned wagon along one of the military roads.

It didn't matter, for the wagon's floor, old as it must have been, did not leak much. It wasn't exactly like he was sleeping in his own bed or under a roof, and the ground was soaking wet. He could hear running water cutting a trench underneath the wagon. Yet it was as close to shelter as he would come, and he thanked the Lord for it. He moved to what he believed must be the center of the wagon, drew up into a ball, still clutching the rifle, and squeezed his eyes shut.

The rain did not lessen.

The storm did not leave.

Yet somehow, James Mann fell asleep.

CHAPTER SEVEN

Mackey's Salt Works

"Know 'im?" Sergeant John Hashtula asked.

Jackson Sixpersons glanced at the bloated body, shook his head, and pulled the tarp — no pine box for this outlaw — over the man's head to reduce the smell. Yet he could assume this man had been shot during the bank robbery across the border in Greenville, Arkansas. The McCoy-Maxwell Gang kept getting thinner all the time. Like most outlaw gangs, these days.

"The men with him?" Sixpersons asked.

The sergeant thrust his jaw northwest toward Muskogee, Sixpersons guessed, in the Creek Country, where John Hashtula hung his hat.

Hashtula was older than even Jackson Sixpersons. He had run the Choctaw Lighthorsemen back when Sixpersons was riding for the Cherokee Lighthorse Police.

In the early days in the Nations, after the

tribes had been removed from their Southeastern homelands, the Cherokees, Choctaws, Creeks, and Seminoles had formed their own police forces, most of them taking the name of Lighthorse, named after General Henry "Lighthorse Harry" Lee of the white man's Revolution against King George.

Actually, the Cherokee police force dated to 1797, although they wouldn't begin calling themselves "Lighthorsemen" until the 1820s. Sixpersons figured, giving the lesser brains of the Creeks and Choctaws, those tribes naturally borrowed the "Lighthorse" name for their own tribal police. In 1844, the Cherokee National Council had made things official, by authorizing a Lighthorse company — a captain, lieutenant, and twenty-four policemen — empowered to arrest Cherokee fugitives. By 1874, the Cherokees had their own prison at the national capital in Tahlequah, but that was the year the white man's government in Washington City had consolidated the Indian agents for the Five Civilized Tribes.

Muskogee's Union Agency had become the headquarters — a slight to the superiority of the Cherokees and Tahlequah, Sixpersons knew in all his heart — and in 1880, Colonel John Q. Tufts, the Union Agency's

Indian agent, had organized a new group of policemen. So Hashtula and Sixpersons moved from their Lighthorse police to the United States Indian Police.

Hashtula had his job with the U.S.I.P. Sixpersons also had his commission as a deputy marshal for Judge Parker's court.

"Muskogee," Sixpersons said.

Hashtula nodded.

"Four men?" the Cherokee asked.

The Choctaw shrugged. "Five, six, ten?" He pointed toward the white men and Indians working at the salt stills and springs. "They don't know."

"You find a trail?" Sixpersons asked.

Hashtula's head shook. "They're good."

The trail ended at the salt works. McCoy, Maxwell, and what was left of their gang could be riding to Muskogee. Or west, deeper into Indian Territory. They might follow the Arkansas River on up into Kansas. More than likely, they would catch the first Katy train and jump off somewhere in Texas. Either way, once they were out of the Nations, they were out of Sixpersons' jurisdiction, which meant that he would go on to Muskogee, even though he clearly knew what he would find. Some white men — four, five, six, ten? — had sold their horses and tack at one of the city's livery stables and hadn't been seen since. Nobody would remember them at the depot, and maybe they would have taken separate trains. Certainly they would not have boarded the train together. But if Link McCoy and Zane Maxwell had sold their horses, that meant they had hurried south to Texas.

Judge Parker and the marshal would be disappointed, but until McCoy and Maxwell returned to the Nations, there wasn't anything Sixpersons could do. Against those bad men. Yet the white men in Fort Smith weren't all stupid. They had given Sixpersons plenty of other warrants. He would meet up with the posse at Eufaula and start hunting. Link McCoy and Zane Maxwell would have to wait.

For now.

Denison, Texas

Jeff White barged through the batwing doors of the Railroaders Saloon, stopped only long enough to see Link McCoy, and stormed over to the corner table where he nursed a beer alone. Uninvited, White pulled up a chair, sat heavily down, and slammed a newspaper on the table.

"Spell your name wrong, Jeff?" Sarcasm accented McCoy's voice.

99

"What this says is that the McCoy-Maxwell Gang made off with more 'n a thousand bucks!" He slid the paper angrily toward McCoy's beer stein. "You give me and Tulip jus' a hunnert."

Ignoring the paper, McCoy picked up the stein, and sipped his beer. He waited for the barmaid to walk by, and when she stopped, and looked at White, McCoy said, "Bring him a whiskey. And you might as well bring me another pilsner, sweetie."

With a smile, she hurried back to the bar.

Only then, did McCoy turn the *Morning Call & Telegraph* around and read the story on the front page. It didn't take long. Texas didn't really care much about what the McCoy-Maxwell Gang was doing in the Indian Nations or Arkansas, which was why the law pretty much left the gang alone in Denison and over in the Hell's Half Acre district of Fort Worth.

He counted two paragraphs and three typographical errors. Maybe four. "Wouldn't be the first time a newspaper has made a mistake. Or a bank official lied."

"Wouldn't be the first time some smart dude has cheated me, neither," Jeff White said. "And —" Dumb as he was, White was smart enough, savvy enough, and experienced enough to shut up when he heard the saloon gal coming up behind him.

She placed the shot glass and bottle in front of White, and the new beer beside McCoy, and took the empty stein and McCoy's greenback away.

Before White could say something else, McCoy cut him off, his voice a cold whisper. "Most of those boys we left dead in Arkansas and at the salt works had been riding with Zane and me a lot longer than you, White." He let those words sink in.

"What are you sayin'?" White reached for the bottle. He didn't bother with the shot glass.

"Meaning I ain't knowed you long enough to miss you when you're gone."

"If yer cheatin' —"

"Drink your whiskey. Take your bottle back to your room. Get drunk. And keep your mouth shut. The paper's wrong. We got four hundred bucks from that robbery. They probably hadn't found the gold-filled sack Clete McBee died for. Go on. The whiskey's on me."

White swore, slammed the bottle on the table, and reached for the *Morning Call & Telegraph.*

"Leave the newspaper," McCoy said.

The outlaw cursed again, but obeyed.

McCoy made sure he left the saloon,

watching him through the front window as he stormed across the boardwalk, crossed the muddy street, and made his way toward the hotel across the street.

Only then did McCoy sip his beer, then pick up the newspaper again. He wasn't vain. He didn't care about what the ink-slingers wrote about him or Zane Maxwell, and could care less if the newspapers reported he had stolen $400 or $4 million. But above the newspaper fold, and far more detailed, was another article.

That one, he read with interest.

Fort Worth, Texas

Twenty hours on a Fort Worth–Denver City train was about as much as Millard Mann could stand, and when he stepped out of the coach onto the crowded Fort Worth depot, his clothes reeked of cigar smoke and sweat. The air around the cow town didn't make him feel any better, but he knew where to go.

The first man he saw was heading across the street toward the nearest saloon, and he didn't like it one whit when Millard Mann stopped him.

"Who was the yard boss when the south-bound came in the other night?"

"How in the —" The railroader must've

seen something in Mann's eyes that warned him. His tone changed quickly, and he took a couple steps back. "On the F.W. and D.C.?"

Mann's head nodded.

The railroader wet his lips. "Flannery Finn. Be my guess."

"Where do I'd find Mr. Finn?"

The railroader shrugged. "If he ain't in jail or Boot Hill, try the café yonder." He pointed.

"Thanks." Carrying his grip and Winchester, Millard weaved through the porters, passengers, and greeters, stepped down the steps, and waited for an omnibus to pass before crossing the busy street toward the Iron Rail Café.

The place was packed, and the smell of greasy food and hot coffee reminded him of the last time he had eaten. But food could wait. He picked out Flannery Finn instantly, and moved quickly, turning sideways to avoid a petite blonde carrying plates of food, and squeezed between two seats at the counter. "Finn."

He was a big, burly Irishman with red hair, a full beard, and a face pockmarked with scars. The man crushed out his cigarette in the runny yolks of what remained of his eggs, and turned. "Who wants to know?"

"Mann. Boss a crew in the Panhandle."

"I boss the yard at Fort Worth. And I'm eatin' me breakfast."

"You've finished eating," Mann pointed out. The grip fell to the floor, and as Finn began to rise, the barrel of the Winchester found itself between two buttons on the center of the big brawler's chest.

The Irishman sank into the stool. A few diners nearby decided their stomachs were full, and left in a hurry.

Millard smiled. "My treat, by the way." Holding the rifle with one hand, the stock braced against his hip, he fished a dime from his vest pocket and dropped it on the plate near the cigarette and leftover crumbs. He had fetched two coins from that pocket. The forefinger and thumb of his left hand held a Morgan dollar. "Information?"

Flannery Finn smiled. "Now what can I bloody well do for a kindly gentlemen like yeself?" His massive left hand came up, palm open, underneath the coin.

"Any riders on last night's southbound F.W. and D.C.?"

Finn understood the meaning was vagabond freeloaders. "Aye. There was one."

Millard breathed a little easier, but did

not lower the rifle. "Where might I find him?" His finger tightened on the trigger.

The big man's laugh boomed across the café. "I left the cur dog with Doc Gertrude. Across from the Donovan Brothers mercantile on Weatherford."

Millard felt the blood rushing to his head, and he had to fight for control. Finn's eyes turned troubled, and the grin vanished.

Millard Mann spoke, though his words were quiet. "You . . . beat . . . up . . . a . . . teenaged . . . boy?"

Just about everyone in the café stopped eating. Most of them, including Flannery Finn, held their breath.

"Are ye off yer bloody rocker?" Finn pushed up his Irish cap. "A boy? 'Twas a man full grown. A brute named Clanton that I've warned ten thousand times not to let me catch him ridin' on our line's dime ag'in. He deserved ever' busted bone I give him, he done. Ask anyone in Fort Worth, and ye'll hear it true. Flannery Finn doesn't beat up children."

"Be glad you didn't." The coin dropped into the Irishman's ham-sized palm. Millard picked up his grip, and backed out of the café, never lowering the Winchester's barrel until he was out the door.

■ ■ ■ ■

An hour later, Millard Mann sat on a bench in the shade at the depot, grip at his side, '73 Winchester across his lap.

He had found Clanton at the doctor's office above the bank next to the mercantile on Weatherford Street. He had given Millard the news . . . as best as he could with his jaw broken and teeth busted, plus four broken ribs and a fractured skull.

After Clanton finished his confession, Millard decided the hobo had been lucky. He would probably have killed the bum.

According to Clanton, James had boarded the boxcar at the water tank by Comanche Springs. They had gone maybe a mile or two before the boy leaped off. Clanton didn't say why, but Millard knew. The sorry cuss had probably tried to rob James of everything he had, which wouldn't have amounted to much — except for the Winchester '86 rifle.

A mile or two from the stop, and just a few miles from home. And there sat Millard, some three hundred miles south of McAdam. He prayed that the frightening experience with Clanton would have ended James's dreams of . . . of . . . of whatever he planned on doing and sent the boy back home.

Yet even as he closed his eyes and clasped his hands, even as he prayed his hardest to God, he knew James would not have gone home. He would have taken off.

But where?

CHAPTER EIGHT

Along the north fork of the Red River, Texas
"Reckon that twister blowed his carcass here?"

Spit. "Else he sprouted from all that thar rain." Spit.

"Is he dead?"

"Shore oughta be."

Instantly, James Mann came awake, realizing that those voices were not from a dream and that he wasn't dead. He fought to grip the Winchester, trying to find the lever, but slammed his head into something hard, which knocked him back down onto the cold, soft, soaking ground.

He remembered he had found shelter underneath a wagon out on the Llano Estacado.

As stars and blazes of orange and white and red circled around him, laughter rang louder than the sudden pounding in his head.

Har! Har! Har!
Har! Har! Har!

Forcing his vision to clear, James made himself lift his head and shoulders, and the rifle. Two figures squatted just ahead of him on the wet ground, between the two left wheels of the wagon. When he had stumbled onto the wagon during the fierce storm, he had thought the vehicle was some old abandoned relic from those wild and woolly days. The two figures told him otherwise.

Both wore buckskins and slouch hats still soaking wet from the rain. One had a full beard — thick, greasy, and silver — and no teeth. The other, much, much younger, had a mouth full of pearly whites and no beard, not even stubble. Just mud. His unkempt hair was the color of corn silk, his eyes a deep blue. The old man had only one eye.

James wished he would put a patch over that hole in his face.

"Careful with that cannon, bub," the old man said, pointing a finger — or what was left of a finger, the pointer missing the first two joints — at the Winchester. "Barrel's clogged with mud. Pull that thar trigger, an' I expect she'll blows up in yer face."

The younger one cleared his throat. "Iffen we wanted you dead, the devil'd be introducin' hisself to you by now."

Said the old man, "Name's Lamar. Wild-cat Lamar. This here's me boy, Robin." Slowly the old man rose, knees popping like gunfire, reaching for the front wheel to help him find his feet. His boots were caked with reddish mud. "Got coffee boilin'. Jerked venison and cold biscuits. Ain't much of a feast to celebrate survivin' that eternal storm of yesttiday, but it'll keep yer belly from rubbin' ag'in yer backbone."

The younger one's blue eyes danced. "He's a right fair hand at cookin'." Then he, too, started moving away from the wagon, boots splashing in the puddles that even the parched patch of land had not yet soaked in.

James rolled out from under the wagon. It was huge. Even the rear wheels stood over his head. The eight-feet-high wheels had to be six inches wide, and the tires had been double-rigged, to prolong their wear. Sixteen feet long, the wooden sides of the wagon stretched up at least ten feet, and although the big freight wagon had the bows for a canvas cover — like one of those old prairie schooners from the Oregon Trail days he had read about — the ribs were empty. It was no Conestoga, but bigger. Considering the lack of cover, whatever those two folks were carrying in the back, was soaked from the hail and rain.

"Help yerself to the grub." Wildcat Lamar slurped some coffee from a tin cup. "Got a heavy load, so we ain't goin' nowheres till the ground dries a mite. Don't fancy gettin' stuck out here."

James rubbed his head, shifted the rifle to his left hand, and looked up at the wagon. "You could fit a stagecoach in there," he marveled.

"Two more 'n likely." Lamar finished his coffee and tossed the cup to James.

He fumbled with it, dropped it, and knelt to pick it up, but not before making sure Robin Lamar wasn't ready to jump him.

After that incident in the Fort Worth–Denver City boxcar, James wasn't trusting anyone.

"Ain't got an extry cup to share," Lamar said. "Didn't expect to have no comp'ny payin' us a visit."

Robin moved around James, giving him a wide berth, and squatted beside his father. "How come you landed underneath our wagon?"

James scanned the countryside, puzzled.

The old man laughed. "Twister run off our oxen, iffen that's what yer lookin' fer."

"It is," James admitted, and moved toward the fire. The smell of coffee proved more than he could stand. He filled the cup, sipped some, and finally relaxed.

"How come you landed underneath our wagon?" Robin asked again. He piled two biscuits and some huge bits of jerky on a plate, and slid the plate across the slick grass toward James's boots.

"The twister dropped me here." James smiled as their eyes widened. "I'm kidding." The biscuits practically broke his teeth, and the jerky felt even harder.

He kept trying to make himself more presentable, but the ripped shirt and everything else about him made that impossible. Before long, nothing mattered. The coffee, even the tough food became his sole focus. He didn't speak further until he had cleaned the plate. Neither the old man or his boy spoke, either.

"I'm bound for Fort Smith," James said at last.

Coughing, Robin spit out a mouthful of coffee, and his father leaned forward, mouth agape. "Afoot?" the old man roared.

The coffee tasted finer than even the chicory Ma brewed. But after all that time without food or anything other than hard water, anything would have tasted good. Well, maybe not the granite-like biscuits and jerky.

James lied. "Lost my horse a ways back."

Old man Lamar seemed to accept that, nodding. "It'll happen. Lost yer way, eh?"

James eyed the man curiously.

Wildcat laughed and found a pouch that hung from the belt over his waist. He opened the piece of fringed leather and pulled out a twist of tobacco, from which he bit off a sizeable chunk and began softening the chaw with his gums. "Ye ain't followin' no knowed trail to Fort Smith," he explained after a moment.

"Yesterday's storm," James offered as an explanation.

Again, the old-timer took that lie as gospel, too, and looked at his son. "What you think, kid?"

Robin shrugged.

After spitting tobacco juice into the fire, Wildcat wiped his mouth with the back of his buckskinned sleeve, and nodded. "Ya can ride along with me and my boy." He laughed. "We's bound for Fort Smith, ain't we, son?"

The kid rolled his eyes. "Eventually." Robin sighed.

First, of course, they had to find the oxen — eight in all — that pulled that large wagon. The old man decided to break camp, sending Robin and James out after the beasts, hoping the animals had not strayed too far during the storm.

The sun dried out James's clothes quickly, but after an hour, James had his doubts. They had found only one animal, and it was dead. He and Robin spread out, trying to cover more ground, although he would have preferred sticking close, just for the conversation. Robin looked to be about James's age, slimmer, fairer, and with the worst haircut he had ever seen. Even the drunkard at the tonsorial parlor in McAdam, who only cut hair part-time (his main source of income being the postmaster, if that was a full-time affair in a place like McAdam), gave a better haircut that the one Robin Lamar had been given. It looked as if Wildcat had cut his son's hair with a knife, a dull knife at that.

Another ox had been killed, too. They saw the turkey buzzards circling before they found its carcass.

James begin to realize how lucky he was to be alive. "Did you see the twister?"

Robin stood just a few feet from him, the two of them looking down into an arroyo, still running with water, and what once had been a beast of burden.

"Heard it," he said. "Storm come up on

us so fast, didn't have time to find shelter or nothin'. We'd just turned the stock loose, and we leaped into the back of the wagon." He looked away from the dead animal, and at James. "Didn't hear you when you come in, else we'd have invited you inside." He grinned, a wonderful smile, full of life. "Don't want you a-thinkin' we ain't hospitable."

James laughed. "I'm surprised the tornado didn't haul your wagon off."

Robin shrugged, moving on, calling out the animals' names. "It's heavy enough," he said after walking several rods, and then his head shook. "If any more of our oxen is kilt, we won't be haulin' nothin' nowhere." That gave him a moment's pause. "Which might not be a bad thing."

"What do you mean?" James had just caught up with the lad.

"Nothin'." Robin changed the subject and pointed at James's ripped clothing. "I gots a shirt you can wear. Yer a mite bigger 'n me, so it might not fit that good, but it's better than what you's wearin'." Without waiting for a reply, he started walking across the plains. "July! August! Where are you knuckleheads?"

By dusk, they had found July and August, November and March. They had been driven into another arroyo, miles south of where the Lamars had been forced to camp, and the narrow slit in the ground had likely saved those four oxen from joining April and October in death. Not bad graze down in the little cut, either. The four animals were obedient, and November took the lead, so that all Robin and James had to do was clap their hands and let out a whoop every now and then to keep the oxen moving. The other two beasts they never found. Robin said four would have to do.

"Too late to make much progress," Wildcat said when they returned to camp. "Let the sun bake the ground some more." He staked the animals a ways from camp and began to get the fire going again.

"Sorry about April and December, Mr. Lamar," James said as he accepted the coffee the one-eyed man had poured. "And the two we just couldn't find."

"October," Wildcat corrected. "December was their ma. She got called to glory back in Missouri."

"Right." James sipped the brew. "October."

"Four's enough," Wildcat said. "They's good oxen. Can pull six tons, I'd bet, and we ain't haulin' that much — jus' enough to make our trip profitable. And them other

116

two . . ." He gestured toward the flat expanse of land. "This country swallers things up, all the time."

"What are you hauling, sir?" James stared at his cup. Anytime he looked at Wildcat Lamar, his eyes almost immediately locked on that hole where the man's right eye should be.

"Supplies." The answer was curt and final.

"For Fort Smith?"

"We'll get there directly. We'll make some stops in West Cache Creek, Elm Springs, old Fort Holmes and some places."

Those names meant nothing to James, but he nodded as if it all made sense to him.

The man kept on talking. "Sell some of our wares there. Good profit to be made in Indian Territory, but it can be dangersome. So I'm glad we got you and your Winchester cannon."

Maybe that was why they had invited James to accompany them on their journey to Arkansas. They needed an extra gun for protection. James swallowed, and almost told Wildcat that he lacked any shells for the repeater. After all, they were decent enough to let him ride along with them. If fate hadn't led James to their wagon, he'd probably be feeding carrion like October and March. No, April. Yet something stopped him. He just couldn't trust these two merchants. Not yet. He didn't know why.

Wildcat spit juice into the fire, and continued. "Cross the Arkansas River again and pret' much jes foller it out of the Nations and to Fort Smith. Big town. Mighty fancy."

James wanted to ask more questions, but didn't want to show them — especially Robin — just how green he was.

Robin told his father to fetch an extra shirt for their new companion.

James expected the supper to be unappetizing as the biscuits and jerky, but as dusk fell, Robin disappeared into the back of the wagon and came out with a double-barreled shotgun, toting the gun and a sack slung over his left shoulder. "I'll see if I can't rouse up a grouse or some pheasant."

Relaxing, James eased his hand away from the rifle's lever, wondering what he would have done had Robin trained those long twelve-gauge barrels on him. Club him? Run? Beg for his life? Wet his britches?

The old gun's barrels were enormous, almost four feet long, but Robin seemed experienced holding such a huge weapon.

The shotgun belonged to another age, probably before the Civil War. It was a muzzleloader, the barrels, affixed to the stock by barrel keys surrounded by egg-shaped escutcheons of German silver, were dark brown and rough from a life of abuse.

"Got yer caps?" the old man asked.

Robin pulled a capper, full of the copper percussion caps, from the pocket of his vest.

"Birds." The old man cursed and shook his head. "Well, maybe with James a-joinin' us with that big ol' Winchester of his 'n, we'll eat us some antelope or a mule deer afore too long."

Suddenly, James frowned. The coffee didn't taste that good anymore, and he hated himself for fooling these good people. Even if he couldn't quite trust them completely.

He went to bed with his stomach full and wearing a new blue-checked collarless shirt, a little tight on him, especially after savoring the taste of sage hens. Robin proved a good shot with that old shotgun, and the old man could cook after all. Roasted sage hens, sourdough biscuits, and fine coffee. He felt as if he had been treated to a supper at the eating parlor in McAdam.

When he woke the next morning, he crawled out from underneath the wagon and found the Lamars hitching the team to the wagon.

"Hungry?" Wildcat asked.

"No, sir," he answered honestly. "Not really."

"Good thing, on account that we et last night." He moved with the harnesses, chains, and curved wooden yokes like a dancer, with ease, unaffected by having lost one eye. "An' we gots miles to make up."

"Can I help you?" James asked, hoping the old man would say no.

"Nope. 'Bout done here anyhows. But take the spade from offen t'uther side of the wagon, and make sure that fire is out. Cover it good. Like we was never here. Do that fer us?"

"Sure." He walked to the end of the wagon, found the spade, and went to work.

Like we was never here.

Fat chance of that happening, James thought, staring at the giant wagon with its massive wheels, pulled by the four behemoth oxen. Anybody would be able to follow that trail.

Suddenly, he paused, and a shiver raced up his spine. *Even Pa.*

"Hey, boy!"

The old man was calling him, so James took the shovel with him and hurried to the front of the wagon.

"Spade goes yonder," Wildcat ordered.

"Then come back here."

When he had finished returning the tool to its proper spot, James found that no one sat in the driver's box. For the first time, he realized that he would not be riding to Fort Smith.

They would be walking alongside the oxen and wagon.

All the way across Indian Territory.

The end of a long blacksnake whip dragged on the ground in front of Wildcat's boots. "Ever skint a mule, boy?" the one-eyed man asked.

"No, sir," James answered honestly.

"Well, we ain't got mules. Just mule-headed oxen. Ever driven one of 'em ignorant beasts?"

"No, sir," he said again.

Wildcat handed the whip, handle first, toward James. "Time ya learnt."

CHAPTER NINE

Denison

Link McCoy picked his room at the Draper House Hotel perfectly. On the second floor right above the hotel's bar, which brought in travelers and cowhands and railroad workers and gamblers and had the loudest, most out-of-tune piano in the county, played by a drunk whose two thumbs had been cut off by a soiled dove five years earlier down south in San Angelo. Nobody ever wanted that room. Nobody could get a good night's sleep in such a place — which was why Link McCoy picked it.

Above the din, he laid the Denison newspaper on the dresser, right in front of the pistol-grip Winchester shotgun, and motioned the others to get closer. When everyone, including Jeff White, had gathered around, he tapped the end of his unlighted cigar on the story.

LONE STAR CATTLEMEN
NEGOTIATE GRAZE LEASE

Below that, in a smaller point size

TEXANS AGREE TO PAY HEFTY SUM
TO HEATHENS

And then in slightly larger type and italics

$25,000 in Gold Going to Chickasaws

He waited as Zane Maxwell read the headline and the story to Tulip Bells, who grinned.

"It'll have to be easier than robbing banks," Zane Maxwell said. "I reckon we learned that in Arkansas."

"Same as Jesse James and his crew learned in Northfield," Bells said, "and the Dalton boys learned in Coffeytown."

"Coffeyville," Maxwell corrected.

"I know that. I was jokin'."

Jeff White merely took another pull on the bottle of rye.

"We do run the risk," McCoy said, "of riling a bunch of Texas ranchers."

"And Chickasaws," Tulip Bells pointed out.

"Indians we can handle," Maxwell said.

"Texans can be another matter, and we won't be far from the state."

"Where's the money go?" Jeff White finally spoke. "It don't say that in the story."

"The Bank of Tishomingo," McCoy replied. "In the Chickasaw capital."

White stepped back. "How you know that?"

McCoy grinned. "I have sources."

"You know when?" Maxwell asked.

"It won't be until after the cattlemen's association finish their meeting in Fort Worth," McCoy said. "That's where they'll be collecting the grazing fee for the Indians. They'll take the train up through here, I expect, then escort their money across the Red River and to Tishomingo. That's where we'll hit them. That money won't reach Tishomingo."

Downstairs in the saloon, a fight broke out. Some chirpy screamed. Men cursed. Glass shattered.

"In town?" Tulip Bells sounded as if he had had enough of committing armed robbery in towns. The incident at Greenville, Arkansas, had put the fear of God — or, rather, the fear of farmers and city folk with rifles and shotguns — in him.

"South of town," McCoy said, and saw the faces of White and Bells relax. Even

124

Maxwell nodded his approval.

"At Fort Washita," McCoy said.

"A fort!" Jeff White took another pull on the bottle.

Below in the saloon, a shotgun roared. The Denison law had come in to break up the fight. More curses, a few shouts, and then someone below told the piano player to get with it.

"A fort, but no army," Maxwell said. "Bluebellies gave up that post twenty years ago. Probably even longer than that. Indians have been using it since then."

"So have the whiskey runners," McCoy said.

Tulip Bells was the first to understand everything. He snapped his fingers. "Yeah. I've bought me some Choc beer there before. And whiskey, too." He laughed and slapped his thigh. "Those Texans, those devils. So that's their plan."

White frowned. "I don't get it."

McCoy didn't expect the blowhard to have understood. He grinned, and had to speak up. The piano player was hammering out "Hot Time in the Old Town Tonight."

"Get the Indians liquored up," McCoy said. "Cheat those Chickasaws out of that twenty-five grand."

"And those Texas waddies riding guard

for the cattlemen's association," Maxwell guessed, "will be roostered pretty good by then, as well."

"Maybe," McCoy said.

"Easy pickings." Jeff White had come around.

"Don't go spending that gold before we've got it," McCoy cautioned. "Any number of things can go wrong, and I'm not going through another massacre like Greenville again. This is my last score. After this, I'm taking my share and riding to Mexico. Figure on buying me a hacienda and sitting back with nothing to do but drink tequila and watch Mexican women feed me grapes."

"Grapes?" Tulip Bells asked.

"Red grapes. I like grapes."

They laughed.

Below, a banjo and some fool on a Louisiana accordion joined the piano player, along with another idiot playing the triangle. Loud. Real loud.

Just the way Link McCoy wanted it.

"Zane will take the train to Fort Worth, pretend to be a reporter from Kansas City, since Kansas City has an interest in what goes on with Texas cowboys because of all the packing plants. Nobody around here would likely know of some ink-slinger with a Missouri newspaper. As soon as the meeting breaks up, and the money is loaded on the train, he'll send us a telegraph."

"That says the gold's comin'!" White was drunk and excited.

"Well, not quite in those words," Maxwell said.

"Right." McCoy picked up his shotgun. "We take the Katy north to Durant. That's just over the Red in the Choctaw Nation. Tulip will already be there. With good horses. Then we ride over to Fort Washita."

The rest of the plan was easily explained. Maxwell and Bells listened. White finished the rye.

"We'll need a few more men," Maxwell said.

"I figure six men, including us," McCoy suggested, and Maxwell and Tulip Bells agreed. Not too many men, so the split would be higher for all of the robbers.

White just giggled, already counting his share of the loot.

"A good or bad whiskey runner," McCoy concluded. "And some liquor."

Bells stepped away from the dresser, picked up McCoy's bedroll from the end of the bed, and rolled it onto the floor.

White turned around. "What are you doin'?"

"Getting ready to turn in," Bells said, and stood.

"In here?"

"That ruckus downstairs don't bother me."

"Crazy fool." White drank more from the bottle. He grinned at Maxwell. "So we need just two more fellers for our job."

"Three," the outlaw leader said.

"Three? We got four already."

McCoy shook his head. "No, you won't be with us, Jeff." The barrel of the shotgun pressed against White's belly button.

The bottle fell to the floor, and White reached for the butt of his pistol, but stopped suddenly, hearing the noise downstairs, and smiled. "You won't kill me. Not here. Even that racket downstairs won't drown out a blast from that —"

Suddenly, he gasped as if sucking for breath that could not, would not, come, and Tulip Bells withdrew the Arkansas toothpick he had plunged into the man's back.

"You drink too much," McCoy said as Bells dropped the knife onto the bedroll, and slid his arms underneath Jeff White's armpits as the man fell back, his mouth moving, eyes darting every which way.

White tried to speak, but no words could come.

"And," McCoy said, "I don't cotton to be called a thief."

Slowly, Tulip Bells laid the outlaw on McCoy's bedroll. No need in getting blood all over the floor. The management would frown upon such things, might even fetch the law, and with a $25,000 payday coming, McCoy could splurge on a new bedroll. In a town like Denison on a loud Saturday night, they could sneak the body out and deposit it where no one would find it for years.

Zane Maxwell pulled a watch from his vest pocket, opened the case, looked at the dying Jeff White, and said, "I'll say three minutes."

"Two," McCoy said.

Maxwell stared at the watch.

Tulip Bells said, "Since I know where I stuck him, I don't reckon I can bet."

All three men looked down at the floor, listening to the awful music and clamor below, waiting to see how long it would take Jeff White to die.

Downstairs, the piano player banged out "There Is a Tavern in the Town."

Mulberry Station, Texas
Millard Mann returned to where he had found his son's hat.

129

He had taken the Fort Worth–Denver City northbound back to McAdam and gone home — only to find, as his head had told him over his heart's wishes, that James had not come home. Millard had then ridden over to Charles Goodnight's spread, bought the best horse and pack mule the old rancher had, and ridden south back to Mulberry Station, where he had discovered James's hat the morning after his oldest son had run away from home.

Millard cursed. He should have looked at the sign closer, realized that James —. Millard stopped that thought. The boy had hopped the freight right there. That much had been clear. There was no way to even guess that he would have jumped out of the car just a few miles down the tracks.

Millard rode carefully, dismounting often, trying to find some track, some bit of trail he could follow. Two miles he covered. Then two more. Then he rode back north a mile, two, three, four.

There was no sign. The massive storm that had hit earlier had wiped out anything he might have found. All he had was . . . nothing.

"Fort Smith."

He was squatting on the east side of the rails, looking at something that might have

130

been a footprint. How old? He had no idea. Many workers went up and down those rails. So did hobos. Anyone might have made that track.

The voice whispered into his ear. *"Fort Smith."*

He looked north, then behind him, standing. The horse, a broad-chested blue roan, snorted. The mule grazed contentedly. Millard saw nothing. No one around to have whispered. The closest person was a few miles up the line at McAdam. The voice . . . Millard shivered. It had sounded . . . just like Jimmy's.

Only then did Millard realize that no ghost had spoken those two words. He had whispered them himself. He said it again. "Fort Smith."

He turned and looked east, across the Staked Plains. It made sense, good sense. James had taken the big rifle and his uncle's badge. He planned to follow Jimmy's footsteps, take a job as a deputy U.S. marshal — as if the federal lawman or Judge Isaac Parker would hire a fool-headed, strong-willed seventeen-year-old kid.

Millard shook his head. Jimmy wasn't that crazy. He would have waited for the next southbound, not traipse off across the Llano Estacado. The rains *could have* washed away the tracks that would have shown James hopping another southbound.

No. Millard sighed. His son had decided to walk. East.

Four hundred miles. With summer heating up the temps. Across the Indian Territory. Through the reservations of the Comanches, other old warrior tribes, and then through the lands of the Five Civilized Tribes. A country full of men who would cut a person's throat for a nickel to buy a bottle of contraband beer.

Swearing again, Millard Mann stood and swung into the saddle, patted the blue roan's neck, and turned the horse around. He rode east, pulling the pack mule behind him.

Along the north fork of the Red River
In the distance, Millard saw turkey buzzards circling, and his heart fell like a stone. His throat turned dry, but he refused to waste water. Slowly, he kicked the blue roan into a trot, and headed across the Staked Plains.

He found debris scattered all over the plains, a few dead animals, and two uprooted trees. Strips of canvas from what appeared to have come off a covered wagon. Sprigs from a clump of sage that had been driven, like a nail, into an old headboard

132

that marked a grave, the year carved into the marker too faded to read.

A tornado had come through recently, and he might have marveled at what he had just seen. The twister had had enough force to drive a needle from a sagebrush into a practically petrified piece of wood. Yet the wood, marking a grave, remained un- touched.

The circling carrion, however, blocked out anything to marvel at.

He rode on, knowing he was on his son's trail. He found a few bits of sign, some tracks made by a not-too-heavy lad afoot. Every now and then, he found spots not wiped out from the storm, tracks made by James's boots and the stock of that big Winchester .50-100-450 rifle he was toting with him.

Closer to the turkey buzzards, he left the trail and rode toward the edge of an arroyo. He caught his breath, steeled himself for what he might find, and then dismounted, ground-reined the blue roan, and walked the last forty feet to peer into the arroyo.

Wolves were at the carcass, keeping the buzzards at bay, but the big beasts did not care about Millard Mann.

His heart eased, and he let out a heavy sigh. An ox. How long it had been dead, he didn't know, but he doubted if it had been more than a few days. It was a big animal, and there were only six wolves tearing at its flesh.

He moved back to the horse and mule, mounted, and rode away a few feet, then stopped. "An ox? Here?" That struck him as peculiar, but a few miles back on the trail, he found something even stranger.

The tracks led east. Toward Indian Territory. The best he could tell, he was following a big wagon, a Murphy maybe, or something like that. It was carrying quite the load, pulled by four oxen. Three men were walking with the wagon, which left tracks so deep a blind man could have followed them. The tracks disappeared into the horizon, but for once Millard felt a little bit of relief.

Maybe James was still alive. Luck had found him. The boy was in the company of a couple teamsters, and Millard should be able to catch up with them . . . if not today, then certainly tomorrow.

Luck, he decided, had also smiled upon him. He would soon be reunited with his son.

Two miles later, the blue roan came up lame.

CHAPTER TEN

Deep Fork, Creek Country

It figured.

Virgil Flatt was with the big black man, Moses Hunter, keeping an eye on the prisoners in the three tumbleweed wagons back by the creek bed along with two other deputies. Malcolm Mallory had volunteered to ride up onto the hill behind the log cabin and keep an eye on the back door. Boston Graves had found a comfortable position behind a stand of live oaks, and brought out his long Remington Rolling Block rifle with the brass telescopic sight to keep everyone covered. Other deputies found other places, well protected, and cocked their Winchester repeaters, their Sharps carbines, or their Colt revolvers — which left Jackson Sixpersons to walk up to the door and serve the arrest warrants for Chebona Bula and his brother.

It was raining, too.

Sixpersons borrowed Deputy Marshal Tom Truluck's orange slicker and stuck the Winchester '87 underneath it, the stock under his left armpit. He found a good walking stick, gripped it in his left hand, and walked out of the woods, past the well, corral, and barn, faking a limp, coughing every now and then, and making a beeline for the cabin's front door. Smoke wafted from the chimney. Water dripped of the soggy brim of the Cherokee's black hat.

He stopped just in front of the cabin, not even climbing the two steps to get under the porch's awning and out of the rain. Most cabins in Creek country had no steps.

"Hërs'cë!" he called out, speaking in the Creek language.

"Hello yourself!" came a reply in English from inside, followed by a question in Creek, which, loosely translated, and without the expletives meant *What do you want?*

Jackson Sixpersons' answer in Creek, loosely translated and without the profanity, came out as *To get out of the rain.*

The man inside laughed.

Fitting, Sixpersons figured. *Chebona Bula* meant "Laughing Boy."

The door squeaked as it opened only a hair, just wide enough for the barrel of a single-shot rifle to stick out.

"Come ahead, old man," Chebona Bula said. "But without your stick."

The wooden branch dropped into the mud, and Sixpersons, crouching, stepped out of the rain. He moved like a cripple. Carrying a Winchester shotgun under his arm certainly helped with that act; it wasn't comfortable at all. He coughed, waiting.

The rifle barrel withdrew from the opening. Footsteps backed away. "Come ahead," Chebona Bula said.

Jackson Sixpersons walked through the door, water cascading from the slicker and his hat and running through the cracks in the cabin's wooden floor. Most cabins in Creek country had dirt floors, maybe stone. Not wood. Still, the inside felt toasty and the aroma of coffee smelled pleasant.

Chebona Bula had backed all the way to the far wall, training the rifle on Sixpersons, who lifted his left hand, removed the soaking black hat, and hung it on an antler rack beside the door. The fire in the stone fireplace invited him, and he nodded at it. "Mind if I get warm?"

Chebona Bula laughed. "It'll be mighty hot for you real soon." The Creek smiled as he added, "Jackson Sixpersons."

Something caught Sixpersons' attention near his feet. Without lowering his head, he

137

quickly studied the floor and looked back up into the Indian's smiling face. "You and your brother killed two men at the Seminole Agency. One was a white man."

Chebona Bula laughed again.

Sixpersons spoke in Creek. "They have asked me to deliver the arrest warrants to you. And request that you submit to the proper authorities to be delivered to Fort Smith where you will be tried." Then he switched to English. "And convicted. And hanged. Where's your brother? I have a warrant for him, too."

Chebona Bula laughed.

Of course, Jackson Sixpersons knew where the Creek's brother was. He had seen the figure through the cracks in the floor's wooden planks. That's why the cabin had steps. A cellar. Or, at least, a hiding place.

"May I remove my slicker?" Sixpersons asked, sliding over to his left just a hair.

"No." Chebona Bula said in English, and he no longer laughed.

"Very well." Letting the Winchester slide down his arm and chest, the Cherokee marshal slipped his finger into the trigger guard, and fired the shotgun into the floor.

The man hiding beneath the floor screamed in agony while Sixpersons moved to his right, feeling the blast from Chebona

Bula's single-shot rifle as the bullet slammed into the door.

Sixpersons worked the lever, brought the twelve-gauge up, and ducked as Chebona Bula threw the empty rifle at him like a boomerang. It slammed against a closed shutter, and dropped to the floor. The Creek jerked a Bowie knife from a sheath on his left hip, and charged.

Again, the shotgun spoke, and Chebona Bula was catapulted back against the log walls, sliding to the floor, both of his shins a bloody mess.

Almost immediately, Sixpersons fell to the floor, crawling toward the front door as bullets thudded into the cabin's walls. Most of the bullets didn't penetrate, but the deputy marshals with the .50-caliber Sharps managed to blow pretty big holes through the shutters, and those slugs slammed into the wall over Chebona Bula's head.

When the firing ceased, Sixpersons cursed his comrades in Cherokee, and then yelled in English. "Stop shooting, you fools! I have Chebona Bula and his brother!"

Virgil Flatt managed to patch up Chebona Bula's mangled legs, though Sixpersons figured the left leg would get cut off by some sawbones when the prisoners reached

139

Fort Smith. Chebona Bula's brother, Harjo, had fared a little better, the thick slabs of pine absorbing most of the buckshot before the other pellets tore off his left ear, and split his cheek.

The prisoners whimpered. No longer did either one of them laugh.

"Good job, Jack!" Boston Graves said.

Sixpersons reloaded the Winchester. He despised anyone who called him *Jack,* but he had despised Boston Graves long before that.

Graves continued. "The Seminoles have offered a big reward on those two Creeks. Looks like we'll collect a bonus once we get them to Fort Smith."

Sixpersons paused, then fed the last shell into the Winchester's chamber. "You're taking them to jail?"

"Might as well. One of the tumbleweed wagon's already full, and those two Creeks you shot up need medical attention. We'll stop at the doctor in Eufaula, let that Indian medicine man patch them up as best as he can, then go on to the jail. I'll give you your share of the reward if you get back."

If. Sometimes, Sixpersons thought being an outlaw would be better than being a deputy. An outlaw could kill a man like Boston Graves.

"You want me to stay out here then?" Six-persons knew the answer. After all, Marshal Crump had said that Graves would be the lead marshal. The Cherokee just wanted to hear Boston Graves say it.

Graves didn't disappoint. "There are plenty of warrants left to be served."

"Including those naming Link McCoy and Zane Maxwell."

Graves sniggered. "I don't think you'll see them soon. Else, I'd stay. But you have two more tumbleweed wagons, and a handful of deputies if they do. Good luck, Jack."

Southeast of McAdam, Texas
Dust rose from the Llano Estacado into the pale blue sky, getting closer to Millard Mann as he led the lame horse and the pack mule. He had seen the dust for some time — one rider. Heading toward him. Millard kept walking, but had pulled the One of One Thousand from the scabbard, and when the lone rider came into view, he eared back the hammer.

The blue roan whinnied a greeting at the approaching horse, which slowed down. Dust swallowed horse and rider, yet only briefly, as the rider reined up. When the dust passed, the rider's hand rose, and he eased the horse into a slow walk, keeping right hand up in a friendly greeting and to keep his hand away from any weapon.

Millard Mann did not lower the hammer on the .32-caliber rifle.

"Halloooooo!" the rider called when he was closer, still with his hand up. He wore a linen duster, had high black stovepipe boots, chaps, and a blue shirt. The rider's hat was black; so was his horse, a good Texas pony. Something glimmered on his vest.

Millard relaxed just a hair. "Come ahead! I'm friendly."

"You're holding a rifle or carbine!"

"I'm also cautious."

The rider chuckled. "I don't blame you, stranger." He kicked the horse into a fast walk, still keeping the right hand up.

Millard could see that he wore a holster, which carried a pistol with an ivory-handled butt. The badge on the man's vest was a badge he had seen many times in Texas over the past twenty years.

It was a circled five-point star, cut out of a *cinco* peso, a Mexican five-pesos coin. "Star-in-the-wheel," folks called it. The badge of a Texas Ranger.

"Name's Alan Clarke," the rider said. "With Company C."

"Millard Mann."

"Mind if I lower my hand?"

In answer, Millard eased down the hammer of the rifle, and brought the Winchester up, resting the barrel on his shoulder.

The Ranger had a thick walrus mustache, and a sunburned face. He pushed back his battered, dust-covered hat and wiped the sweat off his face with the ends of his bandana. "Had some trouble, I see."

Mann nodded. "Horse went lame yesterday. Threw a shoe."

"Happens." Clarke brought out the makings and began rolling a smoke. "Need a hand?"

"McAdam's not far. Blacksmith's in town. I'll be fine. Thanks."

Alan Clarke offered the sack of Bull Durham to Mann.

"No, thanks." The sack and the papers disappeared into the Ranger's pocket, replaced by a match, which flared to life after a quick strike on the Colt's handle and lit up the cigarette dangling between Clarke's lips. "Trailing two folks. Figure they're bound for Indian Territory. Traveling in a big wagon. Maybe you've seen them?" The last sentence came out hopefully.

"Murphy wagon?" Millard asked.

"Nah. Don't think so. Seen a few of them freight wagons, but this one's different. Big, though. Carrying quite the load. Pulled by

143

eight oxen."

"It's four now." Millard watched the Ranger's eyes brighten. "Lost four in that storm that blowed in the other day, at least one of them dead."

"You've seen them!"

Millard shook his head. "Just their tracks." He gestured to his horse. "That's as close as I got."

Ranger Clarke considered this, but held any questions for the moment — mainly because Millard Mann beat him to the inquiry.

"What's the law want with those two boys?"

"The old man is Lamar Bodeen. There's a whole list of charges against him in my book." Clarke patted another pocket.

Millard didn't need to see the book. He had heard of it. List of Fugitives from Justice, the little black book was printed by the state about every year — or whenever Austin had enough money — and delivered to its Rangers, listing the criminal's name, descriptions when available, suspected crimes, indictments and convictions.

"I'm after him because he sold some bad whiskey up in Mobeetie." The Ranger's tone changed. "Three people died, and those weren't easy deaths. One was a twelve-year-old boy."

Mobeetie had been established up on Sweetwater Creek, originally as a buffalo hunters' camp called Hidetown, back in '74. From those raw beginnings, the place had grown into something fairly substantial, by Panhandle standards, along the Jones and Plummer Trail that ran up to Dodge City, Kansas. The army had established Fort Elliott nearby in '75, and that's when Mobeetie really boomed. There had even been talk of landing a railroad.

But a town's dreams can die quickly. The army closed the post in 1890, the railroad never came, and people began moving out. Even worse, in 1893, Mobeetie held a revival meeting. Three hundred people were saved. Reformed, they closed all the saloons, which caused many other folks to leave town.

"Bodeen — he goes by about a half dozen other names — was coming down the old buffalo hunters trail. Snakehead whiskey. Likely, you know the type."

Millard nodded. His son wasn't much of a drinker. If James had hooked up with this Bodeen character, he prayed that his son wouldn't try any of that rotgut whiskey the man was obviously hauling. "Those tracks from that wagon were mighty deep."

The Ranger's head nodded. "Like I said, he's carrying a lot of merchandise. Ain't full, mind you. He'd need a twenty-mule team if that wagon was full. But one barrel's got enough poison. Preying on folks' needs, after they got religion and prohibition." Ranger Clarke grinned, but without humor. "They probably wish they'd left at least one grog shop opened. But it ain't funny. Not what Bodeen done. Twelve-year-old kid."

With a sigh, Millard said, "Well, I think you're out of luck."

Again, Clarke nodded. "They've reached the territories?"

"Probably. They were only a few miles from the state line when I had to turn back."

"Why were you trailing them? If you don't mind my asking?"

"Looking for someone." Millard turned, pointing his rifle barrel toward the north and east. "I found the trail on the south bank of the North Fork of the Red. Big storm we got wiped out most of the sign, but that was some rainfall — which we always need in this country — so you can pick up the trail and follow it real easy. At least until the ground dries up. It dries up fast out here."

"Barrels and barrels of poisoned whiskey.

Still should be able to follow it." Clarke
sighed. "Till he crosses that border.
Then . . . well . . . I don't know. Best move
on. Appreciate your time."

"Good luck." Millard didn't mean it. He
didn't want the Texas law to catch up with
that whiskey runner yet if James was with
him, but he wasn't worried. If the Ranger
followed the law by the book, he would not
cross into Indian Territory in search for
Lamar Bodeen, no matter how many people
he had killed with his rotgut. Something
told Millard that the Ranger had a personal
and deadly interest in the whiskey runner . . . but he probably wouldn't go after
him alone, not in Indian Territory.

Clarke tossed the cigarette away and
kicked his horse into a walk. He had just
ridden past the pack mule when Mann
called out, "What about the man Bodeen's
traveling with?"

"Ain't a man," Clarke called back without
stopping. "It's that old reprobate's daughter."

Denison
"The fella you want," the gravely voiced,
pockmarked man whispered as he lighted
another cigarette, "is Bodeen. Wildcat
Bodeen." He shook out his match, and drew

deeply on the smoke, then blew a long stream of smoke toward the ceiling already cloudy with smoke.

"Bodeen." Link McCoy tested the name.

"Uh-huh. One of his names anyhow." Still holding the cigarette, the man reached for his tumbler, downed a shot, refilled the glass, and returned the smoke to his thin lips.

The saloon was dark, and they sat alone in a corner. Most of the patrons hovered about the bar, which was nothing more than a plank nailed to two empty whiskey kegs. Two men were in the corner near McCoy and the smoking man, but McCoy didn't think they would hear anything. One had passed out fifteen minutes earlier. The other had gotten his head pounded with the butt of a Colt by a man drinking at the bar.

All that sat on the table were the man's sack of Bull Durham and papers, two glasses, the bottle of rye whiskey — Old Overholt — and McCoy's pistol-grip Winchester '87 shotgun.

The rye was the man's idea, but since McCoy didn't know or trust him the shotgun was his own. The smoking, pockmarked man didn't even appear to notice the ten-gauge. He had black hair, black eyes, and looked part Indian. Probably a breed. Rail thin, with slender fingers, and a scar across his left hand. He wore a homespun shirt, a faded blue bandana, flat-brimmed straw hat, store-bought boots about ten thousand years old, and duck trousers. The only weapon appeared to be a sheathed knife on his left hip. McCoy didn't yet know the man's name. He had been recommended by a mutual associate named Carter. McCoy did not trust him either. His fingers dribbled easily on the table just inches from the big Winchester.

The smoking man spoke again. "I'd expect you could find him north of the Red already. He ain't likely comin' back to Texas no time soon."

"How come?" McCoy had to wait until the man smoked and drank some more.

"His whiskey ain't . . ." The man's grin revealed tobacco-stained teeth, which did not surprise McCoy one whit. He could feel tar beginning to stain his own teeth just from sitting in that saloon on the wrong side of the railroad tracks.

"Well, it ain't tasty, that's for certain. Been known, in fact, to kill some folks. It ain't Old Overholt." The man downed another rye and flicked what little was left of his cigarette to the floor, not even bothering to crush it with his boot.

"Poison?"

The pockmarked man grinned even wider. "That's why the rangers want him. Or at least one Ranger. Real bad."

McCoy smiled back. The Bodeen fellow was just what they needed. "And you can take me to him."

"For a price, sure. Me and Bodeen know each other right well. But that price . . . it don't include the Old Overholt you're gonna have to provide." The man was already rolling another smoke. " 'Cause I sure ain't drinkin' Bodeen's liquor."

CHAPTER ELEVEN

Kiowa-Comanche-Apache Reservation, summer 1895

It just seems weird, James Mann thought, *the way Wildcat Lamar and his son Robin travel.*

Traveling in such a big wagon, he figured the Lamars would have wanted to stay on main trails. Not that the roads were all that good, but certainly it made sense to follow the Camp Supply–Fort Sill or Camp Supply–Fort Reno roads. But Wildcat Lamar seemed to prefer following arroyos or deer trails — almost as if the mere thought of meeting up with some stranger on the road scared the old man.

Maybe James just felt impatient. He wanted to get to Fort Smith in a hurry, but they were stuck on some reservation, traveling about as fast as a man could go on a thirty-year-old blind, lame mule. Besides, the work proved hard. Tending to the oxen, hitching up those mules, eating dust, hunting for food or something to burn so they could cook any game they managed to find.

The summer heat had turned fierce, and since that tornado and brutal thunderstorm, he had not felt a drop of rain or even seen many clouds. Sand blasted his face, stung his eyes, and coated his lips and tongue. He had advanced to the point where he could work that blacksnake whip without tearing off much of his own flesh, and the calluses on his hand had hardened so that he no longer had to pop the blisters on his fingers and palms. Yet every time he figured he'd just call it quits, bid the Lamar family goodbye, and make out for Arkansas by himself, the old man would say something to change his thinking — as if Wildcat Lamar could read James Mann's mind.

"You're a pretty good hand, kid," Lamar said that morning after a breakfast of hardtack soaked in coffee. "Might make a teamster after all."

James grinned without much humor and sipped the bitter black brew. "Thanks, but I have another occupation in mind, sir."

That got the old man to laugh hard and then slap his knee. "Hard work don't suit you, kid?"

Beside him, Robin Lamar stared at his

own coffee, refusing to look up or offer any comment.

"I don't mind hard work. My pa —" James stopped, thinking sadly about his family, and knew he'd have to fight another urge. One that told him he should turn west, return to Texas, go home. To his surprise, that homesickness passed almost instantly, and he went on. "Pa worked for the railroad. On the line so much, I had to do most of the work at home. My brother and sister were too young to help Ma too much. So I worked hard."

Well, maybe not this hard. Back around McAdam, Texas, he had never hitched oxen, driven the beasts, and popped a whip with such regularity. He had never gone to bed so tired. Or awakened with every muscle screaming and burning.

Suddenly, he realized something else. Not only had his hands hardened, so had his muscles. His worn clothes fit a little tighter now, and at least a week or more had passed since his muscles had burned with such fierce pain. His boots no longer hurt, even though he had worn his socks till they were basically filthy pieces of thread.

"Sounds like you had a nice family, eh?"

James turned. Robin stared at him with soulful eyes.

"Well . . ." He didn't know how to answer. "Sure. I mean . . ." He understood. His life had been pretty good, better than most on the harsh frontier.

"Had me a nice family oncet," Wildcat said, and his voice, one eye, and face darkened. "Injuns ended that. Dirty, thievin', ugly, woman-killin' injuns. I hate 'em. Hate 'em all."

"I'm sorry." James was looking at Robin, who had again lowered his head, but not before James saw the tears welling in the boy's eyes.

"No need to be," Wildcat said, his mood abruptly changing, his spirits lifting. "Happens. Folks die."

James looked down himself and wiped his eyes, remembering his two late uncles.

Wildcat quickly changed the subject with a belly laugh followed by a burp. "So, James, you don't wanna be a teamster or haul freight or skin mules or whip oxen. What is it you've a mind to do oncet we gets you settled in Fort Smith?"

James steeled himself, made sure the tears had not broken loose, raised his head, and took a sip of coffee to steady his nerves and calm his voice. "I will ride for Judge Parker's court." He had not said that he *hoped to* or *would apply* for the job. He'd said he *would ride* for the court. He had to. No matter what it took. "I'll be a deputy marshal."

Robin's head shot up. His mouth dropped. The boy had not bothered to wipe the tears from his face, for muddy trails had been left on his dirty cheeks. "A marshal!"

The old man laughed so hard, he cut loose with a fart, didn't bother to excuse himself, and tossed the coffee into the wreck pan. "A deputy lawdog? Well, that's somethin' to shoot for." He winked. "Or shoot at." Knees popped as he rose to his feet. "Make sure you scour the cups and pot with sand, boys. We's burnin' daylight." He kicked out the fire, snorted, spit, and walked to the team of oxen, but the laughter had died in his voice and in his eyes. He began cursing bitterly under his breath as he prepared for the day's journey.

James emptied the dregs onto the smoldering remnants of the fire and then he turned to see Robin Lamar staring at him.

"Marshal?" the boy said, although his voice had turned so high, he practically sounded like a girl.

"It's something I have to do."

"Why?"

Luckily, James didn't have to answer, to form those words, to tell someone — a stranger, for all intents and purposes —

155

about his uncle, the late Deputy U.S. Marshal Jimmy Mann. Or to tell Robin why he carried that Winchester '86. Wildcat Lamar began cursing the two of them, screaming at them that they had to move, that time was a-wasting, and that they had an appointment in two days with some big customers.

Camp Creek, Indian Territory

It had taken Millard Mann weeks to find the trail of oxen and the big wagon, and he'd figured he would be on to that scoundrel and James in a day or two after making a good trade in McAdam, though his current ride, a chestnut gelding, had cost him the pack mule and his lame horse. He had decided the pack mule just slowed him down anyway.

However, as the blistering sun began to fade and sink in the west, Millard wondered if he would be alive in a day or two. Or in a half hour.

For hours, he had seen the dust trailing him. At first, he'd thought nothing of it, deciding that the wind had stirred it up, what with the weather so dry and miserable. That feeling had passed quickly. Dust didn't blow so steadily and in such a direct line paralleling his trail. Men on horseback

156

were causing the dust.

He rode on until he found a spot where the creek he was riding along hadn't dried into oblivion. Shade trees — well, shade scrub — and a pool of water that looked halfway clean and thoroughly inviting offered a respite. Only a fool would pass up water and a good place to camp. Besides, if he died in the next hour or so, it seemed as good a place as any.

And that flat piece of driftwood he spotted might just save his hide.

He went about his chores, filling his canteens and letting his horse drink. He unsaddled the gelding and picketed the horse in a shady spot, hobbling it for added security before he moved about setting up camp, stopping briefly to pick up the driftwood, blowing the sand and grit free, and returning to find a good spot for it on his saddle. He nodded in satisfaction before continuing his work.

If the riders came in from the west, the sinking sun behind them, this side of the creek bed might do the trick. He left his Winchester '73 leaning against the bank, hidden behind some scrub that might some day grow into an oak. He checked again. The dust had stopped.

The horse snorted, wanting to be grained.

Millard moved to his saddlebags, put some grain in the feedbag, and walked back to the liver chestnut, configuring the bag so the horse could eat and rubbing the horse's side with his gloved hands.

After wetting his lips, he soon had a fire going from the scrub and driftwood along the mostly dried creek. Once he had his coffeepot filled with water and grounds and resting atop the small fire, he unbuckled his shell belt, wrapped the belt around the holster, and laid it on the bedroll. Back by the saddlebags, he fidgeted with his gloves, trying to calm his nerves while looking off to the west where he had last spied the dust.

Waiting.

But not for long.

Three riders appeared, and Millard breathed in deeply, exhaled, and looked for more. Nothing. There were just three — what he'd been expecting based on the amount of dust he had spied.

In a saddlebag, he found what he wanted, unwrapped some salt pork, dropped a piece in the small cast iron skillet, and returned to the fire, dropping both gloves on the ground. After a moment, he rose, pretending that he had just spotted the strangers. He shielded the sun with his hands, and stared long and hard, hoping to find that the riders were Indians.

They weren't.

Indians he could expect. Even welcome. Most of them, even the Cheyennes and Arapahos were a friendly bunch, generally looking for some food or maybe some illegal whiskey. They would come to trade.

But white men . . . ?

His prayer asked that the riders be led by that Texas Ranger. What had been that man's name? Clarke. That was it. Alan Clarke. Or had it been Adam? Millard couldn't remember and didn't care.

From the lawman's appearance and tone, Millard had sensed that the Ranger wanted Lamar Bodeen, killer and whiskey-runner for something other than justice. His eyes had burned with hatred. Ranger Clarke had a personal score to settle with that felon.

It would not have surprised Millard to see the Ranger trailing Bodeen's trail or his own.

No matter. By the time the three men were fifty yards from the camp, Millard knew they weren't Rangers, and the one riding in the center was not Mr. Clarke.

He had to chuckle without much humor as he remembered the saying *There's no law, and no God, in this part of the territory.*

CHAPTER TWELVE

Limestone Gap, Choctaw Nation

"Wait here." Winchester shotgun in his right hand, Jackson Sixpersons swung down from his horse and handed the reins to Deputy Marshal Malcolm Mallory.

Setting the brake on the tumbleweed wagon, Virgil Flatt blew his nose with one of the tied ends of his bandana. Neither argued with the old Cherokee's orders. Neither tried to talk him out of walking to the log cabin down below.

Sixpersons hadn't expected them to. The fact, however, that neither volunteered to wait in the woods behind them, came as a mild surprise. He pulled his hat on a little tighter before unfastening one of the saddlebags. His left hand disappeared into the leather bag and came out with a long pouch. Liquid sloshed from inside the bottle inside the pouch. Keeping the shotgun in his right hand pointed at the cabin, Sixpersons walked down the path, past the well and the rawhide corral that was falling apart, and stopped before stepping onto the rotting porch. The place hadn't been lived in — permanently — for years, but smoke rose from the chimney. Even outside, Jackson Sixpersons could smell and taste pungent tobacco smoke.

He did not announce himself. Did not knock. Just waited in the hot sun.

"You alone?" a hoarse voice called from inside.

"You know I'm not," Sixpersons answered.

From inside came a slight chuckling. "Yeah, you are."

Jackson Sixpersons had to smile. "I reckon you're right." He tried to pick out the most solid of the rotting wood and eased his way onto the porch without breaking any planks — or his leg or neck — and pushed the creaking door open with the barrel of the twelve-gauge. Slowly, he stepped into the one-room cabin, not stepping into the shadows, but staying in the slip of sunlight.

Any furniture had been taken with whoever had once lived there. He could see the small fire, the occasional orange glow of a cigarette, and the figure of a man sitting on the hearth. Now that he was inside, other odors assaulted his senses.

Dust. Dead rats. The musky smell of a skunk. Or maybe that was just Newton Ah-ha-lo-man-tubbee. For the four years Six-persons had known him, the half-breed Choctaw had smelled of nothing except Bull Durham and sweat.

"You sent for me," Sixpersons said.

The shadow rose. The orange glow disappeared, followed by the sound of a butt hitting the floor. Newton Ah-ha-lo-man-tubbee never crushed out a smoke with his foot, never used an ashtray. He'd probably burn to death in a fire one night. No, he would meet his end from a bullet. In fact, he should already be dead.

The breed glided across the room, but stopped before the sunlight hit him. Still, he stood close enough for the Cherokee lawman to see him.

The ragged clothing. Sweat dripping down his face. The straw hat, the sheathed Bowie on his hip, the cigarette paper, the sack of Bull Durham. He was already rolling another smoke. Jackson Sixpersons could even see the scar on Newton Ah-ha-lo-man-tubbee's left hand.

"I hear," the man said in a tobacco-strained voice, "you want the McCoy-Maxwell Gang."

Sixpersons head shook. "I want nothing.

The law wants them."

"I can get 'em for you."

"Last I heard, they were in Texas."

The Choctaw licked the paper, sealed the cigarette, and put the smoke between his razor-thin lips. A match flared, and Newton Ah-ha-lo-man-tubbee brought the Lucifer to the cigarette, which flared to life. He took a long drag, held it in, blew out a stream of blue smoke, and then pointed a thin finger at the shotgun in the Cherokee's hands. "The younger one, the meanest, smooth-talkin' one" — the cigarette returned to the man's lips, but he kept talking — "his scattergun's fancier than yourn. Mean lookin'. Blow a man's head off."

"Maybe yours."

The half-breed Choctaw smiled. "Maybe so."

"If I don't do it first."

Newton Ah-ha-lo-man-tubbee laughed. "You ain't done it in four years."

"We Cherokees are a patient people."

The half-breed took another drag on the cigarette, held it, exhaled. "Link McCoy."

Sixpersons said nothing.

"Made me a proposition in Denison."

"That's Texas. Not my department."

The thin man grinned again and removed

his cigarette. "But he wants back in the Nations."

Again, Sixpersons kept quiet.

"Asked me to find Lamar Bodeen for 'im."

"Don't know him."

"Whiskey runner. Bad whiskey. Last I heard, the Rangers want him bad in Texas. Made a bunch of folks sick in some Podunk town in the Panhandle. Killed a few. Including one Ranger's kid."

"Like I said, that's not my department."

"Is if Bodeen's in the territory."

"Bodeen, maybe. Not McCoy."

The breed laughed, smoked again, and pointed the cigarette under Sixpersons' nose. "Thought you said you got no interest in Link McCoy. Or Zane Maxwell."

Flattening his lips, the Cherokee waited.

"McCoy asked around down Denison way. He wants to partner up with a big-time whiskey runner, and he ain't after no small-time Choc or Creek. Even a Cherokee. He don't want none of the big boys, but a small-time man with a lot of whiskey and no morals. I figured that described Lamar Bodeen to a T."

When Newton Ah-ha-lo-man-tubbee took another drag, Sixpersons said, "You telling me that McCoy, Maxwell, Tulip Bells and whoever is left are turning to running liquor in the Nations?"

"You don't pay me to make no guesses, Jackson. Just for information."

Sixpersons brought the pouch up and waved his hand so that the liquor in the bottle inside the pouch sloshed.

"Old Overholt?" Newton Ah-ha-lo-man-tubbee asked.

The Cherokee's head shook.

"You know that's my brand," the breed complained.

"Rye's not allowed in the Nations," Sixpersons said. "You get what I can confiscate."

The man's scarred hand came up and took the pouch. "Runnin' liquor is a felony, Mister Marshal, or so I hear tell."

"That's a down payment. Now you pay me."

The cigarette flashed through the light and doorway and disappeared in the afternoon. Newton Ah-ha-lo-man-tubbee's right hand disappeared into the deep mule-ear pockets of his duck pants, and came out holding something that glittered in the sunlight.

Jackson Sixpersons could hear the ticking of the watch. The breed let the watch dangle in the light from his right hand.

It was gold. Sixpersons could tell that

much as the watch spun on its chain, back and forth. After a moment, the Choctaw half-breed jerked the watch to his hand, put his thumb on the key, and the watch opened. Sixpersons couldn't read the manufacturer's name on the dial, but he could hear the music. The lid snapped shut. Newton Ah-ha-lo-man-tubbee held the watch in his hand, and Sixpersons saw the engraved initials on the hunter's case. *MRC*

"Familiar?" Newton Ah-ha-lo-man-tubbee asked.

"Is it a Waltham?" Sixpersons asked.

"I wouldn't know. I can't read. Or tell the white man's time from a white man's toy."

Sixpersons knew. Only one watch like that could be found in Indian Territory, and it had been stolen by the McCoy-Maxwell Gang from a teller named Mike Crawford at a bank in Greenville, Arkansas.

Suddenly, Jackson Sixpersons felt something he rarely felt.

Sweat.

Not from nerves. Not even from the heat. From excitement.

"Whiskey," he said.

"Not just any whiskey. Bad whiskey. That's what Link McCoy wanted. And I told him I could take him to Lamar Bodeen."

"Bodeen." Jackson Sixpersons wanted more than the whiskey runner's name.

"One of his names. Wildcat Bodeen. Wildcat Lamar. B. C. Bodeen. Bill Lamar. Whiskey Bill. Rotgut Wildcat. For about sixteen months, he's been bringin' whiskey from No Man's Land and across the Panhandle, fillin' the railroaders and cowboys bellies with rotgut, then driftin' into Indian Territory. He don't get up into Creek or Cherokee country. Stays south. The wild savages to the west of us. Then Chickasaw and Choctaw lands. Heads down to Texarkana. But, since he's riled the Rangers, I don't reckon he'll do that no more. Appears to me he wants to make one last score then get out of the business."

"They just made a score. More than seventeen hundred bucks from a bank in Greenville. That should last them."

The half-breed's head shook. "What I hear tell, they didn't get near that much. Maybe four hundred. So Link McCoy wants a whiskey runner. And Bodeen's just the kind of man Link McCoy needs."

"For what?"

Newton Ah-ha-lo-man-tubbee busied himself removing the bottle from the pouch. He held it in the light, but his tobacco-stained teeth disappeared in a frown.

"You been samplin'?"

"I don't touch the stuff. Anymore."

"Somebody did."

"The man I confiscated it from."

His teeth reappeared, but only to pull out the cork, which he spit into a hole in the floor, and drank long and greedily. Half the bottle was empty when he lowered it and coughed violently. He blew his nose and shook his head. "Who'd you say you taken this rotgut from?"

Sixpersons had been waiting for that. "Bodeen."

The bottle dropped to Newton Ah-ha-lo-man-tubbee's side, and his face seemed to pale, but only briefly. He cursed, took another pull, wiped his nose with the sleeve of his homespun shirt, and cursed Jackson Sixpersons in Choctaw, Cherokee, English, French, and Spanish. "Funny, for a thievin' Cherokee."

"What does Link McCoy want with a wagon full of whiskey?"

Newton Ah-ha-lo-man-tubbee's head shook. "Don't know. He don't tell me much. Not yet."

"When are they to meet?"

Again, the breed shook his head. "We ain't talked terms."

"Name them." Jackson Sixpersons had

168

heard and seen enough.

"Three horses. One a stud. Fifty dollars. I keep the watch. You keep the rewards. I just tell you where and when. You don't know me. I don't know you. You take the horses and the money to my wife. And if I get killed, you still pay your debt."

"You know I will."

"Yeah, but I want to hear it."

"You just did."

"If you get killed, I still get paid."

"I'll tell my wife. That I lost a bet."

"I trust her more 'n I trust the likes of you." Newton Ah-ha-lo-man-tubbee held up the bottle. "And a bottle of rye, but not this slop. Old Overholt. No, two bottles."

Jackson Sixpersons agreed and asked the question again. "When will Bodeen and McCoy meet?"

The half-breed grinned. "Don't know. But the way McCoy tapped his fingers on the table, it appeared he was anxious and eager to get things movin' along right soon."

"Where?"

Newton Ah-ha-lo-man-tubbee drained the bottle, dropped it through the floor, and began rolling another cigarette. "Like I says, I got to find Bodeen first."

"Be careful, Newton."

Another match flared, and the cigarette

flared to life. He shook out the match, stuck the cigarette in his mouth, and smiled. "You, too, Jack."

"Don't call me Jack. You sure you can find Bodeen?"

"Sure. Providin' he ain't riled the Comanches or Kiowas with his poison and gotten his hair lifted. Or his kid's."

"Kid?"

Newton Ah-ha-lo-man-tubbee took another drag, exhaled, and let out a smoker's heavy cough. "Girl. Fifteen. Sixteen. Some such. The old man tries to pass the petticoat off as a boy, but only an idiot would think that lass be a he."

Kiowa-Comanche-Apache Reservation
After making camp, Wildcat Lamar strode off afoot to the north, leaving the two boys on their own.

"What in blazes are you doing?" Robin Lamar roared.

"I have to go!" James Mann sang out, desperately trying to unbutton his britches. "I've been holding it so long, my kidneys are about to rupture!" Relief — from his bladder and from the fact that he had not wet his pants — came instantly as he sprayed the bush with urine. Too much coffee that morning, he decided, and the old

170

man had been pushing him, Robin, and the oxen hard all day. James finished relieving himself, buttoned up his pants, wiped his hands on the sand, and turned to Robin Lamar.

But Wildcat's son had gone. Practically tripped, it appeared, to get away from James. He scratched his head, then chuckled, thinking that the boy must have thought that he might have peed on him. *Crazy.*

By the time Lamar came back to camp, the oxen were unhitched and camp was being set up, but he flew into a fit, cursing, yelling, kicking out the campfire, knocking over the tripod that held a kettle full of rabbit stew, and screaming at his son that he knew better. Then he pointed a thick finger at James. "Get that team hitched, boy! Now. Comp'ny's comin' and . . ." The rest of the orders were lost in a cacophony of curses and gestures.

They had just finished breaking camp, the team hitched, though ornery at feeling the leather of harness again.

The whole blasted family, father and son, were mad as a couple of mercury-addled hatters.

It all made about as much sense as sticking to game trails or blazing their own paths in that wild country. Company was coming.

So why get ready to break camp? It would be dark before long. Sundown was coming at a high lope, so how much farther could they travel without a road to follow?

On the other hand . . . James began to calm down. If they left camp tonight, they might reach Fort Smith sooner. He stepped around the rear of the wagon, which had been opened by the old man.

Wildcat stepped to the end and tossed James the Winchester '86. "Keep it handy, boy."

James dropped the rifle in the sand. The old fool had thrown it hard.

Another litany of curses came out of Wildcat Lamar's mouth. "Ain't you got any sense, boy?"

James picked up the rifle, blew the sand off the receiver and lever, and checked the barrel to make sure it wasn't clogged. It looked clean.

"What are you talking about?" It might have been the first time James had ever raised his voice against Robin's pa, but frustration was building, and he felt a headache coming on. Fast.

"You can shoot that big gun, can't you, kid?"

"Sure." James hesitated. Well, he thought he could. Yeah, he knew how to work a rifle.

Uncle Jimmy had helped teach him. "Yeah," he said with a little extra confidence. *I can shoot a gun,* he told himself. *Even this rifle.*

If I only had any bullets.

A large barrel rolled out of the wagon.

James stopped it from rolling over him, and read the stamp branded into the oak. MALASES. He sniggered.

"What's so blasted funny, boy?" Wildcat was in poor humor.

James used the barrel of the rifle to tap the word. "*Molasses* is misspelled."

"Like 'em dirty bucks know how to read." The old man hopped from the high wagon, his knees popping. He grunted and pushed himself up. "Robin!" he thundered. "Where be ya?"

"Here," the boy said without much enthusiasm, and stepped around the side of the wagon.

His eyes met James's, and quickly the kid looked away, staring at his feet, practically blushing.

"Ever'thing loaded up, boy?"

"Yes, sir."

"Blacksnake whip in the box?"

"Yes, sir."

"Brake ain't set, right?"

"Yes, sir."

"Fetch yer shotgun."

173

The kid looked up and wet his lips.

"Do it!" Wildcat accented the order with more profanity.

"Yes, sir." Robin climbed into the back of the wagon, disappearing behind other barrels and boxes.

James looked at Wildcat Lamar, who was wiping his sweaty palms on his britches and wetting his own lips.

After a few moments of nervousness, he found a twist of tobacco in his pouch and tore off a mouthful. "Oughten to be here by now." He tried to spit, but couldn't. He wiped his brow again, his mouth working furiously against the hard-cured tobacco

"Who is coming? Who is company?" James lowered the barrel and ran his left hand through his sweaty hair. He looked across the prairie, but saw only the endless expanse of Indian Territory — a few broken hills, grass, and dips of arroyos. Only a few trees seemed to appear way off in the distance. A man could see clear to Kansas off to the north, maybe even Nebraska or the Dakotas. But no one. No body. Not even a horse, rabbit, or tarantula.

"Shut up. I smell 'em. Smell 'em lyin', thievin', connivin' savages. Ro-bin!"

"Here I am." The boy jumped from the wagon, wielding the shotgun.

"Get into the box. Down low. Keep down. Not a word, kid. Don't hardly breathe. Hide till we needs you. You savvy?"

The kid's head bobbed, and then he was running to the front of the freight wagon, climbing up on the front wheel, lowering the shotgun into the driver's box, and then climbing over and disappearing inside the box.

Finally, Wildcat Lamar spit brown juice into the dust. James stepped closer, and the old man sucked in a deep breath, held it, let it out, and nodded to the north.

"Knowed it. Smelt 'em, I did. Here they come. Rifle handy, boy. Rifle handy."

James Mann saw a dozen or more men on horses, mostly paints, but a few roans and one bay. They had appeared as if from magic, climbing out of one of the arroyos. They rode free, easily, long hair hanging in braids, decorated with feathers, although the leader had a buffalo horn headdress. Behind the riders, walked two or three women followed by a dog.

James Mann let out a soft curse. Then he let the .50-caliber Winchester fall into the dirt. "Indians," he said, before his voice box just quit working.

The riders had spread out wide. The one in the center had donned a massive black hat and bandoliers criss-crossed his chest. Dust caked most of his clothes and his black beard.

Millard Mann rose behind the fire and studied the riders as they reined in. The one in the black hat with the bandoliers had a repeating rifle in the scabbard and two revolvers holstered butt forward high on his hips. A big knife was sheathed in his left boot.

To his left, a rawboned man with a wandering eye sat on a sorry looking horse. A fellow that skinny would be hard-pressed to keep his britches on his hips, and this one kept his up not with suspenders, but a piece of rope. Something moved in his long beard. Something alive.

Even from the fire, Millard could smell the thin man. The way Millard figured things, the man didn't need that old revolver on his left hip. The stink alone would kill most people.

In the corner of his eye, Millard considered the third rider. Lean, leathery, wearing stovepipe boots. His red silk bandana danced with the wind, and he wore a linen duster over a black broadcloth coat. Like a circuit rider. Only a sky pilot would be dressed in that outfit in such heat, yet Millard knew the man did not preach the gospel of the Lord. His preaching came from the barrels of the nickel-plated, ivory-handled Remington .44s stuck inside a red sash.

"Evenin'," the one in the red sash said.

"Howdy." Millard was surprised to find he could even speak. It had been far too many years, yet he felt a calm overcome him The nerves faded like they had back in his youth, before marriage, before the railroad, before the children. He felt odd, as if Jimmy and Borden were standing beside him.

Standing with him.

He had to keep himself from glancing to his side to see if the ghosts of his dead brothers were there.

He knew better. To let one of those men out of his sight would mean his death.

The one with the bandoliers raised a hand — his right hand — and pointed at the small campfire. "Yer coffee," he said, his accent a mixture of French and Spanish. "It smells inviting."

Millard smiled. "Does it?" The pot hadn't been on the fire long enough to emit any smell. All he could smell was his own sweat, and the stinking man's foul odor.

"Been travelin' quite a while," the one with the fancy pistols in the red sash said.

"So have I," Millard said easily. "Heading to Fort Smith. My brother works there." *Worked there,* he thought sadly. "Deputy marshal for Judge Parker's law."

"Is that a fact?" Duster Man said.

The stinking man finally spoke. "We might know 'im."

That caused the one with the bandoliers to laugh. Duster Man showed no emotion except his eyes hardened. He would be the one to watch. He was the deadly one. The other two were . . . well . . . idiots.

"You a law?" Duster Man's jaw tilted at the holstered revolver resting on Millard's bedroll, well out of Millard's reach.

The one in the bandolier gave a quick wink and flashed a finger at the saddle where that piece of driftwood resembled the stock of a Winchester in the scabbard. At least, Millard hoped it would fool the three bad men.

He made himself chortle. "Hardly. Work for the railroad."

"What brings you out here?" asked Bandolier Man.

"Got a leave."

The one who stunk like a dead coyote straightened in his saddle. "You gets a

178

leave . . . and you come" — his hand swept toward the barren prairie — "here."

"It's fine country." *So is Hell.*

A long silence passed. Millard wiped his palms, suddenly clammy, on his trousers. He waited. It was a game of waiting, but the three men would not have much patience. It would happen. Soon.

Real soon.

Said Stinking Man, "Sure would fancy a cup of coffee."

"And, we can pay," added Bandolier Man.

Millard wasn't in McAdam. Wasn't in civilization. He was a long, long way from home. He shook his head. "No. I've never turned anyone away from my camp and I've never charged anyone for sharing coffee or grub. Come along." He slid toward the fire, dropped behind it and the pot, and tilted his jaw toward Bandolier Man. "Light down. Rest a spell." *Some of us will be resting till Judgment Day before anyone thinks this coffee is fit to drink.*

The tin cup lay on its side. He picked it up with his left hand, blew the dust out of it, righted it, and started for the coffeepot with his right, before shaking his head, laughing at his stupidity and looking at the three riders. "Liked to have burned my hand. Reckon I'm a mite green."

The three riders stared at each other, but only briefly.

Bandolier Man grinned at Stinking Man and lowered his right hand to the pommel of the saddle. His left hand reached for one of the revolvers.

Green? Millard thought. *Yes. But not stupid.* He picked up the glove for his right hand as if to use it for a mitt as he reached for the handle of the blue-speck enamel coffeepot.

Bandolier Man gripped the butt of his revolver as Stinking Man began to laugh. Duster Man was the only one who seemed wary, as if he could read Millard's mind.

"Don't have any milk" — Millard laughed good-naturedly — "but do you take your coffee with sugar?" He grinned, and the deerskin glove came up. "Or just lead?"

That triggered the senses, the instincts, of Duster Man. He dropped his reins, and both hands darted down for the Remingtons. Millard swung the glove toward him and the deerskin leather exploded in smoke and flame.

E. Allen & Company made few of its 1st Model Derringers, patented just before the end of the Civil War, probably not even two thousand between 1865 and the early 1870s. Millard's, probably manufactured back in 1871, had a barrel of no more than two and a half inches, probably a tad less. The grips were two-piece walnut, but he couldn't feel them beneath the glove's leather. He couldn't even feel the hammer, but he had cocked it before he had dropped the derringer into the glove. The top was flat, the barrel a tad loose. Over the past twenty years, he had taken the .41-caliber rimfire out at Christmas only to clean. He hadn't been sure it would even fire.

Of course, it did fire. He'd aimed from instinct, the way his father had taught him, not at Stinking Man or Bandolier Man with the pistol already palmed and coming up. Millard remembered to kill the deadliest one first.

As soon as the .41-caliber pistol fired, blasting his nostrils with the scent of gun smoke and scorched leather, he leaped over the saddle and ran toward the creek bed, diving just as a bullet whistled over his head.

CHAPTER THIRTEEN

The derringer shot hadn't killed Duster Man — Millard had not expected to get that lucky — but the shot had startled all three men. Bandolier Man reacted first, popping two wild shots as Millard ran.

He landed hard in the soft sand, came up, and the Winchester rifle practically leaped into his hands.

The rifle had been a gift from the governor of Texas, back when Millard, Jimmy, and Borden had been much younger, much wilder — before Millard had become a family man and turned to the railroad for a steady, less dangerous life. A third-model that fired .32-caliber Winchester Center Fire cartridges, it had been manufactured in 1883, sporting a twenty-four-and-one-quarter-inch octagonal, blued barrel, walnut stock with checkering, and a hard-rubber butt plate. His name was engraved on the frame below a Lone Star flag. Also richly engraved with *One of One Thousand,* it was worth better than one hundred dollars.

The excellent weapon had come with a standard rear sight, the sporting style, but Millard had added one of Winchester's midrange vernier tang sights behind the hammer. It weighed nine pounds. It held fourteen rounds. Charged by twenty grains of black powder, that Winchester had been made for killing deer or varmints.

The last man he had killed had been killed with that rifle.

By the time Millard had the Winchester, Duster Man had dived off his horse, come up to a knee with the fancy Remingtons, and popped a shot that kicked up dirt in Millard's face. All the while, Stinking Man was trying to keep from getting thrown off his wildly bucking mount.

Millard loosened one shot, heard a scream, and quickly ducked, levering another round into the Winchester. His rifle lacked the power and range of Jimmy's old battered .44-40 carbine. A .32-caliber bullet and twenty grains of powder could affectively kill at maybe one hundred yards. These men were a lot closer.

In firearms parlance, the word *grain* did not mean gram weight or granules of powder. It had been used since the 1870s to measure the weight of powder and bullet, based on the weight of a grain of rice — and that type of measurement dated to the Roman era.

Two more shots rang out, hooves pounded, and the one who spoke in that mix of Spanish and French cursed in English. Millard sprang up quickly, fired, ducked, and heard the man still aboard the bucking horse scream out. The Remingtons answered.

Bandolier Man yelled, "Eddie!"

Duster Man said, "He's done for. Kill that —" Screams, hooves, and gunshots drowned out the man's curse.

Millard chanced a quick look, caught his breath, and made his heart stop beating so out of control. Stinking Man had been pitched off his horse, his left foot caught up in the stirrup. His badly frightened horse had taken off, dragging the man behind him as he galloped several yards up the creek bed, through the mud, gravel, and pieces of driftwood. Millard watched it leap up the far side, lunge up, and race off toward the east, carrying the dead man and his stink, far, far away.

That left two deadly killers.

Millard took off his hat, wiped the beads of sweat popping out on his brow, and moved along the bank, keeping his head down. He stopped and fed two more shells from his vest pocket into the rifle. For a moment, he looked at the bedroll, his gun belt resting atop it with the old converted Colt, and wondered if that had been a mistake. No, he decided, the Richards-Mason .44-caliber conversion had more power, but not the range of the .32 rifle. Besides, although a Colt felt natural on his hip, he had never been much of a hand with a short gun. Only Borden had ever shown much instinct with a six-shooter. Jimmy and Millard, like their old man, had always preferred their long guns.

Another shot kicked up sand above the bank where Millard had been. Again, he wet his lips and looked over at his horse, dancing around in its hobbles. He had been smart to use those hobbles on the chestnut's forefeet. Providing, of course, the two outlaws did not kill the beast out of spite.

"Hey, gringo!" Bandolier Man called out. "Let us talk. This makes no sense. *Quelle sottise!* We come for coffee. You shoot at us. You kill Eddlie."

Millard wished his horse would stop snorting and dancing so. He wanted to hear. Not what the man with the bandoliers was saying. He was listening for something else.

185

He said nothing.

"Gringo? Talk to me. Ay, caramba, this is just a misunderstanding. Gringo? Gringo, are you dead? *Mince alors!* Did one of our shots kill you?"

The voice sounded as if it came from Millard's left, so he looked to his right, listening, not answering, not making any sound, not even moving. Briefly, he glanced at the Winchester, felt his thumb on the hammer. It was cocked. He knew Bandolier Man didn't want to talk. He just wanted to find out where Millard was hiding behind the bank.

The bank began to drop, leaving him with only about fifteen or twenty yards of cover. If he kept going toward the pistol and his makeshift camp, he would be caught in the open. The creek bed wasn't wide, either, and cover was hard to find. If he tried for his horse, they'd gun him down.

So there was nothing to do . . . but wait.

To their advantage, the sun had been to the riders' backs, making him stare at them into the sun, even as it had begun to sink. In the dark, that might help him. Slowly, softly he rolled to his back and raised the Winchester rifle. Once more, he wet his lips and kept waiting and looking.

"Amigo. *Mon Dieu.* Let us talk. We do not

wish to harm you. We merely want coffee."
Bandolier Man laughed. His voice told Millard that the man was not moving.

The chestnut stopped dancing, but shook its head, snorted, and kept its ears flat on its head. He appeared to be staring up the bank. Millard decided Duster Man would be coming from there. Bandolier Man began talking again in French, Spanish, and English, but no longer did Millard listen to anything he had to say. He kept his eyes on the bank, but mostly on the ground. Waiting.

Waiting.

Waiting.

The long shadow first appeared barely over the edge of the embankment, beyond the scrub where the creek turned to the south. It hung there for the longest while, then grew a bit longer, and stopped again. Bandolier Man kept on talking, screaming, no longer pleading, mostly cursing. Millard knew it was to keep him from focusing on the one in the duster, the one whose shadow moved again, just a bit, and stopped.

Patience.

That often proved the key to surviving a fight. Duster Man, he of the two Remington .44s, had the patience of an oyster.

Another inch the shadow lengthened.

"Amigo! *J'en ai ras-le-bol!*"

Suddenly, the shadow moved dramatically, and Millard followed it with his Winchester.

The black-clad man in the dirty linen duster sprinted the last few feet, leaping off the bank and firing the Remingtons in both hands — where Millard Mann had been earlier. He quickly realized his mistake, probably seeing Millard in the corner of his eye, and adjusted his aim. He was fast, quick, deadly.

Even before he hit the ground, he was raising both Remingtons, shooting the one in his left hand first, but that shot went wild.

His knees buckled as he hit the ground, but he did not fall. He came up, firing again with the .44 in his left hand. That slug slapped past Millard's right ear.

Then the Winchester .32 boomed.

Millard was lying flat on his back, staring at the killer with the twin Remingtons.

Through the smoke, he saw the one in the duster flinch, but not fall. The Winchester barked again. He saw blood spurt from the man's chest, and the slug drove him back against the cut of the bank.

Millard's ears rang from the sound of the guns, he smelled smoke, and he tasted fear, but he was not afraid.

The horse danced and whinnied, fighting

the tether and hobbles, but Millard could pay no attention to the gelding. He jacked another round into the rifle, and the Winchester spoke.

The bullet caught Duster Man higher, and his left hand dropped as he pulled the trigger, shooting himself in the foot, quite an ignominy for a gunman. Again, Millard pulled the trigger, and saw dust and blood fly off the man's chest. The pistol slipped from the killer's left hand, falling into the dust by his bloody, mangled boot, but he still held the other Remington in his right hand.

That might be a threat, but Millard knew he couldn't focus on that man any longer. He heard those French curses and rolled to his knees, levering the rifle, bringing it up to his shoulder just as the man with the bandoliers appeared.

The big man's gun roared, and Millard felt the shot graze his head, burning his hair.

As the outlaw thumbed back the hammer of his revolver, Millard fired the '73.

The bullet split the bandoliers, and sent the burly man flying backward. Almost immediately, Millard turned again to the one in the duster. He had managed to bring up the Remington in his right hand and pulled the trigger, but that bullet didn't come close to Millard.

Millard aimed, but did not fire.

The man didn't have the strength to thumb back the hammer. The pistol weaved wildly in his right hand before it dropped into the dust. He leaned back against the wall of the bank, spit out froths of blood. Millard couldn't hear what the man tried to say, but he could read his lips.

It was an insult to Millard's mother.

He shot the dying man right between the eyes.

He didn't bother to watch the man crash to the ground. He came up, jacking the lever, moving to where the banks dropped off, and stepped up toward the big man with the massive hat — which the wind had blown off — and the bandoliers.

He lay spread-eagled on the ground, the pistol far from his hand, fingers curled.

Millard went to him, and slowly eased down the hammer of the smoking .32. Bandolier Man stared up at him, or rather, up at the sky, but those eyes did not see Millard. They saw nothing. At least, not on earth.

In another world, those eyes were probably staring at Lucifer.

Their horses had galloped off, not after the one carrying the stinking man, but north and west. Millard toed the burly man's side with his boot, just to be sure he was indeed dead. Satisfied, he walked back down the creek bed, fishing out .32-caliber cartridges, which he quickly fed into the rifle as he approached the one in the duster.

He lay on his side. Millard didn't have to toe him to make sure he was dead. That last shot had blown out the back of his skull, but he would have died anyway. The other bullets had been mortal, but he was one tough customer.

Millard considered burying them, but he had no shovel, and they would not have buried him had the outcome turned out differently. He walked back to the bedroll, lowering the hot Winchester and picking up the gun belt, which he buckled around his waist and adjusted the holster on his hip.

His horse had stopped dancing, sensing that loud gunshots would not be heard again. Millard certainly hoped that would be the case. He moved to the saddle, pried out the piece of driftwood from the scabbard and tossed it away. He was shaking. He held both hands straight out, and watched them tremble.

Twelve years had passed since he had done anything like that, back when James was just a kid. Thinking of his son did not steady his nerves. In fact, the thought made him shake even more, until he balled his fingers into tight fists, and steeled himself.

He looked off to the east and south at the broken land. Somewhere out there was James. In Indian Territory. In the lawless world. With a murdering whiskey runner and his ragamuffin daughter. Millard had managed to survive, but how many more rogues would he run into?

"Jimmy," he said softly, just whispering his dead kid brother's name. "I could use your help now." He grinned, thinking back to those early, wild, rawhide years. "You, too, Borden."

But he would have to do it alone.

His fists unclenched, and he held them out again. No longer did they shake. He was just out of practice.

The horse snorted, and Millard said, "I hear you." He picked up the blanket and saddle and lugged them over to the liver chestnut gelding. He did not bother rubbing down the horse. They wouldn't be riding for long, not with the sun gone, but he wasn't about to stay there. He saddled the horse, shoved the .32 Winchester into the scabbard, and walked back to his bedroll — which is when he smelled the coffee.

He remembered what the big man with

the massive black hat and the bandoliers had said just a few minutes earlier.

"It smells inviting."

It hadn't then. The man had lied. But now that the pot had been over flames, it did smell good. Mighty good.

He found the cup, blew out the sand, walked to his glove, and picked it up. It stank of gun smoke and burnt leather. He shook out the E. Allen & Company .41-caliber derringer. After blowing the barrel, he dropped it into a pocket. He reloaded, then distanced himself from the two dead men and set up another camp down the road. He would make two camps. One for supper, then travel on another few miles and spend the night elsewhere, without a campfire or food. To be safe.

A man had to be careful in Indian country.

He actually used the glove to lift the pot and pour the coffee into the cup. Then he sat down and tried to enjoy the taste of the coffee.

But he kept looking off in the distance, thinking of his son, worrying, and wondering just what James was doing.

CHAPTER FOURTEEN

Kiowa-Comanche-Apache Reservation
"Pick up that rifle, you dern fool!" Wildcat Lamar snapped. "You tryin' to get us all kilt?"

James fumbled with the heavy Winchester and brought it up, trying to wipe off the dirt and dust. "They're Indians!"

" 'Course they is. What did you expect? A bunch of Frenchies?" Wildcat cursed. "Keep that rifle handy, boy."

"Mister Lamar." James could barely talk.

The old man had started out, toward the approaching Indians, but cursed and turned back to face James. "What is it?"

He wet his lips. "I . . . I . . . this . . ." He held up the rifle a tad. Took a deep breath, exhaled, and came out with it. "It's empty. I don't have any bullets."

The man's face paled, then turned beet red with fury. One hand dropped for the knife and the other reached for James's throat, but both stopped, as did the curse on his lips. "Jes don't let 'em savages know it." He whirled around, brought both hands up above his head, and began speaking in some guttural language as he walked toward the Comanches.

James had seen Indians before, back when he was a kid, but most of the Comanches and Kiowas had surrendered to the U.S. Army before he had even been born. Reservation Indians were supposed to be tame Indians. That's what folks said over at the post office and barber shop and mercantile in McAdam. Those in front of him did not look civilized, or tame, or anything but wild. Yet as far as he could tell, none carried any rifle or musket, not even a shotgun. However, all except the women and the dogs had quivers full of arrows. A few sported hatchets, and the one with the buffalo horn headdress carried a lance. James hoped it was for ceremonial purposes only.

They rode in, or walked, circling Wildcat Lamar before the one with the buffalo horn headdress said something and dismounted. He kept the lance, wrapped in leather strips dyed red and with brilliant beads and feathers hanging from the shaft, in his right hand.

The dogs barked until one of the women hit one with a switch. That one ran back to the north. The others fell quiet and scurried well out of the woman's reach.

James tried to keep his heart from leaping out of his mouth. Tried to breath. Every once in a while, he had to wipe away the sweat that poured down his face, burning his eyes. His shirt already felt damp on his back and under his armpits.

The one with the lance and Wildcat Lamar did all the talking, but most of it was said with their hands, occasionally saying something in a throaty language more bark than words.

Finally, the leader stepped back and turned toward some of the braves. He spoke briefly, and a tall, lean man wearing only a breechclout and moccasins walked to his horse. James couldn't see what he was doing; the skewbald blocked his view. When the Indian returned, he held a pouch in his right hand, and even from where James stood, he could hear the clinking of coins.

Without a word, he stopped and tossed the pouch at Wildcat Lamar's feet. The old man did not move, but stared hard at the tall brave. "Boy, come here and pick it up."

It took practically an eternity before James realized the old man wasn't talking to the brave. He meant for James to do the errand. Wildcat Lamar wouldn't take his eyes off the lean, mean, silent warrior.

James went at a hurry, feeling every Indian, even the women, possibly the dogs, staring at him as he raced the short distance and knelt down. Actually, they weren't looking at him. Their eyes were glued on the .50-caliber repeating rifle. He kept that in his right hand, and picked up the pouch, heavy with coin, in his left. Backing up, eyes locked on the lean warrior, he offered the pouch to Wildcat Lamar.

"Yer learnin' kid. Taught you good. Never let that one out of yer sight." Wildcat hefted the pouch, smiled, and nodded at the one in the buffalo horn headdress. "This concludes our transaction, gents." He nodded at the barrel of molasses.

James didn't know what a barrel of molasses went for in Indian Territory, but the weight of that pouch told him that the Indians were being robbed. He didn't say anything, just backed away with Wildcat Lamar toward the team of oxen, the wagon, and Robin hiding in the driver's box.

The leader said something and a few other Indians hurried toward the barrel, reaching it long before James and the old man had made it to the wagon.

"It's all right now, boy," Wildcat said as they walked. "We'll just mosey on along. I'll get in the box. You climb into the back. But don't let 'em bucks see you lower that gun." He whispered, "No bullets," and cursed again, but quietly.

James tried to walk calmly toward the back, thinking that none of them had ever ridden in the wagon but glad to do so.

Two of the Indians had drawn their hatchets, the blades iron and not stone, and hacked away at the top of the oaken barrel. Others waited. A few licked their lips. The one in the buffalo horn headdress frowned. The thin, lean one who had fetched the money stared with bitter, angry eyes, first at his comrades, then, with more hatred, at James.

Liquid splashed from the busted top of the barrel, and one of the Indians screamed something, tossed his hatchet a few rods away, and plunged both hands into the jagged opening. He came up, brown water running through his fingers, and drank greedily, then shook his hands and his head, and howled like a coyote toward the sky.

Other Indians quickly ran to the barrel to drink. One pushed another out of the way. Before James had managed to pull himself into the back of the wagon, those two were fighting. None of the others seemed to care. They gathered around the barrel, shoving one another, yelling in that wild language, waiting to get at the barrel. To drink.

The wagon lurched forward, slowly, but picking up speed. The blacksnake whip snapped and bit, and Wildcat Lamar urged the animals on with curses and leather. Oxen generally did not move fast, but these moved faster than normal. Not quick enough to escape all of those Comanches on horseback, but they didn't seemed interested in anything other than the barrel.

"Molasses," James whispered as the wagon pulled away. "Molasses."

He knew. He leaned against another barrel and didn't look at what was stamped on it.

Right, he thought. *Molasses is thick. It doesn't flow like . . . like . . .* liquor.

He cursed his luck and cursed Wildcat Lamar and his son. Those two weren't anything but a pair of miserable, low-down whiskey runners. Criminals. Turning a bold and brave Indian people like those Comanches into wild, crazy, foolish drunks.

Fort Worth
Usually, Zane Maxwell spent his time in Fort Worth in the saloons, gambling halls, and bordellos along with the drunks, gamblers, outlaws, idiots, cowboys, dancehall

girls, and saloon girls that populated the red-light district known as Hell's Half Acre. Now that he was a respectable member of the press . . . he stopped at a business at 705 Main Street and looked at the prints in the window. A kid and a dog. A photograph of the courthouse. A stiff-lipped man with a woman in what appeared to be her wedding dress. Cattle in the stockyards on the north side of town. All good photos.

The bell over the door chimed, and a man stepped out onto the street. "Good day, sir. Might I interest you in posing for a photograph? Not a tintype, sir. I can use dry plates and sell you as many prints as you desire."

Maxwell looked at the sign on the window. SWARTZ VIEW STUDIO. "You're Swartz?"

The photographer bowed. "John Swartz, at your service."

Maxwell extended his hand. "Butch Curry. With the *Kansas City Enterprise*." Both names came to him on the fly. He didn't know anyone named Butch or Curry and wasn't sure if there was a newspaper in Kansas City called the *Enterprise,* but who cared? And who in town would know?

They shook, and the man gestured inside. "A photograph, sir? You'll find my fees and services quite reasonable."

Maxwell laughed and shook his head. "Afraid not. I'm like an Injun. Fear a photograph might just steal my shadow. But good luck to you, sir. I must make my way to the meeting of the Lone Star Cattle Growers Association. Maybe someone else'll pose for you. Make you famous."

He walked away, shaking his head. Him. Posing for a studio portrait. Wouldn't the Pinkertons and the U.S. marshals love that? Somehow getting their mitts on an actual photograph of a notorious outlaw. That would bring about the downfall of the most notorious outlaw gang since the James and Younger boys. Maxwell chuckled as he walked down Main Street toward the hotel, wondering what kind of fool an outlaw would have to be to do such a thing.

The meeting of the cattlemen started at Fort Worth's fanciest hotel on Monday. Yet nothing much went on. In fact, from where Maxwell sat in the back of the meeting room, with nothing to drink but coffee, it appeared all those old boys did was talk about cattle and grass and politics in Austin and Washington City and the weather, with a few brief discussions and lamentations on weather and cattle and grass and politics in Austin and Washington City. He knew he could never be a cattleman or a newspaper reporter. The jobs were just too boring, although the evenings, when everyone adjourned to the nearest grog shop, did have some merit.

He met a few other reporters and discovered that newspapermen weren't any better than cowboys and cardsharpers. They just seemed to drink more. So passing himself off as a journalist came easy, especially since the ink-slinger from one of the Dallas papers said nobody from Kansas City had ever covered a cattlemen's meeting in Cow town.

"How long do you think this deal will go on?" Maxwell asked.

The meeting had adjourned for the day. The cattlemen, being of higher class and with thicker wallets than the journalists, had gone out to eat dinner. A few Chickasaw Indians had gone with them.

The Dallas reporter raised his beer stein. "You mean this?" He laughed, drained a healthy portion, and wiped the suds of his mustache with a bar towel. "The meeting?" He shrugged. "Three days probably. They won't get down to serious matters till Thursday. Finish up Friday. Have the weekend to drink. Go home Sunday after church."

"That's what I thought, too," Maxwell said. He was utterly clueless. "Just wanted to . . . confirm it from another source."

The man drained his beer, slapped the empty stein on the bar, and motioned for the bartender for another. "Got to get our facts right. Or at least confirmed. What paper you say you're with?"

"Enterprise."

The place was filled with people. The man yelled at the bartender when he hadn't responded with another beer.

Maxwell waited until the bartender finally brought another stein, and the Dallas scribe reached for his nickel, before slapping a silver dollar on the bar. "This one's on me, and all the others till it runs out."

The barkeep took the coin, nodded at Maxwell, and brought him a beer. No wait. Not for a man with that kind of money, even if it was only a buck.

"You Kansas City boys are all right."

With a laugh, Maxwell clinked his stein against the Dallas writer's. "We aim to be."

They drank. And then Zane Maxwell, alias Butch Curry, reporter for the *Kansas City Enterprise,* said, "Maybe you can confirm a few other facts for me . . ."

Maxwell met reporters and two or three

cattlemen, and those men enjoyed to gab. They talked. Talked a lot. About anything — to anyone, as long as someone, typically Maxwell, kept them in bourbon and beer.

Everyone told him the same thing . . . the meetings would go on for a while, just to build up for some serious drinking and gambling and eating, but everything would be determined on Thursday morning.

Thursday was a long time coming, it seemed to Maxwell, but finally it did arrive. And, just as everyone had told him, that's when everything was set. Firm. The Indians signed. The Texans signed. They shook hands, posed for a few photographs, and the reporters hurried off to file their stories for the next day's or next week's newspapers.

And so, when the cattlemen and the Chickasaws and the ink-slingers broke for their noon dinner, Maxwell gathered his notes and his bowler, and walked out of the hotel and to the telegraph office. Chatting with a handful of reporters from Fort Worth, Dallas, and Austin had indeed confirmed a few significant facts. He filled out the yellow slip of paper to send a wire to Ben Storm, the alias Link McCoy was using in Denison, Texas.

FIND PREACHER SOON STOP WED-
DING DATE SET JULY 4 STOP SHOULD
BE GREAT CEREMONY STOP

BUTCH CURRY KC ENTERPRISE STOP
HOTEL SAM HOUSTON STOP FORT
WORTH TEXAS

He handed the paper and the greenback
to the telegrapher, and stepped back, watching as the man quickly tapped out the message on the key. He also looked at the
calendar hanging on the wall over the
telegrapher's head. The bespectacled man
in the striped shirt and sleeve garters had
crossed out the days with a red pencil,
marking that day as June twenty-fifth.

The Texans were delivering the gold to
the Chickasaws at Fort Washita on Independence Day, the Fourth of July.

He hoped that McCoy would get that
message, that he had already located the
whiskey runner they wanted to help pull off
the score.

June 25. Eight days.

He frowned, then making sure the telegrapher was not looking, did that little number,
tapping his knuckles and the gaps between
then, reciting the months of the year, just
the way the schoolmarm had taught him all

those years ago. He didn't have to go through the entire year. He smiled. Not eight days. *Nine.*

June didn't have thirty-one days.

CHAPTER FIFTEEN

Denison

The moment he heard the batwing doors pounding and the singing of the spurs, Link McCoy looked at the three men who just walked into the saloon and wished he had his Winchester '87 with him. But he was in a respectable joint on the right side of the railroad tracks, and the owners and the law did not care for weapons. Of course, no one had noticed the brass .31-caliber pocket derringer with the pearl grips in his vest pocket.

"By grab!" shouted Denison's mayor, who had bellied up to the bar a couple hours ago and was still nursing his beer while talking shop with the bartender and saloon owner. "Ranger Clarke! What brings you to Denison?" The mayor hurried across the floor and extended his soft hand at the leathery looking Texas Ranger.

The Ranger shook, but did not seemed

interested in anything the mayor had to say. Covered in dust, he must have ridden halfway across Texas to get there — which made McCoy, who was typically anything but paranoid, think that maybe the Rangers were after him.

Yet the two men who had entered the saloon with the Ranger did not wear the cinco pesos star of the Texas Rangers. They did carry guns — against the city ordinance in town proper. On the other side of the tracks, no one cared who carried what or who killed who. Two guns each, on their hips, while one toted a double-barrel Greener and the other a Winchester carbine.

Link McCoy pulled down his hat, lowered his head, and spied on the three newcomers.

Ranger Clarke would be Alan Clarke. He had earned a bit of a reputation in the Panhandle. McCoy didn't know the one with the shotgun, but the one with the walrus mustache, the brown patch over his left eye, the missing left ear, and the Winchester carbine . . . that one he did know.

Jared Whitney. Hired killer. He was even wanted in Texas. For murder. If McCoy Link remembered right, Whitney had even killed a Texas Ranger.

So what is a Ranger, a lawman like Alan

Clarke, doing siding with a hired gun, a cold-blooded killer? A man with no respect for the badge.

That thought made Link relax. He didn't think the men were after him. He left the brass derringer in his pocket, finished his whiskey, and when the mayor had escorted the three men to the bar, he casually rose, and walked out of the saloon. He would leave Clarke, Whitney, and the third man to their drinking. Besides, he needed to get to Indian Territory. To find that man who drank Old Overholt and smoked like the stack of a Baldwin locomotive. And then find the whiskey runner wanted for poisoning some folks up in the Panhandle.

Elm Spring Station, Chickasaw Nation
Link McCoy and Zane Maxwell did not have a monopoly on crime in Indian country. Proving that, a tumbleweed wagon full of prisoners and its deputies and driver had lit out for Fort Smith weeks ago.

Jackson Sixpersons was alone, unless he counted Mallory and Flatt, who was driving another tumbleweed wagon carrying prisoners.

Two young Creeks, arrested on John Doe warrants for running whiskey, leaned against the iron bars. The one with his left ear bit-

209

ten off waved a bell crown hat to cool himself in the sun. The one wearing a yellow brocade vest was snoring logs and curled up in a fetal position.

On the other side of the wagon sat a white man with black teeth and a gray mustache, who denied that he was Larry Dundee, accused of murdering a peddler named Jameson outside of Muskogee. He sure fit the description on the wanted poster and had been captured with the gold Saint Christopher medallion known to have been in Jameson's possession. He had busted Malcolm Mallory's nose during the arrest, which satisfied Jackson Sixpersons. Mallory kept spouting in his nasal voice that Judge Parker should add a year to Dundee's sentence for resisting arrest and assaulting a federal peace officer.

"You think Judge Parker will leave him swinging for a year after he's hanged for murder?" Jackson Sixpersons asked.

Virgil Flatt laughed at that one. So did the Creek Indian who wasn't snoring. Malcolm Mallory did not laugh, just sulked.

They had made camp in a clearing about a quarter mile from the old stagecoach station at Elm Spring. The old mud wagons and Concords had not traveled through there for a number of years. In fact, the only people hanging around the abandoned cabin were Salvationists, mostly Presbyterians who were trying to set up some sort of mission at the old spring.

"Goin' to a camp meetin', Jackson?" Flatt asked with a laugh. "Yer shore gettin' dressed fer it."

Ignoring the driver, Sixpersons fed another buckshot shell into the shotgun. He worked the lever, and loaded one more round into the twelve-gauge, then stood. "You coming?"

Mallory looked up and slowly lowered the wadded-up soaked bandana. He muttered a curse and whined, "My nose is busted, Jackson."

"What I figured." The old Cherokee pulled down the brim of his beat-up hat and walked to his piebald gelding. He swung into the saddle, not sheathing the Winchester in the scabbard, and rode to the station, hearing the minister or wannabe minister leading the congregation in "Shall We Gather at the River."

Most of them were old people — gray beards and silver heads. Even the person waving the hymnal had to be older than Jackson Sixpersons. Slowly, the leader lowered the book, and stared, his mouth agape, at the lawman as he dismounted and walked to the people sitting on rocks and camp chairs, or on blankets, or just on the grass. The congregation stopped singing and turned to stare, too.

That was good. Those people could not carry a tune in a burlap bag.

One man did not turn. He probably had not been singing anyway. He just sat there in his linen duster and wringing the black slouch hat in his hands, head bowed.

"This is a prayer meeting, sir!" The preacher man had found his voice and pointed a long finger at Sixpersons.

The Cherokee stopped and looked at the young man. "Ben Fellows, come with me."

The man just kept wringing his hat.

Sixpersons brought the shotgun to his shoulder and drew a bead on the young man.

The congregation parted like the Red Sea. A few of the old women screamed. Two of the graybeards protested.

"Let's go," Sixpersons said. "Or I blow your head off."

"Now hear me, you savage Indian, murder is a sin," the preacher said.

"So is rape." Sixpersons' words caused one of the women to faint into a graybeard's arm. "Ben Fellows," he repeated.

The hat fell onto the grass, and the man

turned. His eyes were vacant. He stood, pushed back the linen duster to reveal a Navy Colt tucked inside his waistband.

"You don't want to do that," Sixpersons said.

"Please!" one of the women begged.

Fellows sighed. "No, I don't."

Slowly, he tugged the Colt free with fingers and thumb, touching only the walnut butt of the old pistol, which he dropped by his feet. He extended his arms, offering his hands for the manacles.

Only then did Jackson Sixpersons lower the shotgun.

He walked Ben Fellows out of the prayer meeting. The tumbleweed wagon was filling up.

The next stop was Fort Sill. If only he could drop off the prisoners and his two associates there — but that's not the way the law or the army worked in Indian Territory.

What a shame.

CHAPTER SIXTEEN

Fort Washita, Chickasaw Nation

The post had been abandoned by the army years ago and didn't look formidable. Maybe it never had.

When first established in 1842, it had been the army's most southwestern base, set up to protect the Choctaws and Chickasaws who had been kicked out of their homelands in the southeastern states and forced to make a new home in Indian Territory. The Yankees had pulled out early during the Civil War, and Rebels from Texas had turned the fort into a Confederate base. After Appomattox, the U.S. government had given the fort to the Chickasaws.

Link McCoy rode through the entrance beneath the watchtower and saw only Indians. Not the one he was looking for, but that was to be expected.

He swung down from the bay, wrapped the reins around the hitching post, and looked around the grounds. Finally, he saw the glow of a cigarette from the middle window in the watchtower he had passed under. Looked like a log cabin built on top of a rock wall. He found the ladder, climbed it, and stepped inside the dark room, smelling cigarette smoke.

"You took your time," the gravelly voice said.

McCoy frowned. "I'm here. And we don't have much time."

"So you said. Fourth of July?"

"Yes."

"Be some party."

"I hope it's a good one. For you and me. And everyone."

"It should be."

McCoy looked down at the grounds. No one seemed to care that he was up there talking to that Indian who smoked constantly. Typically, Indians minded their own business.

"You've found Bodeen?" he asked.

"I've sent for him. He should be heading this way."

"What did you tell him?"

"Just sent him a message through a Choctaw I know. That we'd meet him."

"Then let's go meet him."

The man who smoked laughed. "You

might want some help."

"To find a whiskey runner?" McCoy laughed back and shook his head. "I think we can handle him and his kid."

"Yeah. I'd hope so." The cigarette went flying out the window. "But can you handle the entire Chickasaw Nation?"

"What do you mean?"

"I mean that those Indians . . . and a whole lot of others . . . aim to kill Lamar Bodeen. You might have asked for a whiskey peddler who don't poison Indians."

Fort Sill, Indian Territory

The army post closest to the Kiowa-Comanche-Apache reservation had quite the history. It had been serving the army since 1869, back when the buffalo soldiers of the 10th Cavalry had lowered their beat-up carbines and turned into brick masons and carpenters to build the post. They'd done a good job. Many of those buildings still stood almost thirty years later, and while most frontier forts had been abandoned since the last of the Indians had surrendered — even the wily Apache Geronimo was living on the reservation nearby — Fort Sill remained vibrant, alive, and needed.

Indians still called the fort "the Soldier

House at Medicine Bluffs."

Leaving Malcolm Mallory and Virgil Flatt outside with the tumbleweed wagon, listening to Geronimo talk to some reporters, Deputy U.S. Marshal Jackson Sixpersons walked into the post hospital.

An orderly rose, saw the badge, turned toward a man in a white robe, and called out a name that Sixpersons did not catch. The white man turned, removed his spectacles, and walked to the old Cherokee.

He was heavyset and balding although his Dundreary whiskers, heavy with white, flowed. The tie was loosened around his neck. The face was flushed pink. The man's chest heaved. Jackson Sixpersons figured he might drop dead of a heart attack before he even introduced himself. He started to extend a hand, stopped, and studied the Winchester shotgun Sixpersons held in his left hand.

Sixpersons said nothing.

The doctor cleared his throat, looked away from the shotgun and into Jackson Sixpersons' eyes. "You're from Fort Smith?"

Sixpersons nodded.

The doctor cursed and swung a fat arm across the room lined with beds. Most of the patients were white men, probably half not even sick — except of the mundane chores given to a peacetime army — but a few of the patients, way off in the far back corner, were Indians.

"None of them have died, but one is touch and go, and I fear if she cannot hold any food or water in her stomach, she will be called to Glory before two more days. The others are still with us only by the grace of the Lord. Nothing I've done." He sounded like he hailed from Boston. Jackson Sixpersons had heard a lot of Boston accents, mainly from lawyers in Judge Parker's court. Lawyers for the defense. He had grown mighty sick of men from Boston, but the sawbones, well, he seemed all right.

"How long ago?" Sixpersons asked.

"Two days." The doctor began walking across the big room, and Sixpersons followed.

One white soldier stopped him and asked if he was going to shoot the Indians. "You know" — he cackled and gestured toward the men who had gathered at his cot to play cards — "put 'em out of their memory. With that." He pointed a bandaged finger at the twelve-gauge lever-action shotgun. "Like you'd shoot a horse with a broke leg." He giggled.

His companions, with better sense, did not.

218

Sixpersons looked at the joking man and lifted his shotgun, pointing the barrel at the man's ruddy face. "I don't shoot horses."

The man dropped his cards, and his eyes widened. His lips trembled, and he stuttered out an apology before Sixpersons lowered the shotgun and hurried to catch up with the doctor, who had not even stopped walking or talking.

"We get bad whiskey all the time. That comes with the territory. I know you lawmen have been trying to stop those runners. Most of them run whiskey, maybe not the best you'll find, maybe not much better than Taos Lightning, but it doesn't kill. Or come close to killing. Not like this. This" — he stopped, drew a handkerchief and wiped the sweat off his face — "is murder. Plain and simple."

Jackson Sixpersons had never cared for hospitals. He didn't even like visiting the holy people in Cherokee Country. White man's hospitals smelled of medicine and alcohol and white men, but mostly, of death. He wanted to get out quickly, but he needed to hear what the doctor had to say first.

"Strychnine. A nasty way to die." The doctor said, pointing a fat finger at an Indian. A girl. Most Comanches were on the stout side, but this one had lost so much weight, she looked like copper skin melting onto bones. Her breathing was ragged. Her eyes closed.

"Bodeen?" Sixpersons asked.

"I don't know the runner's name. The Comanches don't know him either. Just call him Wildcat." The doc saw recognition in the Cherokee's eyes. "I figure him to be the one you marshals are after."

"Not just the marshals. Rangers, too."

"And likely Comanches, Kiowas, Apaches and every Indian on every reservation in this territory. Good. I hope you catch him and kill him." The doctor sighed. "He had a boy with him, maybe two. And a big wagon pulled by oxen. That's all I could get out of the Indians and the Indian agent who brought him here."

That was all Jackson Sixpersons needed to hear. It was Lamar Bodeen. Wildcat Bodeen.

"The Comanche chief — he's on the wagon, just leads his people to the devil. Not Quanah. Not the big man of the Comanches. Just the big boss of his village. Anyway, he said they wanted to go after the man — the ones who had come to buy the whiskey and get drunk. Once those people started getting sick, coughing blood, sick and dying, they had another notion. Figured they could ride down a man in a wagon that size. But the whiskey made them all sick real quick. There was nothing to do but get them to help."

Sixpersons considered that and asked. "They come here first?"

The doctor shook his head. "No. To their medicine man. He couldn't do anything. Didn't have the *puha* or whatever the Comanches call it. Three of them died there. So they brought the others here."

"Two days ago," Sixpersons said.

"That's right."

"How long was Bodeen in their camp?"

"Just a day. Maybe two."

That gave Lamar Bodeen and his son a four-day head start. But in a wagon that size and that slow, Sixpersons figured he could catch up with that crazy killer with booze fairly quickly. A whiskey runner like Bodeen would want to clear out of the federal reservation as fast as he could. He'd go southeast into the Chickasaw Nation. Sell his poison there. Then move out again into the Choctaw Nation.

"What became of the liquor?" Sixpersons asked.

"The major sent a few troopers down to West Cache Creek. That's where the fiend sold his poison. They found the tracks.

Destroyed the barrel — it was in a barrel marked *molasses* or something like that. Listen." He moved close to Sixpersons, too close, but the Cherokee did not move.

"I know Judge Parker probably can't hang a man for killing a bunch of Comanches, but he can for killing a white man, can't he?"

Sixpersons said nothing.

"Well, one of the troopers decided that destroying the liquor — which was the major's orders — meant drinking it." The doctor shook his head. "He was dead before they even got back here. You can hang the runner for that, can't you?"

Sixpersons shook his head. "I don't hang anyone. That's up to Judge Parker and the court." But he was staring at the girl and thinking *this time I might just make an exception.*

Wild Horse Creek, Chickasaw Nation
Millard Mann had ridden far since killing those two — no, three — outlaws back along Camp Creek. Lost James's trail in a dust storm. Found it again. Lost it in a river and it had taken two days before he crossed the trail again since the old man kept off the main trails. Millard couldn't figure out how a man could hide a trail so well when

222

he was traveling in a giant wagon heavy with whiskey.

He had found one small camp southwest of Fort Sill and a busted barrel of whiskey marked MALASES — meaning molasses, he figured — the word obviously misspelled. Drops of blood, vomit, a mixture of tracks from unshod horses, the wheels of the big wagon, and the oxen indicated something had happened there. He surmised a trade for whiskey, and something had gone wrong. The whiskey barrel wasn't even half empty.

Whatever had gone wrong had left its mark in the air and had spooked him. And his horse. They had left early, seeing dust rising from the north. Maybe Indians. Maybe soldiers. Millard hadn't stuck around to find out.

That had been days ago.

He stopped to give the horse a breather and hooked a leg over the horn, resting, too. He was slaking his thirst from the canteen when the chestnut gelding's head came up, and he looked into the wind blowing in from the southeast.

Following the horse's gaze, Millard studied the countryside. It wasn't the same as the reservations to the west and north. What he saw was hilly, wooded, and even hotter than the furnace he had been riding

223

through. He couldn't see much through the growths of timber and scrub, but he could hear. So he listened.

Grunting, heaving, sweating, practically busting their backs and straining every muscle in their bodies, Robin Lamar and James Mann rolled three big barrels out of the wagon.

Wildcat Lamar stopped them with his spade and waited for them to climb out. "Hurry up, children." He fanned himself as though he had done all the hard work. " 'Em bucks'll be here directly." He hurried inside the wagon to fetch something else.

"Come on," James urged Robin, but the kid was weak as a girl. He'd had to do most of the work to get the barrels out of the wagon, and suddenly he gained a higher measure of respect for the railroaders his father had to supervise and boss around. Those men swung sixteen-pound sledgehammers ten to fourteen hours a day.

With Robin using the spade's handle as a shovel, they managed to get the first barrel righted, and began working on the second one when Wildcat Lamar came rushing back toward them.

Thunk.

James whirled to see the old man swinging a hatchet, tearing at the barrel like a crazy man.

Thunk.

Thunk.

Thunk.

Splinters, then chunks of oak sailed into the air as the man worked furiously.

"Come on, James," Robin said.

To the sound of the ax blade splitting the upright oak keg, they went back to work.

As soon as the second barrel was upright, the old man started attacking it.

He probably would have gone straight for the final barrel, if his son hadn't been leaning over its top, exhausted.

"Get up, kid," he said angrily. "They'll be here —"

A horse's snort stopped him and he spun around, the hatchet slipping from his hand and sailing right for the second barrel. James had just stepped around it to see who the new guests were when the hatchet splashed into the open barrel, sending a fountain of amber liquid sailing.

Generally, that would have made him laugh, but it made him cry and fall to his knees. "My eyes!" he screamed, trying to put out what felt like burning kerosene. "Argghhhhh! That . . . b-b-burns."

"Shut up." Wildcat cursed. "Shuts up.

They's here."

Robin went to James's side, helped him up, and handed him a rag to dab his watering eyes.

Listening in the quiet, Millard Mann realized that what he felt wasn't of ghosts and death and an assault on his gut. It was more instinct. He unhooked his leg from the saddle horn and slid both feet into the stirrups, holding the reins to the gelding in his left hand and lowering his right to the stock of the '73 Winchester. He kept his hand there for a moment, still studying the timber and hills, looking for any sign, any movement.

Nothing.

Yet he couldn't shake that feeling.

Deliberately, he drew the .32 from the scabbard, brought it up, and rested the walnut stock on his thigh. His thumb came to the hammer, but he did not ear the hammer back.

James is in trouble, Brother.

Jimmy's voice came with the wind, whispering in Millard's left ear. He shook it off as imagination. He had been in the saddle far too long. Had been in a gunfight, survived, and left three dead men to feed buzzards, coyotes, and ravens. Besides, he already knew his son was in trouble. Didn't need his spooked mind or dead kid brother to remind him of that. James was with a wanted whiskey runner who was peddling poison to white men and red men alike. If Millard didn't find his son soon, the boy would be bound for the dungeon at Fort Smith, Arkansas, and then sent up to Michigan to serve a sentence in the federal pen. Or dead from the poison liquor. Or strung up by vigilantes or angry, but justified, Indians.

Millard studied the horse's ears, listened to how the horse breathed, realizing he had been around trains and rolling stock far too long. He seldom had need for what his father had told him all those years ago, back when he and Borden and Jimmy were barely taller than a fence post. *"Watch the horse. Watch the dog. The heifer. The bull. The rooster. Animals know. They hear. They sense. Long before you will."*

Millard gave a short nod as he remembered. Yeah, whatever it was, it was down to the southeast. Not in the nearby woods, but over the next hill. Maybe two. He didn't know that country, though Jimmy would. As a lawman, he had ridden the Nations for far too many years. Always bragged that he knew every hideout, cave, and creek in the territory.

But Jimmy was dead and buried up on Tascosa's Boot Hill.

CHAPTER SEVENTEEN

"Shut up." Wildcat cursed. "Shuts up. They's here."

Robin went to James's side, helped him up, and handed him a rag to dab his watering eyes.

He had been right. He had tried to convince himself that the deal with the Indians he had witnessed earlier wasn't what he had thought. He had tried to make himself believe something else. He stepped back, lowering the rag, pulling free from Robin. Through blurred vision tried to find the old man. "That's not molasses. It's whiskey!"

"Get to the wagon, boy. You, too, Robin."

"But —"

Robin pulled him away, then pushed him toward the wagon.

He tried to resist, but his eyes hurt too much. For a moment, he thought maybe he had been blinded, but slowly the tears flushed out the terrible whiskey.

"You didn't swaller none, did you?"

It took a while before he realized Robin had asked him the question.

"No." He shook his head. His eyes had swallowed the handful that splashed into his face.

"Climb up."

They had reached the front of the wagon. Once again, old Wildcat had not unhitched the team.

"It doesn't make any sense to hide up here now," he said.

"Do it . . ."

He turned and faced Robin, seeing that the kid's face was white. Afraid. The boy was afraid. And suddenly James understood that Wildcat Lamar was afraid, too.

That was the fuel James needed. He reached out, took hold, put his left foot on the piece of wood, climbed up, and pulled himself into the boot. Robin went in right behind him and grabbed the shotgun.

James stared at the Winchester '86.

"That won't do us no good," Robin said. "Unless you've conjured up some magic bullets."

He sighed, blinked his eyes rapidly, and looked across the camp.

The Chickasaws were farmers, had been even when they'd lived in towns east of the

Mississippi River in the state of Mississippi. Even before they had been removed to Indian Territory, those civilized Indians had had their own laws, their own religion, and their own government. The Chickasaws had shared a reservation — a Nation — with the Choctaws until the Treaty of 1854 had divided the reservations and created the Chickasaw Nation with five divisions.

The story went that the Chickasaws had always been allies of the white men, and had even helped General Anthony Wayne whip the Shawnee. Something told James that the twelve Indians he saw were not allies of Wildcat Lamar.

They dressed well, three of them in black broadcloth suits, five wearing tall silk hats like Abraham Lincoln might have donned, and several with silk cravats. They rode good horses. Yet every one of them carried a shotgun, rifle, or pitchfork.

"Chikma," Wildcat Lamar said, waving his hand.

James figured the Chickasaw word meant hello.

"Ofí!" snapped a silver-haired gent in broadcloth and top hat. He spit.

James figured that word did not mean hello.

The old man lowered his hand and gathered his wits as he glanced at the wagon. A few riders eased their horses up until they had formed a semicircle around him and his whiskey kegs. None of the Indians seemed to consider Robin or James.

"This ain't good," Robin whispered. "Ain't good at all."

"Gots some mighty fine whiskey here, gents," Wildcat said. "Three kegs. Like you asked fer, ol' chief, ol' pard. You got the silver?"

"You don't sell whiskey," the old chief said.

His voice surprised James. He didn't sound like an Indian, at least not like those he had seen back on the Kiowa-Comanche-Apache federal reserve. He sounded prim and proper, except when he had said that one Indian word. Bitterness and contempt had laced his voice then.

"You serve death."

Old Wildcat Lamar started to back away.

From the distance and even with his eyes still not completely clear, James could tell that the old man's face was losing all color. Wildcat was scared. He could sense death.

Realizing if he ran, he would be killed, the crazy man turned back to face the chief and his braves. "No. Yer jes' tryin' to get me to lower my price. Ya ol' skinflint." He laughed, though more fear came out than cackles.

"We will see." The chief's head bobbed, and four men swung down from their horses. "After you drink your own whiskey." Then he barked something in his native tongue.

Wildcat turned, screamed, and ran.

It happened so fast, James wasn't sure he understood any of it.

Wildcat Lamar was running, begging, and yelling for help.

Two Chickasaws kicked their horses and cut off Wildcat, blocking him from their view.

The shotgun roared, blistering James's left ear. He screamed, but couldn't even hear his own shout. The shot had been deafening. He clawed at his ear with one hand as if that might bring back his sudden hearing loss. Only then did he realize that Robin had cut loose with one barrel of the shotgun.

The horse's ears flattened, and Millard pulled on the reins, then stood in the stirrups. The wind blew and carried not only the smell of summer, but sounds.

Gunfire.

Swearing, Millard raked his spurs across the liver chestnut and galloped down the hill, skirting the woods, following the trail.

"Never ride into a fight," his father had told him, *"until you know what you're riding into."*
Millard didn't care.

His son was down there. In trouble.

As Robin thumbed back the other hammer, the second barrel exploded, sending James flying off the wagon and landing with a thud. He rolled over, trying to catch his breath. Shots and screams sounded, but far, far, far away. Like in a dream. He realized he was not deaf, that only one ear could not hear. The other picked up sound.

Robin had fired again, and her shot had knocked a man off his horse. Close by. James heard the horse gallop past him, so close it spit dust and gravel into his face. On his knees, he wondered why the oxen did not take off. Slowly, he comprehended that the brakes had not been unlocked. Those four animals were worn out from the long, hard haul and were not even straining to get away.

A bullet whistled past his ear that could not hear.

Blinking, he made out a tall Indian on a horse aiming a Henry rifle right at him. He swallowed, knowing he was about to die. At the last moment, the Indian switched aim, saw another target, and fired.

Behind him, Robin screamed. He heard it through his good ear.

James's head spun, only to see Robin falling back, dropping the shotgun, which he had been desperately trying to reload, and disappearing into the driver's box.

James looked back. The tall Chickasaw Indian was levering the rifle, sliding off his horse, and aiming at James.

James saw an old Colt revolver lying in the dust, inches from the Chickasaw that Robin had shot out of the saddle. He was dead, his chest a bloody mess.

Robin killed him. That thought was quickly replaced by one more urgent. *And that tall Indian is about to kill me.*

James dived for the Colt, and the bullet from the Henry rifle sliced over his head, barely missing him. Had he reacted a second later, he would be dead, too.

His right hand found the pistol. The tall Chickasaw was coming toward him, jacking the lever, aiming. Once again, he changed his aim and fired at someone else.

"Arggh!"

Robin's voice reached James somehow. He heard a thud behind him and wondered if the Indian had killed Wildcat's scrawny son.

Instinct took over as his right hand came up, his thumb pulling back the hammer.

235

James knew he could not look back to see if the boy lived or lay dead like the Chickasaw. If he wanted to live, he had to kill.

The tall Chickasaw stood only a few feet from him, levering the rifle again, bringing the barrel down.

The pistol kicked in James's hand, and he smelled the bitter scent of gun smoke. The Indian fell backward, clutching his shoulder, sending the Henry rifle sailing over his head. James dived to his side as another bullet cut a swath past him. He fired again.

Once.

Twice.

Three times.

He thumbed back the hammer, pulled the trigger, and heard — through his good ear — that dreaded click.

Pitching the empty Colt away, he scrambled back toward the wagon. Robin lay faceup, bloody, but still breathing. A bullet splintered one of the spokes in the front wheel. Another kicked up dust an inch from his fingers and he scrambled.

For . . . ?

For what?

He saw the Winchester — Uncle Jimmy's old 1886 cannon. James grabbed the rifle, rolled over, backed up against the front wheel, and brought the empty .50-caliber repeater to his shoulder. "Don't move!" he yelled, hearing his own voice . . . through both ears.

Three Indians stopped. Maybe they could see the size of the barrel. Obviously, they did not realize that the rifle was empty.

"Don't move," he said again, quieter. Still, he heard his own voice, heard the echoes of gunfire fading, and saw himself staring down the barrels of rifles, shotguns, and revolvers.

He said it again. "Don't move."

The silver-haired old leader stepped into the center of men, the nearest ones less than ten yards from James.

"He is a boy," one of the Indians said.

"So is the other," said another.

Another, out of James's view, cursed in English, and moaned. "He is old enough to have shot me."

That caused a few of the Indians to laugh.

The chief barked something in the Chickasaw tongue, and the men fell silent.

They had not killed James. Not yet. He found that hard to understand, but he felt immensely grateful.

"Well?" asked one with a Yellow Boy, the old 1866 Winchester .44 carbine, so-called because of its shiny receiver.

"Where's — ?" James shot a quick glance

to find Wildcat Lamar and then wished he had not. Taking his eyes off the Indians could have, should have, been all it took for the Chickasaws to have killed him.

Wildcat Lamar's head was being held in one of the whiskey barrels. Two Chickasaws stood over him, their pitchforks on the ground. The old man struggled, but the Indians refused to lift his head.

"Let him up!" James snapped. He stared at the chief and brought the gun around until the .50-caliber rifle was aimed at his belly. "Do it! Tell them to let him up or I'll kill you."

The Indian leader snapped his fingers, and the two Chickasaws jerked the man's white face, dripping with vile whiskey, out of the keg, and tossed him unceremoniously onto the ground behind them. They wiped the whiskey and its stink on their denim pants.

Wildcat Lamar rolled over, and groaned, moaned, and cursed.

"He is brave," one of the Chickasaws said.

"For a puppy," said another.

"We should let him live. To tell the white men not to bring their poison into our country." This came from one with a silk cravat and a diamond stickpin . . . and a massive Sharps carbine that would have blown James in two.

"He shot me in the shoulder!" moaned the one James had shot.

James kept the '86 aimed at the chief, thinking *How many times can I pull off this bluff?*

The chief answered that question. "Kill him."

Yet the one with the silk cravat and fancy stickpin said, "We've killed two already."

That brought out a series of curses and insults in English and Chickasaw from the old chief. "And how many of our people . . . how many of all Indian peoples . . . would they have killed with their poison? You have heard what they did to the Comanches to the west? He brought this poison to kill as many Indian people as he could. A sick, evil man. Who also killed his own people, his own kind, with this poison in Texas."

"And he has drunk that which will kill him," said the one that James decided was truly civilized. "It is enough. We do not need to kill any more."

James held his breath, but did not lower the Winchester.

"Killing a white man is not an easy thing," said one holding a muzzle-loading shotgun. "The metal shirts will come for us. To arrest us. To take us to Fort Smith. To hang us."

"These are not white men," the old chief countered. "They are not even men. Killers of children. Murderers of women. And they do not kill fast, but slowly, cruelly. Kill him."

James would later think that was what it was like to be one of the Five Civilized Tribes. To talk. To sort out things. To make sure one did the right thing, or at least, what the majority agreed upon. That had saved his life. He figured the Comanches or Kiowas or Apaches would merely have shot him dead and been done with it.

"Think about it, John Yaneka," the chief told the one who had been arguing that James should live. "Think how you would feel had your daughters or your sons have had a swallow of the poison in those barrels. Imagine the deaths we have heard described. Brought on by these with no God, no decency, no souls."

The man with the cravat and stickpin sighed. "You are right, Fochik." James's savior turned to the Indian nearest him. "Kill him."

The Indian with a Remington .44 stepped forward.

For some reason, some crazy reason, James swung the barrel of the empty Winchester toward the Chickasaw, moving in to kill him. The Indian raised the revolver —

the hammer had long ago been cocked —
and James was waiting to hear that . . .

Ka-boom!

CHAPTER EIGHTEEN

The Indian spun around three times, slinging the .44-caliber revolver during one of his revolutions, and spraying the ground about a foot in front of him with a bloody arc before he dropped to his knees.

An Indian wielding a pitchfork sang out a guttural cry and charged, lowering the tines, but again, a rifle roared, and the Indian collapsed in a heap, the pitchfork sailing harmlessly a few feet before landing in the dirt and dust. He did not move again.

James stared at the .50-caliber Winchester, not comprehending until a rapid volley of rifle shots kicked up dust in front of the other Indians. That's when he understood. Someone in the timbers behind them was shooting a Winchester repeater.

The Indians' ponies reared, fighting the hackamores. A few of the women began singing a singsong chant as the others ran. So did the dogs.

James knew, however, that those Indians could still kill him. He tossed aside the empty rifle and bolted for the Remington, already cocked, that lay in the dirt. One Indian brought up a shotgun, but a bullet splintered the stock, sending the single-shot Savage sailing over his head and knocking him onto his buttocks. James felt the warm grip of the walnut butt in his palm. His finger slipped into the trigger guard, brought up the .44, and fired.

Whoever kept shooting that Winchester did not let up, though James had stopped trying to count the rounds. Ten? Twelve? Rifles did not hold many more rounds than that. For all James — or the Chickasaws knew — there could be more than one shooter . . . or one shooter could have more than one rifle.

It didn't matter. James saw an Indian help the wounded one to his feet and shove him toward a horse held by another Chickasaw.

He cocked the Remington, fired. Someone shot at him, sending sand into his eyes. He rolled over, yelling, trying to thumb back the hammer, but that .44 was so old, so antiquated, the mere act of cocking the piece seemed halfway impossible. A bullet singed his hair. He blinked away tears and sand, managed to hear that click, and as he rolled back onto his stomach he fired again.

Dust clouded his vision. Behind him came four more shots. The Indians sang, shouted. Hoofs pounded. But James could not see through the thick dust. He squeezed off another shot. Then another. Tried to remember how many times he had shot.

He kept shooting into the dust, though he could find no target.

Finally, the hammer of the .44 landed with a deafening *click.*

He swore, tossing the empty revolver to the ground, and ran for the pitchfork. Lifting it about waist-high, he waited.

Those Chickasaws would kill him, but, by thunder, he would die game.

"They're gone."

He spun at the sound of the voice to see a man reining in a liver chestnut, a gelding. He saw the beautiful Winchester rifle in the man's hands as fingers deftly found fresh brass cartridges from a vest pocket and fed those .32-caliber shells into the Model '73.

Then he saw the face of the rider. "Pa?"

"They'll be back, though."

Millard Mann racked a fresh round into the chamber and slid from the gelding, staring as the wind carried the thick dust away.

"Horses are gone." Millard turned and looked at the heavy wagon. "All right. No choice. Have to take that wagon." He led the chestnut to the rear wheel, wrapped the reins around one of the spokes, and moved toward the writhing body of Wildcat Lamar.

James wet his lips, wondering if he were dreaming. Then he saw the body of the Indian, the one whose pitchfork he held. The tool fell to his feet. The Chickasaw lay facedown, a bloody hole in his back where his father's shot had exited. The man was dead.

Behind him came a groan, which snapped James into action. Forgetting the dead Indian, he spun on his heels and hurried over to Robin Lamar and rolled the lad over. Wildcat's son squeezed his eyes shut and bit his lip, fighting against the pain.

James saw two bloody holes in the boy's fringed buckskin shirt, one low on the left, the other higher up on the right.

The kid wailed, coughed, and sucked in a deep breath.

James found the sheathed knife in Robin's belt, quickly drew it out, and sliced through the loose-fitting buckskin.

"No . . ." Robin managed to protest through a mouth tight against the pain. He even tried to reach out and grab James's wrist, but just didn't have the strength.

The knife was honed like a razor, and easily sliced through the thin hide. James pulled back the sides of the torn shirt . . . and gasped.

The skin was white, except for the purple holes seeping blood, one in the meaty part of the kid's side, the other around the lowest rib. Neither wound looked fatal. The kid wasn't spitting up blood, and no sucking sound — the sure sign of a lung-shot — came when he breathed. What shocked James was the dirty strips of cloth tied high on Robin's chest . . . trying to keep the boy's bosoms from showing.

Boy's bosoms? "You're . . ." James blinked. "You're a girl!"

A shadow fell across Robin Lamar, and James turned to look into the dirty face covered with beard stubble and sweat of his father.

Millard jerked his head behind him. "I'll take care of her. You get all that poisoned liquor rolled out of the wagon. We'll load the kid and the old man into the back, make for the Red River. Getting into Texas is the only chance we have."

James rose, started to say something to let his father know that he was no whiskey runner, that he was too stupid to have realized Wildcat Lamar was peddling whiskey in the Indian Nations, but he knew better. His father was right. The Chickasaws would come back, and with one dead Indian and a few wounded ones added to the score they'd dearly like to settle with the Lamars, and now, James and his father.

His head bobbed, and he walked past his father, around the chestnut gelding, and shot a glance at Wildcat Lamar, who still lay groaning, moaning, and coughing against one of the barrels of rotgut liquor.

Making himself ignore the one-eyed old man who had almost gotten them all killed, James climbed into the back of the freight wagon. To his surprise, he found an uncommon strength — maybe from adrenaline or the fear of the gunfight — but he rolled over one barrel with hardly any effort, then kicked it, knelt, and gave it a mighty shove. He followed it, guiding it until it rolled off the tailgate and crashed onto the ground and kept rolling a few feet before settling.

He tossed a few canvas and leather sacks and saddlebags into the corner, out of the way, and pushed another barrel onto its side. That one was harder, but where it had once taken Robin and him to get the barrels out of the wagon, James managed to do the task alone. It crashed hard, and the barrel broke open, sending amber liquid pouring from the busted sides. He stared momentarily at three snakeheads that came out with the whiskey, frowned, and went back to work.

The final four barrels also fell from the wagon, the last one making a path directly toward Wildcat Lamar before stopping a few feet from the sobbing old man.

"James," his father called.

James turned.

His father leaned over Robin. Somewhere, Millard had found strips of cloth, which he had used to bandage Robin's bullet wounds. His father pointed to the side of the wagon. "Grab that ax, son, and bust open those kegs."

"Yes, sir." James moved toward the wagon.

"Don't . . . don't . . . do . . . it . . . boy. . . ." Old Wildcat Lamar groaned out the words between gasps.

James didn't listen. The ax blade bit into an oaken keg, and soon the ugly booze poured onto the ground. By the time James had busted all of the barrels, his clothes dripped with sweat, he was out of breath, the muscles in his arms ached, and the ground stank of rotgut liquor.

The only barrel with any liquor in it was the one Wildcat Lamar leaned against, and James walked to the one-eyed man, ready to rectify that situation.

"Don't . . . it's . . ." The old man rolled onto his side and coughed up a bloody froth.

That shocked James as Wildcat Lamar coughed, gagged, cursed. But he knew he had to hurry, so he stepped over the man's buckskinned legs, and slammed the ax into the keg near the iron rim around the bottom. The second swing did the job, and the whiskey belched out of the keg and onto the ground. When enough had poured out, James tilted the keg over, and watched the rest erupt from the busted opening. Once again, a few snakeheads came out with the whiskey.

Wildcat Lamar had righted himself and wiped the blood from his lips.

"Snakeheads," James said. "You put snakeheads in that whiskey."

The man's one eye gleamed. "Give . . . kick . . ." He coughed.

"What else?"

James looked up to see his father standing over the whiskey runner, who stared at the tall man, and then shrugged.

"Tobaccy juice . . ." A cough. "Grain alcohol." Another gag. "Brown sugar." A grimace. "Strychnine."

James sucked in a deep breath, but his father did not appear surprised.

"I ought to leave you to the Chickasaws,"

Millard said.

Lamar's pale face flushed red with anger, and he cursed savagely, finding new strength. His fist came up, and he pointed a busted finger at Millard Mann. "Injuns kilt my wife, my kids. Scalped 'em. I owed 'em sons —"

"Not the Chickasaws," Millard said.

The old fool snorted, and spat, then smiled. "They's all gots red skin, ain't they?"

"What about those folks you killed in the Texas Panhandle?" Millard asked.

James didn't understand that question at all.

Lamar laughed again, spit out another bloody phlegm, and shook his head. "Accident. Give 'em the wrong barrel."

"Accident!" Millard spit bitterly and nodded at James. "Grab his feet."

The man yelped like a coyote, and tears flowed from his one eye when James lifted the man's smelly legs while his father, leaving the Winchester leaning against one of the busted kegs, grabbed under the whiskey runner's arms, and the two managed to carry the big man to the back of the wagon.

"Doooonnn't," Wildcat Lamar begged, but unceremoniously, they swung him up and down, back and forth, until they had enough momentum to send him sailing up onto the big wagon's tailgate. He landed with a thud, rolled over, and vomited.

"We should leave you for the Chickasaws," Millard said again, and walked back to fetch his rifle. "It would buy us some time."

James backed up, saw Wildcat Lamar crawling, vomit and blood dripping from his beard, toward one of the canvas pouches.

"Come on," his father called out, and James followed him toward Robin Lamar. Blood had already soaked through the two bandages, but the boy . . . no . . . *girl* seemed to be breathing at a more normal rate.

They treated her gently and walked toward the rear of the wagon. When they rounded the corner and looked up, James found himself staring down the barrel of a cannon held in the trembling hands of Wildcat Lamar.

Fort Worth

Grip in his right hand, and a .41-caliber Colt Cloverleaf in his coat pocket, Zane Maxwell met the three men waiting for him at the depot. He let a porter carrying the baggage of some ugly spinster pass before he set his satchel on the plank floor and hooked his thumbs in his waistband. "You understand the job." It was not a question.

"Yeah," said the red-mustached man in a

thick Texas drawl. "And we savvy the pay."

"Good."

The man with the red mustache looked like a cowboy, probably was some old saddle tramp who had been bucked off too many times by chuckleheaded horses. He called himself Red, so Maxwell figured he could remember that one's name. Red carried an old Yellow Boy Winchester, the 1866 model with the bronze-brass alloy receiver, a carbine in .44 rimfire with a nineteen-inch barrel and brass butt plate. Resting in a well-worn russet holster on his right hip was a .44-caliber Merwin Hulbert revolver, nickel-plated with two-piece ivory grips. The barrel was a long, sleek, and deadly seven inches. The only things about Red that remained clean were the carbine and open-top framed revolver. He'd do. Do just fine.

Beside Red stood a younger man in a plaid sack suit and bowler hat. His weapons were hidden inside his coat, but Maxwell had seen them before, a matched pair of .38-caliber Colt Lightnings, those self-cocking pistols with three-and-a-half-inch tapered round barrels. Nickel plated, pearl handled, and the dapper-dressed dandy with the hazel eyes and clean-shaven, almost babyish, face could use them. He called himself Steve Locksburgh and probably had yet to clear his teens. Maxwell had seen a wanted dodger on Steve Locksburgh tacked up on the wall outside the post office. Murder and robbery. The description, however, seemed too vague to attract any of Fort Worth's policemen or bounty hunters. Locksburgh had this cocksure attitude about him that made Maxwell think the kid didn't care if he lived or died. He'd do, too.

The third man stood tall, chewing on a match, thumbs tucked inside the gun belt he wore around his black-and-red striped britches tucked inside fancy black boots with white stars inlaid in the uppers. His weapons were Remingtons, butt forward on his left hip and butt facing the rear on his right. Old weapons that had been converted from cap-and-ball percussion to .44-caliber centerfire, also nickel plated but with walnut stocks, and eight-inch octagonal barrels and brass trigger guards. His black mustache was waxed, the ends turned upward, and he never smiled. The handle he used was John Smith.

Original. Maxwell didn't believe that any of those three had been given those names after their births, but he didn't care. Link McCoy and he needed three men good with guns and unparticular about how they earned their pay. Men like that were easy to find in Fort Worth. Now that he was no longer playing the part of Butch Curry, reporter for the *Kansas City Enterprise,* he had rounded up the three men they needed.

He reached inside his coat and pulled out the train tickets, passing them to the three hired gunmen. "You don't sit together." He stopped speaking until two other passengers had headed past them toward the waiting locomotive. "You don't speak to one another. In short, you don't know one another."

The men said nothing.

"Smith, you get off at Denison with me. You check into the Red River Hotel. The next morning, you'll buy a horse at Greene's Livery. Ride north toward Colbert's Ferry, and I'll follow you, catch up before you cross the Red."

Smith did not acknowledge a thing, but he knew what to do.

"You two" — Maxwell tilted his head at Locksburgh and Red — "will catch the Katy and ride north, getting off at Caddo. Tulip Bells will meet you there. He'll have horses waiting for you."

Red grunted. "How's we ta knows what this Tulip gent looks like?"

You could look at the wanted posters ran through Zane Maxwell's mind. What he said was "You don't."

Red frowned and started to grumble, but Steve Locksburgh chuckled and turned to face Red. "Those lavender bandanas. The ones he give us yesterday evenin'. The one you said you'd never wear alive."

Red didn't get it. "Huh?"

Locksburgh chuckled, shook his head, and brought out the makings.

As he began to roll a cigarette one-handed, Zane Maxwell explained. "Caddo's in the Choctaw Nation. When you get off at that depot, you'll both be wearing those two lavender kerchiefs."

"The one you said you'd have to be dead wearin'," Locksburgh said.

Red grunted.

Locksburgh grinned again and stared at Maxwell. "I don't know what this job is, but I do believe if we pull it off, we'll be as famous as the Daltons."

"*When* we pull it off," John Smith corrected.

"Just remember, you don't know me. I don't know you. You don't know each other." That was it. Maxwell picked up his grip and walked away, finding his own ticket. He'd find his berth later after the train had pulled out of Fort Worth.

If everything went well, he and John Smith

would be in Denison and lighting out for Indian Territory, where they would meet up with Link McCoy and track down that man-killing whiskey runner.

That should be easy enough, Maxwell thought.

Then Tulip Bells would find Locksburgh and Red and steer them over toward Fort Washita.

Some soot-faced urchin stood pacing in front of the train waiting to pull out from the station, waving one of the Fort Worth newspapers in his hand, hawking out the headlines. Maxwell stopped to fish out his ticket and a coin for the tyke, which he flipped over. That kid was fast, snatched the coin, dropped it in a pouch hanging from his neck, and whipped out a folded newspaper.

"Thanks." Maxwell climbed up the steps of the smoking car.

The only thing Red, John Smith, and Steve Locksburgh knew about the job was that they'd be paid $500 each, if they lived, and that they'd be riding with Zane Maxwell and Link McCoy. The McCoy-Maxwell Gang, or as Maxwell liked to call it, the Maxwell-McCoy Gang. That's all they needed to know for the time being. The details would be worked out later. Actually, soon.

Maxwell slid into a chair, tossed his satchel onto the cushioned seat across from him, and opened the *Fort Worth Standard.*

He didn't care about the news items, the murder in Hell's Half Acre the other night, the weather, the comments from the cattlemen's association meeting, or how Fort Worth was such a better town than nearby Dallas could ever hope to be. He just looked at the date underneath the newspaper's banner.

GOOD AFTERNOON! TODAY IS THURSDAY, JUNE 27, 1895.

Seven days. One week until the Maxwell-McCoy Gang pulled off their last robbery. He was about to roll up the newspaper and toss it aside, when another headline in the lower left-hand corner caught his eye. Apparently the editors of the *Standard* had picked up an article that had first been published that spring in the *Kansas City Star.*

Zane Maxwell read about young Emmett Dalton, how he walked out of the cellblock at the Kansas pen in Lansing every day. Lock step, single file, right hand on the shoulder of the inmate in front of him, left

257

arm rigid at his side. Walking in unison, right foot high, left foot shuffle, march, march, march. But young Emmett was looking fit and proper, and no longer slumping from the wounds he had received in Coffeyville a few years back. How Emmett Dalton was the model prisoner, reading newspapers, and magazines, and books. Being rehabilitated. Hoping some kind folks might think better of him and issue him a parole or pardon and send him home to live out his days in peace.

Emmett Dalton. The one survivor of the Dalton Gang.

What was that cocky Steve Locksburgh had said? *"I don't know what this job is, but I do believe if we pull it off, we'll be as famous as the Daltons."*

Maxwell felt sweat rolling down his forehead, and he leaned over to open his satchel and fetch that flask of rye whiskey.

As famous as the Daltons.

Certainly, the Dalton boys had earned enough fame to last a hundred years or thereabouts when they had tried to rob two banks at the same time in their hometown of Coffeyville, Kansas. Folks still talked about it almost three years after that bloody event of October 1892. Grat, Emmett, and Bob Dalton had ridden into town with Bill

Power and Dick Broadwell. None had ridden out in one piece. Emmett's brothers were dead, along with Power and Broadwell, and Emmett had been shot to pieces but somehow had managed to live, get patched up, and sent to the Kansas state pen.

Yeah, the Dalton Gang was famous, sure enough. But most of them were dead.

Maxwell let the whiskey pour down his throat, took a deep breath, and slid over toward the window as the conductor called outside, "All aboard."

CHAPTER NINETEEN

Wild Horse Creek

The cannon Wildcat Lamar Bodeen held was a single-shot horseman's pistol, probably one made by I.N. Johnson. Millard Mann's father had carried two of those during the Mexican War. A copper percussion cap would ignite the black powder rammed down the barrel and send a .54-caliber slug straight through James Mann's brain. Of course, Bodeen would have only one shot, but that's all it would take, and at close range, probably blow off James's head.

James held the girl's feet. Millard held the kid's shoulders, his rifle was leaning against the wagon wheel, and he could not reach the Richards-Mason conversion holstered on his hip.

"I'll kill this boy, mistah." The barrel weaved. The dying old whiskey runner had trouble keeping the big pistol steady.

"Then I kill you?" Millard asked.

Bodeen turned away from James and stared. Millard had asked a question, not stated a fact.

"That the idea?" Millard asked.

A tear rolled down the old man's cheek. From one eye. The other eye was nothing more than a dark, ugly hole. The old man did not speak.

Millard knew that the girl, Bodeen's daughter, had passed out — which, he figured, was a good thing.

"Put you out of your misery," Millard said, not taking his eyes off the whiskey runner. "You swallowed enough of your brew to know what's in store for you. The same as those folks you poisoned in Texas. And all those Indians you've murdered."

"Savages," the old man hissed.

Millard said nothing. He just stared, but he could feel the chill racing up his spine, a chill that was maybe a hundred degrees from the heat he felt, heat from anger and the intense summer sun that sent beads of sweat down his face. His hands felt clammy. One wrong move, and Bodeen would kill James. Millard had traveled too far, seen too many men die already — from his own hand — to be the cause of his oldest boy's murder.

He knew what Bodeen wanted. Knew why

the old man was playing this game. And he had an idea how it would end. But if he played the wrong cards, James would be dead.

"I'll . . ." — the whiskey runner shook from a spasm that sent a mixture of blood, vomit, and saliva dribbling from both corners of his mouth — "kill . . . the . . ." — he almost collapsed, but somehow found enough strength to stay alive, and steady the gun a little, staring at James — "the . . . the . . . boy."

"Or me."

The man's eyes locked again on Millard. "No . . . the . . . kid."

Millard said in a steady, deliberate voice, "Go ahead."

Fort Arbuckle, Chickasaw Nation
The old army post sat on the southern bank of the Washita River. Many years earlier, when Jackson Sixpersons was in his teens, the place had bustled with white men. A captain named Randolph Marcy had selected the site to put up a fort to protect the white settlers traveling westward on the California Trail from Comanches, Kiowas, Cheyennes, and Arapahos. The Army would also protect the Choctaws and Chickasaws, those civilized Indians, from being butch-

ered by the warlike Indian tribes.

The fort had been crowded with soldiers, but had never been much of a fort. It was a long rectangle, barracks facing each other from the two longest sides, the quartermaster's compound on the third side and a commissary across from it. Roughhewn log cabins numbered close to thirty or so, but it was not enough for the white men. Before Arbuckle was even ten years old, the army had sent most of the troops stationed there to build another base called Cobb. Texas Rebels took over the fort during the Civil War, and after the rebellion had been put down, the 6th Infantry and the 10th Cavalry, the latter regiment one of the all-black "buffalo soldiers" troops, came back to man the fort.

About all the fort was ever used for was to feed and grain horses and other livestock, mostly during the army campaigns against the Cheyennes in 1868. By the time Fort Sill had been established in 1869, there was no longer any reason for Fort Arbuckle to exist, and the army had abandoned it a year later.

It still looked abandoned.

"They got coffee at this here post?" Virgil Flatt asked.

Jackson Sixpersons did not answer, and

refused to shake his head at the tumbleweed wagon driver's joke. Or maybe Flatt was that stupid.

Malcolm Mallory shouted, "You fool. This fort is named after General Matthew Arbuckle, a great man in this part of the country. Not after Arbuckles coffee."

"Iffen he was such a great general, how come they named this rawhide lookin' outfit after 'im?"

Flatt was right. It was one rawhide-looking outfit, held together by spit and sand, and maybe the wind kept some of those rotting buildings from collapsing in a heap. A few had been burned already, leaving nothing but stone fireplaces as their tombstones. But two horses were tethered in front of a stone powder house, and a tall man in a gray hat stepped outside.

Sixpersons reined in and held up his left hand. His right did not lessen its hold on the lever-action shotgun. *"O-si-yo,"* he called out in Cherokee.

"Don't hello me in your heathen tongue," responded the man in the gray hat. "Come get this man-killer and take him to Arkansas so he can be jerked to his Jesus."

"Open the door," Sixpersons told Malcolm Mallory. "Let the prisoners empty their bladders. I'll fetch Doc Starr."

He rode up to the half-breed lawman for the Chickasaws, and saw the gray-hatted Indian disappear inside the powder house. By the time Sixpersons had ridden close enough to dismount, a thin man sailed through the opening, landed in the dirt with a grunt, tried to stand, but collapsed.

The Chickasaw in the gray hat stepped outside, wiping his hands on his black britches.

"He's all yours, Sixpersons."

The Cherokee lawman nodded before swinging from the saddle. Doc Starr lifted his head, spit out dirt and saliva, and pushed himself to his knees, before he wiped the sand from his lips.

"Doc Starr?" Sixpersons asked.

"Yeah." At least that half-breed did not deny it.

"I have a warrant for your arrest. You are charged with murder —"

"Eat it."

Sixpersons pressed the barrel of the twelve-gauge atop the man's bald head. "Up. I carry you in alive to hang or dead to be buried."

The half-breed rose, stared at Sixpersons' spectacles, and then looked at the barrel of the Winchester '87.

"Walk to the wagon," Sixpersons said.

"Run, I shoot you. Trip, I shoot you. Do anything other that walk straight to that wagon and climb inside and I shoot you." He watched.

Doc Starr was no fool. He did not run, did not trip, did not stagger, but walked straight for the wagon where the other prisoners were climbing back inside. Doc Starr found a comfortable spot on the floor and sat down. A few moments later, Malcolm Mallory was locking the door, and looking across the old fort's parade grounds at Sixpersons.

Sixpersons turned to the Chickasaw in the gray hat. "I'm after a whiskey runner."

The man in the gray hat, whose name was Folsom, nodded. "So are many."

"He poisoned a lot of Comanches a while back."

"I care not for the Snake People," Folsom said. "Let them die."

"I'd like to bring this white man in."

Folsom grinned. "I think he is dead by now."

Possible. Probable. "Then where might I find his body?"

No answer. Instead, Folsom pointed to the blue roan mare next to his sorrel. "I will keep the killing doctor's mare. It is not a bad horse . . . for a white man."

Sixpersons nodded. He could have taken the horse back to Fort Smith, but he knew how to barter with a Chickasaw.

After gathering the reins to the blue roan mare, Folsom swung into the saddle on the sorrel and turned to ride southeast. "I must be at Fort Washita in a week's time."

"Shouldn't take you anywhere near that long."

"No. We will meet the Texans there. They bring us money for grass to feed their beef."

"Good for you and your people."

The Indian nodded. "Maybe."

Sixpersons waited.

Folsom tilted his head. "This man my people know as Wildcat. He was to bring them whiskey."

Sixpersons nodded.

"Wild Horse Creek. At the crossing near the hills."

"I know of it." Sixpersons felt relief. That wasn't more than a day's ride west.

"He was to bring them whiskey," Folsom said again. "My people were to bring him death."

Wild Horse Creek
"What?" The .54-caliber cannon in Wildcat Lamar Bodeen's hand shook wildly, but the whiskey runner recovered and used his free

267

hand to help steady the big pistol.

"You heard me," Millard Mann said. "Kill the boy."

The one-eyed man sneered. "And then you kill me."

"I'd have to drop your daughter to fetch my pistol. Might break her neck."

"Like I give a fig."

Millard made himself look away from the whiskey runner and killer. Those Chickasaws might have found enough courage or help to come back, and those oxen wouldn't make good time. They needed to head out of the place already reeking of poisoned whiskey and death immediately. Else they'd all be dead.

"Son," Millard said easily.

James, his face pale, blinked and stared at his father, his father who had just told a man holding a Dragoon's old horse pistol to go ahead and blow his boy's head off.

"This girl's getting heavy. Let's walk over to that shade and set her down for a spell." Millard waited.

The boy did not move.

Millard couldn't blame him. "It's all right, James. Trust me. Let's go."

Slowly, James took a tentative step back. His Adam's apple moved up, then down, and he took another step. He made himself look at his father as they slowly carried the unconscious body of Robin Lamar away from the giant freight wagon and the one-eyed whiskey runner with that massive single-shot pistol.

"Stop!" Wildcat Lamar Bodeen croaked.

Millard merely nodded at his son, who took another step back.

The old man would be aiming at Millard's back, for James stood in front of his father. If Bodeen pulled the trigger, the .54-caliber ball would tear through the flesh of Millard Mann, and not his seventeen-year-old son.

"I'll kill ye both!" the whiskey runner called.

Millard nodded, and James took another step. Then Millard whispered, "Stop."

"One more step . . . and yer . . . dead!" Bodeen managed to spit out the order.

Slowly, Millard Mann turned. He was staring at the cavernous barrel of the big pistol. "You got one shot, Bodeen. Best remember that. And how that poison you brewed killed all those Indians and white folks in the Panhandle." He turned back around, smiled at his son, and nodded.

James took another step. Millard walked with him.

Another step.

Another.

Bam! They heard the gunshot.

Fort Arbuckle

"That don't make a lick of sense, Jackson." Shaking his sweaty head, Deputy U.S. Marshal Malcolm Mallory slapped his fancy hat, ordered from the Sears & Roebuck Company, against his pants, sending dust sailing into the air.

Not to you, Sixpersons thought, but, in true Cherokee style, held his tongue.

Sitting on the driver's seat of the tumbleweed wagon, Virgil Flatt bathed a beetle with a thin shot of brown tobacco juice. "Ya know what yer doin'?" the cantankerous coot asked.

The Cherokee lawman nodded. "I want you to take these prisoners back to Fort Smith," he repeated. "Once you get there, find Judge Parker, tell him to get Crump and send some good marshals — good marshals, savvy? That don't mean Boston Graves. Send them to" — he had to think — "Fort Washita." That was close enough and in the Chickasaw Nation. It wasn't a real fort anymore, but it was a major stopping point in the territory. If the Chickasaw lawman named Folsom had not mentioned it, Sixpersons didn't know which Chickasaw stagecoach stop, inn, or campsite he would have suggested.

"How many laws?" Virgil Flatt asked, and then shifted the quid of chewing tobacco to his far cheek.

About a hundred and fifty, thought Sixpersons, but he shrugged. "A dozen."

Judge Parker, as good as he was, would be forced to reduce the number to six, and Marshal Crump would dwindle the six to maybe only three. But that would have to do. Unless one of those three happened to be Deputy U.S. Marshal Malcolm Mallory.

"But you know Judge Parker's orders," Mallory said. "No deputy is to travel through this country without someone to back him up."

Then why do I have you and Flatt? Again, Sixpersons merely nodded. "Chances are this is nothing, but I don't want to risk the lives of these prisoners." *Even if the tumbleweed wagon is full of killers, rapists, thieves, and whiskey runners, men who don't give a spit for the law or the Indian people who live in this country.*

Outlaws like Link McCoy and Zane Maxwell would not care if they gunned down a bunch of wanted men, unarmed, riding in the back of a prison wagon. For all Sixpersons knew, those outlaws might even free the prisoners and force them into the

McCoy-Maxwell Gang. All he knew was that that always-smoking Newton Ah-ha-lo-man-tubbee had told him that Link McCoy was looking for a whiskey runner to help him pull off a job, some kind of robbery somewhere in Indian Territory.

And Sixpersons was right close to finding the crazed, killing whiskey runner named Bodeen that McCoy needed. Find Bodeen, and Sixpersons was that much closer to catching and arresting — or killing — Link McCoy and his confederates.

Sixpersons certainly did not need a couple imbeciles named Virgil Flatt and Malcolm Mallory to foul up his chance or possibly, probably, get himself killed.

"But Judge Parker and Marshal Crump won't like this at all," Mallory whined.

"They will if this leads me to who I think it will." Sixpersons was tired of talking. He wanted to get the tumbleweed wagon moving west and wanted to put his horse into a lope toward Wild Horse Creek.

"Well, who is it yer goin' after?" Flatt asked.

"Tell Judge Parker and Marshal Crump it's Link McCoy and probably Zane Maxwell."

That caused Flatt's mouth to fall open, and Mallory to straighten in his saddle.

"Tell them," Sixpersons repeated. He had dallied long enough. He adjusted his spectacles, pulled down the brim of his hat, and, still holding the Winchester '87 twelvegauge in his right hand, he kicked his horse into a fast walk, riding away from Flatt, Mallory and the prisoners in the wagon.

Before Flatt or Mallory could holler some other fool question at him, he kicked the horse into a steady lope.

CHAPTER TWENTY

Wild Horse Creek

Texas had been a hard place for Millard, Jimmy, and Borden Mann to grow up as young teens, and even as young men. It could still be hard. Jimmy had learned that, and so had Millard, up in Tascosa earlier that year. Indian Territory could be just as lawless.

Millard remembered back in 1890 when the U.S. Census Bureau's superintendent had said that the Western frontier of America was history, that the West had been settled, that the frontier was closed, a thing of the past. Maybe two years back, he had read a newspaper account of some talk this historian named Turner had given up in Michigan or Minnesota, maybe Wisconsin, pretty much saying the same thing.

The West might be settled, a part of American history, and the frontier might be officially closed from a population standpoint, but Millard knew that the West could be just as hard, just as mean, just as bloody, and just as tough as it had been back when he and his brothers were growing up. Back when Jimmy and Border were still alive.

"Don't look," Millard told his son. "Just lower the girl to the ground. Gently."

When they had Robin Bodeen lying in the dirt near the destroyed whiskey barrels, he said, "Stay with her," and walked back to the big freight wagon.

Wildcat Lamar Bodeen, or whatever his real name was, had indeed made his one shot count. He had pressed the barrel of the horseman's pistol and sent the ball through his temple. The old one-eyed man lay on his side, still holding the smoking single-shot weapon.

After climbing up into the wagon, Millard pried the warm gun from the dead man's cold grip. The weapon was slick and slender, a fine pistol in its day. Briefly, he studied the gun before tossing it near the wreckage of whiskey barrels.

The Christian thing, the decent thing, to do would be to bury the man, but being visibly dead might buy the living some time. Millard rolled the corpse out of the wagon, heard it crash on the dirt, and jumped down. He dragged the remains of Wildcat

275

Lamar Bodeen to the whiskey barrels and left him with his poison.

He had no time for a prayer or eulogy and doubted if Bodeen would have wanted one anyway.

Millard walked away, back to his son and the still unconscious girl. "All right." He nodded to James, and they picked the girl up and carried her back to the wagon. They did not toss her into the back like a sack of flour, but moved her up gently. Millard had to climb up and ease her into the shady side of the wagon. He found a blanket, covered her, and hurried out of the back, where he picked up the Winchester '73.

James stared at it. "Whose rifle is that?"

"We need to ride. Make for the Red."

"It's a One of One Thousand," James said.

"Can you drive this team?" Millard looked at the oxen. They appeared to be bone-tired and half-starved, but that's all they had.

"Yes, sir." James wet his lips and started to say something else, but his pa interrupted.

"Climb up. I don't want you walking alongside the wagon. In case something happens. You got any bullets for your rifle?"

Your rifle. Not Jimmy's. Millard realized he had said it and was pointing at the Model 1886 repeater.

James picked it up, swallowed, and shook his head.

A quick glance revealed the pitchfork, the empty Remington .44, and a few assorted old weapons, none of which Millard would put his trust — his life — in. The Remington would be the best, but there was one problem. The shells for his Army Colt would not fit the Remington .44 even though his Richards-Mason design used a conventional .44-caliber centerfire cartridge — not as powerful as .44-40s, but strong enough to get the job done — and even though the Remington .44 had been converted from cap-and-ball to centerfire, too.

Truth be told, although both models had been labeled .44 caliber, neither the 1860 Colt Army or Remington's 1858 Army had been truly bored in .44. The balls they had used in the percussion cap days took a ball with a .454-inch diameter, and the barrels were bored .451. Technically, both of those models were actually .45 caliber.

After the Civil War, conversions became the rage, if companies could find a way around Smith & Wesson's patent for bored-through revolver cylinders that chambered brass centerfire cartridges. Colt engineer F. Alexander Thuer had done just that with its Colt conversion by using a cone-shaped round that was loaded from the front of the cylinder.

To Millard, it would have made a lot more sense to have one shell fit any brand of weapon — Colt, Remington, Smith & Wesson — but those firearms companies could be greedy and proprietary. A lot of money was made by selling ammunition that fit only its models, and those companies were also looking longingly for government contracts.

The army had tested several variations of the Remington .44 Army revolvers around 1870, but never bought into the Remington model for its soldiers.

Weapons were always changing. Folks called it progress. Flintlocks had made way for percussion caps, and after the Civil War anyone with a brain could tell that fixed metallic ammunition was the wave of the future.

When Smith & Wesson brought out the American .44 revolver — which chambered Smith & Wesson .44 cartridges — Colt followed the trend by introducing its 1873 single-action Army in .44 caliber. The Army loved it, but asked for a .45 caliber, and Colt complied. That six-shooter became the rage, the most powerful revolver since the old Colt Dragoons of the 1840s. In the late

1870s, Colt and Winchester finally understood a bit about "reciprocation" and Colt
began manufacturing revolvers that fired
Winchester's .44-40 rounds.

Yet Millard Mann still owned a conversion model of his Army Colt. He was too
old-fashioned, maybe, too set in his ways.
And he had never dreamed he would be
forced to use those guns again.

The Indian's Remington would have to
do. He pointed at the pistol. "Get it."

James picked up the weapon. "I've never
fired a six-shooter before."

"Runs in the blood. I'm not much of a
hand with one myself," Millard admitted.
"But it'll have to do. And you won't be
shooting it until I can figure out what to
do."

James pointed at the cartridges in Millard's shell belt.

"They won't fit." Millard didn't explain
the history of firearms and ammunition.

James again looked at his father, and tried
to find the words, but there was no time for
any conversation, any family reunion.

"We need to make tracks," Millard said.

"What about . . . him?" James motioned
toward the body of Wildcat Lamar Bodeen.

"I'm hoping he'll keep the Chickasaws oc-
cupied." It was a hard thing to say, but it

was the truth. The whiskey destroyed and the culprit dead might be enough to keep those Indians from chasing after the slow freight wagon to avenge the Chickasaw that Millard had been forced to kill.

He watched James climb into the box and handed him the empty Winchester rifle. Pulling his hat down low, Millard walked to the liver chestnut, pulled the reins from the spoke, and swung into the saddle.

They'd ride south and east, should cross Caddo Creek if the map he had studied was right, and then follow another creek that fed into the Red River. He wasn't sure how high the river would be, but that big storm from a ways back worried him. The Red could be full of quicksand and driftwood in the dry months. During wet years, it could rage like a mountain river during snowmelt. Nobody could estimate how many cowboys had drowned crossing that big muddy river during the trail-driving years or how many others had perished.

Straight southeast was closer than making for Colbert's Ferry, and Spanish Fort was just across the river in Texas. There might be a sawbones there who could tend to the girl.

If the Chickasaws didn't kill them first.

Everything had gone well, so far. Zane Maxwell had departed the train and watched John Smith ride out that morning. Those other two, Locksburgh and Red, should be disembarking in Indian Territory and meeting up with Tulip Bells, which meant all Maxwell had to do was buy a horse from the livery, ride out of town, and catch up with Smith. Then the two of them could find Link McCoy and that informant he was working with. They'd catch up with the whiskey runner and get ready for the Fort Washita job.

After Maxwell finished his coffee, he left enough money for his breakfast on the table, grabbed his hat off the hat rack, and stepped out of the café and onto the boardwalk.

"Hello, Zane."

He had been fishing a cigar from his vest pocket, and stopped to reconsider, but before his right hand moved for the Cloverleaf .41, the voice said, "Nah, just leave that hideaway gun in your pocket. But you can smoke. Especially if you got a cigar for me, too."

Maxwell nodded and brought out two cigars, biting the end off one and putting it in his mouth, before holding the other out

281

as he turned to face the man leaning against the white wooden front wall of the café.

A body didn't see too many double-action Starr Army revolvers very often anymore. Starr Arms Company of New York had first patented those revolvers early in 1856. Most gunmen preferred more modern weapons, not the old cap-and-balls, but the two fitting snugly in a red sash seemed well cared for. Six-inch round barrels, a blued finish, smooth walnut grips, brass blade front sights. Of course, the man had no need of the two .44 revolvers, for he also carried a Winchester carbine, the barrel pointed, not exactly at Zane Maxwell, but definitely in his general direction.

The gunman's sidearms might be old-fashioned, but his long gun was modern. It was a Model 1892, one of the new lever-actions from Winchester with, like the two Army revolvers, a blued finish. The tapered round barrel appeared to be of a smaller caliber, maybe a .32 or .38, probably twenty inches long with a bead style sight mounted on the front and a Williams folding rear sight in a dovetail. The buttstock and fore end were walnut, smooth, showing almost no damage, and the crescent butt plate appeared smooth.

The man holding the rifle was tall, old,

his face scarred from pockmarks, fistfights, knives, and at least one bullet. That's why he had a brown leather patch over his left eye. His mustache was more gray than brown these days, and his one good eye burned an intense blue. He had no left ear. That one had been sliced off with an Arkansas toothpick in a brawl in Eureka Springs.

A gloved left hand came up to take the cigar, which the gunman put in his mouth, bit off an end, and then refit between tobacco-stained teeth.

"Hello, Zane," the man said again, waiting for Maxwell to light both cigars.

"Jared." Maxwell struck a match against the wall, lighted the gunman's cigar first, then managed to get his going.

Jared Whitney sucked in the smoke and grinned in satisfaction. "Nice flavor."

"El Pervenirs," Maxwell said. "Imported from Havana."

"I like it."

Maxwell hooked a thumb down the boardwalk. "You can get them, two for a quarter, at the mercantile."

"I'll keep that in mind."

"You after a reward?" Maxwell asked.

"You know me, Zane. I like money."

"What brings you to Denison?"

"Money."

Maxwell removed the cigar, flicked some ash, and returned the Havana to his mouth. Jared Whitney, who would kill a man for a cigar or a thousand dollars, would talk when he was ready. Obviously, he didn't want Zane Maxwell dead. That's the only reason Maxwell still breathed.

"I'm lookin' for a whiskey runner named Bodeen," Whitney said.

Maxwell almost gave away his surprise, but he had played too many hands of poker to let that slip. He grinned. "Do you think Link and I want to get out of the bank and train business and start running rotgut?"

"There's been talk," Whitney said.

Maxwell let it slide, but inwardly he cursed John Smith. He should have instructed the hired gunman not to hit one of Denison's myriad saloons when the train arrived, but go straight to his hotel, sleep, and get the horse in the morning without talking to anyone.

"You can get whiskey here," Maxwell said. "A lot better quality that you'd find from a runner in Indian Territory."

"Who said anything about Indian Territory?" Whitney grinned and blew blue smoke from his mouth. Then he talked. "There's a Texas Ranger named Clarke with a score to settle against Bodeen. Seems this gent sold some liquor to some Podunk town up in the Panhandle and left some citizens dead, including the Ranger's son. He's hired me and some tinhorn with a Greener who calls himself Charley Conner to help him bring in that whiskey runner."

"You a lawman now, Jared?"

The killer grinned again. "Ranger Clarke wants Bodeen dead. That's something I can handle."

The town was coming to life. Across the street, businesses were being opened where just minutes earlier the only places showing signs of life were the livery and café. A man wearing two Starr revolvers and holding a Winchester '92 would draw some attention, even in a lawless railroad burg like Denison. Might even attract a lawman.

"I'm heading to the livery," Maxwell said.

"Thanks for the invite." Whitney motioned with the carbine barrel, and Maxwell nodded and turned.

Jared Whitney was too savvy, had lived too long with a gun, to make some fool mistake. He did lower the barrel of the Winchester, but Maxwell knew the gunman wouldn't get too close to him, nor would he give Maxwell a chance if he tried anything. So Maxwell just walked, smoking the cigar, smiling at passersby along the boardwalk and issuing friendly greetings to strangers.

Twice, he even tipped his hat to some ladies.

Behind him, Jared Whitney did the same.

When they reached the livery, Whitney tossed a nickel to a Mexican in jeans and a homespun shirt and told him in Spanish to fetch his horse, saddled and ready to ride.

"You going somewhere?" Maxwell removed the cigar, dropped it in a dirt patch — he was careful to avoid the straw and hay — and ground it out with his boot heel.

"With you," Whitney said.

"Where's that Texas Ranger?" Maxwell tried to remember the name. "Clarke?"

"In the Nations," Whitney said. "Rode out with that assassin with the Greener. They left me in Denison, in case Bodeen loses the law dogs and injuns chasing him in the territory. If Bodeen shows up here, I'll kill him. If Conner or Clarke guns him down, I still get paid. Not as much, but enough." The gunman kept puffing his cigar.

"How much?" Maxwell asked.

"Fifty dollars. In gold coin."

Maxwell nodded as if that amount would impress him. Fifty dollars. Life could come cheap in that part of the world.

"Well," Maxwell said as the Mexican boy brought out Whitney's horse, a thin, short but game cowpony, brown with two white stocking feet. "I think we might be able to do a little better than that."

"Thought you said you wasn't in the whiskey running trade." Whitney took the reins and thanked the boy.

Before the kid could disappear, Maxwell cleared his throat and turned his attention to the Mexican. "I'd like to buy a horse."

The kid fired off something in rapid Spanish and pointed across the street.

"Says his boss is in the store yonder getting some shoeing nails. Back directly."

The kid said something again.

Whitney interpreted. "But there's a good bay mare you can probably have."

More Spanish.

Whitney grinned and nodded at the boy. "Says his boss will start at fifty bucks, but he'll settle for fifteen, which is about what the horse is worth and five more than what his boss paid for her."

Maxwell looked at the waif. *"Gracias,"* he said, and the kid disappeared somewhere in the stables.

"Five hundred dollars suit you?" Maxwell asked.

Whitney removed the Havana and stared long at hard. "Didn't think whiskey running was that profitable."

"It's not, but you might also be able to collect that other fifty from your Texas Ranger. After we pull our job first."

CHAPTER TWENTY-ONE

Walnut Bayou, Chickasaw Nation

They made camp in a small clearing along the meandering creek, thinking that the forest thick with hickory, elm, ash, and hackberry trees would provide them plenty of cover. Several yards from where James was getting a fire going and tending to Robin's wounds, Millard butchered a six-point buck he'd risked a shot on earlier in the evening, knowing and regretting that much of the meat would have to be left behind for coyotes and other scavengers.

So far, luck had favored them. The Indians had not followed them in the two days that had passed since he'd rescued the kids and unceremoniously left the dead whiskey runner lying among the wrecked barrels that once had held his poison.

With enough venison steaks in his bloody hands, he walked back to the camp and deposited the steaks in an iron skillet.

Robin Bodeen, if that indeed were her real name, had finally come back into consciousness. She wore Millard's extra shirt he'd put on her. It fit her like a short dress. She stared at him, trying to figure out just who he was.

"That's my pa," James said.

Millard washed his hands, dried them off, and picked up the One of One Thousand Winchester. He kept it on his thighs as he kneeled beside her. "How do you feel?"

"All right. I reckon."

He waited a few moments then decided there was no use bandying words and beating around the bush. "Your father's dead." He did, however, have enough compassion not to let the child know that her old man had taken his own life.

"He weren't my pa," the kid said.

James gasped. "What?"

" 'Bout two years back, my pa traded me to Wildcat."

James sang out in shock, "He traded you?"

"For some whiskey."

It didn't surprise Millard. Oh, it might have, a few weeks earlier, but he wasn't working for the railroad any longer — wondered if he'd still have a job when he got back to McAdam, Texas — and had covered too many miles in too lawless a land to be shocked by anything anymore.

"It wasn't pizened." Her face hardened. "Though sometimes I wished it was."

Millard leaned over, lifted the shirt to check the bandages, and said mainly to change the subject, "One of the bullets went through. Clean shot. I just drew a silk bandana through it to clean it. The other one" — he nodded at the one through the ribs — "I had to dig out." He grinned at her. "You were tough. Tough as nails."

"Don't remember it," she said.

"That's good." He peeled back the bandage and nodded in satisfaction. "I got the slug out. Didn't go too deep, and don't think it hit any vitals. It doesn't look like infection has set in, but I want to get you to Spanish Fort first. Find a doctor there. Let him finish what I started."

He noticed James staring at him.

"Where'd you learn to do surgery like that?" James asked again. He had asked earlier when Millard had forced the bullet out with a pocketknife blade he had held over a small fire the first night out of Wild Horse Creek.

Millard had not answered, and might not have replied again had not the girl's penetrating eyes locked on him.

He stood, forcing a smile. "My brothers

and I kinda ran into some trouble when we were growing up." Surprisingly, that sentence made him feel pretty good, better than he had a right to feel, and memories came flooding through his mind. He could see Jimmy and Borden, younger, full of vim and vinegar, and see himself, much younger, although Borden had always said Millard was the old man of the bunch, even if he were the middle child. "I had some practice, doctoring."

He smiled at his son. It was good to see the boy . . . alive. They had not had a chance to do much talking, for James to explain why he had run away from home — although Millard had a fair idea of that reason — or how he had teamed up with an Indian-hating, man-killing whiskey runner and this girl who had been pretending to be a boy. *That* Millard could understand. Especially with rogues and ruffians — those who scoffed at the law and killed without cause — running loose.

He remembered the three men he had killed earlier, and the smile faded. That was one side of him he had hoped his children would never have to see.

"Bring me that Remington," he said, and watched James tug the revolver from his waistband and hand the .44 over, butt forward. Millard set down the Winchester, took the revolver, and began plucking the casings from the cylinder. "Fry up those steaks while I do this."

James went to the skillet and Millard worked on the Remington.

He had found the powder flask in the leather pouch, along with a smaller pouch of lead balls. Those would work, though he'd have to melt them down and use the bullet mold, also in the pouch, to make the bullets. It would take a while, and he wasn't sure it would work, for he would have to trim the .54-caliber slugs with his knife to fit into the .44 — actually, .45 — caliber chambers for the revolver.

Years, practically a lifetime, had passed since he had made his own reloads. He moved to the fire to begin the process, Millard melting down the lead bullets, and James across from him, frying venison steaks for supper.

The steaks smelled better.

He heard James's sigh over the sizzling of the deer and grease in the skillet, followed by his son's soft voice. "I'm sorry, Pa."

Millard lifted his gaze, but all he could do in response was just nod.

"I didn't mean for all this to happen."

After exhaling, Millard's head shook. "You

figured your mother and I'd just let you run off."

"It was just . . . I just . . . well . . . I had to."

"To do what?"

James forked the steaks, turned them over. "Follow Uncle Jimmy."

Millard let out a mirthless chuckle. "Be a lawman? Pin on that tin star?"

"Yes, sir. Something like that."

"Seventeen years old. I'm not rightly sure, but I think even in Fort Smith they'd want a man old enough to vote to enforce the laws and keep the peace."

"I figured —"

Millard laughed with humor. "To lie about your age." He waited.

His son's head bobbed. "Yes, sir."

"There are easier ways to get to Fort Smith than travel in a freight wagon with a whiskey runner."

"Yes, sir." James proceeded to tell him everything that had happened, about the ruffian in the boxcar — Millard did not interrupt to let him know he knew about that fiend — the tornado, and finding himself underneath the wagon after that savage storm.

Millard liked hearing his son's voice. It had been a long time, and now that he had to think about it, he had never really had much of a father-son conversation with James. Maybe the whole situation was Millard's own fault.

There was no *maybe.* Millard could have been a better father. He could have taught his son how to shoot, instead of leaving that more or less up to Jimmy. The railroad, that job, had just kept him so busy, and he'd left most of the child-rearing to Libbie. If anyone should be apologizing, he realized it was him.

"Well," Millard said when James had finished. "You're all right. I'm all right. We'll get this girl to Spanish Fort, then head back to McAdam." His eyes hardened. "Your mother, brother, and sister will want to see you."

James's mouth turned into a hard frown, and Millard knew his son was still bent on making it to Fort Smith.

"I want to be a lawman," James said. "I have to be one."

Millard's head shook. "It's not all that it's cracked up to be, son."

"But you wouldn't know —"

"Wouldn't I?" Millard's head tilted toward the Winchester '73 leaning against the wagon's wheel. "Your two uncles weren't the only ones in that line of work. That's one reason I got that rifle."

"I'd never seen it." James motioned at the belted old Army revolver. "Or that?"

"That's because it was history. To me. A part of my life" — he almost said that he wanted to forget, but found other words — "that came mostly before you and your siblings."

"You were a lawman?"

"For a while. Sheriff's deputy . . . and Jimmy, Borden, and I all served with the Texas Rangers briefly."

James could only stare for the longest while. Like he was in shock. Sometimes, thinking back to those years shocked Millard himself.

"Why didn't you . . . let us know?"

Millard's head shook. "It never came up." He stared at the pot, wishing those balls would start to melt. "People change. Jimmy was cut out for that kind of life. And Borden, too, in his own way. I wasn't. It never came easy for me, and I never really liked it. Then I met Libbie. Then you came along." He had to think back. "I reckon you were maybe five years old when I decided it was time to turn in that tin star, find something different to do, something safer." He found the words. "I didn't want your mother to be a widow. I didn't want you,

Kris, and Jacob to grow up without a father. That's why Jimmy never married, you know. That's the kind of life you'll have if you go to Fort Smith, if you somehow pin on a badge. And about all you can hope for . . ." He couldn't finish.

Borden had been lucky. He had a wife to grieve over him, and a funeral that had attracted many to that Kansas town where they'd lived. Jimmy had been buried in the worn-out cemetery in a fading Texas town that would be blown away in a few years.

"It's still something that I have to do," James said.

Millard's head shook wearily. "When you're twenty-one, you can see —"

"How old were you?" James cut him off.

That took Millard back. He had been younger than James when he had first held a Winchester Yellow Boy. Jimmy had been even younger. He had been in his early twenties when Winchester had introduced its 1873 model.

"Times were different then," he said, but that sounded and tasted like a lie on his lips. Because it wasn't true. He had realized that when he had been forced to cut down those three outlaws up on Camp Creek. The Indian Territory could be just as wild and brutal as Texas had been back when he and his two brothers had ridden for the law.

Millard nodded at the skillet. "Those steaks are burning."

After James had flipped the meat again, he pointed the fork at the now-sleeping girl. "What will the law do to her?"

"I'm not turning her into a sheriff. She goes to a doctor — if there's a sawbones in Spanish Fort."

"What'll happen to her?"

Millard looked at the girl and again at his son. No romance between the two. By thunder, James had not even realized Robin was a girl until after she had been shot by the Chickasaws. "That's up to her."

"She's had a hard life." James shook his head sadly. "A father . . . who'd sell . . . his own flesh and blood . . . for whiskey!"

"It's a hard life," Millard said. "For everyone."

He studied his son. He would always imagine him, always see him, as that five-year-old boy who had laughed a lot or a boy not yet in his teens, but those years had flown by. James was no longer that boy, not even a kid, but a man. Inexperienced, sure, but growing up and learning fast. He probably would pin on a badge, no matter how much Millard and Libbie protested. What's more, he'd make a fine lawman.

"She's old enough to make her own way," Millard said, just to keep talking, to push aside those thoughts that told him that eventually James would find his own path, and was likely already choosing it. "She can choose her own path now that she doesn't have that —" The rest he left unsaid.

"What about the Chickasaws?" James asked.

"I don't think we have to worry about the Indians," Millard said. "If they wanted to attack us, they'd have hit us before now."

"So why make bullets?"

Millard smiled, but once again, the humor had left him. "Indians aren't the only ones a body has to worry about in the Indian Nations."

CHAPTER TWENTY-TWO

Wild Horse Creek

The piebald gelding fought bit, reins, and stirrup as Deputy U.S. Marshal Jackson Sixpersons eased toward the ruins of a campsite. He couldn't blame the horse.

Death hung in the air.

When he had forced the gelding a few more yards, he reined up and swung down into the dust. He wrapped the reins around a limb, but just to be safe, withdrew the hobbles from the saddlebag, and secured the paint horse's black front feet, as well. He did not want to be left afoot.

He found several blood droppings, casings from a Winchester — a small caliber — some other brass cartridges, and the remnants of a few copper percussion caps. In front of him lay the smashed remnants of whiskey kegs. Nearby that lay the body of a white man vultures and other carrion had picked over.

The corpse wasn't going anywhere, so Sixpersons tried to piece together what had happened. Horse tracks showed riders had come in from the north and left that way in a hurry. Chickasaws. The heavy wagon and oxen had gone south and without the dead white man. One horse, shod, had gone with the wagon. The Indians had later returned and followed.

There couldn't be any whiskey left in the load, not with all those busted barrels. Maybe the Indians had destroyed the batch of poisoned brew.

Jackson Sixpersons knew how to be patient and precise. He worked methodically, studiously, and carefully, piecing everything together. The wagon had arrived without a horse — that shod horse had ridden in from the south then left with the wagon. The Indians had come from the north, left in a hurry, and a few more had come back. Those had scalped the dead white man, but had they destroyed the contraband liquor? That he could not make any sense out of.

Yet he knew a fight had broken out, a quick but deadly one. Bodies, wounded or dead, had been carried away when the Indians had retreated. Probably attributed to the arrival of the man from the south, the rider with the good horse. Only later did the Chickasaws, if they were Chicka-saws, had returned.

One of the members of the wagon crew had been wounded, possibly killed, and most likely had been loaded into the back of the wagon, but the whiskey runners had not taken the dead man with them. Why not?

He went to the dead man, used his right foot to roll him over, and knelt beside the already bloated, stinking body. One eye had been missing for a long time. The other had fed a raven after the man's death. The dead man's tongue was missing, cut out. That had been after his death, probably by the Indians when they had returned.

However, the man had not been killed by Indians. The old Cherokee lawman could see the powder burns on the corpse's tem-ple, as well on the rigid fingers of his undisturbed right hand. He had put a gun to his head and shot himself. The large-caliber slug had not exited, because his skull was thick and hard.

Sixpersons saw few other wounds. He rose, knees popping, and spit the bitterness out of his mouth. He stared down at the corpse. "Lamar Bodeen, you saved me and Judge Parker a lot of trouble."

Behind him, the piebald snorted and

stamped his feet nervously.

There was nothing more for Sixpersons. He walked back to the piebald, removed the hobbles and returned those to the saddlebags, gathered the reins, and mounted again. His report would say that he had found Lamar Bodeen, whiskey runner, dead, apparently by his own hand. His report would describe the powder burns, the single entry wound of a large-caliber bullet, and a description of the man that would likely convince all of the courts that it indeed was Lamar Bodeen, alias Wildcat Lamar, alias Wildcat Bodeen, alias, alias, alias.

Maybe Sixpersons would see, eventually, a little bit of the reward money the state of Texas had posted on this killer — yeah, about the time he got a fourth set of teeth. He would leave out the fact that the man had been scalped. Not that Sixpersons cared much about the Chickasaws, but he did not want to bring anymore anger to any Indian people, and white men did not like to hear about white men, even outlaws, being scalped by Indian hands. The cutting out of Bodeen's tongue would fail to make his report, too, for the same reason. However, the next time he went to Fort Sill and ran into any Comanches on the federal reservation, he might let it slip to those Indians what had become of the fiend who had killed so many. Not that he cared much for the Comanches, but they were Indians . . . and so was he.

He would not say that he had buried the dead felon, because that would be a lie. Maybe the white peace officers would just assume that he had buried the dead man as that would have been the decent thing to do. Maybe he would have taken the time to bury the dead man, had Lamar Bodeen shown any decency during his wretched, wicked life.

Sixpersons kicked the piebald into a walk, then a lope, for the horse — and the deputy marshal himself — wanted to get away from the foul, evil place.

The tracks of the wagon were easy to follow.

Six miles south, he ran into other tracks and realized that he was not alone. The Indians following the whiskey wagon had turned back, but someone else was following the wagon of the whiskey runners. On shod ponies. Likely, those men were not Indians.

He decided to check the loads in his Winchester '87 before continuing south toward the Texas border.

*Along the north bank of the Red River,
Chickasaw Nation*

The river ran red.

Muddy, high, it was an angry torrent that
sent logs spearing downstream like torpe-
does. Texas longhorns and trail-weary
cowhands used to cross there on their way
to the Kansas cattle towns before the trail
moved westward and Dodge City had become the Queen of the Cow Towns, but no
trail boss in his right mind would have tried
to ford the Red when it raged like that.

Millard Mann could scarcely find the
bank, the water had risen so high. He spit,
slogged through the mud back to where he
had ground-reined his liver chestnut, and
looked at the wagon. The girl and James sat
in the driver's box, anxiously waiting. Robin
could sit up, which made Millard less
nervous about his doctoring abilities.

"Might as well light down," he said as he
led the gelding toward the oxen. He looked
at the sun. Still enough daylight to make a
few miles, but they could eat their supper
before moving downstream a ways and run
a cold camp. The Chickasaws were not coming after them, but he still did not want to
take any chances or lower his guard while
in Indian Territory.

"We're not crossing?" James asked.

"Not here. Unless you two swim like an otter." Millard smiled.

The two kids grinned back with utter relief. They had seen that river. To attempt to ford there would have meant a sure, wet death.

After wrapping the reins around the rear wagon wheel, Millard tilted his head eastward. "We'll follow the river. There's a ferry at Willis. We can cross there and head to Denison instead of Spanish Fort. Better chance of finding a doctor in Denison anyway. At least, a doctor who works on people more than horses and mules."

Usually, the Red stretched only one hundred yards or so there. Back in the late '80s, some entrepreneur had stretched a cable about twenty feet above the water line, put together a rope-and-pulley system, and built a wooden ferry that could carry people, horses, and wagons with the east-southeast current.

He should have headed for the Willis Ferry to begin with. Denison was much bigger than Spanish Fort, which wasn't more than a cattle crossing and farming community, and the railroad ran through Denison. He would leave the girl with the doctor, and board a train for Fort Worth. He would begin the long journey home with his son, back to McAdam. He would be a better father. Take the kid hunting. Fishing. Maybe get him a job on the railroad, if Millard could talk his way back onto the crew himself. He never had expected to be gone as long as he had. Anyway, in Denison, he would send a telegraph to Libbie and the kids. Let them know he and James were all right, and that they were coming home.

With the last of the deer meat frying in the skillet, and the last of the coffee boiling in the pot, Millard brought out the Winchester rifle, ejected all the shells, and began cleaning the .32-20.

"That's a One of One Thousand," Robin said, eyes wide with wonder.

Millard nodded.

Winchester Repeating Arms began advertising its One of One Thousand series around 1875. If you believed the company, every sporting rifle was tested, but some barrels proved to be significantly better than others — though all, Winchester proudly claimed, were mighty fine and all shot true. Yet those top barrels seemed worth their weight in gold, so the One of One Thousand series had been created, at a price of one hundred dollars. You could, of course, elect to buy the not-quite-as-good-but-better-than-many rifles known as the One of One Hundred, which added just twenty dollars to the model's factory price.

Granville Stuart, the famed Montana rancher, had a One of One Thousand. So did the legendary sharpshooter Doc Carver. Millard Mann never thought he deserved one. After all, there had not been many special rifles made. In fact, when it was all said and done, Winchester produced only one hundred and thirty-three One of One Thousand Model 1873s, while the One of One Hundreds would be even rarer, with no more than eight produced. The company had also produced One of One Thousands and One of One Hundreds in its 1876 Centennial Model, but Millard had never seen many of those big monsters in any version.

"How did you get one?" Robin asked.

Millard lowered the rag he was using to wipe the receiver. "You know about guns?" He didn't think the girl had picked that up from a rogue like Lamar Bodeen.

She nodded. "My pa" — she looked away — "rode with Buffalo Bill Cody's Wild West for a while. Till the whiskey got him."

"Whiskey'll do that," Millard said.

"Where has that rifle been all this time?" That question came from James.

"In a scabbard. In a trunk." Millard patted the butt of the old Colt revolver. "Along with this."

"You never —"

"It's part of my past," Millard interrupted his son. "Never saw any need of it once I got the job on the railroad." He tried to smile at James. "It would have been yours, eventually. Will be yours, someday." He focused on the rifle.

"My name's Gillett," the girl said.

James and Millard looked at her. "Ain't Bodeen. Gillett. Robin Gillett."

Millard nodded. "I once knew a Texas Ranger named Gillett."

She laughed. "Wouldn't be no kin to my pa."

He went back to cleaning the rifle. "No, I expect you're right."

The girl wanted to talk, to get everything off her chest, and suddenly she was spilling it all out, no holding back, tears streaming down her face.

Mal Gillett drank more liquor than even Buffalo Bill Cody, only Robin's pa couldn't hold his booze. It got to the point where he couldn't fork a horse or hold a rifle, and for a hard-riding, sharp-shooting cowboy in one of the biggest shows in the world, that wouldn't do. Colonel Cody had fired the drunk, and Mal Gillett had returned home, six months later, to Baxter Springs, Kansas.

His wife and his children — Robin had two sisters and three brothers — were happy to have him home. For a short while. His drinking picked up, and he wasn't a happy drunk. Liquor made him mean.

"Before that, he was a good pa," Robin said, dabbing her eyes with the tails of the long cotton shirt Millard had given her. "I was the oldest. Tomboy. He'd take me huntin'. It was him who taught me how to shoot. But then he found likker. Maybe it found him. Or they jus' found one 'nother."

So Mal drank. And drank. His wife had to get a job in town, clerking in some mercantile, and before long the two oldest boys were working. Just trying to make ends meet. Robin had to care for the little ones, staying home, and she had to put food in the pots, and that she did by hunting.

That was all fine and dandy until someone in town jokingly told Mal that Colonel Buffalo Bill Cody had hired the wrong Gillett. Cody should have hired Robin, and not Mal, and that maybe Robin could have challenged Cody's sharpshooting girl, Annie Oakley, and won over all of America's hearts.

It was the wrong thing to say to Mal Gillett.

A week later, Wildcat Lamar Bodeen happened through Baxter Springs, on his way to sell contraband whiskey in the Indian Territory, and he sold a few jugs to Gillett.

Mal Gillett didn't have any money to pay for hooch, but he had a daughter that he jealously despised.

"So he beat me and tossed me in the back of that wagon," Robin said. "An' that's the last I ever seed of my ol' man or my family."

CHAPTER TWENTY-THREE

Near the Red River, Chickasaw Nation

It had been pure luck that they had come across the trail, picking it up at the crossing of Caddo Creek and then following it south. A large freight wagon and a shod horse. It simply had to be Wildcat Lamar Bodeen and his poisoned whiskey.

The only scare came when maybe two dozen Chickasaws — at least, that's what the smoking Indian said they were — rode up on them, but Link McCoy turned around his horse and showed them the working end of his sawed-off Winchester '87 ten-gauge with the pistol grip.

That would not have been enough, except McCoy had plenty of company.

Zane Maxwell jacked a .44-40 round into his Winchester rifle, and Tulip Bells filled both hands, thumbing back the hammers of the nickel-plated Smith & Wesson No. 3 and the Starr Army — even though the .44 was double-action.

There were more. Locksburgh found one of his self-cocking Lightnings, John Smith palmed a Remington .44, Red opted for his Yellow Boy, and Jared Whitney ignored his old Starrs and drew his Winchester '92 carbine. The only rider who did not draw a weapon was the constant-smoking Choctaw breed, Newton Ah-ha-lo-man-tubbee, who calmly rolled another smoke and said, "They're Chickasaws."

Staying a good two hundred yards from them, the Indians watched the gunmen and talked among themselves before turning their horses around and heading north.

"What was that about?" McCoy asked.

"Probably after Bodeen." Newton Ah-ha-lo-man-tubbee fired up a match and lighted his cigarette. "Same as you."

It was enough to cause the outlaws to slow down and keep a keen eye on their back trail. McCoy and Maxwell did not trust Indians, not even Newton Ah-ha-lo-man-tubbee.

When the half-breed Choctaw said, "Chickasaws are cowards. They won't trouble you," McCoy figured the smoking man said that about every Indian tribe and probably even white men.

The outlaws slowed down, but they were

chasing a heavy freight wagon pulled by worn-out oxen. And the Red River would be impossible for a wagon like that to ford. Soon enough, the McCoy-Maxwell Gang would catch up to the whiskey runner.

As they neared the Red River, McCoy knew they were close to catching up. He called a halt to rest their horses, dismounted, and took time to load some shells for his ten-gauge.

He never trusted factory loads, the kinds to buy in a mercantile or hardware store. He trusted himself, and only himself. All he needed was gunpowder and a shot dipper. He found a piece of wood to use as a base, set the empty shell on that, punched out the primer, then turned the primer punch around to push the wads in the shell. Pliers, powder and shot funnel, and he was practically ready . . . except he enjoyed making his loads personal.

Years back, he had read about a deputy marshal in New Mexico Territory who had put cut-up dimes in his shotgun shells. McCoy had grown up poor, knowing only a fool or a filthy rich man would destroy good currency, but that newspaper account had given him an idea and he had sprinkled some barbs from barbed wire, chunks of metal, sometimes even glass in some shells.

He used a heavy pair of scissors to cut the thin metal of some keenly honed razors he'd bought from a barber in the new unincorporated town of Addington and dropped the sharp chunks into his shotgun shells.

"Plan on giving someone a close shave?" Maxwell asked.

"So he'll never have to shave again," McCoy answered with an evil grin.

When he had finished with the last shell, he pushed four of his new creations into the ten-gauge, jacked the lever to chamber a round, and slid in one more two-and-seven-eights inch shell. He rose and walked to his horse. "Let's ride."

No one protested.

He didn't know what to expect from Lamar Bodeen when they finally caught up with the whiskey runner, but doubted if the man would mind earning $500 for his whiskey. Not that McCoy had any intention of paying a fool like Bodeen. McCoy didn't plan on paying the gunman Maxwell had brought along, either. Jared Whitney would sell his own mother out, but McCoy didn't blame his partner for letting Whitney tag along. They could use a few extra guns. That's why they had brought in Locksburgh, Red, and John Smith. But once the job was said and done, and they had all of that gold coin from the Texans and Chicka-saws, Link McCoy was counting on a three-way split. Tulip Bells and Zane Maxwell were men to ride the river with. The others were men to get killed, after the job was done.

"How far's the river?" he asked the half-breed Indian riding on his right.

For once, the smoking man had no ciga-rette in his mouth, nor was he in the process of rolling one . . . but he had fished out his sack of tobacco. He jutted his jaw toward the south, Indian-fashion.

Along the north bank of the Red River
"Why don't you try that Remington?" Mil-lard Mann, full from the last of the deer meat, removed the straw from his mouth and pointed at the old .44 conversion in his son's waistband.

"Sir?" James asked in surprise.

"See if those loads I made will actually shoot . . . and not blow off your hand." He grinned to let his son and Robin Gillett understand that he was joking. At least, Mil-lard hoped it was a joke. Those old pistols had been known to misfire.

He had relaxed and decided it was time to be the father he should have been for a long, long time. "Go ahead. Just one shot. See if

316

that old thing works."

Reluctantly, James rose from where he was seated beside Robin and started to tug on the walnut grips of the converted .44, but stopped and nodded at the oxen and horses.

"I think those oxen are deaf," Millard said, grinning. "And too tired anyway. And my chestnut" — he stopped, remembering — "is used to gunfire." *By now.*

He thought back to thirty years earlier, when he would have been a long way before leaving his teenage years, and later, riding with the Texas Rangers. In those days, Borden, Jimmy, and he had trained their horses not to be spooked by gunfire.

James walked a good way from camp, drew the revolver, and looked back at his father, the barrel of the Remington pointed at the ground, his index finger resting on the trigger guard, but not inside.

Good, Millard thought. *Be careful. Don't put your finger on the trigger until you're ready and willing to shoot.*

"What do I shoot at?" James called out.

"Blackjack on the bank," Millard said, pointing with the straw.

Nodding, James turned, brought up the .44, eared back the hammer, aimed, and fired. The gun boomed like a cannon, and the gelding danced around a bit, flattening its ears, but then quickly settled as the echo of the Remington's shot faded into the evening air. White smoke enveloped James's right hand, but the breeze quickly carried it away as he lowered the pistol.

Near the Red River
Newton Ah-ha-lo-man-tubbee was about to answer when the gang heard a gunshot.

They reined up, guns instantly at the ready.

"Quarter mile south." the breed said, returning the tobacco pouch to a pocket. Smoking was a bad habit in a gunfight, or when trying to surprise some whiskey runner. Someone might see the glow of the cigarette, the smoke you blew, or smell it on the wind.

"Shooting a rabbit maybe?" Zane Maxwell asked. After all, it was closing in on supper time.

Newton Ah-ha-lo-man-tubbee shook his head. "Pistol shot. I doubt he was hunting."

"Warning shot?" Tulip Bells asked.

The half-breed shrugged and grinned at McCoy. "But I do believe you have found your whiskey."

"We'll split up," McCoy said as he eased his horse forward. "Indian, you'll stay with the horses when we get close. We'll come in

318

from all sides, but remember this, every one of you, and remember it good. The whiskey runner, Bodeen, ain't no good to us dead."

Along the north bank of the Red River
The tree stood a good thirty yards from James's position, but Millard had seen bark fly off one of the lower limbs. "What were you aiming at?"

"The center of the trunk." He began walking back to the camp, letting the barrel cool before returning it inside his pants.

Millard grinned again. James was a Mann, all right, all the way through. A mighty fine shot with a long gun, but a tad shaky when it came to firing a revolver.

"That gun kicks," James said as he sat down.

"It oughta," Robin said. "You see'd the size of the load your pa packed, an' that bullet he had to whittle down with his knife so 'em ca'tridges would even fit in that relic. 'Bout like a cannon, that pistol be."

James pointed toward the freight wagon, where the empty Winchester Model 1886 rifle sat. "Wish we had bullets for that."

"We'll get you some. Once we're in Denison." Millard pulled himself to his feet. "Let's put out the fire, get ready to move camp." He pointed the straw downstream, then tossed the straw away. "We'll move two or three more miles, run a cold camp, get an early start in the morning for the ferry at Willis. With luck, we should be there in two days."

Robin, feeling better and having regained much of her strength, helped James get the wagon ready to move — although James did most of the work and all the heavy lifting. Millard saddled the gelding.

As soon as the two kids had climbed into the front box of the big freight wagon, he led the liver chestnut ahead, shoved his One of One Thousand into the scabbard, and had put his left boot in the stirrup when a voice called out.

"Hallloooo the camp!"

Millard came down ready, turning toward the voice but also turning the gelding to use the animal as a shield. The Winchester was sheathed on the other side, but his right hand darted down and gripped the butt of his converted Army Colt. He waited.

A man stepped out of the brush. Afoot. He held a shotgun in his hand, not threatening with the weapon, just letting Millard see that he was armed and was not green. "Was hoping for a taste of coffee."

"Sorry," Millard called out to the stranger. "Dumped it on the fire."

"You pulling out?"

Millard nodded his head.

The man grinned. "Careful, ain't you?"

"It pays to be." Millard started to pull the .44 from its holster and heard a rifle cock behind him. At the metallic click of the rifle's lever, he detected two men walking on his left.

"Pa!" James called out, pointing at the bank.

Two men had climbed up from the soggy bottoms, brandishing six-shooters.

James's right hand started for the Remington in his waistband.

Millard shouted, "No." Lowering his voice, he said, "No sudden moves. Keep your hands up and away from that .44. Both of you, just sit still." He did not move from the horse, but looked over the saddle at the man with the shotgun, who resembled the cat that had eaten the canary.

The other men began walking toward camp.

Millard cursed his stupidity. He'd acted like a greenhorn, letting James fire that revolver. It had given away their position. That's how people got killed in the Indian Nations . . . or anywhere in the West, even in 1895. He had made a bad mistake, thinking they were safe, relaxing, lowering his guard. He didn't know what these men wanted, but he could tell they were not law-abiding citizens.

He leaned onto the saddle, keeping his right hand away from the holstered revolver — like he could do anything with his six-shooter against seven men — and made himself smile at the one with the shotgun on his shoulder. "You must want coffee mighty bad."

The man laughed and started crossing the clearing.

Millard observed him closely. Average height and weight, clean-shaven except for the stubble, and fairly well dressed. Brown boots, trousers of brushed cotton, a fancy light blue vest with yellow paisley designs and a shawl collar, a black silk puff tie with a shiny stickpin in the center, white shirt, camel-colored wool frock coat and nice hat with a flat crown, the color of pecan. Dressed like a gentleman, until you considered the shotgun he pointed in the general direction of Millard and the chestnut.

It was a Winchester '87, lever-action, but Millard knew it had not left the factory in New Haven, Connecticut, looking that way. A smooth pistol grip instead of the traditional stock, beaded leather covering the fore end, and a sawed-off barrel, casehardened and blued.

He also knew only one man in the West was known to carry a shotgun like that, but he did not mention the name of Link McCoy.

"Now before anyone gets fidgety and gets killed, let's all relax. I'm not here to rob you, kill you, but to offer a proposition. One that could bring us all a lot of wealth." McCoy took another step. That sound fine?"

Millard nodded.

"But, just so no one does get fidgety and then gets killed, why don't you drop your six-shooter and step away from that fine-looking horse?"

Slowly, the .44 conversion cleared the leather then slipped from Millard's two fingers and thumb and landed on the wet grass. He turned toward the wagon and gave a nod at James and the girl.

James stood, showing the two men coming up from the banks of the Red River the .44 Remington, which he let fall over the side. "I'm going to pick up a shotgun and drop it."

"Do it right careful-like," said one of the men coming from the bank, a pockmarked fellow with a gray mustache, sliver of a beard under his lip, and a bell crown hat. The man cocked a shiny revolver just to get

323

his point across.

Robin cleared her throat, bent down, and picked up the double-barrel shotgun, which she pitched over the side and onto the grass.

"That all?" called the leader.

"You see the Winchester in the scabbard," Millard told him.

"That ain't what I asked," said McCoy.

"That's all." Millard saw no point in telling them about the old horseman's pistol in the back of the wagon or his son's .50-caliber repeating Winchester. If the outlaws found the weapons, and Millard figured they would, it wouldn't matter. Both guns were empty. Besides, a man like Link McCoy would have expected a lie.

"That's fine, then," McCoy said, but he did not lower the fancy shotgun. "I'm hoping you got plenty of leftover whiskey, because that's what brung us to you, Wildcat Bodeen."

CHAPTER TWENTY-FOUR

McCoy told one of the men who had approached from Millard's right to go help with the horses.

The man with a red mustache, dressed like a dollar-a-day cowhand and armed with a Winchester Model 1866 carbine, nodded. His spurs rang out a tune as he jogged off to the north. Most of the men wore lavender bandanas.

"So you want to hear my proposition, Bodeen?"

They think I'm the whiskey runner. It might buy some time. "Sure." Millard grinned as he added, "Link."

The gunman grinned at such recognition. "You flatter me."

"As you do me. Teaming up with" — Millard slowly turned, sought out until he recognized the one who had to be Zane Maxwell, and gave that man a soft salute — "the McCoy-Maxwell Gang would be an honor." Then he made himself sound like a businessman. "If the price is right."

"It is," Maxwell said from behind him.

"All we want, really, is your whiskey," McCoy said. "But just to be safe, and so you'd really earn your share of our haul, we'll want to keep you with us. Till we make the score."

Millard nodded. "I see." There was just one problem, he realized.

So did the man with a patch over one eye who had placed himself at the back of the big wagon. "Zane! There ain't no whiskey in here!"

McCoy's expression changed instantly. He shoved his way past one of his men and strode toward the wagon, where Robin and James were climbing out, watched by the pockmarked man in the bell crown hat. That one, Millard figured, had to be Tulip Bells. The others he didn't recognize. Then he remembered. Most of the others were already dead.

McCoy jumped into the back of the wagon, but there wasn't much to see. He didn't look for weapons — a stroke of luck — though Millard couldn't figure out what he'd be able to do with two empty guns against seven outlaws bound for the gallows or a shallow grave.

Almost immediately, McCoy leaped out

of the wagon and went back to Millard, stopping a few feet from him, bringing up the shotgun, waist-high, and slipping his finger against the trigger. "You couldn't have sold all that liquor, mister. I heard you was carrying a ton."

Millard shrugged. "You weren't at Wild Horse Creek."

McCoy glanced at Maxwell, then at another gunman, asking a question with his eyes.

"North of where we picked up the trail," said the one with the eye patch. He also was missing a left ear. A name flashed through Millard's mind. He remembered seeing a wanted poster on him at the Fort Worth depot. *Jared Whitney.*

"Well." McCoy demanded.

"Chickasaws jumped us," Millard said.

"They didn't like getting cheated and poisoned?" Maxwell asked.

Millard shrugged, wondering how much longer he could pull off the faux bravado. "I didn't ask them. Had to shove out the barrels just to save our hides. Killed one of them. Maybe more." He decided to chance another lie, just in case they had seen the body of the real Lamar Bodeen up at the site of the gun battle. "Had one renegade white man with them. Killed him, too."

McCoy cursed. Maxwell echoed it with his own round of profanity.

"Do we really need hooch?" asked Whitney.

"Yes!" McCoy snapped.

Millard made himself smile. "Boys, y'all don't know me well, I reckon. But you ask anyone in Indian Territory, and they'll be sure to tell you that Wildcat Lamar Bodeen can brew up some good liquor. Right quick like. Me and my boys." He gave James and Robin a short wave.

"You must not know me very well," said the tallest one of the outlaws. An edge accented his voice. He had a match dangling between his teeth, dancing underneath the neat black mustache, wore fancy Texas boots, and carried a brace of old Remington revolvers. "But this fellow ain't Wildcat Bodeen."

Millard's throat turned to sand, but he scoffed. "Then who am I?"

McCoy and Maxwell didn't seem to hear Millard. They stared hard at the one who had been talking.

"What do you mean, Smith?" Maxwell asked.

"Bodeen the whiskey runner is knowed to have only one eye. Like Whitney yonder."

The gunman with the brown leather patch

over his left eye didn't appear to enjoy having his imperfection singled out.

McCoy stepped forward, not stopping until the sawed-off barrel of his ten-gauge pressed against Millard's shirt.

"And," Millard said, trying to sound calm, "Link McCoy wears a wheat sack over his head when he's pulling a job on a bank or train. So does Zane Maxwell."

"So?" Link asked icily.

"So it's a disguise, you blasted fool." Millard shook his head in disgust. "You think I could get along without landing in Judge Parker's dungeon or up at the federal pen in Michigan if I showed everyone how handsome I actually am." He laughed then sighed, finally letting out a long breath. "You fellows been known to change clothes after a bank or train robbery. You go from looking like men who ought to be in the calaboose to respectable, law-abiding citizens. I heard that once you even pinned on deputy sheriff's badges so you could fool real posses into thinking you was actually looking for yourselves." He slapped his thigh. "That was a good one. A bona fide stroke of pure genius." He pointed at his eyes. "I see fine. And I make whiskey fine."

"Or not so fine." At least McCoy had lowered his shotgun.

"What's your pleasure?" Millard asked.

"The worst you can brew."

Millard grinned, but before he could speak, Zane Maxwell shot out, "We don't have a whole lot of time. Let's forget about this whiskey angle —"

"It ain't eighteen-year-old Scotch I'm making, boys," Millard said quickly. "It's rotgut." He had to think fast. If they decided against whiskey, he — and James and Robin — were dead.

"I tell you this ain't Bodeen!" cried out Smith.

Thankfully, McCoy and Maxwell didn't appear interested.

"What'll you need?"

"Raw alcohol," Millard said. "Sugar. I'll burn it. Unless you can find me enough oak sawdust to do the job. Adds color. And some taste. Plugs of tobacco. Cures it, adds some mighty fine whiskey color to the brew, and gives some bite. Some chopped up rattlesnake heads. And strychnine."

"Strychnine," Maxwell repeated.

Millard nodded. "Gets the heart started again."

"Or not?" McCoy asked.

Millard made himself grin. "Or not. You see, in the old days, my grandpa used to make good corn liquor. A bushel would

330

produce three gallons of pure whiskey, if it was the best corn my grandpa growed. But then some distillers learned that if they could mix a bit of strychnine in their yeast, they'd be able to average four bushels per gallon. Take three cents worth of strychnine and a gallon of water, and put that atop the brewed three gallons of pure whiskey . . ."

They stared at him with blank faces.

"I reckon you don't rightly care to hear about stramonium. Some folks like to use it rather than strychnine. Easier to find. Or was, back in Grandpa's day. The problem with stramonium is it makes one's stomach a little irritable, but you can cure that by adding some opium. But then you got to take the opium into account, counteract it, you see, and you do that by just a pinch of potash. That'll give you the right smell, pretty fair taste. Wouldn't cost no more than four cents, maybe five, to make a lot of good sipping whiskey. Back in my Grandpa's day."

"This gent ain't Wildcat Bodeen!" Smith snapped.

"And who is you?" Millard put a challenge in his voice.

The man started to swing the rifle toward Millard, but stopped and answered, "John Smith."

Millard laughed hard, though he had to

summon every ounce of strength just to make himself laugh and slap his thigh. He almost doubled over. "Well, that's mighty original, fellow."

Smith started to press against the trigger, but one word from McCoy and one move of his shotgun made the outlaw back off.

"You say he's not Bodeen," McCoy said.

"I know he ain't."

"You know Bodeen?" McCoy asked.

"Well . . ."

"Have you ever seen him?" Maxwell tossed in.

John Smith frowned. "Not exactly. But I know of this whiskey runner. Heard him described plenty of times. I got friends —"

"You don't have one friend in the world." Millard figured that was absolutely true.

The conversation was interrupted when Tulip Bells jumped out of the back of the wagon and came running with the old single-shot horseman's pistol and the Winchester '86. "Look what I found, gents!" he announced proudly.

"They're empty," Millard said. "Traded with some injuns for a barrel of fine sipping whiskey."

"Well," Bells had to agree, "they ain't loaded. That's for sure."

Millard decided to go back to talking

about whiskey. "You can also use cocculus, but it's hard to find. Comes from Africa, or so Grandpa used to tell me, and it can make a body sick, even cause prostration. Unless you use too much. Ten grains would be enough to send a good oxen or strong horse into convulsions and spasms and kill it. Some tribes in India, I hear, would even poison wells with cocculus. And —"

"Shut up!" McCoy snapped.

"He sure talks like a whiskey runner," Jared Whitney said.

"Look," Millard said. "You want whiskey and you want it in a hurry. Who's it for?"

McCoy glanced at Maxwell, and then Maxwell said. "Chickasaw Indians and Texas ranchers."

Millard nodded. "Well, you don't want to tell the injuns that I brewed the whiskey. But Chickasaws and Texans don't have much in the way of taste buds. They want liquor. They want to get drunk. That's what I can deliver." He began counting off items on his fingers. "Raw ethyl alcohol for starters. I'll toss in some chewing tobacco, tea, coffee — prune juice if we can lay ahold of some. Nah. Forget the prune juice. Too hard to come by. Red pepper and gunpowder. If you can't get me no sugar — burnt sugar's the best, but molasses can do in a pinch. I can even get some sagebrush if need be. Or creosote." He looked at the sky, nodded to himself, and went on. "Tartaric acid. Maybe sulfuric acid. Or ammonia. No, those aren't gonna be readily available. But you can get strychnine anywhere there's wolves, and there are wolves and coyotes aplenty. So strychnine. Maybe some turpentine."

He waited.

"Rattlesnake heads?" Jared Whitney asked.

"The snakeheads ain't what kills the drinkers," Millard said. "It's the strychnine. Or colossus. Stramonium don't quite do the job if you want to kill someone. Make them sick, stramonium's fine. All the snakeheads do is add a bit of power to my busthead."

He didn't let any silence linger, but wondered how long he could keep on talking. "Ask folks anywhere, and they'll tell you that Wildcat Lamar Bodeen knows everything you needs to know about bug juice, coffin varnish, gut warmer, nose paint, tanglefoot, tongue oil, skull bender, sheep dip, stagger soup, leopard sweat, corpse reviver, widow-maker, phlegm-cutter, widow-maker, scamper juice, John gas-remover Barleycorn, snake poison, pop skull."

"Only he ain't Bodeen." John Smith wouldn't let that notion die.

"We're about to find out," McCoy said.

That made Millard sweat. "Now I can also make you some halfway decent champagne cider. It'll get you roostered, but won't kill you. Just need brown sugar, water, yeast, and I'll add a little grape juice to it. Cost you only five dollars a quart."

"Here they come." Maxwell pointed his Winchester barrel off to the north.

Slowly, everyone turned around.

Millard eyed the new arrivals. The waddie with the Yellow Boy Winchester — the one with the red mustache — was coming back, herding along the other horses. He wasn't alone. Another rider came along, smoking a cigarette. Millard couldn't tell who the man was, but he knew enough to figure his impersonation of the whiskey runner was about to end. Along with his life.

The rider was tall, but from the color of his skin, the length of his hair, and the way he forked a paint horse, Millard knew the man was an Indian.

Still, he'd run his bluff as long as he could.

"You see," he said to no one in particular, "you heard tell of sink-taller whiskey, I presume. No? Well, if the whiskey has been diluted, you can drop in a piece of tallow. Beef usually, but mutton'll work. If that taller sinks, well, that's how you know the

335

whiskey ain't what it once was. But in good bona fide rotgut hardcore John Barleycorn, that chunk of taller will just sink like an ironclad to the bottom of the keg. And . . ."

A few of the gunmen went to help with the horses, ground-reining or hobbling them, while the Indian remained in the saddle.

"Hey, breed!" Maxwell shouted. "Ride here. We need you to settle something for us."

Millard wet his lips, glancing over toward the wagon to warn Robin and James with his eyes that the game was up, that they should make for the river, run, swim, hide, just get out of there before they were all gunned down. All he could see, however, were the faces of a few of the gang members.

He kept looking, kept his face turned away from the Indian, just to hold out a little longer. The paint horse's hoofs clopped slowly — an eternity — each sound of the unshod hoof on the ground driving nails into Millard's heart, into his coffin. He had to steel himself not to break through the men circling him. He wet his lips again.

The horse stopped.

"Smith says this ain't Bodeen," McCoy said. "You tell us."

That was Millard's cue. Slowly, defiantly,

he turned around and looked at the long-haired, slim, old Indian sitting on a worn saddle but one mighty fine horse. The Indian, Choctaw — at least part Choctaw — from the looks of him, busied himself sprinkling tobacco onto a paper in his fingers. The pouch dropped into a vest pocket, and he rolled the cigarette with one long-fingered hand, brought the smoke to his thin lips, then found a match, which he struck on this thumb.

The Lucifer flamed to life, and his hand brought the match up to the cigarette, which flared to life. Finger and thumb held the smoke in his lips then pulled it out. The Indian raised his head toward the darkening sky and blew out white smoke.

"Is this Wildcat Bodeen?" Link McCoy asked.

The Indian looked directly into Millard Mann's paling face.

CHAPTER TWENTY-FIVE

"Of course it is," the smoking Choctaw half-breed said. *"Halito,* Bodeen. *Chish nato?"*

Millard Mann breathed out a sigh of new life. While a couple outlaws were shaking their heads at or cussing out the man called John Smith, Millard nodded at the smoking Indian. "Hello yourself, Newton Ah-ha-lo-man-tubbee." He waved at the Indian. "Been a long time. And" — he couldn't help but grin and shake his head in wondered amazement at his good fortune before answering the Indian's question — "I'm doing mighty fine." *Now.*

It was a puzzlement. Holding the reins to his paint horse in his left hand and the Winchester shotgun in his right, a kneeling Jackson Sixpersons studied the signs. The tracks of the massive freight wagon led right into the roaring, flooding waters of the Red River.

Yet the oxen had not pulled the wagon into the river. Several men had pushed the wagon into the Red and the current had pummeled what had been left of Wildcat Lamar Bodeen's whiskey hauler. The remains must be resting on the bottom or smashed along the banks farther downstream.

Several men had come across where the wagon had been parked, approaching on foot. Later, horses had joined them, and they had ridden not along the riverbank, heading for one of the ferries downstream to go into Texas, but north and east. The oxen had been scattered by a rider on a good cow pony.

What did it all mean?

Well, for one, they didn't want or need the wagon. But they wanted the three people with the wagon. Also, they weren't going to Texas, but staying in the Nations.

Chickasaws? No. Those Indians had turned back earlier. The riders had come in from the east, but they weren't Choctaws. At least, most of them weren't. Sixpersons had known Newton Ah-ha-lo-man-tubbee long enough to recognize the half-breed's moccasin prints. He'd also spotted the markings of the shoe on his pony's left forefoot. He had made a note of that track when the cigarette-addicted Indian had told him about the whiskey runner Bodeen.

Counting the rider who had held off the Chickasaws when Bodeen had been killed, Sixpersons knew he was chasing eleven. Newton Ah-ha-lo-man-tubbee? There was no telling which hand the Choctaw breed would play. He might help out Sixpersons; he might kill him. The three from the wagon? He didn't know them or anything about them, other than he could arrest them for running contraband spirits into Indian Territory. The others? Well, he had a good inkling those would be Link McCoy, Zane Maxwell, Tulip Bells and whatever other gunmen they had recruited.

Sixpersons studied the twelve-gauge. He would need a whole lot more firepower to tackle that gang, and he had more than a fair idea that those marshals he had asked to rendezvous with him at Fort Washita were probably still in Arkansas.

Sixpersons started to stand then heard the twin clicks of a double-barrel shotgun being cocked behind him.

Orr, Chickasaw Nation
There wasn't much to the town (*settlement* might have been a better word) of Orr — yet — but it had what the McCoy-Maxwell

Gang needed. It was so new, not enough years had passed to fade the whitewash on the frame buildings. It had boasted a post office since '92, and although probably fewer than two hundred people called Orr home, it brought in farmers, Indians, and traders for business. After all, in that part of the Indian Nations, cities and stores could be hard rides apart from one another.

Orr dreamed of having a famous city square like Santa Fe, New Mexico Territory, or Fort Worth, Texas, but the merchants had yet to buy into the city founder's fancy, evidenced by the dominant feature of vacant lots. A few single-story buildings had been erected, and business boomed in two buildings cattycorner from one another. Both general stores boomed because anything could be purchased at either of the mercantiles.

Like raw ethyl alcohol.

Like sugar.

Like plugs of tobacco.

Like red pepper, gunpowder, and strychnine.

"What's the poison fer?" asked the mustached clerk in sleeve garters and an Irish cap.

"What else?" Millard Mann answered. "Wolves and coyot's."

The clerk nodded. "What else you need?"

"Five pounds of bacon," Millard answered. "Sack of flour. Sack of corn meal. Tub of lard. Some of those cans of peaches and tomatoes, about ten each. Let's say a half-dollar's worth of those penny candies you got in that jar. And three or four cans of that." He pointed to the shelves behind the clerk's head.

The clerk had written it all down on his order form, then licked his pencil, made a few additional notes, and nodded as he stuck the pencil above his right ear. "Take me a while to get it all fer you."

"No rush. Let me have one of those plugs of tobacco, and me and my pard'll wait on the bench. Just holler when it's all ready." Turning, Millard nodded at the mustached villain called Red, picked up the tobacco the clerk slid in front of him, and walked out onto the boardwalk in front of the store. He sat on a crate that served as a bench, leaned against the rough frame wall, and opened the tobacco.

"I heard what all you told that fella." Red leaned on the wooden column that held up the awning and stared hard at Millard.

"Wasn't a secret." Millard bit into the tobacco, tore off a chunk, and pitched it to the gunman, who caught it, studied it, smelled it, and finally decided it wasn't poisoned.

He bit off a fair-sized wad and began softening it with his molars. "That coffee and such. Maxwell didn't tell you to order that."

"You don't drink coffee?"

"You know what I mean."

"Tell Maxwell. Tell McCoy. Tell anybody." Millard paused to let a couple Indian women carrying paper-wrapped packages to pass, worked the tobacco some more. It had to be the lowest grade he had ever tried to chew. "Two strangers come into this store, buy nothing but what anybody in these parts knows is usually bought to make forty-rod whiskey, and what do you think that clerk's going to do? He's going to alert the town law, if a place this size has a law —"

"It ain't." Red grinned. "That's how come Maxwell picked it."

"But Tishomingo's not far from here, and that clerk would be letting the United States Indian Police know his suspicions. Or some federal deputy. Ordering coffee and that other stuff makes the clerk thinks he's outfitting a couple new settlers to the territory, ones who have a coyote and wolf problem and like to chew a lot of tobacco." Millard spit perfectly between Red's boots.

"Well . . ."

Thinking, Millard knew, was not Red's strongest suit.

"Well . . ."

"Well," Millard said, "I told McCoy that if he wanted not to attract suspicion, he shouldn't buy everything in one store."

He had told McCoy no such thing, and actually, the gang leader was across the town square — empty except for a well and some hitching posts — buying a few other items, including kegs to put the poisoned whiskey in, kettles to help brew the concoction, and, if he had more brains than Red, flour, bacon, coffee, and tobacco to throw off any suspicion. Maxwell was over at the livery off the town square, buying two wagons, one to pick up the supplies McCoy was ordering and one to haul the strychnine and alcohol and other items to wherever it was that they planned to brew the liquor.

Millard looked across the street. He couldn't see McCoy inside still dickering with a clerk, but he could see Tulip Bells, Jared Whitney, and Steve Locksburgh positioned at various points in case something went wrong and gunplay erupted in the small but busy town of Orr. Bells waited closest to the livery. Undoubtedly, he'd be driving one of the wagons. The man called

John Smith had stayed outside of town in an arroyo with the half-breed Choctaw, keeping a watch on Robin Gillett and James.

Millard scratched the palm of his right hand with the barrel of his holstered Colt. The outlaws had let him keep his sidearm, knowing it would look strange for a man in that part of the world to ride into town "undressed," as the saying went. Of course, they had unloaded the converted Colt before shoving it back into his holster, and the only cartridges in his shell belt were empty casings for the Colt and his Winchester repeater. They had let him keep the rifle in his scabbard on the saddle. Likewise, they'd unloaded it as well.

He took off his battered hat to fan himself in the heat of the day and smiled pleasantly as farmers and farmers' wives walked about town. He wondered what Libbie and his youngest children would be doing.

Things had happened quickly after Newton Ah-ha-lo-man-tubbee had told McCoy and the ruffians that Millard was indeed Wildcat Bodeen. They had unhitched the team of oxen, and Red had driven them off toward the west, and while the cowboy-turned-renegade was doing that chore, the rest of them, including Millard, his son, and Robin, had shoved the heavy wagon into the Red River.

The current had taken the big wagon almost instantly, and it had capsized in a white foam and disappeared in the mad torrent.

As soon as Red returned, they had left, Millard riding his liver chestnut between McCoy and Locksburgh. John Smith had ridden double with Robin, and James had been forced to ride with Tulip Bells, but only until they had reached the first farmhouse a few miles northeast of the river.

The McCoy-Maxwell Gang had stolen two mounts — an old mule and a gray horse blind in one eye — but the animals were game enough to carry Robin and James. The owners of the animals hadn't been home, so no one had been killed. Millard's luck still held.

The stolen animals had been left in a gulley a few miles south of Orr, and James and Robin had been forced to ride double again until they reached the arroyo where they had been left under guard. Millard didn't think any harm would come to them. At least, not until he had brewed the poison whiskey.

He spit again.

Tulip Bells mounted his horse and eased the animal to the livery. A few minutes later, he had tethered his mount behind a farm wagon and was driving the team of big mules pulling it toward the general store across the street. Ten minutes after that, Zane Maxwell exited the livery in a covered wagon, his bay mare tied behind it, and made for Millard and Red.

The wagon stopped, and Maxwell dismounted without a word after setting the brake. He gathered the reins to his horse, checked the cinch before swinging into the saddle, and rode away. South. Toward the arroyo where they would rendezvous later to pick up the others.

The clerk stuck his head out of the door, left open to allow a breeze on the stifling afternoon. "Your stuff's read, mistah."

Millard spit and wiped his lips with the back of his hand. "Let's get moving, Red. I've a hankering to get back to our spread and eat some fresh biscuits." He smiled at the clerk, who turned and disappeared inside the store.

Red just blinked in confusion, but followed.

"We can help you with that," the clerk said as Millard handed Red the flour and cornmeal.

"No. We like to do our own work, sir." Millard watched Red carry the heavy load toward the waiting wagon.

Red stopped at the door, waiting.

"What's the final damage?" Millard asked.

The clerk told him.

Millard suggested a few dollars less.

The clerk grunted.

Red moved onto the boardwalk and carried the flour and cornmeal to the wagon.

"Tell you what," Millard said softly, "how about a box of .32-20 Winchester?"

Frowning the clerk dropped behind the counter to fish out the box of cartridges, and Millard fished out the gold coins McCoy had given him.

That had troubled Red, too, but Maxwell had told his gang member that he didn't trust Red with money, that Red wouldn't know if the store clerk was cheating him, that Red might even try to cheat Maxwell.

Red was back, heading toward the counter, when the clerk came up and slapped a box of cartridges on the counter, but Millard positioned himself in front of Red, blocking his view. He found the boxes of poison and sugar, and loaded those onto Red's big arms, and as the man snorted and carried that load to the wagon, Millard turned back to pay the clerk.

Quickly, he opened the box of Winchester rounds, emptied a handful into his hand,

and dropped those into the pocket of his pants. Red was coming back inside, so Millard pushed the box behind the counter.

The clerk stared and tried not to curse Millard for his clumsiness.

"Sorry," Millard said, gathering his change and pushing the greenbacks and coin into his pocket.

The clerk disappeared behind the counter to pick up the scattered rounds, and Millard helped Red with some of the merchandise.

Outside, Millard watched Tulip Bells drive the wagon full of kegs, kettles, and other items around the corner.

McCoy rode straight toward Red and Millard. He stopped at the rear of the wagon, struck a match on the horn of his saddle, and fired up a black cigar. "Five miles south of Fort Washita along Caddo," he said just loud enough for Millard and Red to hear, "there's a dugout. That's where you'll find us. Get there as quick as you can and don't let anyone follow you." He puffed on the cigar and pointed it at Millard. "If he gives you any trouble, Red, kill him." An icy, unfriendly grin then spread across McCoy's face. "But he won't give you any trouble. Because he knows, if he does, those two children . . . will be dead before he is."

CHAPTER TWENTY-SIX

Along the north bank of the Red River

He did not lower the Winchester '87, but kept the barrel pointed at the ground as he slowly rose, releasing the reins to the piebald, and carefully turning around to face the man with the shotgun.

Actually, there were two men.

The short, stocky one wore nondescript clothing, had a nondescript face, cavalry gauntlets on both hands, and a pair of Colt revolvers holstered on his hips. The one on his left had the butt facing forward. Sixpersons, however, would not call the Greener shotgun nondescript, not with those sawed-off barrels aimed at his gut. The white man held the double-barrel at his waist, his face grim, his fingers ready.

Beside him, holding the reins to two horses, stood a tall man with a black hat, blue shirt, linen duster, black stovepipe boots, gray pants, adobe-colored chaps, and a silver badge. The badge was a five-point star cut out of a coin. A Texas Ranger. His face had been relentlessly beaten by the sun, and while his mustache seemed permanent, the beard covering the rest of his face appeared a more recent growth. An ivory-handled Schofield revolver was holstered on his right hip.

With his left hand, Sixpersons pulled back the vest to reveal the badge on his shirt.

"Indian police?" the Ranger asked.

"And a deputy U.S. marshal," Sixpersons answered.

"Charley," the Ranger said, and the double-barrel Greener's hammers were softly lowered.

The Ranger did not introduce himself, but led a big black horse and a smaller dun toward Sixpersons, who picked up the reins to his paint horse, but kept an eye on Charley with the Greener.

"Looking for Bodeen," the Ranger said. "The whiskey runner."

Sixpersons pointed the barrel of his shotgun at the tracks. "His wagon went into the Red."

Charley with the Greener snorted and spit tobacco juice into one of the footprints. "He wouldn't be fool enough to cross here."

"Bodeen has crossed another river," Sixpersons said.

The Ranger straightened, his eyebrows knotted, and his fists clenched. "What do you mean?"

"Bodeen's dead."

For the longest while, the only sound came from the river, the wind, and the chirping birds. At last, the Ranger released his fists and sucked in a deep breath. He exhaled, and stared hard at Sixpersons. "You kill him?"

The old Cherokee shook his head. "Killed himself."

That caused the Ranger to stagger back. He wet his lips, rubbed his bearded chin, and asked, "Why?"

Sixpersons shrugged.

"Why?" the Ranger asked again.

"If I had to guess, I'd guess that he had a belly full of his poison. Decided to take the coward's way out."

Charley with the Greener snorted. "He wouldn't drink that stuff."

"Don't think it was his own idea," Sixpersons said.

"Whose?" the Ranger asked.

"Chickasaws." Sixpersons tilted his head north. "Happened about two days' ride that way. That's where I found his body. Whiskey barrels were destroyed. The wagon came this way." He pointed to the river. "Till some others caught up with them here."

"You sure it was Bodeen?" the Ranger asked.

"Crazy-looking white man. One eye missing, like it had been plucked out years ago. Wore buckskins."

The Ranger said nothing, but his face revealed that, indeed, the dead man had been the whiskey runner. "I wanted to kill him," he said finally.

Sixpersons nodded. He had figured that much. Texas Rangers typically did not cross the Red River and leave their jurisdiction unless they felt like it.

"He killed my kid," the Ranger said. "Killed some other white men. I wanted to kill him."

"He killed plenty of Indians, too," Sixpersons said, but the Ranger did not appear to hear.

Charley with the Greener sighed and shoved the shotgun into the scabbard of his horse, the puny dun. "Reckon I don't get no money. Figger to ride down to Spanish Fort and get good and drunk."

Sixpersons thought about letting the man ride off, but as soon as Charley had swung into the saddle, the old Cherokee cursed his luck and said reluctantly, "How much was the Ranger offering you?"

That got the attention of both men.

"Enough," Charley said.

Enough could have been five dollars, Sixpersons guessed, for a man like Charley with the Greener.

Again, Sixpersons pointed his shotgun barrel at the tracks. "I'm after these men."

The Ranger blinked, but otherwise showed nothing.

Charley with the Greener spit tobacco juice and shook his head. "What's that worth? Two bucks for an arrest. Split between the three of us. Think I'd rather get drunk in Spanish Fort."

"I figure the rewards for the McCoy-Maxwell Gang will tally a bit more than two dollars," Sixpersons said.

Without a word, the Ranger mounted the big black, pulled down the brim of his hat, and locked his gaze onto Jackson Sixpersons. "What about Bodeen's kid?"

Sixpersons shrugged. "Likely rode off with the rest of the gang." He pointed northeast.

"I don't care about a reward," the Ranger said. "You two can split that up. I'll just kill Bodeen's spawn."

Remembering what Newton Ah-ha-lo-man-tubbee had told him back in the cabin at Limestone Gap in the Choctaw Nation,

354

Sixpersons wet his lips. "That kid's a girl. No more than sixteen years old."

"She's a whiskey runner and killer, just like her old man. I couldn't kill Bodeen. But I will kill that kid. An eye for an eye." The Ranger spurred the big black and rode out, leaning low in the saddle, trying to pick up the tracks.

Charley with the Greener grinned and followed, and Jackson Sixpersons mounted his piebald, all the while wishing that he had kept his big mouth shut.

The bend of Caddo Creek, Chickasaw Nation
It was beginning to smell like whiskey.

Following his father's orders, James Mann stepped out of the dugout to gather more firewood. It was a relief to step out of the sweltering hole in the ground and feel a light breeze, if blistering sun, on his skin. Behind him limped Robin Gillett, and the two made for the pile of wood under the careful eye of the gunman called Steve Locksburgh.

They said nothing, just walked past the half-breed who sat cross-legged and rolled a cigarette while coughing savagely.

When each had an armload of wood, they went back, sweating profusely, and ducked to get back into the dugout, followed by

355

Locksburgh.

Millard stooped in front of the fireplace, stirring the contents in a blackened caldron. He stepped back, motioned for James to dump his load on the fire, and directed the girl to drop her wood beside the fireplace. James blinked sweat from his eyes and quickly backed away from the scorching fire. He looked at his father, whose clothes were so wet with sweat they stuck to his skin.

"Reminds me of when I was younger than you kids," Millard said with a grin, "and Pa would be boiling goober peas. Hot work. Hot work." He winked at the gunman. "But worth the sweat. Same as this."

"I ain't drinkin' yer rotgut," the gunman said, fanning himself with his hat.

"Not if you want to live," Millard said with another wink. "At least, not this batch, but I'll make some special for all y'all." He went back to stirring the pot.

As the new wood flamed to life, the heat intensified. James had to guess that it must have been at least one hundred and twenty-five degrees in there. And about to get hotter.

Two minutes later, Steve Locksburgh said he had had enough and hurried outside into the ninety-degree day to cool off.

As soon as the gunman had left, the smile

vanished from Millard's face, and he left the stick in the caldron, grabbed a canteen of water, and stepped back against the wall. "You kids all right?" he asked, wiping his mouth with his wet sleeve.

James wiped the sweat from his face, and nodded. Robin did the same.

"Just hang on. We'll get out of this . . . somehow." Millard tossed the canteen to Robin, who took several long gulps.

She pitched it to James, who really wanted to just empty the contents on his baked head, but he knew better. Ma and Pa had always drilled into him that water was precious, not to be wasted. He took two short drinks, and screwed the cap back onto the canteen to reduce any further temptation.

"How . . . ?" James had to swallow, summon up strength just to talk. "Where'd you learn to make whiskey?"

His father grinned. "Kids, I'm what you call winging it."

"But everything you said back at the river crossing . . ." Robin said.

"Well, first" — Millard wiped away more sweat — "you learn a few things when you work with mostly Irish railroad workers. And" — he cleared his throat — "I've known quite a few men handy with a still in

357

my day."

James blinked, not just sweat, but surprise. He had always thought of his father as the taciturn, hardworking man with no sense of humor, one who'd never even lived, just worked. Recently, he had found out that his father — his very own pa — had been a lawman, could shoot almost as good as Uncle Jimmy could, had done his share of raising Cain, and knew a lot more than how to survey or grade a railroad line.

James hooked a thumb toward the open door. "That Indian out there. The half-breed . . . you knew him?"

Millard gave a short nod. "Lucky for us." He motioned for the canteen, which James picked up and tossed to his father. Once Millard had taken two more sips, he said, "Newton Ah-ha-lo-man-tubbee. Choctaw father. White mother. All Indian. Jimmy worked with him some in the Nations. I knew him years back in Texas."

"He's a lawman?" Robin asked.

Millard set the canteen on the ground. "Not hardly. Mostly he's what we called an informant."

"You mean . . . you pay him for information?" James asked.

"That's right."

"So why did he lie, tell those men out

there that you are Wildcat Lamar?"

"For money," his father replied. "Newton Ah-ha-lo-man-tubbee doesn't do anything free. We get out of here alive, he'll be well-rewarded."

"And if we don't?" Robin asked.

James waited, wondering how his father would answer.

Millard shook his head. "We'll get out."

"But if we don't?" the girl insisted.

"Then Newton Ah-ha-lo-man-tubbee will be well-paid by Zane Maxwell or Link Mc-Coy. He plays both hands." Millard's head nodded as if in satisfaction or appreciation. "Like I said, Newton Ah-ha-lo-man-tubbee doesn't do anything for free."

"Will he help us?" James said. "When we escape?"

Again, his father surprised him with honesty. "Only if the percentages favor us."

As far as James could tell, they would not.

The doorway darkened, and Millard put on his grin again, fanning himself while one man, then another, came into the dugout. Almost instantly, both men began fanning themselves with hats.

"How's it coming?" Zane Maxwell asked.

"Getting there," Millard answered.

"How much longer?" Link McCoy asked.

"Well, usually, I age my whiskey ten weeks."

"You have two days," McCoy said flatly.

"Two days'll work, too. Just have to keep the brew hot longer. You fetched the rattlesnake heads? Need six per keg, and you bought six kegs."

"Smith and Red are out hunting now," Maxwell said.

Millard's head bobbed. "Good. Good."

"Is it poisoned?" McCoy stared at one of the kegs for a long time, then looked at the cauldron filled with bubbling brew.

"Strychnine I add last," Millard said, pointing to the containers of poison. "You want to taste?"

The killer answered with a grin. "I bought some rye."

"Good for you. But I'm glad you brung up the poison, because that leads to another important question."

"Which is?" Maxwell inquired.

"How dead do you want them?"

The outlaws eyed one another then looked back at James's father, their faces stunned.

"I like to kill my people slow," Millard said. "Make them suffer."

James stared at his father in utter wonderment. His pa seemed to be a natural thespian, taking on the role of Wildcat Lamar

Bodeen the way one of the Booth brothers might have tackled Hamlet or Macbeth.

"How long till you want them dead?" Millard snapped his finger, which caused Robin to jump as if she'd been struck. "Quick. Take a sip and keel over deader than a doornail? Make them cough up blood and die in agony a week later? I got to know those things, boys. To figure out the proportions and all that. This is science. Pure science. Ask anyone in Indian Territory, and they'll tell you that Wildcat Bodeen is a regular scientist, an apothecary."

Seeing the look on the men's faces, Millard laughed, walked over to one of the boxes, and pulled out the small bottle of strychnine, holding it up. A skull and crossbones appeared on the label. He slipped his pinky finger into the lanyard and pulled out the cork. James could not take his eyes of the tiny bottle, maybe holding one-eighth of an ounce of the pale grains. The poison had been manufactured by a chemist in Baltimore.

"You two boys know nothing about strychnine, do you? Well, here's the way it works. Not much color to it, as you can see, but it tastes bitter as gall. The sugar and the pepper and all that tobacco will disguise that bitterness when folks is drinking their liquor. First they'll get sick to their stomach, puke their guts out, but nobody will think nothing of it because that's what drunks do when they've gotten themselves liquored up. They'll wish they was dead. That's also what drunks do when they've had that much whiskey.

"Just when they think they can't get no sicker, the convulsions will start up then get longer. And longer. Then they'll be frothing at the mouth like one of them hydrophoby dogs. That's how it'll go. Worser and worser, until their guts start with spasms that'll double them over. They'll beg for death, and it'll come. Not soon enough. But it'll come. They won't be able to breathe. And they'll get lucky because the spasms will knock them out. And when they wake up, they'll be in hell."

He shook his head in delight. "That's what you want to know, ain't it? What you want to hear?"

Maxwell did not answer, but stared hard at his partner, which led James to believe it was McCoy's show. Well, it was the *McCoy*-Maxwell Gang.

McCoy stopped fanning himself and put on his hat. "Not instant death. But quick."

"Hour? Week? Month?" Millard fired off the questions like rifle shots.

"Six hours."

To James's surprise, McCoy's words came out like a tremble.

"No more . . . than . . . say . . . eight. . . . No less . . . than . . ." — he swallowed — "um . . . four. No, six. No less than six. No more . . . than eight."

Millard grinned. "Troubles you, don't it?" He followed that with a slap of his knee and a belly laugh. "You like to kill quick. That's why you cut down that old Winchester shotgun of yours. Kill quick. This ain't your game, is it?"

"Just do your job. Or I'll kill you quick." McCoy stormed outside to breathe in fresh air, to get away from the stink.

Maxwell stayed inside for another minute, still fanning himself, and finally put his hat on. "You sure this'll work?"

"On my end, absolutely. I don't know nothing about what you're planning, but this whiskey, it'll kill . . . in six to eight hours. That much I can promise you. All the rest? Well, that's up to you and him." Millard pointed at the open doorway through which McCoy had exited. "Will that plan work?"

"It'll work," Maxwell said. "We can guarantee you that."

Even James could detect the false bravado

363

in the killer's voice. Their plan wasn't a bank robbery, a stagecoach holdup, or some train job. The McCoy-Maxwell Gang was branching off into a new territory.

"Reckon you'll see," Millard said.

Maxwell had turned to climb out of the dugout, but he stopped, turned, and stared hard at Millard. "You'll see, too, Bodeen. Because you'll be with us."

CHAPTER TWENTY-SEVEN

They had taken his converted Colt, and the Winchester rifle remained sheathed in the scabbard on his saddle, which lay in a lean-to next to the corral. So far, none of the outlaws had even noticed that the rifle was a One of One Thousand, but the handful of cartridges Millard had managed to shove into his pants pocket wouldn't do much good without that rifle. He knew he had to be patient, wait for the right time. To rush his move would mean his death. That didn't worry Millard. What worried him was the knowledge that it would also lead to the murders of Robin Gillett and his oldest son.

So he brewed whiskey.

He had grown up in East Texas, where he had known quite a few peddlers of whiskey. Stills had been common, and a drunk could find good corn liquor, or bad corn liquor, whiskey distilled from potatoes, or anything from the champagne cider he had talked about back along the Red River to the worst rotgut whiskey that would eat off the taste buds on a man's tongue.

He kept the dugout a furnace, which kept most of the outlaws outside, and brewed whiskey. When he figured he had the alcohol hot enough, he got Robin and James to help him and carefully poured the scalding liquid into one of the kegs, in which he had evenly distributed the plugs of tobacco. Pretty soon, he had three of the six kegs filled. Then all six.

He decided to burn the sugar, which he then dumped into the kegs.

"Bodeen, when do you add the poison?" McCoy had dropped in again to hurry up the whiskey man, to make sure Millard remembered the deadline.

"Last. I done told you that. Then we seal up the kegs, so the strychnine will settle. Load it up and haul it off to" — he smiled — "Fort Washita."

That turned McCoy's cold eyes icy in the hellhole. "Who told you about Fort Washita?"

Millard smiled as he noisily scraped the burned sugar from a cast iron skillet into one of the kegs. It had been a guess. "Closest place. And I've heard a lot of whiskey peddlers make stops there. What's happening? Some sort of whiskey runner convention?"

"Just brew the stuff, Bodeen." Gripping his wicked-looking Winchester '87 ten-gauge, McCoy hurried out of the swelter box.

When he had left, Millard pulled another skillet filled with smelly burned sugar from the fireplace and stepped to the next keg. In the corner, Robin sat dividing the red pepper evenly into tin cups.

"When *do* you add the poison?" James asked.

"I don't." Millard rested the heavy skillet on the rim of the keg of steaming raw ethyl alcohol. "I'm not killing anyone. Not even by accident."

He had already taken care of that during the first night at the dugout. As soon as the kids were asleep, and most of McCoy's and Maxwell's gunmen drunk in the yard, Millard had opened all of the poison bottles, which took a good length of time, with those boxes full of eighth-ounce bottles. He'd dug a hole, dumped the poison into it, covered the hole, and used the leftover sand to fill the bottles of poison. The whiskey he brewed might have some sediment in the bottom, but it wouldn't kill anyone. He had even washed the severed rattlesnake heads before adding those to the barrels.

"This whiskey might make some people sick, but it won't kill them." He laughed. "By Jacks, it might even taste halfway decent."

The smiles on the teenagers' faces pleased him.

His mother had always told him that as long as you laughed or smiled, life would turn out all right. "I'm holding you to that, Ma," he said thoughtfully.

"What?" James asked.

Millard shook his head. "Nothing." Then he thought better of that. "No, it is something. Something my mother, your grandma, told me and Borden and Jimmy. Smile and laugh. Smile and laugh. Keep that up, and life will turn out just fine and dandy. Don't forget it."

All right, Millard thought, *I've taught my son everything he needs to know. I can die now.* His smile faded. *Because pretty soon, I'll likely be killed.*

Orr

If there was one thing a Cherokee was good at, it was listening. Jackson Sixpersons had the patience of an oyster, which was a good thing, because the clerk at the general store in Orr talked forever.

The Ranger, whose name turned out to be Alan Clarke, did not have patience. "They didn't say where they were from?" he practically shouted when the clerk stopped for a breath.

Frowning, the store clerk answered. "No, sir." His eyes fixated on the cinco pesos star, and he knew the Texan was out of his jurisdiction. "No, sir. I didn't ask them." He went on, counting on his fingers the merchandise purchased by the two farmers or ranchers or maybe prospectors — if there was anything in that country other than dirt, dust, and dung to dig up. "Bacon. Flour. Cornmeal. Lard. Some cans of fruit. Candy. Let's see." He thought a moment. "Castor oil. Ain't figured that out yet. And a box of .32-20 slugs for a Winchester."

Jackson Sixpersons didn't care about those items. What had interested him was the raw alcohol, sugar, tobacco, red pepper, and gunpowder. Key ingredients to a man who wanted to make contraband forty-rod whiskey.

"Oh, strychnine," the clerk added. "Bought a lot of that. Said they'd be used for wolves and coyotes."

"Strychnine." The word hung like death on the Texas Ranger's tongue.

"How much?" Sixpersons asked.

369

"Four boxes."

That was more than enough for coyotes and wolves, not to mention the little dose some whiskey peddlers would add to their scamper juice — to get the heart started again.

A quick glance at Clarke told Sixpersons that the Ranger was thinking maybe someone else . . . like old Bodeen's daughter . . . planned on poisoning Indians and kids with rotgut whiskey.

"Middle-aged men, you said," Sixpersons reminded the clerk — and the Texas Ranger.

"One in his forties," the clerk said, nodding in agreement. "The other I'd say in his thirties. Whiskers on their faces. Usually first place a man like that goes to is the barber, but not these boys. They rode out of town. Funny thing about that. They bought that wagon at Kennedy's Livery over yonder." He nodded in some general direction. "Had their horses tied behind the rig when they left."

Ranger Clarke leaned forward. "Which way did they go?"

The clerk's thumb jerked. "South. Way they come."

"Kennedy sold two wagons that day," the clerk said. "Big day for him."

That, Sixpersons already knew. They had

stopped at the store across the practically vacant square first, learning that two men had purchased kegs, kettles, and other sundries — and also had loaded their merchandise into a new wagon purchased from Kennedy's Livery.

"South," came from Charley with the Greener. "Back fer Texas maybe."

Clarke had the same thought as Sixpersons. "No." The Ranger shook his head. "No, that's a ruse. They'll be going north. Or east."

"What about west?" Charley asked.

Sixpersons answered. "Not unless they want their hair lifted by Chickasaws, Comanches, Kiowas, or Apaches."

The clerk started talking again. "A right fair amount of gunpowder, too. Right fair." He smiled at the attention the lawmen gave him. "I was thinking same as y-all. That they was buying that to brew whiskey. Contraband, you know. But . . . no . . . you don't put that much gunpowder in whiskey." He paused, paled, and added. "Least, that's what I've heard tell over at John the Barber's."

"To reload their cartridges?" Charley with the Greener asked.

The clerk laughed. "Not unless they're part of an army."

That caused Sixpersons to think they might be an army.

"But I figured they'd just blast out some of them wolf dens."

Sixpersons had all the information he needed, but he couldn't quite figure it out. What would Link McCoy and Zane Maxwell need those supplies for? Why had they destroyed Bodeen's wagon and bought new ones? He nodded at the answer that formed in his head. Mules and horses would pull those small wagons a lot faster than oxen could pull that giant freight vehicle.

Whiskey. Poison. Gunpowder. The gunpowder he could understand. To blow open a safe. Orr wasn't that far from the Katy railroad, but the McCoy-Maxwell Gang had not robbed a train in years.

He thanked the clerk again and stepped toward the door.

"One more funny thing about one of them boys," the clerk said.

Clarke and Sixpersons turned, sighing heavily. Charley with the Greener stepped outside and went to his horse.

"What's that?" the Ranger asked irritably.

"Well, one of the gents, the older one, he asked for that box of .32-20 shells, like I said. Spilled some, then knocked the whole box onto the floor. I went to pick them up, and . . . well . . . when I started putting them back into the box, he said he didn't need any more. Took only, I don't know, four, five, six maybe. Those he stuck in his pocket."

Clarke saw nothing funny or peculiar about that and stormed outside.

Sixpersons started to do the same, but stopped. "The older one?"

"Yep. Other one was outside. He was coming in when the one who'd asked for the shells knocked them to the floor."

"And when did he tell you he didn't want them, just the few he had put in his pocket?"

The clerk thought about that. "Well, right after I had —"

"Was his partner in here?"

The clerk thought again then flattened his lips. "I couldn't tell you. Sorry. Don't remember everything."

"Wait till you get to be my age," Sixpersons said and went out the door.

The bend of Caddo Creek

Robin and James were the first ones through the door, shielding their eyes from the bright sun.

Then came out Millard, that supposedly loudmouthed whiskey peddler and killer, waving a jug over his head. "It's whiskey, boys," he announced proudly and pitched the heavy piece of stoneware at Tulip Bells.

Thinking that maybe the poison would kill him just by touching the jug, the outlaw caught it before he let it fall onto the grass and backed away as if it were a grenade.

"Har!" The whiskey runner spit tobacco juice and shook his head. "It ain't been doctored with that magical element called strychnine, gents. Just wanted you guys to get a sample of what I cook."

Link McCoy rose easily, shifting the Winchester '87 shotgun he had been cleaning to his left hand and waking past Tulip Bells. Kneeling, McCoy picked up the jug and held it out to Jared Whitney.

"No thanks," the killer said.

"Just pull out the cork," McCoy ordered.

Whitney did as told, but reluctantly, squeezed his eyes shut, and jumped back when the cork popped out.

"Bottoms up," the blowhard of a whiskey runner said with a grin.

McCoy did not drink. Did not even smell. He simply walked over to the peddler, and shoved the jug at Millard. "You first."

He grinned, slapped his thigh, and took the bottle. His Adam's apple bobbed three times, and when he lowered the jug, he smiled, smacking his lips.

"Have another," McCoy said.

"Glad to." Millard drank again and followed it with a loud belch that smelled just like bad whiskey. "You want me to take another snort, boss? To prove to you that I ain't built up no immunity to the poison?"

McCoy waited.

"Or is you yellow?"

He could have, maybe should have, killed the crazed whiskey runner for that, but he accepted the jug and drank a wee taste. It burned. It was bitter. But it had kick, and when it went down, it wasn't any worse than some of the rankest rotgut he had tasted in his life.

"It ain't Irish. It ain't Scotch. It ain't rye. It ain't gin. But she'll do the job, and do you right proud." Millard took the jug again, drank another sip, and pitched the container to Zane Maxwell. "You told me to have it ready by today. Well, it's ready. Want me and the kids to start loading?"

"Yeah." McCoy walked over to Maxwell.

They passed around the jug, and watched as Millard and the two kids rolled one keg out of the dugout and to the covered wagon. The Choctaw breed went over to help. None of the others seemed so charitable. They even bragged that the whiskey tasted mighty fine.

"Well?" Maxwell asked.

McCoy just nodded. The jug was empty. No one looked sick. No one was dead. No one was even drunk.

The outlaws watched the others work until the wagon was loaded with all six kegs, and the sweating whiskey maker, the Choctaw and the two kids walked over.

"I go with you, eh?" Millard asked.

"Yes," McCoy said. "We'll go this afternoon. It's your whiskey. You'll serve it. You'll sell it. Then you'll head back here to pick up the two kids."

"And my money?"

"Your split will come to you in Paris, Texas. In two weeks. Can you find that?"

"On the Texas-Pacific line. I also know some things about railroads." Millard's eyes brightened as though he had just told some inside joke.

"Get moving," McCoy told him. "Breed. You ride with him. You, too, Smith."

McCoy waited for a minute and then looked at the two kids. "You two just wait here. Don't do anything stupid. That'll get you killed. By him." He jerked his thumb at Whitney.

"How's that?" the gunman asked.

"You stay here," McCoy said.

"And miss out on the deal? I'll be —" The

next thing Jared Whitney knew he was doubling over from the punch of the sawed-off Winchester shotgun in his stomach.

"I don't take arguments." McCoy nodded, and Zane Maxwell and Tulip Bells straightened the coughing gunman. McCoy stepped closer. "You won't miss anything, Whitney," McCoy whispered. "I need every gun I can muster. Wait here. For a day. Then ride hard, real hard, for Fort Washita."

"What . . . about . . . the kids?" Whitney gasped.

"Kill them right before you leave."

CHAPTER TWENTY-EIGHT

No wagons. Just one horse in the corral, but using his spyglass, Jackson Sixpersons could see enough horse apples to know that several mounts had been there recently. And someone was still in the dugout in the arroyo. Smoke drifted from the chimney along with the smell of bacon and coffee.

Charley with the Greener snorted. "What kind of fool builds a soddy in a danged arroyo?" He spit tobacco juice. "Place must get full of water during the rainy season."

Slapping the spyglass shut, Sixpersons backed away from the edge of the arroyo suddenly aware that Charley with the Greener wasn't as dumb as he had thought. Caddo Creek curved just a mile east of the soddy, and the arroyo would carry rainwater to the creek. Only it had not rained lately. The country was mighty dry and hot.

"Who'd look for a hideout here?" Sixpersons asked, and Charley with the Greener understood. From Orr, they had picked up the tracks left by the riders and the two wagons.

Those men had played things mighty carefully, trying to cover their trail, crossing streams and riding through pastures of grazing cattle. They were not homesteaders, not squaw men, but professionals. Outlaws. Hiding something.

Sixpersons had lost their trail twice, only to pick it back up a few hours later. He didn't know what Link McCoy or Zane Maxwell had planned, but he knew he was following those two hombres.

"How many do you think are down there?" Charley asked.

Sixpersons backed away for the arroyo's edge. He answered Charley, "One horse," but he looked at the Ranger, whose expression remained blank.

Years ago, Jackson Sixpersons and his wife had lost two children. Young, of course, still in diapers. It hurt, naturally, hurt deep, but you had to accept that as part of life. Some lived. Some died. It was a hard life in the Cherokee Nation. Three others had survived, and Jackson was a proud grandfather. Maybe the boy who had died from Lamar Bodeen's rotgut had been Clarke's only child. He didn't know. He did know that

Clarke's look troubled him.

"So one man?" Charley grinned, liking the odds.

Sixpersons shook his head. "Why would McCoy and Maxwell leave one man behind?"

"Could be an ambush." Charley began looking around, but there was no likely spot to set up an ambush . . . unless a half-dozen men were waiting inside that dugout.

Sixpersons found that possibility highly unlikely. He figured McCoy and Maxwell had left Bodeen's kid and maybe the other bootleggers behind, but he wouldn't make any more guesses. He didn't have time for that.

He pointed below with the spyglass. "I'm going to make my way down to the lean-to. You two stay up here and cover me."

"Why?" At last, the Texas Ranger had found his voice.

"Because you have rifles." With his other hand, Sixpersons held up his Winchester twelve-gauge. "I have this." He dropped the spyglass and went into a crouch, making his way a few yards before dropping off the edge and into the arroyo.

Still morning, the sun had yet to turn the country into an oven, but Sixpersons had worked up a sweat as he eased toward the corral. The horse lifted its head from the scattered grain, snorted, and stared at him, ears showing alertness but no anger or surprise.

As long as he could remember, he'd had a connection with horses. They did not fear him. He didn't think he actually communicated with them somehow, but they just realized that he posed no threat. He nodded at the horse. It did not whicker, merely snorted again and went back to its breakfast.

Sixpersons eased behind the corral, keeping an eye on the doorway to the dugout. No sound came from inside the sod house. He figured breakfast had been cooked, and the occupants were chowing down. He put both hands on the Winchester '87 and moved toward the lean-to, took a deep breath, held it, watched the doorway, and sprinted the ten yards through open country until he disappeared inside the lean-to. Bales of hay made up the wall nearest the dugout, and butts of cigarettes and one empty stoneware jug littered the ground. He glanced back at the soddy, then used his left hand to pick up the jug. He sniffed and tossed it aside.

Whiskey. Low-grade. Rotgut.

Maybe his posse had been right. Maybe

whoever had taken the wagon away from the late Lamar Bodeen was back in the business of running contraband spirits throughout Indian Territory. Sixpersons frowned. But was that whiskey poisoned?

He leaned past the bales of hay and studied the dugout. No more smoke came from the chimney. He had the perfect spot. All he had to do was wait for whoever was inside to come out of the dugout.

"What I can't figger out," Jared Whitney said, "is how come a pup like you got a cannon like this." Slowly, the gunman drew back the lever on James Mann's Winchester '86 .50-100-450. "Fifty caliber." He smiled. "Hundred grains of powder. I'm guessing it has a muzzle velocity of fourteen, maybe fifteen hundred feet per second. Blow your head off at this range." He finished cocking the rifle.

James knew that the outlaws had bought rounds for his rifle at one of the stores they had visited in Orr. And he'd figured out why one man had been left with him and Robin. To kill them. But to wait until his father was too far away to hear a shot. Wait a day, kill the kids, and join the group of outlaws at Fort Washita. As soon as Jared Whitney caught up with the outlaw gang, James thought he understood that they would kill his father, too.

Robin Gillett had just emptied the coffeepot onto the fire. Following Whitney's orders to clean, she stooped to shove the pot into a canvas sack on the floor.

When she rose, James yelled, "Run, Robin! Run!" He kicked back, pushing up the table as the big rifle roared.

Inside the close confines of the dugout, the shot proved deafening, and the muzzle flash, so close it scorched James's left ear as he fell back, almost blinded him. Yet his move had worked. The table had knocked the barrel of the Winchester, spoiling Whitney's aim.

Over the roar of the blast, James heard Whitney's curse. The table and kick of the massive rifle had knocked him onto the dirt floor. James staggered to his feet, tried to find his bearings, saw the open doorway.

Robin was already through it.

He tried to follow, but Whitney was a pro. A survivor. The gunman had jumped to his feet, and saw James. Instead of cocking the rifle, he swung it hard and savage. The barrel caught James straight across the forehead, and that was the last thing James Mann remembered.

■ ■ ■ ■

Sixpersons' wait lasted three minutes. A figure exploded from the doorway.

An incredibly loud shot had followed the shout, and he'd gone to his knees, pressing the butt of the shotgun to his shoulder, drawing a bead on the open doorway. He had enough sense to relax his finger on the trigger, seeing it was one of the kids.

The boy — no, it had to be a girl — staggered, tripped, and came up to her feet, running, screaming some name, looking back as she zigged and zagged, unsteadily, heading for the corral.

He had no time to think. Only to react. Coming to his feet, he stepped away from the lean-to. "Over here!" he called out. "Over here."

Another figure appeared in the doorway to the dugout.

Sixpersons saw the barrel of a rifle, touched the trigger, and buckshot sprayed just above the doorway. The rifle and the man disappeared back inside the dugout. Sixpersons could have held his shot just a second and killed the man, but he hoped to take him alive. If possible.

Quickly, he worked the shotgun's lever. It

wasn't the fastest action, but John Moses Browning had made it simple, and the '87 responded perfectly. Keeping an eye on the doorway, Sixpersons brought up his left hand to his mouth and shouted again. "Over here!"

A bullet kicked up dust in front of the girl's feet.

The first thought racing through the old Cherokee's mind was that Charley with the Greener had been right. It was some sort of ambush. A second later and a glance up the high bank of the arroyo told him otherwise. He swore and ran toward the girl, firing a quick blast at the dugout's doorway, just to keep the gunman inside from getting any peculiar notions.

Another bullet whined off a stone on the ground, and Sixpersons cursed again. The Ranger, that crazed old grief-struck Texan, had mounted his big black horse and was firing, leaping the horse down the bank.

Clarke wasn't trying to help Sixpersons. He was trying to kill Lamar Bodeen's kid.

It's my own fault, Sixpersons thought. *Should've kept my mouth shut. Done this alone.*

A few second later, Charley with the Greener was riding just a few yards behind Clarke, no longer carrying his shotgun, but a Winchester carbine.

The girl stood, shocked, stunned. She saw Sixpersons running toward her, but thankfully, did not move. He grabbed her wrist and pulled her toward him. A bullet tore through the old Cherokee's long gray hair and then he was falling.

From inside the cabin, a rifle roared. It hit top of the stone well and bounced away. Jackson landed behind the cover of the well, dragged the girl with him, and jacked another load into the shotgun.

Cursing, he fed fresh shells into the twelve-gauge. "Stop it!" he yelled at the hard-riding Ranger.

The Ranger levered his Winchester and the rifle spoke. A bullet whistled past Sixpersons' ear.

Another round came from the dugout, destroying the well's bucket. Sixpersons didn't know what kind of rifle that man inside was firing, but he guessed it to be a baby cannon.

Clarke shot again. Reins in his teeth, he rode hard, jacking another round into the rifle, pulling the trigger, cocking the Winchester again.

Jackson Sixpersons did not hesitate. He had given the Ranger enough chances. He brought the shotgun up and fired. Not waiting to see if he had hit Clarke, he swung the barrel toward the cabin and sent buckshot through the open doorway.

He dropped down, crawled around the side of the well, and saw the black horse gallop past him. The horse in the corral whinnied a greeting as the black, eyes wide with freight, galloped off to the north.

Sprawled in the dust lay Ranger Alan Clarke.

Sixpersons swallowed, sucked in a breath, and worked the Winchester's lever, wondering what hand Charley with the Greener would play. The air smelled of gun smoke. His eyes burned.

"Stay down," he told the kid, who had covered her ears.

Seeing the Ranger in the dirt changed Charley's thinking. He leaped off the horse and fired a quick blast at the doorway, figuring he stood a better chance against the outlaw than the Cherokee lawman's shotgun.

Charley shot again, but a round boomed from inside the dugout, and Charley was knocked a good five yards back, leaving a pink mist hanging in the air. His rifle clattered on the ground. He did not move. Nor did Alan Clarke.

Sixpersons backed away, cursing Texans

for their stupidity. He was alone . . . unless he counted the girl. He didn't.

Sometimes a bluff worked, so he called out, "You in the cabin. I'm a federal marshal. I got ten other deputies out here and a stick of dynamite."

From inside the cabin, a gunshot roared, sending splinters from the near post of the well.

Usually, of course, the bluff never worked.

He tried again. "You got nowhere to go, But hell."

"I'll see you there!"

Sixpersons looked at the girl, reached behind his back, and pulled out a pistol. He put it by the kid's right hand. "That's all I got. Five-shot .22. Hide it. Use it when you have to." He had confiscated the Remington Elliot rimfire from a soiled dove he and Jimmy Mann had arrested in the Creek Country two years back. It featured a three-inch fluted group of blued barrels and two-piece rosewood grips.

"Hey, Deputy Lawdog!" the man inside the dugout shouted.

Sixpersons kept quiet.

"I'm coming out. With a kid. So hold your fire."

He slid to the other side of the well and watched.

Sweat dripped off the ends of the outlaw's thick walrus mustache. A brown patch covered his left eye, and he had no left ear. His right hand held the big Winchester across a boy's chest, blood congealing on the boy's forehead and across his face. The outlaw's left hand pressed a Starr revolver directly under the kid's throat.

He looked over at Charley with the Greener's horse standing halfway between the cabin and the corral. "I ain't gettin' kilt by you or hung by Parker. I'll kill this boy right now. Blow his head clean off. Lessen you toss that scattergun aside and stand up. You got five seconds, law dog."

In the old days, Jimmy Mann would have been somewhere with his Winchester, covering Sixpersons. Jimmy had been such a marksman, he would have put a round right between the outlaw's eyes. Would have killed him before he could have even squeezed the trigger and killed the hostage. But Jimmy Mann was dead and gone.

Knowing he couldn't use his shotgun — it would kill both the outlaw and the hostage, Sixpersons looked at the girl. "Remember what I said." He held the shotgun up, stood, and got ready to die.

CHAPTER TWENTY-NINE

"Shotgun in the dirt."

Carefully, Jackson Sixpersons laid the Model 1887 on the ground. As he stepped away from it, the outlaw released the boy and shoved him back into the dugout, never taking his eyes off the Cherokee.

"An injun." The outlaw chuckled. "Injun with a badge. You can't arrest white men, injun. Don't you know that?"

Sixpersons thought *but I can kill them.* He held his hands, not over his head, but above his waist.

"Where's the runt?" the outlaw asked.

Sixpersons gestured with his head. "You killed her."

James Mann had landed in the dugout with a grunt. His head felt as if it had been cleaved into with an ax, but he was still alive — and had no intention of dying without a fight. That would be Jared Whitney's fatal blunder.

He staggered to his feet, only to trip over the sack on the floor and sprawl again.

He heard voices from outside. Something about an injun. Then a strange voice saying, "You killed her."

Killed her. That no-account rogue Whitney had killed Robin Gillett. Murdered her.

James did not think. Only hours later would he remember what happened, vividly and in slow detail.

A blinding rage replaced the pain he felt everywhere, but mostly in his head. His hands grasped around for anything he could use as a weapon. He touched something hard and cold and iron. The handle to the cast-iron skillet. Cleaned with bacon grease, it still smelled like breakfast.

He was on his knees, jerking the skillet from the canvas sack, and next he found his feet. Blood and sweat he could taste on his lips, but he felt nothing but rage. Uncontrolled anger. He vaulted through the doorway and into the morning light. All he saw, all he heard, was Jared Whitney.

"Balderdash." The gunman smiled. Slowly, he brought up the Starr revolver, pointing it at Sixpersons. "But I reckon I will kill you."

Hearing James, Whitney turned quickly, but he wasn't fast enough. Cursing savagely,

James swung the skillet with all his might. The iron pan caught the outlaw on the jaw, and blood and teeth sprayed from the stunned killer's jaw as he slammed to the ground.

The momentum sent James sprawling. He landed, still holding the pan, and came up.

Whitney had risen too, his jaw busted, mouth pouring blood, but gunmen knew how to deal with pain. Often, living with pain meant living, period. The rifle he had lost, but the Starr revolver was still in his hand, and he aimed it directly at James.

The skillet came up as the gunman fired. James heard the whine of a bullet, and his hands stung as the cast iron pan went flying off to his left. The skillet had saved his life, but it was gone, and James had been flattened by the impact. He came up quickly to charge that man, that beast.

Looking like a clown with his shattered jaw and blood everywhere, Whitney spit out more teeth, bloody phlegm, and a piece of his tongue. He aimed the pistol again at James, but instinct . . . or something . . . told him the danger lay behind him. He spun, snapped off a shot at the lawman, an Indian in a black hat, blue shirt, long gray hair, and . . . eyeglasses.

The bullet sailed over Sixpersons' head as

he dived for the shotgun.

Whitney's Starr barked again.

A moment later, another figure appeared — Robin Gillett! — standing behind the well. Something popped in her hand, some sort of derringer.

Whitney turned again to aim at her, but James yelled at the killer, charging and cursing as he ran.

The killer turned back toward him.

Something told James to dive to his left. He ceased his charge and found himself flying out of harm's way.

Robin's five shots missed as he landed on the ground. Whitney did not fire, mumbled something, and turned forward yet again, trying to snap a shot at the old Cherokee.

If the killer got off a shot with the revolver, James didn't hear it. All he heard was a deafening roar. All he saw was blood spraying from Whitney's chest as the killer was lifted up a full foot before he landed on his back, still gripping the smoking Starr, his eyes staring vacantly at the beautiful morning sky.

I am not dead. Jackson Sixpersons didn't understand it, certainly didn't believe it, but he looked over the smoking barrel of the Winchester shotgun, and saw the killer sprawled in the dirt, deader than he'd ever be.

First, Sixpersons sucked in a breath. Then he put his right hand on the wall of the well and used it to help him stand. The shotgun felt as if it weighed a ton. He leaned against the well for a moment and looked around.

The girl was on the other side of the well, the little Remington Elliot smoking in her hand. The boy, his face a bloody mess, came up slowly, dusting off his shirtfront. The Ranger and Charley with the Greener lay still. Dead.

"James!" The voice came from Bodeen's daughter, who dropped the derringer, and stood. She reached for the crank of the well, noticed that the bucket had been shattered by one of the killer's shots, and ran toward the corral.

Jackson Sixpersons wondered if he could move that fast, even fifty years ago.

She had a canteen and hurried back to the boy, who blinked away confusion.

The girl took him by his right arm and led him to a crate that served as a bench in front of the dugout. She began to wash the boy's face. A wicked gash creased the kid's forehead, and a bruise was likely forming beneath all the blood and dirt. A concussion or possibly a fractured skull.

Sixpersons decided to walk . . . to see if he *could* walk. He came to the dead outlaw. He had wanted to take the man alive, but he wasn't sorry to see him dead. Actually, he wasn't sorry to see anything at that point. He was alive. He had to thank Bodeen's kid, but mostly, the young, tall boy.

The old Cherokee did not recognize the outlaw, but a man with one eye and one ear and Starr revolvers should not be hard to identify. Probably a reward on him. Next the lawman moved over to Charley with the Greener. The hole in his breast was the size of a fist. The Ranger's chest was pock-marked with bloody holes from Sixpersons' shotgun. That might be hard to explain to the Texas Rangers, so maybe he would just leave that part out in his report in Fort Smith. No, Rangers didn't like to have one of their own go missing. He'd just say that the Ranger, who certainly had no jurisdiction in Indian Territory, had been killed during the assault. Have him die a hero. Him and Charley with the Greener. Killed by the outlaw with the Starr.

A lie. Sixpersons shook his head. *No, not a lie. Just a smart falsehood.*

He had been hanging around with white men too long.

Changing gears, he went to work. His

piebald would be hobbled up atop the arroyo's bank. Charley's horse had run off about fifty yards during the last round of gunfire, but didn't appear to be leaving anytime soon — too much good grass to eat — and the outlaw's horse stood at the far end of the corral. So they had horses to ride.

Leaving his shotgun in the dirt, he grabbed the Ranger's boots and dragged the dead man into the dugout, taking him all the way to the back. He did the same for Charley with the Greener and the dead man, taking them inside, but not before going through the man's pockets. About seventeen dollars and a gold-filled, open-faced Hamilton pocket watch. Unfortunately, one of the buckshot had shattered the watch's face, stopping the time at 7:23. The bills were bloody, too, but looked like they would still spend. Sixpersons pocketed the cash but left the ruined watch by the dead man's boots.

He also went through the pockets of the other two dead men. Charley had just a few coins, a rabbit's foot, and chewing tobacco. Nothing that would help identify him when it came to notifying any next of kin. The Ranger had a wallet with some papers and cash money. Those, Sixpersons would hand in at Fort Smith, along with Clarke's badge so they could be returned to the Ranger's family in that Panhandle town. He did not look at the papers. He did not want to know anything else about Alan Clarke, who would have killed him and the girl. Clarke had lived the past weeks on nothing but hate. That had killed the Ranger. With help from buckshot from Jackson Sixpersons' shotgun.

The last thing the Cherokee lawman did was close the dead Ranger's eyes.

With no door to the place, he dragged several hay bales from the lean-to to serve as a barricade. The boy, still being tended to by Bodeen's daughter, asked if he could help, but Sixpersons did not answer . . . because the girl did.

"You just sit here," she snapped, wiping off more blood and dirt. "You ain't doin' nothin' yet. That skull of yourn might be busted."

The kid pouted, causing the girl to smile. "Not that you got nothin' resemblin' a brain inside that thick skull of yourn."

Sixpersons managed to heave the last bale of hay into place. That would hold the bodies, since he had no time to actually bury those men, and if the Rangers or anyone else wanted to claim them, they could. At least, unless there came a hard rain, and the arroyo flooded, and those waters carried the dearly departed to Caddo Creek to feed the catfish lurking on the creek bottom.

He brushed the hay off his shirt and pants, wiped the sweat from his forehead, and walked to pick up his shotgun. He wiped the barrel and receiver with his bandana, and then reloaded the twelve-gauge. It would get a thorough cleaning later. He just wanted the weapon ready to fire, in case the McCoy-Maxwell Gang was close. The girl was still working on the boy, so he rounded up the horses, his and Charley's, and put them in the corral but not unsaddling them.

They walked over to drink from the tin pail in the center of the corral. The Cherokee watched them for just a moment, and heard something. He turned and almost smiled.

Birds chirped. A raven soared overhead. Peace slowly but certainly began to settle over the hideout. The violence would soon be forgotten, and some sort of normalcy would return to that section of the Chickasaw Nation.

The boy and girl sat on the crate, the boy holding a wet rag against his forehead. The blood and grime had been cleaned off his face. He had picked up the big Winchester rifle the outlaw had been firing, and it was cradled on his lap.

"You two all right?" Sixpersons asked.

The girl nodded.

The boy dropped his rag.

And that almost dropped Sixpersons to the ground.

James blinked. That old Indian, who had saved their lives from Jared Whitney, looked as if he had seen a ghost. For a moment, James thought the lawman might drop dead of an apoplexy.

The old man's mouth opened, but no words came out. He stared, studied, took a tentative step closer, and then pointed a long finger at James. "You . . ." was all he managed to say.

"Yeah . . ." James shot a glance at Robin, but her eyes were locked on the Cherokee.

Slowly, the Indian came closer and looked at the Winchester '86 on James's lap. Something clicked in the old man's mind, and those dark eyes lost that vacant stare. "You're Jimmy's . . . nephew."

Something registered with James, too. "You're Jackson Sixpersons. You rode with Uncle Jimmy."

Jackson Sixpersons did not grin. He nodded. "What the Sam Hill are you doing here?" The Cherokee lawman no longer sounded stunned.

Slowly, James slid his left hand into his back pocket, found what he wanted, withdrew it, and held it in an open palm for the lawman and Robin to see. It was the six-point star with DEPUTY U.S. MARSHAL stamped in bold black letters in the center.

"You're a lawman?" Robin asked in surprise.

James shook his head. "No, but I want to be. I've got to be. Just like . . . Uncle Jimmy."

"A deputy? You? Like Jimmy?" Sixpersons shook his head. "We'll get all this straightened out later. Right now —"

James cut him off by standing. "Right now, we have to catch up with those others. Stop them. And save my pa."

For some reason, the Cherokee did not protest. Maybe he knew that James had shown his worth.

That's what James wanted to believe. And he had. If not for him, Sixpersons would be dead. So would James. So would Robin. It had taken all three of them to kill Jared Whitney, but that outlaw was dead. And so were those other two. Two lawmen. *Killed.* *Like Uncle Jimmy.*

Sixpersons nodded. "All right. Where are we going?"

CHAPTER THIRTY

South of Fort Washita, Chickasaw Nation

He had planned the heist perfectly, and everything had come together. Satisfied, Link McCoy drew the flask of rye from his trousers pocket and tossed the liquor to Tulip Bells, who sat across the dying campfire alongside Zane Maxwell. The rest of the gang, the cigarette-smoking Choctaw breed, and the man they all thought was the whiskey runner Bodeen stood by the wagon. The outlaws were loading or cleaning their weapons. "Bodeen" and Newton Ah-ha-lo-man-tubbee were hitching the team to the covered wagon they would drive into Fort Washita in an hour.

After unscrewing the flask and taking a snort, Tulip Bells wiped his mouth and said, "But I still don't see why we need him." He tilted his bell crown hat toward the wagon.

"The poisoned liquor," Link explained as he fed the last two and seven-eighths-inch shell into his cut-down ten-gauge. "The Chickasaws won't care about the stolen gold. They'll be chasing him halfway to Texas, and he'll be running for his life. That's how come he's alive. That's the only reason."

Bells considered that, took another drink, and tossed the flask to Maxwell. "But it's their money we'll have stole."

"Indians are different from white men, Tulip," Link said with a grin. "They value the lives of their loved ones higher than gold. Remember how we had to scare them off from taking Bodeen's scalp?"

Bells nodded. "And the law? The law that ain't injuns. You know, them deputies from Fort Smith?"

Link let his partner answer.

"Deputy marshals won't be there," Zane said after swallowing a healthy portion of the rye. "They'll be way up in the Cherokee Nation. Seems that the Maxwell-McCoy Gang plans to rob a train near Gibson this afternoon."

"McCoy-Maxwell Gang," Link corrected.

With a sly grin, Maxwell pitched the flask to Link.

Tulip Bells laughed. "What about the Indian coppers?"

"Won't be any," Maxwell said and wiped

his nose. "That's something else I learned from hanging out with all those ink-slinging reporters in Fort Worth. The U.S. Indian Police lets money do the talking. Those Texas cattle barons paid a fair amount to the commissioner in Muskogee to make sure no police would be around Fort Washita today. Texans like their liquor."

"Until they get a snootful of Bodeen's," Link added.

The flask was back in Bells' right hand. "So . . . all we got to worry about is the Texans guarding the gold payment."

Maxwell and Link nodded, and Link pointed a finger at the men they had brought into the gang. "That's what they're for. And while they're fighting off the Texans, killing each other, we'll be riding south. With enough gold to send the McCoy-Maxwell Gang into retirement."

Maxwell cleared his throat. "The Maxwell-McCoy Gang."

Everyone, even Link, laughed heartily, until Tulip asked one last question. "Where's Whitney? Shouldn't he be here by now?"

"He should be," Link answered as he stood. "But if he doesn't make it in time, that's just one less man we'll have to kill — if the Texans don't kill him first."

Along Caddo Creek, Chickasaw Nation

Everything finally clicked for Jackson Six-persons, a slow, methodical man who waited until he knew everything before making a decision. It had kept him alive in Indian Territory.

Fort Washita.

He recalled his conversation with the Chickasaw up at Fort Arbuckle. Folsom had told him that he had to be at Fort Washita where the Texans would be bringing "money for grass to feed their beef." Knowing Texans, knowing how hard and dry things had been in the Lone Star State, those cattlemen would be paying a tidy sum for all that grass to feed their cows. *The lease price.* That was what Link McCoy and Zane Maxwell planned on stealing.

Sixpersons kept thinking. He had sent Flatt and Mallory to bring back more law-men, and by a stroke of luck, had asked for the deputy marshals to rendezvous with him at Fort Washita.

The Cherokee marshal almost felt satis-fied until he saw the dust up the trail. He reined in and motioned for the two kids, James Mann and Robin Gillett, to stay behind him. Sixpersons pressed the shot-gun's butt on his thigh and waited.

A rider came into view, stopped, stared,

and then slowed his horse to a walk, approaching slowly, carefully.

"O-si-yo," Sixpersons called out in Cherokee, for the man rode like an Indian.

The man answered. "Don't hello me in your heathen tongue."

Sixpersons frowned. He knew the voice, and by then he knew the gray hat the rider wore. It was the half-breed Chickasaw lawman, Folsom. The same one who had told him about the meeting between the Texans and the Indians at Fort Washita.

"Thought you were supposed to be in Fort Washita," Sixpersons said when the man reined up beside him.

"Was. Got told not to." Folsom shrugged, reached into his pocket, and pulled out a note. "So I get to play Pony Express rider and deliver you some important message." He held out the yellow telegram.

The two kids, sensing the lack of danger from Folsom, eased their horses alongside the old Cherokee.

Sixpersons studied the telegram after adjusting his spectacles.

MCCOY MAXWELL GANG TO ROB KATY AT GIBSON STATION JULY 4 STOP PROCEED IMMEDIATELY TO ASSIST STOP

Sixpersons crumpled the note in his hand. "How does Crump know the gang's robbing the train?"

Folsom shrugged. "The telegrapher didn't tell me."

One of those confidential informants, Sixpersons figured. It had to be. But probably not as reliable as the half-breed Choctaw Newton Ah-ha-lo-man-tubbee could be. "July Fourth." The Cherokee shrugged.

Folsom laughed. "Yeah. You got some hard riding to do, to get to Cherokee country in . . . six hours."

Sixpersons couldn't have covered that distance even on a train. "What took you so long to deliver this?"

The half-breed pushed back the brim of his big gray hat. "You ain't exactly the easiest lawman to find, Sixpersons."

Turning to his right, the Cherokee lawman considered James Mann for a brief moment then looked to his left to see the slight girl dressed as a boy. *Not much of a posse.* He stared hard at Folsom. "That gang's nowhere near Gibson. They're robbing the Texans delivering that money to you Chickasaws today at Fort Washita."

"Explains why the mighty-mucks at

Muskogee told me not to be there today."

"I'm going," Sixpersons said, but he would not ask, not beg Folsom to come with him, although he did add, "There's a mighty big reward on McCoy and Maxwell."

"Yep." Folsom nudged his horse to the side of the road, riding past the girl, walking at first. "Problem is, you can't spend that money if you're dead." He kicked his mount into a trot.

The lope turned into a gallop as the half-breed Chickasaw left the three sitting their horses in the middle of the trail.

Honestly, in his gut, even Sixpersons considered giving up his foolish notion and riding after Folsom. He thought about breaking his vow and getting drunk. Yet it was the girl who brought his mind back to some sort of reason, if one could call it reason and not insanity.

"I'm going," she said.

The boy concurred. "So am I." James had already pulled the big Winchester '86 from its scabbard.

Sixpersons studied him and shook his head in wonderment. That boy was the spitting image of Jimmy. Had his sass. Style too. And sure didn't lack courage. The old Cherokee only hoped the kid had a bit more discipline than his namesake uncle.

He turned to the girl. She had picked up the dead Ranger's Winchester repeater, and the dead outlaw's Starr revolver. "Can you shoot that rifle?" he asked.

"She shoots better that I do," James answered.

Sixpersons cursed. "That ain't exactly the highest praise I was looking for."

Fort Washita, Chickasaw Nation

From the high point of the road, McCoy watched. Trees grew along the creek banks and on the hills behind the fort, and every once in a while he could see another tree sprouting, trying to take root in what once had been a treeless prairie of gentling rolling plains. *Progress*, Link figured. *In a few more years, actual forests might be growing in this part of Indian country.*

He saw a few tents flapping in the wind outside the fort's walls, and inside the fort, a Texas Lone Star flag flew high and proud. Likely, a Texas flag had not flown over the post since the Civil War. The Chickasaws must be welcoming those Texas cattlemen. That would also explain why the wind carried the notes of "The Bonny Blue Flag" from the fort. A brass band was warming up down there.

"Locksburgh." McCoy waited for the gunman to ease his horse forward. "The guard tower's yours. Get up there. Should be two sentries. Texans. Kill them. Quietly."

"No problem," the killer said.

"When you've done it, lean out the front window, wave that pretty bandana I gave you. That's our signal."

With a solemn nod, the gunman kicked his horse into a trot and headed down the hill toward the old fort.

"Red, you ride with the whiskey runner, but keep your horse tied up behind the wagon."

McCoy waited as the gunman dismounted to lead his old nag to the covered wagon. "Smith, you have —"

"I know." The killer shook his head. "You've told us often enough. Upstairs corner window of the West Barracks. Good cover."

"That's right."

The Army boys had put up those barracks back in '56, finding the limestone at a nearby quarry. Since it had been abandoned, some family had turned the big building into a home, but they were out of town, renting the place to the Texans for their celebration and party.

McCoy grinned. It would not be much of a celebration for those cattlemen, but certainly a party they would never forget. No one would ever forget that Independence Day in the Indian Nations.

"Then get to it." He watched John Smith lope toward the fort then turned to Tulip Bells. "The South Barracks are yours." That's all he needed to say.

That building, finished around 1849, had been made of wood and stone, the lumber coming from seventy-five miles away. It stretched a hundred and twenty feet long and thirty or so feet wide, fourteen-foot high ceilings, with the upper story completely surrounded by a verandah.

During the Army years, the upper story had been used for two companies and the orderlies, while the company, mess, and storage rooms sat on the dark, bottom floor. Bells would find a good vantage point from the upper story. Most of the visitors and dignitaries would be on the parade ground, what they called the cannon pavilion back in the day, but the cannons had left with the Army.

Bells finished his cigarette and grinned before kicking his horse into a trot.

McCoy watched him ride away before turning his horse and moving closer to the covered wagon. "You know where you're going?" he asked the whiskey runner.

"To Hell," Millard said and cackled. "But not today."

McCoy frowned. If he hadn't planned things exactly, he would have sent Bodeen to Hell already. But he still had the idea that the Indians would chase the whiskey runner, and not himself and all that beautiful gold coin. "Don't get smart, Bodeen."

The crazed killer laughed and shook his head, but tilted his hat in the general direction of the fort. "I follow the cobblestone road right down to the spot between the old adjutant's office and the bachelor quarters for the officers. North corner. And start serving up whiskey" — he winked — "and death."

McCoy nodded. With Red covering from those quarters, the gang would have everyone in the fort covered. They'd start shooting, killing the guards when the stagecoach arrived with the gold. During the murderous fire, McCoy and Maxwell would gallop from their spot by the old two-room log cabin, leap into the stagecoach, and drive away with the gold. The others, even poor old Tulip Bells, would have to fend for themselves.

"Then get moving. You ought to be serving whiskey in fifteen minutes."

McCoy did not tell Bodeen or Red what

411

they would learn soon enough. Naturally, the adjutant's office was no longer a place for paperwork or headquarters. It had been built of logs, and when a chaplain was blessed with the fort, it had been his building, too, and he used it to teach school. Back in the late 1840s, privates from some infantry regiment would be assigned "teacher" duty. Not anymore, of course. The Army had gone, but the schoolhouse remained, only now it taught children, not soldiers. Taught Indian kids. He wondered how the folks in the community would like having whiskey being served in front of a schoolhouse . . . and poisoned whiskey at that.

Zane Maxwell pulled out his watch and nodded in satisfaction at the time. He glanced back at the road.

"What about Whitney?" Red asked. "He ain't showed up yet."

The gunman had been assigned the officers' quarters along the northwestern edge of the main part of the old fort, but they could handle things without him. Most of the buildings had been abandoned since the Army had left.

"More money for us," McCoy said, causing Red and Maxwell to smile.

Maxwell knew that the *us* referred to

himself and McCoy, and *only* himself and McCoy.

"There." Millard pointed toward the watchtower, and McCoy grinned at the sight of the lavender bandana flapping out of the center window.

"He works fast, don't he?" Millard said.

McCoy agreed, but did not answer.

"And me?" The smoking Indian breed eased his horse next to the wagon.

"Ride in with the wagon. You know the rest."

The man showed his tobacco-darkened teeth with a mean smile. "When the ruckus starts, I'm at the corral, helping scatter the horses."

"Right."

Maxwell snapped his watch shut. "Time to start the ball, boys." He and McCoy watched the wagon ease down the road with Newton Ah-ha-lo-man-tubbee riding alongside.

They gave the wagon a head start, and then Link McCoy and Zane Maxwell kicked their horses into a slow walk, confident that in an hour they would be riding out of the Chickasaw Nation at a high lope — and filthy, filthy rich.

CHAPTER THIRTY-ONE

"That's my rifle, you know." Grinning like the madman he was pretending to be, Millard Mann pointed at the Winchester rifle Red had on his lap.

"Not no more it ain't." Red flicked the lines, and the wagon picked up a little more speed. "Mine." He shot Millard a bemused look. "One of One Thousand. You probably figgered I didn't know that."

Millard shrugged. "Well, I hope you enjoy it." He looked to his side where the smoking half-breed Choctaw rode alongside the wagon on his horse. It did not surprise him that Newton Ah-ha-lo-man-tubbee had just finished rolling a cigarette and was sticking it in his mouth.

"How about a smoke, breed?" Millard said as the Choctaw struck a match against the saddle horn and brought it up to his cigarette.

As soon as the Indian had the cigarette

fired, he blew out a chimney of smoke and handed the cigarette over. Millard took it, nodded, and placed it in his mouth. He took a long pull and exhaled. "Reckon you better get to the corral, breed. Before McCoy and Maxwell get irritated."

Newton Ah-ha-lo-man-tubbee's head nodded, and he kicked his horse into a lope, moving in front of the wagon, making Millard and Red eat the horse's dust. He rode fast, moving underneath the watchtower that sat above the road into the fort and then veered west toward the corrals.

Like most frontier military posts, Fort Washita did not have a stockade surrounding the grounds. It seemed a tad different from most Army bases Millard had seen — Fort Supply and Fort Sill in Indian Territory; Fort Davis, Fort Sam Houston, Fort Richardson, Fort Griffin, and Fort Elliott in Texas. Fort Washita lacked rhyme and reason, spread out, maybe a bit discombobulated. It had been constructed before the Civil War, but had not been a fort in years. Most of the posts Millard had seen were more modern.

He saw Newton Ah-ha-lo-man-tubbee ride past the baker's oven and the guardhouse and dismount in front of the corral, already full of horses. Somehow, the half-breed had managed to roll a smoke during his lope down the road. Millard could see smoke drifting above the Choctaw's hat. That man had an amazing talent, and one hard addiction.

Millard withdrew the cigarette, checked how much remained, and wiped his sweaty hands on his pants. His heart pounded as the wagon drew closer to the watchtower. He could see Steve Locksburgh in the center window. Millard wet his lips, and returned the cigarette, trying to remember the last time he had actually smoked anything other than a cigar.

"Won't be long now," Red said.

"Yeah," Millard said. "You're right. It won't be long. Won't be long at all."

A shout came from behind the wagon, followed by the thundering of hooves. Red leaned over to look from his side, and Millard peered around the canvas flap on his side.

Zane Maxwell had his horse at a gallop, leaning forward, low in the saddle, reins in his right hand, violently whipping his horse's side with his hat. He rode as if death chased him.

Something did. Millard saw dust down the road to the south.

"Hurry!" Maxwell shouted. "Get moving,

Red! They're coming! Those Texans are coming! Early!"

A second later Maxwell had thundered past the wagon, raising dust for the watchtower and shouting at Locksburgh up in the log cabin on the stone pillar.

"Get moving, man!" McCoy had caught up with the wagon, riding alongside, gripping the pistol-grip shotgun. His hat had flown off his head, but he had no intention of stopping to pick it up.

"What?" Red asked, but already had grabbed a whip and started popping the black-snake above the mules' long ears. "Hiyah! Hi-hay!" He cursed the animals. The Winchester .32-20 bounced on his lap.

"Find your place!" McCoy spurred his horse forward.

"They ain't supposed to be here for another hour or more!" Red bellowed, but McCoy was too far ahead to hear.

For a moment, Millard thought about making a play for the rifle in Red's lap, but bouncing up and down and sideways on the uncomfortable wooden seat, he had to grip the bottom to keep from flying out. His lips pressed to hold the cigarette in place as he thought, *Link McCoy and Zane Maxwell planned everything for this heist. Planned it and timed it perfectly. Yet the Texans have spoiled those plans by arriving early.*

Again, Millard leaned over the side of the wagon. He could make out the stagecoach pulled by a team of six black horses. One driver on the top was popping his own whip, working those horses into a thundering frenzy. The Texas flag flew on a pole affixed to the side of the coach. It flapped and snapped in the wind as the stagecoach bounced along the road.

Those Texans had spoiled some of his ideas, too. He drew hard on the cigarette, and leaned forward.

"Hi-yah! Hi-yah!" Red's whip bit.

The watchtower was closer. Millard glanced through the oval canvas opening at the kegs in the back. *Time it. Time it right,* he thought, making one final hard drag on the cigarette.

He pitched it into the back. A sudden *whoosh* sang out, and the stink of sulfur bit into his nostrils.

"What the —" Red was turning, lowering his whip, but Millard was already moving.

He snatched the rifle from the gunman's lap, kicked up, and jumped, praying he had enough distance, enough momentum to clear the road. He landed hard but kept the Winchester One of One Thousand in his arms, and bounced hard, the breath leaving his lungs. His head pounding, he rolled over and over and fell into a ditch. Instantly, instinctively, knowing what was about to come, he had the sense to cover his head with his arms.

The detonation deafened him. Even a foot down in the dry ditch, an intense heat singed his shirt. He heard bits of wood whistling over him, felt hot embers landing on his back. He rolled over and came up, fighting to regain his breath, fighting to see.

Fighting to live.

Smoke and dust obscured his vision. He coughed, his lungs working again, and stepped into the smoke, yelling. At least, he thought he was yelling. "Go back!" he shouted at the approaching stagecoach. "Get out of here!"

To his amazement, the long-haired driver of the stagecoach didn't slow or even try to stop his team. He steered the vehicle off the road, moving around the destroyed main gate. The coach bounced, almost toppled over, but somehow managed to regain all four wheels as it clipped the fence that ran about twenty-five yards alongside the gate. The driver had the stagecoach — and all that gold — riding straight into the hands of Link McCoy and Zane Maxwell.

Millard couldn't see it anymore. Wind

blew the smoke in an eastward direction, and the stagecoach and its crazed driver disappeared.

What he *could* see was the ruins of the covered wagon and the burning tower.

McCoy and Maxwell had made the mistake of leaving the making of the whiskey and the loading of the wagon to Millard, James, and Robin. Oh, they had brewed some whiskey, but the only poison in it was castor oil. *Just in case,* Millard thought, *they wanted someone to get real sick.*

A lot of whiskey peddlers put gunpowder in their whiskey. To add a little kick to that Taos Lightning. Millard hadn't. He had packed the gunpowder into one keg, and spread a mass of black powder right beside it. That's what the cigarette had touched off. Then that keg had exploded, igniting the whiskey barrels, and sending poor Red — and unfortunately the team of mules and his trailing horse — into oblivion.

It had exploded just as Millard had hoped, right as it passed the tower, which was aflame.

But it had not killed Steve Locksburgh. One of his Colt Lightnings barked.

Millard answered with a shot from the Winchester and hurried toward the scorching hot mass of what once had been a covered wagon. Sweating, smoke half-blinding him, the heat almost unbearable, he levered a round into the Winchester and fired through the floor of the tower. Once. Twice. Three times. Four. He went out on the other side, looking up at the open windows, and put two shots through the center window.

Three seconds later, Steve Locksburgh came down through the trap door. His knees buckled, but he didn't fall. He held a Colt Lightning in each hand and fired from both, but Millard knew that was a fool's play.

You didn't win gunfights being the fastest.

You won them being accurate.

His rifle kicked and Locksburgh was driven into the conflagration behind him. He screamed once, stepped away from the fiery mass, and fell facedown onto the hot ground, his shirt ablaze.

Millard levered another round into the rifle, went over and kicked dirt onto the dead killer's shirt until the body was just smoking. He also picked up both double-action revolvers, sticking the hot weapons into his waistband, ignoring the pain, and moved away from the burning mass, the heat, the smoke, the death, and carnage.

He stared across the ground. The stagecoach had stopped near the flagpole. The driver had set the brake and fired a shotgun at one of the buildings. He leaped down and disappeared. Another man was running straight for the stagecoach, firing as he moved.

Chaos. Panic. Indians and white men ran this way and that, trying to get out of the line of fire. A tuba sounded. Then dropped. Millard could not make out McCoy or Maxwell, but he levered the Winchester as he ran straight into the pandemonium.

It had made absolutely no sense to Jackson Sixpersons as he'd whipped the team of horses pulling the stagecoach into Fort Washita. The covered wagon had exploded just as it had reached the entrance to the compound. Some guy had jumped off, shouted something, and waved before vanishing in the smoke and dust and debris.

At the flagpole, he'd managed to stop the team and slam the lever to set the brake. He dropped into the driver's box, yelling, "Stay down! Stay down! Stay down!"

A bullet sang from the big stone barracks off to the west and clipped the makeshift pole from which the Texas flag waved.

There's one of them, he realized. He came up with the Winchester scattergun, fired, although those barracks were well out of range, and leaped from the coach onto the ground. As he ran toward the stone building, he cocked the shotgun, thinking that he ran pretty fast for an old Cherokee.

A figure with a black mustache appeared in the corner upstairs window and shot again. Realizing the gunman was shooting a revolver, not a rifle, Sixpersons sent another round and saw the buckshot spray the stone wall just to the left of the window.

Ten steps later, he was inside the barracks, finding the stairs, and taking them two at a time.

Something inside him told him to stop. He did and heard a grunt outside. Down the steps he went, moving lightly on his feet and taking a quick glance at the shotgun. He didn't remember doing it, but he had cocked the twelve-gauge already.

From outside came more firing, more screaming. Curses and confusion. As he moved toward the door, he heard the metallic click of a revolver being cocked and then the man with the black mustache and a pair of old Remington revolvers in both hands appeared in the doorway.

The old Cherokee saw the surprise in the man's eyes and the understanding that he was about to meet the devil.

The gunman fired both .44s at the same time. One bullet went far to the left of Sixpersons. The other tugged at the brim of his hat.

With the shotgun braced against his thigh, Sixpersons fired from the hip, and the man with the black mustache and two Remingtons was knocked through the doorway. The Cherokee lawman moved, fishing two-and-five-eighths-inch shells from his pocket to reload the '87 as he reached the doorway. He looked outside to see the man with the black mustache lying faceup, spread-eagled, quite dead on the ground.

McCoy had just dropped from the saddle behind the old log cabin on the other side of the cobbled road — a long way from the fort's main gate and *behind* the log cabin — when the explosion knocked him from his feet. That's how powerful the blast was.

As his horse had scampered away, he'd found the cut-down, pistol-grip shotgun, and hurried through the cabin to the front where he saw the whiskey peddler's wagon and the tower aflame. People were running everywhere.

Suddenly, he saw a man with a long rifle shooting from underneath the tower, firing at the floor, and finally stepping away from the burning wreckage. That man looked a whole lot like the whiskey runner Bodeen. McCoy watched as a figure dropped from the burning log cabin. Guns spoke. And Steve Locksburgh died.

"Bodeen!" McCoy croaked. He uttered a curse and fired his shotgun, though the whiskey runner was far, far out of range for the sawed-off ten-gauge.

Something else caught his eye. The stagecoach driver was running toward the South Barracks where John Smith was watching. They exchanged shots and then the driver, also working a lever-action shotgun — though not as fancy, nor as original as Mc-Coy's own — went inside the building at a dead run.

McCoy smiled, thinking old John Smith would outfox that old man with the long gray hair.

The hired gunman leaped from the window, pushed a trumpet player aside, knocked down the fleeing, screaming, crying band conductor, and moved back inside the barracks, trying to sneak up on the shotgun-wielding old man. Guns echoed inside the dark building, and instantly, Smith came flying out the door, landing on the grass with a thud, his chest a bloody mess.

Tulip Bells came bolting down the stairs that led to the verandah of the bigger barracks on the south side of the parade ground and ran straight for the stagecoach.

The stagecoach! All that gold has to be inside. McCoy started running toward it, too, but Bells reached it first, grabbed the latch to the door, and swung the door.

McCoy stopped running when he saw a flash of flame and smoke belch from inside the stage and a hole as big as a grapefruit suddenly appear in Tulip Bells' back. The killer went flying backwards as that boy, that kid who'd helped the crazed Bodeen, leaped outside, levering the big Winchester .50-100-450 rifle.

The other door opened, and that other waif, the kid — McCoy couldn't remember the urchin's name — stepped out, holding a Starr revolver in each hand. One hand came up, and the old gun spoke, sending a chunk of lead that tore a hole through the side of the outlaw's linen duster.

"It's all gone to hell!" Link spun as his partner rode up, pulling a black horse behind him.

"Let's ride. We gotta get out of here!" Maxwell didn't even slow down but did drop the reins to the black as his horse thundered past. Rifles spoke, and he leaned over the side of the horse, heading straight toward the smoke. Riding south. Getting away.

McCoy understood that he had to do the same. He snatched the reins and leaped into the saddle. Another bullet whistled over his head. He let the ten-gauge roar but doubted if his shot would prove true. He didn't take time to look. He just gouged the horse's sides with his spurs, leaned low in the saddle, and rode as hard as he could, desperately trying to get away.

CHAPTER THIRTY-TWO

James Mann took his time, squeezed the trigger, and felt the savage kick of the .50-caliber Winchester bruise his shoulder. He knew he had missed, for Link McCoy had leaned low in the saddle. Horse and rider vanished in the smoke and dust, following Zane Maxwell.

He looked around, saw Robin Gillett coming from behind the coach, holding those double-action revolvers in her hands. He saw the Cherokee lawman hurrying across the grounds from a big stone building. Finally, he heard a familiar voice, and saw his father — his blessed, living old man — crossing the cobbled road from the south side of the post, moving past a couple stunned Chickasaw women.

His dad shouted, "James!"

Yet something inside his gut told him James had to hurry. Reunions would have to wait. "I'm all right, Pa!" he shouted and started running as fast as he could, gathering the reins to the horse trying to break the tethers holding it to the railing of the stairs in front of the long wooden building. "I'm going after McCoy and Maxwell!"

"No!" That shout, in unison, came from his father, Robin, and even the old Cherokee marshal.

James did not listen. He held the reins, had a foot in the stirrup, and then he was pounding the horse's side with the hot barrel of the Winchester '86, riding into the smoke, going after Link McCoy and Zane Maxwell, the two most feared bandits in that part of the West, maybe all of the West.

Jackson Sixpersons stopped underneath the flagpole, cursing in Cherokee and in English as that fool-headed boy rode out of the fort. He swung his shotgun toward the man running toward them, but quickly lowered it, and blinked. "Millard."

Millard stopped. Tears formed in his eyes, maybe from the smoke, but most likely from watching his oldest kid ride into hell. The brother of Sixpersons' late partner raised his head. Smoke and soot blackened his face and most of his clothes. "O-si-yo, Jackson."

" 'Si-yo," the Cherokee said, and turned toward the girl. "You all right?"

"Yeah," Robin answered.

Another figure came trotting a horse, and bringing two saddled mounts behind him. Newton Ah-ha-lo-man-tubbee reined to a stop. He was smoking a cigarette. "Got these from the corral, Jack."

"Don't call me Jack," Sixpersons said, but he was gathering the reins to the sorrel and swinging into the saddle.

Beside him, Millard Mann mounted the gray.

"What about me?" the girl whined.

"You stay put!" Millard bellowed.

Sixpersons looked at Newton Ah-ha-lo-man-tubbee. "You want to ride with us?"

The Choctaw flicked his cigarette into the dust. "Are you crazy?"

Near the Chickasaw–Choctaw border
James Mann did not know how far nor for how long he had ridden, but his butt hurt. He had been smart enough not to keep the horse he had borrowed in a gallop. He would slow to a trot, then a walk, letting the fine animal catch its breath, then resume into a walk, trot, and gallop. Ahead of him, Link McCoy and Zane Maxwell must have been doing the same, because he'd made sure he could see their dust.

About five miles from the fort, his father

and Jackson Sixpersons caught up with him.

"What do you think you're doing?" his father asked.

"The same as you're doing," he snapped. "And him!" He jerked his head at the old Cherokee.

"We'll need him," Sixpersons said.

Millard turned his anger on the Cherokee lawman. "He's just a kid."

"We still need him." Sixpersons kicked his horse into a walk, following the trail of the two outlaws.

James followed, and, reluctantly, so did his father.

They came to the lightly timbered hills and slowed their animals to a walk, no longer seeing dust. Two rifles and the Cherokee's shotgun were at the ready.

"Cave country, isn't it?" Millard's voice was steady, but quiet.

Sixpersons answered with a nod.

James listened. At that time of year, birds should be singing in the trees on the hills, but the only sound came from the hard-blowing horses.

"Their mounts have to be as played out as our own," Millard said.

Again, the old Indian nodded.

"You circle around," Millard suggested to the old lawman. "Leave James here to cover

431

the rear."

The boy knew why. His father wanted to keep him safe, and the last direction Maxwell or McCoy would run would be north, back toward Fort Washita and the posses that the Chickasaws and probably the Texans had formed.

Millard spoke again. "I'll ride the trail."

James swallowed. That trail led right into open country, through the hills that were filled with caves. A man riding there would be a sitting duck, setting himself up to get shot.

A horse whinnied in the distance on the other side of the hills. That seemed to settle everything. McCoy or Maxwell, or likely both, had dismounted on the far side of the hills, left their run-down horses, and come back around to set up an ambush. They had no other choice . . . except surrender and be hanged by Judge Parker in Fort Smith.

"No," Sixpersons said. "You circle around. I'll ride the trail."

"Why?" Millard snapped.

"Because I'm the only one of you with a badge." The eyeglasses glinted as the Cherokee looked directly at James. "Well" — the Indian grinned — "the only one with a commission."

Millard stared in silence but finally sucked

in a long breath, exhaled, and rode his horse off to the west, moving deeper through the trees, making a wide berth. A short while later, he dismounted. Carrying the Winchester rifle, he moved slowly but confidently in a crouch through the woods that swallowed him.

"Dismount, James," Sixpersons said. "You got a good view from right here."

James obeyed, ground-reining the horse. His heart pounded. His mouth felt incredibly dry. He lay on his stomach, Winchester against his shoulder, and stared up the hill, barren of just about everything except a few rocks too small for anyone to take shelter behind.

"It's harder to shoot uphill," Sixpersons instructed. "Just aim low. Always aim low." He pulled his hat down, kneed his pinto's sides, and the horse carried him out from the trees and up the hill.

Almost an eternity passed. James wet his lips and kept his eyes darting left, right, trying to find someone, some sign. His mouth hung open as he waited to shout a warning as soon as he saw McCoy or Maxwell — just to give that brave Cherokee with the shotgun a chance.

It happened before he realized what was actually happening.

Two figures materialized, springing from the earth on opposite ends of the trail like demons rising from Hades. As soon as James understood what he had seen, the two men were firing, the one on the right with a shotgun, the one on the left with a revolver.

The lawman's horse screamed and fell to its side as Sixpersons dove off, landing with a thud and rolling over. Both men ran toward him to finish the job, to kill the Cherokee.

James fired. He couldn't have told you which one he shot at, McCoy on the right, or Maxwell on the left. All he remembered was that he was charging, firing the Winchester, not even feeling the big rifle's savage kicks.

A bullet whined off a rock in front of McCoy's feet, and James understood that his father was shooting from his position up the hill. His father had McCoy covered, leaving Maxwell to James. He sprinted in that direction, pulling the trigger and working the lever as he ran. He could make out Sixpersons crawling for his Winchester '87, his leg bleeding from several buckshot from McCoy's scattergun. Maxwell ran, too. Both headed straight for the Cherokee.

Maxwell slid to a stop, saw James, and brought the revolver up. James fired. Nothing happened. He felt no kick. Heard no shot. He had shot the weapon empty, yet he did not stop charging, did not stop screaming like some old Rebel in some long-ago Civil War battle.

He shifted the weapon, grabbed the barrel, and swung as hard as he could, still running like a madman as Maxwell's finger tightened on the trigger.

James hit the ground with a thud and came up dazed. The bullet had scorched his side, but that was it. His Winchester was on the ground beside the body of Zane Maxwell, whose skull had been crushed by the heavy rifle.

More bullets sounded on the other side. James turned, saw the smoke from his father's rifle in the woods, saw McCoy dropping back into a hole.

Grabbing Sixpersons' shotgun, James picked it up and ran after the outlaw, following him straight into that hole, straight into the depths of hell.

"No!" Jackson Sixpersons yelled and heard what he thought was an echo, only to realize that it was the boy's father shouting from his position on the hill.

Too late. The kid disappeared into the cave.

Sixpersons fell back onto the ground. His

435

leg hurt, and he cursed in Cherokee before pushing himself up. They would have had McCoy cornered, trapped in that cave like a rat. They could have waited him out, starved him out, or even smoked him out.

But he was in there . . . with the boy. And Jackson's own shotgun.

The ground was slick, hard, cold.

James slid down and dived to his left just as a shotgun blast roared. In the deafening confines of the cave, he felt as if his eardrums had been ripped out of his body. The right side of his face stung, and he thought for a moment that he had been hit by shot from McCoy's fancy weapon. He blinked, felt the blood tricking down his cheek, and understood that the blast had showered him with gravel and sand.

Carefully, he managed his breathing and peeked around the corner. The passageway seemed narrow but not too long. He couldn't tell if there were any side tunnels or side rooms, anyplace McCoy could be hiding.

It wasn't as dark as he had expected it to be. In fact, he could see pretty well. Keeping the shotgun's barrel pointed directly down the cave, he took a step into the open, breathed, and took another step, his finger tight on the Winchester's trigger.

He had to step over some rocks and duck his head. He waited. Sweat burned those wounds on his cheek, but he ignored the pain. He tried not to blink. He stepped again. Slowly. Again. His eyes moved to both sides with every step, then focused on what lay ahead. Just dark earth.

Five yards. Ten. He had to step over more rubble. His ears had stopped ringing. He could hear his feet on the cave's floor. So . . . he wasn't deaf.

Ten more yards and he stopped, leaning into a small depression in the cave's wall. He had come to the entrance of a larger room. Beyond it he saw another tunnel and light shining from the end where Maxwell had jumped up in his futile attempt to kill Jackson Sixpersons.

How long did that tunnel go? James could not tell. Nor did he have any idea how big the room was. It had to be larger than the tight chamber he found himself in. Likely, McCoy hid in there somewhere, but on which side? Left? Right? Or was he waiting in the tunnel on the far side of the room.

For a moment, James looked back, staring at the tunnel through which he had come. He had the urge, a desperate desire, to run back . . . and out of the cave. Back to Sixpersons and his father. Back to where he could see the sun and sky and feel the wind. But if he did that, his back would be to McCoy's shotgun. And he would die.

He fought down the panic and the bile rising in his throat. Just when he felt he would collapse in total fear, a certain calm overcame him, and he thought with complete and total clarity, remembering what his father had told him when he'd first — almost the only — time he'd taken him hunting. *"Patience. Be patient. Make sure what you're shooting at before you squeeze that trigger. This isn't a race. You race, you lose."*

It was not James who had to get out of the cave. It was McCoy, and he would have to do it soon. Before other posses — there had to be men already riding from Fort Washita — caught up with him. James could wait — all day and all night, but McCoy could not get out of the cave without showing his face.

Smiling, breathing normally again, James moved to the center of the tunnel and sat down. He did, of course, keep the barrel of Jackson Sixpersons' twelve-gauge aimed at the opening as he waited for Link McCoy.

James lost all track of time. Ten minutes?

An hour? Five hours? He wasn't sure. It didn't matter. He just sat there holding the shotgun, which never seemed heavy. He never felt tired. He kept quiet, kept listening, and just waited.

And waited.

He felt a presence sitting beside him and knew it was his dead uncle. Oh, he knew Uncle Jimmy wasn't really there, and he didn't turn to look at some ghost. His eyes stayed focus on the opening, but he listened.

"Here's what you need to know, kid," his uncle was telling him, just as he had done all those months ago back at that boxcar turned into a home near McAdam, Texas. "It ain't the rifle. It ain't never the rifle. It's the fella shooting it."

Rifle. Or shotgun. And James understood then that he was a much better man than Link McCoy. He knew he had more patience than an outlaw. He knew Link McCoy was a fool who had planned the robbery but had been outsmarted. He knew McCoy had planned the ambush, only to be outsmarted again. He knew McCoy was as good as dead.

A scream sounded, echoing crazily in the big room in front of James, but he wasn't scared. He simply tightened the shotgun's butt against his shoulder and got ready to dive to his right.

McCoy came from James's left and pulled the trigger first, the sawed-off barrel belching smoke and flame and sending the chopped-up bits of razors splattering off the cave's wall. A few pieces whistled past James's head, and one even clipped the cloth of his shirtsleeve near the shoulder.

James had been smart to sit in the center. He squeezed the trigger. Patiently. Making sure of his target. McCoy had rushed his shot and it had cost him his life.

Above the ringing in his ears and the bitter smoke burning his eyes, James saw the gunman hurled against the wall. James jacked another shell into the chamber and slid through the opening to the large room.

McCoy's shotgun banged and clanged as it clattered across the floor. James brought his weapon up, drew a bead on the outlaw, but relaxed his finger on the trigger. The killer had pulled himself up, moaning, coughing, and was crawling through the opening.

James calmly walked across the room. It wasn't as big as he had imagined. He watched McCoy clawing his way up the entrance . . . or maybe the exit — it didn't matter — into the sunlight.

James stopped to pick up the outlaw's

shotgun and ducked as he went into the tunnel, following the bloody trail the robber and thief was leaving.

He stuck the barrel of McCoy's shotgun through the opening, tossed it onto the ground, pushed Jackson Sixpersons' Winchester into the fresh air, and laid it down gently. His arms came through. He looked at the clear blue sky, and felt himself being lifted out of the cave and onto the top of the hill.

James Mann looked at his father. "Hello, Pa."

His father answered by squeezing him into a bear hug.

James felt as if he could have stayed like that forever, burying his head into his dad's shoulders. He felt like crying but didn't. Finally, his dad stepped back but put an arm around James's shoulders.

Jackson Sixpersons, hobbling on a piece of wood as a crutch, one leg wrapped with bloody white strips of bandages, stood over the body of Link McCoy, who would rob no more banks, trains, Texans, or Chickasaws.

Father and son joined the deputy marshal, but James did not look at Link McCoy. He had killed three men that morning. That would hit him later. And when it did, he would hit back, and hard. Those men would have killed him had he not shot them first. That, he could live with.

"Jackson." Millard stared curiously at the old Cherokee.

James looked at his father, who asked, "How in the Sam Hill did you get that stagecoach?"

CHAPTER THIRTY-THREE

Fort Smith

The way Jackson Sixpersons and James Mann had explained things to Judge Parker and U.S. Marshal Crump in the judge's chambers went something like this.

The Cherokee marshal, Robin Gillett, and James Mann had been riding north toward Fort Washita when they saw the Texans traveling hard in that stagecoach. They dismounted, and Sixpersons stood in the center of the road with his shotgun pointed down and held loosely in his left hand. His right hand gripped the six-point star, which he held out and over his head to let the stagecoach driver know that he was a lawman.

The driver and two guards with double-barrel Parkers sat atop the coach. When it stopped, four cattlemen and four guards stepped out, all smelling of whiskey.

Sixpersons explained what was waiting for

them at Fort Washita and suggested that they leave the gold, already in a Wells Fargo box inside the coach next to the buckets of whiskey and beer — Texans being Texans — and that the guards ride with him and surprise the McCoy-Maxwell Gang.

The leader of the Texas cattlemen, a man named Willoughby, sneered, cursed, and stamped his high-heeled boots, proclaiming that no Indian was going to suggest anything to him, that for all Willoughby knew it was Jackson Sixpersons who was holding them up, and he had half a mind to have his guards shoot down the lot of them.

Sixpersons managed to convince everyone that he was a federal marshal, but none of the guards or cattlemen were willing to go with him so they stayed at the side of the road to protect the box of gold.

That wasn't exactly the way things went.

What had gone down was that when Willoughby was doing his threatening and stamping and cursing, Sixpersons had rammed the barrel of the Winchester '87 underneath the cattle baron's throat and snapped, "Move, breathe, fart, and I'll blow this big windy's head clean off."

Willoughby changed his tune and began singing to the other cattlemen, the stage driver, and the guard. "Do as he says. Do as he says. Do as he says."

The guards were disarmed, as were two of the cattlemen with pocketed pistols, and they were told to drop their pants and grab their ankles. Jackson Sixpersons did leave the gentlemen from Texas with their buckets of beer and whiskey.

"We're comin' with ya!" Robin Gillett jumped inside the stagecoach.

"No, you're not!" Sixpersons cursed when James climbed inside, too. "Get out!"

"No!" the kids said in unison. "Time's wasting!"

"Get out!"

"My pa's with those cutthroats!" James roared. "If you don't want to come, stay with those fools and Robin and I'll get it done ourselves."

So Jackson Sixpersons crawled up onto the driver's box and drove the stagecoach to Fort Washita, happy his made-up story satisfied the judge and the marshal.

"Amazing," Judge Parker said. "And what of the money from the bank robbery in Greenville?"

Sixpersons shrugged. "Never found it."

"Probably spent it," Crump said.

Jackson Sixpersons had his doubts. He had telegraphed the sheriff in Greenville, asking about that teller, Mike Crawford —

the one who had lost his watch (now in the hands of Newton Ah-ha-lo-man-tubbee); the one whom bank president Grover Cleveland had sent to check on that zebra dun that had trotted back to town after the holdup; the same one the bank president had fired, even though Crawford had identified Link McCoy.

Sheriff Whit Marion had replied that Crawford and his family had left town. No one knew where they had gone, although someone seemed to have overheard Crawford mentioning Mexico. The bank had reported a loss of $1,793.67; the gang had allegedly made off with $400.

Sixpersons figured $1,393.67 would replace a gold watch, with plenty of money to spare, but he only shrugged at the marshal's theory.

"Amazing," Judge Parker said again. "And you killed McCoy, Maxwell, and Bells."

"Big reward for you, Sixpersons," Crump added between puffs on his cigar.

"For him." Sixpersons pointed the eyeglasses he was cleaning at James, who sat uncomfortably in a comfortable leather couch. "James got all of them. Saved my hide doing it, too."

"Bully for you, kid!" Crump shouted. "There's a lot of money —"

"I'd rather have something else." James reached into his pocket and pulled out his uncle's badge.

"What?" Judge Parker asked.

"My late uncle's job."

The judge and marshal looked at one another, at Sixpersons, and finally at James Mann.

"Son" — Parker adopted a fatherly tone — "federal deputy marshals die often, far too often, in the Indian Territory. You should —"

"I want that job, sir."

Crump set his cigar on an ashtray. "Are you twenty-one years of age, son?"

It had come to that.

James sucked in a deep breath. Was he willing to lie? Suddenly, he knew that he couldn't. He could not, would not, lie. He knew his uncle, good old Jimmy Mann, would have no regrets, no worries, and would lie — had lied — to get his way. But there was too much of his father in him to lie.

He was about to sigh and answer when the door opened and in walked his father.

"Millard Mann!" Judge Parker exclaimed. "It has been a long, long time."

"That's right, Your Honor." Millard looked at his son then at Crump. "Sorry to barge in on you."

"It's no bother at all, Mann." Crump grinned and picked up his cigar. "Your son here wants to be a lawman. One of my deputies. I'd just asked him if he was twenty-one. But maybe you can answer that for us."

Millard looked at James, at Sixpersons, and finally at Judge Parker. At last, his gaze landed on Marshal Crump and his posture relaxed. He even smiled and looked back to his son before answering. "Well, George, I reckon I'll always look at James as a ten-year-old. Sometimes younger. Guess that's how I'll see him when he's bringing my grandbabies so I can bounce them on my knee." He sighed and turned back to Marshal Crump. "But he's all grown up, George. Time Libbie and I faced that. Is he twenty-one?" Millard laughed, and his head nodded. "He's a Mann. Surely a Mann. A Mann full grown."

Smoke and steam belched from the locomotive as the three men, Jackson Sixpersons, Millard Mann, and James Mann stood on the platform. Pinned to his new vest, the latter's badge reflected the sunlight.

"The girl get off all right?" Sixpersons asked.

James nodded. "Yes, sir. Back to her home in Lincoln, Nebraska."

"You see her off, son?" Millard asked with a grin.

James gave his dad a meek smile, and they laughed.

Robin's mother had divorced that drunken fool and was remarried to a sober, pleasant store owner. The marshals had tracked them down, pooled to buy the girl a ticket, and sent her home.

"She'll do fine in Nebraska," Millard said.

"And it ain't too far away from Fort Smith," Sixpersons said.

The conductor called out. "All aboard!"

Millard picked up his grip and the scabbard carrying his Winchester One of One Thousand. He stuck the rifle under one arm and extended his hand to his son. "You'll write your mother once a week. Let us know how you're doing. What you're doing. And you'll listen to this ornery old man with bad eyes and do exactly — *exactly* — as he tells you. This Cherokee might not look like much, but he'll keep you alive." They shook.

James wasn't certain, but he thought he saw tears welling in his pa's eyes. He couldn't be sure, though . . . because of the tears in his own eyes.

"I'm proud of you, son." Millard cleared

his throat.

"I'm proud of you, Pa."

They released.

The conductor hollered out something else, and Millard took the rifle and hurried for the nearest car.

James and Sixpersons watched him go. They stayed on the platform, watching the train pull out of the station.

Sixpersons turned. "Let's go."

They left the depot and walked until they reached a saloon at Garrison Avenue. The sign above the batwing doors said TEXAS CORNER SALOON.

"This is where the deputy marshals gather," Sixpersons said.

"We going to have a drink?" James Mann grinned.

"No." Sixpersons peered inside and frowned. "Katie Crockett runs it. She's not much older than you. We just came here to pick up your horse. I had Flatt bring it down." He pointed to a brown gelding tied to a hitching post.

James's eyes almost popped out of his skull. He saw the saddle and the Winchester '86 in the scabbard, but it was the horse that he ran to. He rubbed its neck, whispered into the gelding's ear, and turned toward Jackson Sixpersons. "This is" — he wasn't sure he could find the words — "Old Buck. Uncle Jimmy's . . ."

The eyes behind the spectacles revealed no motion. Sixpersons only nodded.

"But . . ."

The old Cherokee finally spoke. "Listen, Crump pays you what some folks might call a salary. Most would call it a pittance. The U.S. marshal does not provide in any way or form clothes, lodging, firearms, weapons, or grub. They will pay for mileage, if it's on official duty, and some minor expenses." He pointed to the upstairs of the saloon.

"Katie will also give a lawman a room. Cheap. Noisy. Not too comfortable." The old man's eyes hardened, and he spoke like an angry father. "Understand this, James. That's all Katie's giving."

James didn't care about that. His thumb jerked to the brown gelding, Old Buck. "But this —"

"Jimmy left it with me when he —" Sixpersons did not finish. He did not have to. "I figure Old Buck belongs to you now."

James smiled. "Thanks, Jackson."

"Don't thank me. You just remember what you got told in the judge's chambers the other day. Marshals get killed out here. A lot. You remember that. And if you ever pull some fool stunt like you did when you jumped into that cave to get Link McCoy, I might just kill you myself."

James's grin widened until the old man reached into his pocket and pulled out some papers. "What are those?"

Cursing, Sixpersons shook his head. "Arrest warrants, you dumb oaf." He spit and swung into his saddle. "Boy, you got a lot of learning to do. Mount up."

James grabbed the reins, swung into the saddle, and backed Old Buck onto the street.

"Ever been in the Winding Stair Mountains?" Sixpersons asked.

"No, sir." James wet his lips.

"We'll meet Flatt and Mallory and another — Riley Monaco is his name, about as worthless as the other two combined — across the river. Try not to get yourself killed before you write your first letter to your ma. You pa would never let me hear the end of it."

It was the most James had ever heard the old Cherokee speak in one conversation.

They rode down Garrison Avenue, in a sight that would soon become familiar to the residents of Fort Smith, Arkansas — the long-haired old Indian on a paint horse carrying a Winchester Model 1887 lever-action twelve-gauge shotgun. And a younger deputy named James Mann, riding a brown gelding and armed with a Winchester Model 1886 rifle in .50-100-450 caliber.

The employees of Thorndike Press hope you have enjoyed this Large Print book. All our Thorndike, Wheeler, and Kennebec Large Print titles are designed for easy reading, and all our books are made to last. Other Thorndike Press Large Print books are available at your library, through selected bookstores, or directly from us.

For information about titles, please call:
  (800) 223-1244

or visit our Web site at:
  http://gale.cengage.com/thorndike

To share your comments, please write:
Publisher
Thorndike Press
10 Water St., Suite 310
Waterville, ME 04901